By Wright Morris

Novels

The Loneliness of the Long
　Distance Writer (1995)
Two for the Road (1994)
Three Easy Pieces (1993)
Plains Song (1980)
The Fork River Space Project
　(1977)
A Life (1973)
War Games (1972)
Fire Sermon (1971)
In Orbit (1967)
One Day (1965)
Cause for Wonder (1963)
What a Way to Go (1962)
Ceremony in Lone Tree (1960)
Love Among the Cannibals
　(1957)
The Field of Vision (1956)
The Huge Season (1954)
The Deep Sleep (1953)
The Works of Love (1952)
Man and Boy (1951)
The World in the Attic (1949)
The Man Who Was There (1945)
My Uncle Dudley (1942)

Photo-Text

Photographs &.Words (1982)
Love Affair: A Venetian Journal
　(1972)
God's Country and My People
　(1968)
The Home Place (1948)
The Inhabitants (1946)

Essays

Earthly Delights, Unearthly
　Adornments (1978)
About Fiction (1975)
A Bill of Rites, A Bill of
　Wrongs, A Bill of Goods
　(1968)
The Territory Ahead (1958)

Anthology

Wright Morris: A Reader
　(1970)

Short Stories

Collected Stories 1948–1986
　(1986)
Real Losses, Imaginary Gains
　(1976)
The Cat's Meow (1975)
Here Is Einbaum (1973)
Green Grass, Blue Sky, White
　House (1970)

Memoir

Writing My Life: An
　Autobiography (1993)
A Cloak of Light: Writing My
　Life (1985)
Solo (1983)
Will's Boy (1981)

WRIGHT MORRIS

The Loneliness of the Long Distance Writer

THE WORKS OF LOVE & THE HUGE SEASON

BLACK SPARROW PRESS · SANTA ROSA · 1995

FICTION

Morris, W

Lit

PS3525
.07475
L66
1995

Black Sparrow Press books are printed on acid-free paper.

LIBRARY OF CONGRESS CATALOGING-IN-PUBLICATION DATA

Morris, Wright, 1910–
    The loneliness of the long distance writer / Wright Morris.
        p.   cm.
    Contents: The works of love — The huge season.
    ISBN 0-87685-990-2 (pbk. : alk. paper). — ISBN 0-87685-991-0 (cloth trade : alk. paper). — ISBN 0-87685-992-9 (signed cloth : alk. paper).
    I. Title.
PS3525.O7475L66   1995
813'.52—dc20   95-47580
                                             CIP

THE

WORKS

OF

LOVE

For

LOREN COREY EISELEY

&

to the memory of

SHERWOOD ANDERSON

pioneer in the works of love

Grown old in Love from Seven till Seven times Seven
I oft have wished for Hell for Ease from Heaven.

—WILLIAM BLAKE

We cannot bear connection. That is our malady.

—D. H. LAWRENCE

If the word love *comes up between them I am lost.*

—STENDHAL

Contents

IN THE WILDERNESS

1

IN THE dry places, men begin to dream. Where the rivers run sand, there is something in man that begins to flow. West of the 98th Meridian— where it sometimes rains and it sometimes doesn't —towns, like weeds, spring up when it rains, dry up when it stops. But in a dry climate the husk of the plant remains. The stranger might find, as if preserved in amber, something of the green life that was once lived there, and the ghosts of men who have gone on to a better place. The withered towns are empty, but not uninhabited. Faces sometimes peer out from the broken windows, or whisper from the sagging balconies, as if this place—now that it is dead—had come to life. As if empty it is forever occupied. One of these towns, so the story would have it, was Indian Bow.

According to the record, a man named Will Brady was born on a river without water, in a sod house, near the trading post of Indian Bow. In time he grew to be a man who neither smoked, drank, gambled, nor swore. A man who headed no cause, fought in no wars, and passed his life unaware of the great public issues—it might be asked: why trouble with such a man at all? What is there left to say of a man with so much of his life left out? Well, there are women, for one thing—men of such caliber leave a lot up to the women—but in the long run Will Jennings Brady is there by himself. That might be his story. The man who was more or less by himself.

His father, Adam Brady, a lonely man, living in the sod house without a dog or a woman, spoke of the waste land around Indian Bow as God's country. It was empty. That was what he meant. If a man came in, he soon left on the next caboose. As a pastime, from the roof of his house, Adam Brady took potshots at the cupola, or at the rear platform, where the brakeman's lantern hung. He never hit anything. In his opinion, God's country should be like that.

Adam Brady's sod house was like a mound, or a storm cave, and after the first big snow of the winter just the snout, like a reluctant ground hog, could be seen peering out. The rest of the year it looked like the entrance to an abandoned mine. On the long winter nights the coyotes would gather to howl on the roof, or scratch their backs on the longhorns put up there to frighten them off. In the spring their tracks could be seen around the door, where the earth was soft.

Adam Brady spent several winters in this house alone. But one windy fall, with the winter looming, he put on his dark suit, his wide-brimmed hat, his military boots from the Confederate army, and rode eighty miles east in search of a photographer. He found one in the up-and-coming town of Calloway. The picture shows Brady standing, hat in hand, with a virgin forest painted in behind him, and emerging from this forest a coyote and a one-eyed buffalo. The great humped head is there, but the rest of the beast is behind the screen.

This picture might have given any woman pause, but there was no indication, anywhere in it, of the landscape through the window that Adam Brady faced. There was not an inkling of the desolation of the empty plain. No hint of the sky, immense and faded, such as one might see in a landscape of China —but without the monuments that indicated men had passed, and might still be there. In that place, remote as it was, men at least had found time to carve a few idols, and others had passed either in order to worship, or to mutilate them. But in this place—this desolation out the window—what was there? Nothing but the sky that pressed on the earth with the dead weight of the sea, and here and there a house such as a prairie dog might have made.

Adam Brady had ten prints made of this picture, and six of them he mailed to old friends in Ohio; four he passed out to strangers, traveling men, that is, on their way east. A man who wanted a woman had to advertise for her, as he did for a cow. And a woman who wanted a man might be led to forget—for the time being—that great virgin forests are not, strictly speaking, part of the plains. That one-eyed buffaloes are seldom seen peering out of them. For there was some indication that the man in this picture lived in a real house, had friends and good neighbors, and perhaps a bay mare to draw a red-wheeled, green-tasseled gig. And that on Sunday afternoons he would drive his new wife down tree-lined roads. There was no indication that the man in the picture had on nearly everything that he owned, including a key-wind watch with a bent minute-hand. On the back of this picture, in a good hand, it was written that the man to be seen on the front, Adam Brady by name, was seeking a help-mate and a wife. And there was every indication that this man meant what he said.

What became of nine pictures there is no record, but the tenth, well thumbed and faded, with a handlebar mustache added, finally got around to Caroline Clayton, an Indiana girl. She was neither a widow nor, strictly speaking, a girl any more. Her independent cast of mind had not appealed to the returning Civil War boys. What she saw in this picture it is hard to say, as both the forest and the buffalo had faded, the coyote was gone, and someone had punched holes in Adam Brady's eyes. But whatever she saw, or thought she saw, she wrote to him. In her letter, sealed with red wax, she enclosed a picture of herself taken at a time when she had been, almost, engaged. A touch of color had been added to the cheeks. She gazed into a wicker cage from which the happy bird had flown. We see her facing this cage, her eyes on the empty perch, a startled look of pleasure on her face, and though she is plain, very plain, there is something about the eyes—

I can see very clearly [Adam Brady replied] *your lovely eyes, with the hidden smile, but I am not sure that I, nor any man, might plumb their depths and tell you what they mean. I fix my own eyes upon you without shame, and I see your face avert for my very boldness, and I can only compare the warm blush at your throat with the morning sky.*

Another place he spoke of the illicit sweetness of the flesh.

The Works of Love

—I can say I know the passions of the men about me, and the heated anguish of the blood, but I have never tasted the illicit sweetness of the flesh.

There was hardly room, in letters such as this, to speak of grasshopper plagues like swirling clouds in the sky, or of the wooden shapes of cattle frozen stiffly upright out on the range. No, it was hardly the place, and when she arrived, the last day of November, Adam Brady had to carry her through drifts of snow while leading his horse. There was no time for her to think, no place to reflect, there was nothing but the fact that a tall bearded man, smelling like a saddle blanket, carried her half a mile, then put her down on the ground *inside* of his house. There it was, right there beneath her, instead of a floor. Had there been something like a road, or a neighboring house, or a passing stranger that she might have called to, Will Jennings Brady, as we know him, might not have been born. But as it was, he came along soon enough. In September, when the grass had turned yellow on the sun-baked roof.

In this sod house, the cracked walls papered with calendar pictures of southern Indiana, Will Jennings Brady, according to the record, was born. The grasshoppers ate the harness off a team of mares that year. That was how Adam Brady, his father, remembered it. Just four years later, in the month of October, Adam Brady put a roll of baling wire around his waist and went up the ladder on the windmill to make a repair. That was all that was known, and the story would have it that Emil Barton, the station agent, found him swinging like a bell clapper between the windmill posts. Adam Brady's boots were given to Emil Barton, as they still had, as was said, life in them, but his ticking watch was put aside for Will Brady, his son.

In the town of Indian Bow there was a dog named Shep, who was brown and white and had a long tail, and a boy named Gerald, about the same dirty color, but no tail. There was also a depot, a cattle loader, several square frame houses with clapboard privies; and later there were stores with pressed tin ceilings along the tracks. In the barber shop were a gum machine and a living rubber plant. Over this shop was a girl named Stella, who ate the boogers out of her nose, and her little brother Roger, who was inclined to eat everything else. Over the long dry summer it added up to quite a bit. But in Willy Brady's opinion it was still not enough.

From the roof of the soddy he could see the white valley road, the dry bed of the river, and the westbound freights slowly pulling up the grade. These trains might be there, winding up the valley, for an hour or more. Sometimes a gig or a tassel-fringed buggy, that had left Indian Bow in the morning would still be there—that is, the dust would be there—in the afternoon. Like everything else, it didn't seem to know just where to go. The empty world in the valley seemed to be the only world there was. A boy on the roof of the soddy, or seated on the small drafty hole in the privy, might get the notion, now and then, that he was the last man in the world. That neither the freight trains, the buggy tracks, nor the dust was going anywhere. But if at times this empty world seemed unreal, or if he felt he was the last real man in it, he didn't let this feeling keep him awake at night, or warp his character. He grew up. He went to work for Emil Barton, the stationmaster.

Emil Barton passed most of the day near the stove where he could tip forward and spit in the wood-box, or open the stove door and make a quick frying sound on the hot coals. Then he would twist his lips between his first finger and his thumb. That always left a brown stain on his thumb, and he would sit there, rubbing the stain between his fingers, and when it seemed to be gone he would hold those fingers to his nose. The smell never rubbed off. It always seemed to be there when he sniffed for it.

Will Brady remembered that, as he did the deep

scar on Emil Barton's forehead, which turned bluish white in winter as if the bone was showing through. It was said that this had happened over a woman, in a fight. It was said that Emil Barton had lost the woman, but the other man had lost his right eye, which Emil Barton kept in a whisky bottle at the back of his house.

As Emil Barton's assistant, Will Brady wore a cracked green visor with a soft leather band, black sateen dusters, and an indelible pencil behind one ear. During the long afternoons he sat at the window looking down the curving tracks to the semaphore, the switch near the cattle loader, and the bend in the river called Indian Bow. Now and then the Overland Express roared through, blowing on the windows like a winter gale, rocking the lamps in the station, and leaving a fine ashy grit on his teeth. Once or twice a year the express might stop, to pick up some cattleman or let one off, and when this happened the dining-car windows would throw their light on the tracks. Through the wide diner windows Will Brady would see the men and women from another world. They seemed to think Will Brady was as strange a sight as themselves. They would stare at him, he would stare at them, and then the train would take them off with just the blinking red lights, like a comet's tail, showing down the tracks.

Otherwise he might have stayed there, seated at the wide desk, listening to what the chirping ticker said, married Stella Bickel, and watered the rubber plant in her father's shop. But Stella Bickel married a brakeman on the C., B. & Q., and Indian Bow being on the Union Pacific, she moved east to Grand Island, where she could keep an eye on him. And just six months later, early in March, having made up her mind to go home to Indiana, Caroline Clayton Brady went to bed and died. The decision, Emil Barton said, was too much for her. He didn't say, in so many words, that it would soon be too much for Will Brady, but he let it be known that there were more things opening up down the line. East that is, down the grade toward Calloway. There was a roundhouse there, and a man could go to Omaha on week ends.

And Emil Barton was there, his hat in his hand, the sleeting rain cold on his bald head, when they stood on the raw pine board at the edge of his mother's grave. Over the wide valley spread a dim rain, the slopes of the hills grained like a privy clapboard, and the wind blowing a cloud of mist, like smoke, along the tracks. There was no woman at the station to see a man off—or ask him to hurry back. There was no dust to follow the dead wagon back into town. This desolate place, this rim of the world, had been God's country to Adam Brady, but

to his wife, Caroline Clayton, a godforsaken hole.
Perhaps only Will Brady could combine these two
points of view. He could leave it, that is, but he
would never get over it.

2

WHEN the eastbound freight pulled over on the
siding, about half a mile west of the town of Calloway, Will Brady put on his shoes and came out on
the platform of the caboose. Just north of the siding was a lumberyard where several men were
working, piling new lumber, and beyond the yard
was a long frame building with a flat roof. Eight or
ten young women were out on the roof, drying
their hair. When they saw Will Brady two of the
girls jeered at him. They were very young, with
loud voices, and this may have had something to do
with the fact that Will Brady took a great interest
in the lumberyard. One of the men in the yard wore
a carpenter's apron, with deep nail pockets at the
front, but another seemed to carry all the nails he
needed in his mouth. He fed them out, one at a
time, as he hammered them.

Now, these goings on seemed to interest Will
Brady very much. He had never seen so much

wood before—perhaps that was it. Nor so many women—though he preferred one woman at a time. And there was one, oddly enough, seated on the porch. This woman had also washed her hair, and one man might have judged it golden, like corn silk, while another might have found it somewhat brittle, more the color of straw. But there it was, anyhow, drying on her head. She wore a green kimono with faded red dragons on the loose sleeves. In her hand she held a magazine, but so great was her interest in the lumberyard, and in what the men were doing, that it was placed face-down in her lap. When the men dropped the timber she watched the yellow sawdust rise in the air. She saw it collect in the dark beard of the man who ran the saw. Perhaps it was the smell, like one out of a garden, or the noon sun beating down on the yellow timber, or the white arms of the men now that it was spring and their sleeves were rolled, but whatever it was, it seemed to her a marvelous sight. Not once did she raise her eyes to the young man in the wide-brimmed hat, his face in shadow, standing on the platform of the caboose. Would that explain what came over him? Why, as the express roared past, he took the wide-brimmed hat from his head and sailed it out on the air, as if the wind had sucked it off? There it sailed through the air, the woman looking at it, and as the freight began to move, the young man threw his wicker bag into the ditch, jumped after it. After all, that had been his father's hat. There would be another train, but perhaps in all the world just one hat like that. So he went after the hat, and it would be hard to say whether the woman with the yellow hair saw or did not see what a fine young man he was. A little narrow in the shoulders, but with his father's long legs. And now that his hat was off, there was his mother's wavy hair. Whether she saw these things or not there is no telling, as his hat was on, his face was in shadow, when he walked past her toward the town. No telling what she thought, but every indication that she sized him up.

Through the window of the Merchant's Hotel he could see the potted palms at the front of the lobby, and the row of oak rockers, with leather seats, facing the tracks. In one of the rockers sat a man with a black linen vest. He wore elastic bands on his sleeves, and in one pocket of the linen vest were several indelible pencils with bright red caps. The man was large, but he didn't look too well. His face was about the same color as his light tan button shoes, and when he got out of the rocker he took his time, as if he needed help. But he was friendly enough. As they walked back to the desk he rested one hand on Will Brady's shoulder and with the other slipped a chew of tobacco into his mouth.

"Young man," he said, "I take it you missed your train?"

"I got off," Will Brady said, "I was getting off."

"My name is Bassett," the big man said, "two esses and two tees." He smiled, then he said: "There's nothing in Omaha we haven't got right here." He let that sink in, then he said: "You know what I mean?" Will Brady nodded his head. The man laughed, then went on: "Hotel on the European plan, girls on the American plan—you know what I mean?"

"Yes sir," said Will Brady, as his mother had brought him up right.

"Young man," said Mr. Bassett, and took from the case a box of cigars, placed it on the counter, "I could use a man like you right here if he wasn't afraid of work." He let that sink in, then he said: "Have a cigar?"

"No, thank you, sir," Will Brady said, "I don't smoke."

"You don't smoke?" said Mr. Bassett.

"I just never started," said Will Brady.

"You like a drink?" said Mr. Bassett.

"Thank you very much," Will Brady said, "but I don't drink."

"What is your name, son?" Mr. Bassett said, and put his hands on the counter as if for support. His mouth stood open, and Will Brady saw the purple pencil stain on his lip.

"Brady, sir," he said, "Will Jennings Brady."

"You don't drink an' you don't smoke," Mr. Bassett said. "Tell me, boy—you anything against the ladies?"

"No, sir," said Will Brady, and took off his hat as his face felt hot. From the pocket of his coat he took a clean handkerchief and blew his nose into it.

3

As THE night clerk in the Merchant's Hotel, Will Brady wore a green visor, quite a bit like the old one, and a vest that Mr. Bassett ordered for him from Omaha. There were pockets in the vest for indelible pencils, a new stem-wind Dueber-Hampden, and the cigars that traveling men might offer him. "Just because you don't smoke, son," Mr. Bassett had said, "don't think you're any better than the man who does." By that he meant to accept the cigar and keep his mouth shut. Give it back to the man the next time he came around. In the last pocket, pinned there, was the key to the coin drawer. In the coin drawer were stamps, fifty dollars in silver, and a Colt revolver with five deep notches in the mother-of-pearl handle. During the night the Colt was slung in the holster strapped to the leg of the desk.

Most of the day Will Brady slept in a room with several copper fire extinguishers, a stack of galvanized buckets, and about sixty feet of cracked canvas hose. A good many traveling men fell asleep while smoking their cigars. Others were apt to doze off in the lobby, a coat pocket or a vest burning, and the smell in some cases was not much different from that of the cigar. He would have to leave the desk and walk up front for a look at them. On the back of each room door he nailed a sign bearing the signature of Ralph O. Bassett:

PUT OUT CIGAR
Before
PUTTING OUT LIGHTS

Twelve hours a night he sat in the lobby facing the map of the state of Nebraska, or the Seth Thomas clock which he wound once a week. On the wall with the clock were five or six railroad calendars. A man with time on his hands might imagine himself in the Royal Gorge, crossing the Great Divide, or with the honeymoon couple as they motored through the Garden of the Gods. There were no pictures of Indiana, nor of holy men feeding the birds, but, thanks to his mother, he was at home with calendars. They were alike, in that the scenes were all far away.

Nearer at home was the map of Nebraska, with the chicken-track railroad lines, and the dark-ringed holes that the traveling men had burned with their cigars. One at Calloway, Grand Island, Columbus, and Omaha. Every now and then a town was added, the name printed in by the man who had found it, with the help of other men who had been there or had some notion where it was. The country was booming, as one man said. This man could prove it to you, pointing at the map, but the truth was that Will Brady, who seemed bright enough in some ways, had a hard time visualizing such things. He could stare for hours at the hole in the map without seeing very much. Eyes open, all he saw was the map; and eyes closed, all that came to mind was the smell of the floor mop and the ticking of the Seth Thomas clock.

He had arranged with Ralph Bassett to take the night off once a week. What was there to do with it in a place like Calloway? A married man, of course, didn't face the same problem, but when Will Brady took the night off he walked down the tracks to the building where the girls washed their hair on the roof. At the side of this building was a sagging flight of stairs with a lantern at the top. If this lantern happened to be burning, it was Will Brady's night off. The wire handle on the lantern would be hot from the flame, and he would have to wrap his handkerchief around it before he took it down from the hook and opened the door. With the smoking lantern in his hand, he would step inside. He had learned to set it on the floor, not the rug, but he had still not learned how to take off his shoes, or his socks, without sitting down on the side of the bed. He would tap the cinders in the heels of his shoes into the palm of his hand. If it was summer and warm, he might even take off his socks.

What was he up to? Well, the woman in the bed had a word for it. He was a lover. That was her way of putting it. Her name was Opal Mason and she talked pretty frankly about some things. That might seem an odd way to describe a man who brought nothing along, said nothing loving, and left a good deal up to the woman, to say the least. A lover in some ways perhaps, but not too bright. He went about his business and then he rolled over and went to sleep.

He also slept very well, while she seemed to sleep indifferently; sleeping was something she could do, as she put it, at another time. It was not something she did when she had other things on her mind. The lover lay on his side, his heavy head on her arm, his breath blowing wisps of yellow hair in her face, and she lay on her back listening to the engines switch around in the yard. A big woman, with straw-colored hair, Opal Mason usually cried when somebody died, when babies were born, or when certain men slept with her. Like the lover, for instance. Something about it struck her as sad. In her opinion, a woman's opinion, there was something very lonely about a lantern, the tooting of switch engines, and the way men were inclined to fall asleep. Something strange, that is, about lying awake with a man sound asleep. Perhaps this struck her as the loneliest thing of all. The town of Calloway struck her as lonely since she had the smoking lanterns, the tooting engines, and the sleeping lover all at one time. It made her strangely melancholy. It was a pleasure for her to cry.

Every lover took time as well as patience; and lying awake, Opal Mason had come to have the notion that men did not come, the lovers did not come, merely to sleep with her. No, they came into the room, the lantern in their hand, for something else. In her opinion, all of these strong silent men were scared to death. Of what? Perhaps they were scared of themselves. They were all such strong, silent men, and they all seemed to think they would live forever, make love forever, and then drop off

to sleep as they always did. They were like children, and if they came to her—more, that is, than
to the younger women—perhaps she reminded
them of what the situation really was. There were
all sorts of men, of course, there were those who
seemed to know this and those who didn't, and
then there was this lover, Will Brady, who didn't
seem to know anything. That might be what she
liked about him. Lying awake she often wondered
if that was what he liked about her.

"You men!" she would say, wagging her head,
and as this sometimes woke him up, he would rise
on his elbow and ask her what the trouble was. For
all that, she never seemed to know. She would tell
him to please shut up and go back to sleep. From
the pocket of the green kimono that she wore she
would take the package of Sen-Sen, put some in
her mouth, and then lie there whiffling through her
nose and sucking on it. It was not the kind of thing
a man like Will Brady could appreciate. If the
weather was bad, or the room was cold, he would
lie there and try to ignore it, but on the warm summer nights he would get up and put on his shoes.
On his way out he would blow out the lantern before he hung it back on the wall, and if the night
was clear he might remember to look at his watch.
He didn't like to get caught along the tracks when
number 9 went through, at three in the morning,

so he might stand there till he heard the whistle far down the line. He would still be there, later, watching the receding lights on the caboose.

Sen-Sen, of course, was a small matter, but there was nothing small about her old friends, several dozens of them, who might pop up at any time. Men from as far away as Salt Lake City and Cheyenne. Busy men who found the time, somehow or other, to stop off. And from June through September, four pretty long months, Opal Mason met all of her old friends in Denver, where she liked the climate better, as she said, for a woman in her work. Also, why did she have to mention it? These things were not small, they were serious, and they had led better men than himself to see the weakness in the American plan. It wasn't women he wanted—what he wanted was a woman for himself.

Ralph Bassett, for example, had one, and Will Brady saw quite a bit of her as she spent most of the day on the wire-legged stool in the Hotel Café. She kept Ralph Bassett's books, and once a week typed out a new menu. As there wasn't too much for her to do she spent a good deal of time peering into the pie case, where there was a mirror, and adjusting the hairpins in her heavy black hair. With her arms raised, the bone pins in her mouth, she would arch her broad back and turn on the stool to look at her face, and her hair, in the pie case. Part of Will Brady's trouble over the summer was certainly due to the fact that the long summer days, and the heat, were hard on Ethel Bassett's hair. She spent a good deal of time with her arms raised, fixing it. On the wall behind her was a mirror, so that Will Brady saw her both front and back, in the round so to speak, while she looked him straight in the face. Which was odd, as she never seemed to see anything. A wall might as well have been there, but none was. Ethel Bassett had large dark eyes, and a face that any man would call handsome, but it would be hard to say what she had on her mind. The phases of the moon? Well, she sometimes spoke of that. He had once seen a book with pictures of the stars open in her lap. There was also her son, a boy named Orville, who liked to hug his mother most of the time, and there was some indication, Will Brady thought, that she egged him on. Anyhow, it didn't help a young man settle his mind. Over a long hot summer, while Opal Mason was cooling in Denver, he had nothing to do but watch Ethel Bassett put up her long black hair.

Suitable women, as Ralph Bassett liked to say, were pretty damn scarce. They were safe at home in one of the tree-shaded houses some man like Ralph Bassett had built for them, or they wore sunbonnets and walked about among the flowers with watering cans. Or they were very young, their hair in long braids as in the album pictures of his mother, or they were too old, peering at him over a line of wash, clothespins in their mouths and another woman's baby at their feet. He saw the arms of these women, from time to time, drooping from some hammock like a strand of rope, and other times he heard them at the back of a lawn, in a creaking lawn swing. Their age was uncertain, but it was known they were spoken for. They were as near and as far as the women he saw in the dining cars.

"And now what is it?" Opal Mason would say, as she couldn't stand a man thinking. A man lying *there* and thinking, that is.

"Can't a man just lie here?" he would say.

"You're not just lying there—you're thinking!" she'd say, and there was no use asking such a woman what was wrong with that. He could lie somewhere else, she would tell him, if he wanted to think. But he didn't. It was just that he thought while lying there with her. Trying to think what a suitable woman would be like.

For the important thing about Opal Mason, a "very unsuitable woman," was that he knew what he knew, and she knew, and that suited him. The only unsuitable thing was some ten or twenty other men. The only way to settle a thing like that was to make her a suitable woman, to buy a ring with a stone and make this woman his wife. With the summer coming on he made up his mind, ordered a ring with a stone from a house in Grand Island, and near the middle of May, a warm spring night, he shaved and rinsed with bay rum. He wore the vest to his suit so that he could take the ring along. He walked down the tracks, on the ties this time, to keep the cinders out of his shoes, and with the smoking lantern he stepped into the room, softly closed the door. For reasons of her own, Opal Mason was awake, playing solitaire. Not many women look good sitting up in bed, whether they're playing solitaire or not, and the idea crossed his mind that maybe the time was not right. But he had waited too long, and what he had come to say came out. Still holding the lantern, he said: "Opal—I want you for my wife."

It was some time before she said anything. Before she moved, or anything like a thought crossed her broad face. In that amount of time he saw the board in her lap, a packing-case board with the name RORTY on it, and fanned out on the board her very soiled deck of cards. At the moment he spoke, her right hand had been raised, the thumb ready to flick the tip of her tongue, and the tip of that thumb was white as a blister, the dirt licked off. He saw all of that, then he realized that where he hurt —for he hurt somewhere—was the wire handle of the lantern burning his right hand. "Ouch," he said, but not so much in pain as in what you might call recognition. Then he bent over to lower the lantern to the floor. He was still bent over when he heard Opal Mason begin to laugh.

Now, the thing is that Opal Mason never laughed. In order to account for what he did later you have to keep in mind that Opal Mason, a big sad-eyed woman, often cried a good deal but she never laughed. She grinned now and then, but nearly always covered her mouth, as if her teeth hurt her if she felt a smile on it. A laugh was such an odd sound, coming from her, that the man with the lantern doubted his senses, bending nearer as if to make sure for himself. But the woman was laughing, there was no doubt of it. Perhaps it was the *ouch* that struck her as funny, coming right at the time it did, rather than the sober, simple statement she had heard. Perhaps. Or the fact that he didn't find it funny himself. There's a pretty good chance that if he had laughed she would have married him. But he was an odd one, no doubt about that, and while Opal Mason laughed herself sick he picked up his lantern and went out on the porch. He hung it back on the hook and made his way to the foot of the stairs. There he found a light in the front hall as it was still early, around midnight, and four or five girls had come out on the porch to see what was wrong. Nobody had ever heard Opal Mason laugh before. To these girls, standing there together, one of them in a shawl she had wrapped around her, Will Brady said: "Is there one of you girls that would like to get married?" That did it. They began to laugh, they saw the joke. "I'm not joking," Will Brady said. "Is there one of you girls that would like to get married?"

One girl stopped laughing and said: "Mickey. I guess Mickey would."

"Who is Mickey?" he said, and stepped up on the porch. He was shy of young girls who were bold and named everything freely, but right at the moment he was not shy. He was bold himself. "Where is Mickey?" he said, and for some reason took off his hat.

"My God!" said one girl. "Go get him Mickey!" and they held on to him, holding his arms, while they ran down the long hall to the rear, then came running back. "Here's Mickey," they said, and brought the girl out. She was a kid, maybe fifteen, sixteen years old. She was a thin, flat girl with her hair in braids looped up like stirrups, and there were scratched mosquito bites on her arms and skinny legs. A girl not so thin wouldn't have looked so pregnant, so swelled up.

"I understand you would like a good man," he said, in a friendly way, and smiling at her, but this kid stepped forward and slapped him full in the face. It left his cheek numb, and one eye seeing double, but she stood right before him, her fists clenched, and in the quiet he could hear her gritting her small pointed teeth. He just looked at her, he didn't raise his hand and give her a cuff. After all, just an hour before, he had shaved himself, rinsed with sweet-smelling water, and come down the tracks to ask a woman to be his wife. In the right-hand pocket of his vest was a ring, with an eighty-dollar stone. It makes a difference, something like that, and perhaps even this kid felt it as her teeth stopped gritting and she began to snuffle through her nose. She didn't want to let on that she had started to bawl. There were freckles straddling her nose, and tangled in with her braids were strips of colored ribbon, but looking at her Will Brady didn't feel very much. He was thinking of himself, and what he was doing, and what a fine thing it was for a man like himself to behave so well with a kid like that. No, he didn't feel much of anything till she slapped him again. With her left hand, across the other side of his face. You have to give it to a kid like that, a kid with that kind of spunk. Until that occurred you might even say that Will Brady hadn't really thought about her, but as a boy he had always taken his hat off to spunk. He didn't have a whole lot of it, put it like that. Before she

29

slapped him again—and he saw it coming—he bent over and scooped her off her feet, and she beat on his head with her fists doubled up, smashing down his hat. Then she suddenly stopped, hugged him tight, and began to bawl.

He carried her down from the porch and along the fence that went around the sawmill, down through the ditch, then up the steep gravel bank to the tracks. He walked on the ties toward the red and green lights in the semaphore. Although she was a skinny girl, she was a little heavier than she ought to be, and not the right shape for carrying more than a quarter mile. Near the water tank he had to stop and put her down. His arms were asleep, his hands were prickly, and he stood there holding her hand and listening to the waterspout drip on the tracks.

"How much further are we going?" she said.

He hadn't thought. He hadn't thought about that part of it.

"Before we go any further," she said, "I think I better tell you we can't get married."

"We can't?"

"I'm already married," she said. "I'm as good as married, that is."

As he was still holding her hand he put it down and said: "I've got a ring here—now why don't you use it?" He took the ring from the pocket in his vest, put it in her hand. "As I won't need it now, you use it," he said. There was a moon behind her, and she turned so that the light fell on the stone.

"Is that the real McCoy?" she said.

"That's the real McCoy," he said. She closed her hand on it and put that hand behind her back.

"What's your name?"

"Brady," he said, "Will Brady."

"My name is Mickey Ahearn right now," she said.

"I'm down here in the hotel," he said, and pointed down the tracks past the semaphore. "The Merchant's Hotel. I'm in the lobby most of the time."

"I'll remember," she said, "I always remember everything."

"Well," he said, rubbing his hands, "it's getting pretty cool, you better run along." She ran off like a kid for about thirty yards, then she stopped. She stood there between the tracks, looking back at him. "You shouldn't run like that any more," he said. "You're not a kid any more, you're a lady."

"That's what I just remembered."

"Well, now you go along," he said. He turned and walked a little ways himself, but when he turned back she was still there. "Now you go along," he said, and shooed his hand at her, like a friendly dog, but she didn't move, so he turned and walked away. When he looked back from the station platform, she was gone.

4

IN NOVEMBER Will Brady was sitting in the lobby, waiting for the local to come down from North Platte, when he saw Mickey Ahearn on the platform of the eastbound caboose. She was standing there, her hands on the brake wheel, beside a boy by the name of Popkov, one of the section hands on the C., B. & Q. One of those foreign kids with curly hair that seemed to grow right out of his eyes. He had one hand on her arm, and with the other he held a large duffel bag. Mickey Ahearn looked straight down the tracks toward the sawmill until the caboose passed the hotel, when she turned her head sharply as if she had thought of him. But the sun was on the window, and besides he was behind a potted plant. This kid Popkov might have seen him but there was no reason for him to look, and he kept his eyes, like those of a bird, right down the tracks. So did Will Brady, until the eastbound freight had pulled out of sight.

* * *

In the Wilderness

Early in the spring, about the first week of March, Fred Blake, the Calloway station agent, called Will Brady up and said that he would like to speak to him. "Right away, Brady," he said. "Got something over here with your name on it."

That was a Sunday morning, the one he liked to sleep, but Will Brady got out of bed as it wasn't often anybody sent him anything. As he crossed the tracks he could see that Mrs. Blake, a big, motherly woman, was sitting there in the office with a wicker basket in her lap. The basket was covered with a cloth, like a lunch, but a red American Express tag, fastened on with a wire, dangled from the handle on one end.

As he opened the door Will Brady said: "Somebody put me up a good picnic lunch?" as Fred Blake himself was quite a kidder and liked a good joke.

"This ain't exactly a picnic," Fred Blake said, and though it was too early for flies in the office, he waved his hand over the basket as if there were. Then he raised one corner of the towel, peeked in. "No, this ain't no picnic, Will," he said, and still holding the corner of the towel, he stepped aside so Will Brady could see for himself. No, it was no picnic. A sausage-colored baby lay asleep on its face. A soiled nightshirt, or whatever it is that babies wear that leave their bottoms uncovered, was in a wadded roll around its neck. On the baby's left leg, tied there with a string, was another American Express tag, and Will Brady turned this one over to see what it said.

My name is Willy Brady

and that was all.

"It's a boy?" Will Brady said.

"He's a boy," said Mrs. Blake, and rolled him over on his back, and he was a boy, all right. Around his neck was a strand of black hair with a gold ring braided to it. The ring had what looked to be about an eighty-dollar stone.

"How old you reckon he is, Mrs. Blake?" he said.

"He's about five weeks," Mrs. Blake said, and then she put the knuckle of her little finger in the boy's mouth. She let him suck on it for a bit, then she took it out, sniffed the knuckle, and said: "The poor little tyke—a bottle baby." She shook her head sadly, put the knuckle back again.

"There's an orphanage in Kearney," Fred Blake said. "Think they call it Sister something or other. They say it's not a bad place, don't they, Kate?"

"It's not bad," she said, "as them places go."

"Unless you was thinking," Fred Blake said, "of something yourself."

Had Will Brady been thinking? No. But now he would.

"If it was a girl," Mrs. Blake said, "now I wouldn't know what to think. But there's nearly always someone, it seems to me, who wants a fine boy."

"Don't get in a hurry now, Kate," said Fred. "After all, this boy's got Will's name on him. Maybe Will here would like a husky boy himself."

Mrs. Blake smelled the knuckle of her little finger again. "The poor little tyke," she said, "the poor little tyke."

"Mrs. Blake," Will Brady said, "what would you say he'd need besides a good bottle?"

Mrs. Blake opened her mouth, wide, then she seemed to change her mind.

"What'd you say he'd need, Kate?" said Fred.

"He could use a good woman," Kate Blake said, and scooped the baby up. "You mind I take him home and feed him, Will?" she said.

"Why, no," Will Brady said.

"Kate," Fred Blake said, "what do you say we just keep him till Will here picks up what he needs?"

"Won't that take him some time?" Kate Blake said, and they stood there, looking at her. "You men!" she said, and with the boy hugged tight she went through the door. Then she put her head back in and said: "Now I'll tell you when to come around. I don't want you, either of you, moping around the house." With that she let the door slam, and through the wide window they watched her cross the tracks.

"That's the way they get," Fred Blake said. "Just let a kid come along and that's the way they get." He turned to the basket and said: "What'll we do with this—you won't be needing it."

This Willy Brady was an odd one for a boy, as he wasn't much bigger than a rabbit, and he had the dark unblinking eyes of a bird. They were neither friendly nor unfriendly, nor were they blue like Will Brady's, the watery blue of the faded summer sky. They were more like the knobs on a hatpin than eyes. They seemed to pick up, Will Brady thought, right where his mother's eyes had left off, staring at him from the top step of the porch.

It also seemed to be clear that somebody had made a mistake. If Will Brady had fathered this boy—as Fred Blake liked to say—then Prince Albert was the son of Daniel Boone. The little fellow was also, as Mrs. Blake said, pretty bright. He seemed to have taken after his mother in most respects.

If Will Brady took exception to this he never

let on, nor troubled to deny it, but just went about the business of being a father to the boy. That is to say that once or twice a week he bounced the boy on his knee in a horsey manner, and let him play with the elastic arm bands on his sleeves. Mrs. Blake referred to him as Daddy, to herself as Grandma, but she might call the boy any number of things. Sometimes she called him Cookie because of his black currant eyes.

"Now give Cookie to his grandma," she would say, and swing the boy in the air by his heels; but let Will Brady try that and there would be hell to pay. The boy would scrounge around, grunt like a pig, or hold his breath till his black eyes popped. He would turn a grape color and scare Will Brady half to death. "Here, give him to his granny," she would say, and of course he would.

Other times the boy would just sit in his lap like a big cat, watching his face, and making Will Brady so self-conscious he couldn't move his lips. He never said a word about it, naturally, but he knew long before the boy had said a word, any more than da-da, that talking was going to be something of a problem for both of them. Fred Blake could make a fine assortment of faces, barnyard noises, and the like, but as for Will Brady he couldn't even whistle properly. Nor was the one face he had strictly his own. He knew that whenever the boy stared at him. It was just something that he wore that people like the boy saw right through. About all that he could do was wear arm bands with bright metal clips, or gay ribbons, wind his watch with the key, and keep penny candy in the pockets of his vest. Once a month he would bring the boy something special from Omaha. Something he could eat, ride, put together, or take apart.

Will Brady went to Omaha with the idea that almost any day, any warm Sunday morning, he might find Mickey Ahearn out walking on Douglas Street. He might see her in one of the doorways, or leaning out of one of the upstairs windows, with that boy Popkov, or somebody just like him, right at her back. He would be a foreigner, and the hair would be growing right out of his eyes. He also looked in jewelry stores, or better-class pawnshops, thinking he might find her choosing a ring, one with a stone that would be the real McCoy. All he wanted to do was to tell her what a fine healthy boy she had, but that it wouldn't hurt him any if he had his own mother one of these days. That was all. He wasn't going to force anything on her. In his wallet he had a picture of the boy seated on a wire chair, like those they have in drugstores, holding a wicker bird-cage and a Bible in his lap. The boy's mouth was open and you could see his three front teeth.

In the Wilderness

He would find her and show her this picture, and while she looked at the picture he would study her face, trying to make up his mind if she would be a good mother or not. If he thought she would, he would repeat what he once said. Let bygones be bygones, he would say. If she didn't look healthy, or didn't seem to care, or if she was still married to this Popkov—if that was how it was, why then he would have to think of something else.

He didn't have to think, as it turned out, very long. He never saw nor heard of Mickey Ahearn again, but the spring the boy was three years old, by Mrs. Blake's reckoning, he brought him a birthday present from Omaha. An Irish Mail, with a bright red seat—one of the many things the boy would have to grow into—Will Brady brought it back with him on the train. As he got off, down the tracks from the station, he saw a large funeral passing through town, and he stood there wondering whose funeral it was. In the lead buggy was Reverend Wadlow, and there at his side, wrapped up in a robe, was the widow—a woman who didn't look any too old. She was dressed in black, with a veil, and as the buggy rocked on the tracks she lifted this veil, deliberately, and looked at him. The same kind of look, whatever it was, that Ethel Bassett usually gave him in the pie-case mirror, she now gave him directly, then lowered the veil. In the buggy behind her was her son Orville, with members of her family, who were said to be Bohemians, and who had driven down from their farm near Bruno to be with her. Will Brady stood there, watching, until Fred Blake came along and picked him up.

That same evening, driving the team that Ralph Bassett reserved for Sundays, he drove the widow to the evening service at the church. From there he drove her home, put the team in the barn, and seeing that the spring grass needed cutting, he came back the following day and cut it for her. It was no more than Ralph Bassett's widow had the right to expect. She brought him a cool glass of grape juice, and while he stood there in the yard, sipping it, she sat in the chain swing behind the wire baskets of ferns.

The place needed a man, she said—needed a man to keep it up.

He agreed with that, and when he finished with the grape juice he said that the place needed a man, the way a man with a boy needed a home.

He didn't wait to see if she agreed with that or not. He put the glass on the porch and walked the mower through the grass to the back of the house.

5

THE HOUSE Ralph Bassett had built for his wife was full of furniture made in Grand Rapids, and in the gables were diamond-shaped pieces of colored glass. When the sun shone through the glass it reminded a railroad man, like Will Brady, of the red and green lights in the semaphores. Inside of the house, it was one of the things that made him at home. In the summer these colors might be on the floor, or cast on the goldfish bowl near the table, but in the winter they made a bright pattern on the wall. Or on the man who now sat at the head of the table, whoever he was. The food on the table was sometimes red, but the man at the table was usually green owing to the way he liked to lean forward, his head cocked to the side. The green light could be seen on his forehead, his wavy dark hair. Out of habit, perhaps, Will Brady—the man who now sat at the head of the table—liked to cock his head and keep one eye on the green light. That was what he liked to see down the spur of tracks, where the switch was open, and in the brakeman's lantern at the top of Opal Mason's stairs. Green. There was something friendly about it.

When the green light was not on his face Will

Brady might see, through the rippling bay window, the shrubs that were cut to look like giant birds, or little girls holding hands. Men who thought the house looked like a caboose might not see them curtsy in the wind, or the rambling rose vine that crawled up their arms to put flowers in their hair. But on Sunday, beyond the arbor, any man with eyes could see the tasseled buggies that scoffers drove by, very slowly, to see the house for themselves. Or to remark that Will Brady, seated in the chain swing, or mowing the lawn, had the look of a man who felt at home about the place.

Another man might smoke, or take it easy, but getting up from the table Will Brady would say: "Well, this isn't getting the grass cut," and hang his coat and vest on the back of his chair. He was not much of a hand with shrubs, but he could mow a lawn. As it happened to be quite a piece of lawn, maybe half an acre if you counted in the barn, by the time he was through in the back it was long in the front again. Not that he minded. Maybe he needed the exercise. As a matter of fact he liked a big lawn, with a few big shady elms around it, and a house with a swing and a wire basket of ferns on the front porch. He had a taste for the good things. Maybe it came natural to him.

When Ethel Bassett had to go and visit her people he slept in the house, in the guest room, as she felt better with a man in the house, as she said. Her maiden name was Czerny, and this helped to explain some of the things he felt about her, as foreigners were apt to be different in funny ways. When her father drove over for her he first spoke of his horses, wanting feed and water for them, then he spoke of his family, the weather, or whatever might come to mind. Ethel Bassett would go home with him, over Sunday, helping her mother with the Sunday meal, and then visiting the cemetery, where the stones were marked with foreign names. Some of them like her own, others hardly pronounceable. Ethel Bassett's feelings about these things was what Will Brady would call religious, as distinct from what he was apt to feel himself. He liked it. It was a thing to respect in her. There was something there, something to go back to, that he didn't seem to have, and he saw that it gave her an advantage over himself. It was part of the finer things she had around the house. It was his own suggestion that he stay in the house—look after these things, as he put it—so she wouldn't have something like that on her mind.

He slept in the guest room, which was on the south side of the house, facing the tracks, but a different air seemed to blow in the window from that in the hotel. It smelled of the grass he had cut himself. The bed seemed to be softer, and even his sleep seemed sounder, though he was a sound enough sleeper, normally. Something about the idea of a place of his own. The keys in his pocket to the cellar door, the lock on the barn. In the morning he served himself a good breakfast, eating his bacon and eggs in the kitchen, but putting off the coffee until he stood in the dining-room. Later he would walk from room to room, his feet quiet on the Axminster rugs.

No, it doesn't take long to get used to the finer things. All you need are the things, and a man with the taste for them. A woman with bird's-eye maple in her room, and small cut-glass bottles, with large stoppers, and an ivory box with long strands of her combed-out hair. Dark and soft as corn silk, not at all wiry like her red-haired boy. Somehow, he didn't care for the boy—his own boy struck him as a good deal finer, and the only thing in Calloway that went with the house. An imported look, like the glass chimes on the front porch. But there was nothing wrong with Ethel Bassett, nothing that he could see. A quiet woman, not given to talk, with something of a religious nature, she seemed to rely on him now that Ralph Bassett was gone. She left it up to him to shovel the snow from in front of the house. And when the snow was gone, it was up to him to cut the grass. He used a grass-catcher on the mower, but when the grass was damp, or he walked a little fast, it would miss the catcher entirely and stick to his pants, so he would need a broom from the kitchen to sweep himself off, and if it was summer he would need a cooling drink—grape juice, with a lump of ice in it, or fresh lemonade. And after putting away the mower he would walk around to the side of house where there was a faucet, and rinse off his hands. It was her own suggestion that he do that in the house. One thing like that leads to another, so he got in the habit of using the kitchen, and she got in the habit of standing there with him, holding the towel. Now, he didn't need a towel—that was what he always said. But she would wag her head, as women do when they find something like that in a man, and he would take the towel but only use the corner of it. And when he rolled down his sleeves, she would hold his coat for him. That was all. There was no need to say anything. Perhaps this was why the night that she spoke he was not at all sure that he had heard her, or that she had said what he thought he had heard.

"Yes—?" he said, and stood there, holding his hat.

What did he think of all the talk, she had said. So he had heard it all right. That was what she had said.

"Talk?" he said. "What talk?" and put his right hand into his pocket, as he did when the boy put a hard question to him. With the boy all he had to do was give him something.

There was talk of their getting married, she said, and he stood there, his hand in his pocket, then he took the hand out and looked at the rusty tenpenny nail. He used the nail to clean his thumbnail, then he said that if there was talk of that kind, he hadn't heard it, but if he had heard it he wouldn't have done much of anything. What he meant to say was that talk like that didn't bother him. That was what he said, then he put the head of the tenpenny nail in his mouth and saw that she was looking at him as she did in the pie case, her eyes wide. He saw that this blank expression, this look she gave him, was meant to be an open one. He was meant to look in, and he tried, but he didn't see anything.

There was talk of their getting married, she repeated, so he raised his voice and said that if that was the talk, why he had no objection. That was all right with him. If that was the talk, he said, his voice ringing, why, let them talk.

Would he be able to wait, she said, another three months?

Would he be able? Why, yes. He nodded his head. Yes, he repeated, he would be able to wait three months. Then he followed her out on the porch, full of wonder about what he had been saying, and picked up the paper, the Omaha Sunday paper, he had left on the swing. He put his paper in his pocket, then he took it out and waved to a man in a passing buggy, then he went down the seven steps and crossed the lawn. There was a brick sidewalk, but he stepped across it, waded into the road. From the park across the street a boy ran out, circled him twice, then ran off crying:

> *Strawberry shortcake,*
> *Huckleberry Pie,*
> *Pee in the road*
> *An' you'll get a sty.*

Somehow it made him feel better, and without looking back he walked off through the park.

IN THE CLEARING

1

THEY WERE married in Bruno, a Bohemian town in the rolling country just south of the Platte, four or five miles' drive from where her father had a big farm. They were married in the church where Ralph Bassett had married her. It sat on the rise, overlooking the town, and as it was June the door stood open and Will Brady could see the buggies drawn up beneath the shade trees out in front. An elderly man was combing sandburs from a dark mare's tail. It was quiet on the rise, without a leaf stirring, but in the sunny hollow along the tracks a westerly breeze was turning the wheel of a giant windmill. It looked softly blurred, quite a bit the way the heat made everything look in Indian Bow, with the air, like a clear stream of water, flowing up from the hot earth. Near the windmill a man was sinking a post, and the sound of the blows, like jug corks popping, came up in the pause that his mallet hung in the air. Fred Blake had to remind him—nudging him sharply—to kiss the bride.

They went to Colorado Springs, where he sat in the lobby, reading the latest Denver papers, and giving her time, as he said to himself, to compose herself. A little after ten o'clock he went up, and as he opened the door he saw her, seated at her dressing-table, her face in the mirror. The eyes were wide and blank, just as they were in the pie case. She did not smile, nor make any sign that she recognized him. Could he bring her something, he asked, but when she neither moved nor seemed to hear him, he closed the door and walked to the end of the hall. There was a balcony there, facing the mountains, and maybe he stood there for some time, for when he came back to the room, the lights were off. He did not turn them on, but quietly undressed in the dark.

As he had never been married before, or spent a night in bed with a married woman, there were many things, perhaps, that he didn't know much about. That was why he was able to lie there, all night, and think about it. The woman beside him, his wife, was rolled up tight in the sheet. She had used the sheet on top for this purpose so that he was lying next to the blanket, a woolly one, and perhaps that helped keep him awake. She seemed to be wrapped from head to foot, as mummies are wrapped. It occurred to him that something like that takes a good deal of practice, just as it took practice to lie, wrapped up like a mummy, all night. It took practice, and it also took something else. It took fear. This woman he had married was scared to death.

When a person is scared that bad, what can you do? You can lie awake, for one thing, in case this person might be lonely, or, like Opal Mason, in case she didn't like men who fell asleep. But it was hard to picture Opal Mason rolled up in a sheet. Or what it was now in this room that frightened this woman. As he had never been married before, he was not as upset as he might have been, for it occurred to him that there might be something he hadn't been told. In the marriage of widows, perhaps, a ceremony. A ritual that called for spending one night rolled up in a sheet. He had heard of such things. It was something he could think about. There was also the fact that this woman was a Bohemian, a foreigner, and perhaps she had foreign ways. But nobody had told him. And while he wondered, she fell asleep.

In time he fell asleep himself, but not too well beneath the woolly blanket, which may have been why he dreamed as he did, and remembered it. He

saw before him Ralph Bassett, standing behind the
desk. He had a large paunch, larger than he remembered, and the front of his vest, between the lower
buttons, was worn threadbare where he rubbed
against the handle of the coin drawer. A strange
dream, but Will Brady fathomed it. All these years
—and it seemed very long—Ralph Bassett had
rubbed the coin drawer during the day, then he had
gone home to rub against his mummy-wrapped
wife at night. It didn't strike him as funny. Nor did
it strike him as out of this world. If a woman has
lived twelve years with a man, and the nights of
those years rolled up in a sheet, and this woman was
now your wife, it deserved serious thought. And
while he thought, this woman, his wife, snored
heavily.

Their honeymoon room had a view of the mountains, with Pike's Peak, and a cloud of snow on it,
and as it was warm these windows were open on
the sky. The glass doors stood open on their balcony. Through these doors he could see the light on
the mountains, which were barren and known as
the Rockies, and toward morning the eastern slopes
were pink with light. He got out of bed and stood
for a while on the balcony. There was a good deal
to see and to hear, as the city below him was rising,
and in the blue morning light the woman on the
bed seemed out of this world. Still wrapped in the

sheet, she looked prepared for burial. He dressed
in the bathroom, and when he came out her white
arm lay over her face, shutting out the light, so he
closed the doors to the balcony. What did he feel?
What he seemed to feel was concern for her.
Neither anger nor dislike, nor the emotions of a
man who had been a fool. No, he felt a certain
wonder, what you might call pity, for this man
once her husband, now dead, and for this woman,
his wife, who was still scared to death. He felt it,
that is, for both of them. They were out of this
world, certainly—but in what world were they
living? Greater than his anger, and his disappoint-
ment, was the wonder that he felt that there were
such people, and that they seemed to live, as he did,
in the same world. Their days in the open, but
their nights wrapped up in a sheet.

Practically speaking, a honeymoon is where you
adjust yourself to something, and Will Brady managed this adjustment in two weeks. He worked at
it. He gave it everything he had. He learned to
sleep, or to lie awake, indifferent to her. And when
he learned these things this woman, his wife, gave
up her sheet. There it was, back where it belonged,
between Will Brady and the woolly blanket, and
let it be said for him that he recognized it for what
it was. A compliment. Perhaps the highest he had
ever been paid.

The truth was that he was flattered, and it was her own suggestion, plainly made, that he learn to do the things her red-haired boy had done. Draw up her corset, and fasten the hooks at the side of her gowns. In the lobby this woman walked at his side, her hip brushing his own, and coming down from carriages she seemed loose in his arms. Another compliment? Well, he could take that too. He had taken something out of this world, learned to live with it. He had discovered, in this strange way, something about loving, about pity, and a good deal about hooks and eyes and corset strings.

He had this concern for her, and she seemed to be proud of him. Her handsome face was blank, with the pleasant vacant look again. They ate a good deal, in rooms overlooking the city, or in cool gardens with flowering plants, or they rode in buses to look with others at prominent views. It was not necessary, eating or looking, to say anything. Everything necessary had already been said.

If in three weeks' time two strangers can manage something like that, working together, who is to say what a year or two, or a summer, might bring? Who is to say what they might have made of something like that? But in three weeks' time he had to help her into her suit, with the hooks at both sides, and kneel on the floor and button her high traveling shoes. Then he held the ladder for her while she climbed into the upper berth. She was wearing a veil, the car was dark, and it might be said that the last he saw of the woman he knew was her high button shoes and the dusty hem of her petticoats. Whatever they had managed, between them, whatever they had made in the long three weeks, went up the ladder and never came down again. It remained, whatever it was, there in the berth. When she started down the next morning, calling for him to steady the ladder, the woman who spoke his name was a stranger again, his wife.

"Ethel," he said, taking her hand, "you're home again."

2

OVER the summer he liked to sleep in the spare room, with the window open, as he could see down the tracks to the semaphore. When the signals changed, this semaphore made a clicking sound. On quiet summer nights he would hear that sound and then roll on his side, rising on his elbow, to watch the coaches make a band of light on the plains. The rails would click, and when the train had passed, there would be little whirlwinds of dust and leaves, and a stranger might think that a storm was blowing up.

Beyond the semaphore was the cattle loader, the smell strong over the summer, and down the spur to the west, past the sawmill, the house of a man named Schultz. This man lived alone on a ten-acre farm. In his bedroom, along toward morning, a yellow lamp would be burning, and now and then the shadow of this man Schultz would move on the blind. A hard man, a bear for work, it was known that he had married a city girl, but that the caboose that had brought her to town also took her away. He kept the lamp burning, it was said, in case she came back.

An hour or so after the Flyer went by, the west-bound local came along from North Platte, and Will Brady had got into the habit of meeting it. Now and then important men stopped in Calloway. Once a month, for example, the local came along with T. P. Luckett, the man who had charge of the U.P. commissary in Omaha. A big man in every way, around two hundred sixty pounds, Mr. Luckett had his breakfast in the hotel, and while sitting in the lobby, smoking his cigar, he seemed to feel like talking with someone. At that time in the morning Will Brady was the only man there. In T. P. Luckett's opinion, that of a man who spoke frankly, Calloway was dead and didn't know it— a one-horse town with the horse ready for pasture, as he put it. Nebraska had spread itself too thin, he said, the western land was not particularly good, and what future there was, in anything but cattle, lay in the east. Within a day's ride from Omaha, that is. The whole state was tipped, T. P. Luckett said, low in the east, high in the west, and the best of everything had pretty well run off of it, like a roof. The good land was along the Missouri, near Omaha. The good men, as well, and in T. P. Luckett's opinion it was high time a young fellow like Will Brady gave it serious thought. Saw which way the wind was blowing, that is, and got off the dime. Calloway might always need a jerkwater hotel to meet the local, but a jerkwater man could take care of it. This fellow Luckett made it clear that a man like Will Brady, with his oversize head, was doing little more than wasting his time.

Will Brady had never thought of himself in such terms. Whether he was an up-and-coming man, and ought to be up-and-coming with the east, or whether what he was doing or not doing was wasting his time. He simply did it. That was the end of it. But it doesn't take a man long to acquire a taste for the better things. All he needs are these things. The taste comes naturally.

No, he had never given it a thought—but he did now. Running a hotel was little more than sitting in the lobby, between the potted palms, and facing the large railroad map of the state on the wall.

There on the map any man could see for himself. There were ten towns in the east for every one in the west. Did it matter? Well, it did when you thought about it. When you're married, in a way, and have settled down, and have stopped, in a way, thinking about women, you find you have time now and then to sit and think about something else. Your future, for instance, and whether you're currently wasting your time.

T. P. Luckett, for example, was a man who had given up thinking about women in order to spend all of his time thinking about eggs. He thought about eggs because fresh eggs was one of the big dining-car problems, and T. P. Luckett was the top dining-car man. This problem kept a big man like Luckett awake half the night. Wondering how he could just put his hands on an honest-to-God fresh egg. Eggs were always on this man's mind, and perhaps it was natural that Will Brady, with nothing much on his mind, would get around to thinking about them. He made T. P. Luckett's problem something of his own. Take those eggs he had for breakfast, for instance; at one time he would have eaten them, that was all, but now he examined the shell, and marked the weight of each egg in his hand. He broke them into a saucer to peer at the yolk, examine it for small rings. He considered the color of the eggs, and one morning he made the observation that the whites of some eggs, perhaps fresh ones, held their shape in the pan. Other eggs, perhaps older ones, had whites like milky water, the yolk poorly centered and slipping off to one side. T. P. Luckett thought this very interesting. *His* particular problem, T. P. Luckett said, looking at him in a friendly manner, was to determine something like that with the egg in the shell. Then he laughed, but he went on to say that any man who could study like that, his own eggs, that is, might well discover anything. He put his hand on Will Brady's shoulder, looking him straight in the eye, and forgot himself to the extent of offering him a good cigar.

A week or two later, toward morning, a time that Will Brady did most of this thinking, the solution to T. P. Luckett's problem occurred to him. The way to get grade-A fresh eggs was to lay them, on the spot. Get the chickens, the spot, and let the eggs be laid right there. Day-old eggs, which was about as fresh as an egg might be. All T. P. Luckett needed was a man to raise as many chickens as it took to lay the required number of eggs. That might be quite a few. But that's all he would need. This egg would be white, as the white egg, by and large, looked best in the carton, just as the rich yellow yolk looked best in the pan. And what chicken laid an egg like that? White Leghorns. It just so happened that a white chicken laid the whitest eggs.

T. P. Luckett listened to all of this without a word. A bald-headed man, he took off his straw and wiped the sweat off the top of his head, peered at the handkerchief, then stuffed it back in the pocket of his coat.

"All right, Will," he said, "you're the man."

"I'm what man?" he said.

"I've got five thousand dollars," T. P. Luckett said, "five thousand simoleons that says you're the man. That'll buy a lot of chickens, that'll even buy you some nice hens." Will Brady didn't have an answer to that. "Tell you what I'll do," T. P. Luckett said, "I'll throw in ten acres I've got near Murdock. Murdock is a lot better chicken country anyhow."

Will Brady had an answer to that. He said: "Mr. Luckett, I've got a wife and kids to think of. My wife has a home, several pieces of property right here."

"You think it over," T. P. Luckett said, and wiped his head again, put on his hat. "You think it over—right now you could sell all this stuff for what you got in it. Twenty years from now you won't be able to give it away."

"In a way," Will Brady said, "I like it here."

"Tell you what you do," T. P. Luckett said;

"you put the little woman in the buggy and some fine day you drive her over to Murdock, show her around. Leave it up to her if she wouldn't rather live in the east."

"I'll see what she says," Will Brady said.

"I'm not thinking of eggs. I'm thinking," T. P. Luckett said, "of a man of your caliber sitting around in the lobby of a jerkwater hotel."

"I'll think it over, Mr. Luckett," he said, and T. P. Luckett took off his hat, wiped his head with the sleeve of his shirt, put his hat on, and went out.

As a man could marry only one woman, Will Brady had once brooded over such matters as the several thousand women he would have to do without. As no one woman had everything, in the widest sense of the term, neither did any egg have everything. But he came to the conclusion, after months of consideration, that the Leghorn egg had the most for the "carriage trade." This was how T. P. Luckett referred to those people who were something. What we've got to keep in mind, he always said, is how the carriage trade will like it. A very neat way of putting things, once you thought about it. Will Brady had seen a good many of such people through the wide windows of the diners, and on occasion he had spoken to some of them. Offering a match, or the time of day, as the case might be. It was very easy to tell such men from those who dipped their napkins in their water glasses, then used the napkin to clean their celluloid collars, their false cuffs. With a little experience a man could tell the real carriage trade from that sort of people, as easily as the real carriage trade could tell a good egg. Nine out of ten times it would be a Leghorn.

Well, that was the egg, but what about the chicken laying it? Did it take two, maybe three of them, to lay one egg? Did they quit after a while, die over the winter, or get the croup? To determine these and like matters, he bought three dozen Leghorn hens, kept them in sheds behind the barn, and bought a ledger to keep their record in. This ledger he kept in the basement, and every evening he entered the number of eggs, the amount of grain eaten, and the proportion of large eggs to the case. He compared this with the figures at the local creamery. Every morning he cracked two eggs, peered at the yolks, then fried them, slowly, in butter, or he boiled them and served them in an official dining-car cup. He had never been of much use with his hands, he hurt himself with hammers, cut himself with knives, but it seemed that he could handle an egg with the best of them. He could take five in each hand, right out of the case, and hold them gently, not a shell cracking, or he could take two eggs, crack them, and fry them with one hand. There were people who would like to have seen that, his wife perhaps, and certainly T. P. Luckett, but he did it alone, just as a matter of course, every morning. He studied eggs, just as a matter of course, every night. As all of his own eggs were fresh and didn't need to be candled, he had a case of cold-storage eggs sent out from Omaha. He mixed them up with his own eggs, then sorted them out. It took him several weeks, but he learned—without anyone around to tell him—how a fresh egg *looked*, and about how old a storage egg was.

In April he took a Sunday off to drive his wife over to Murdock, a town of several thousand people and some big shady trees. Just east of town was a two-way drive with a strip of grass right down the middle, lamps on concrete posts, and a sign welcoming visitors to town. There was nothing to compare with it in Calloway. T. P. Luckett's ten acres were just a half mile north of town. A nice flat piece of ground, it lay between the new road and the curve of the railroad, and there was plenty room for several thousand laying hens, maybe more. Along the north side of the land was a fine wind-break of young cottonwood trees.

They had their dinner in town, at a Japanese restaurant where there were paintings on the walls, and violin music played throughout the meal. They sat in a booth, with a dim light on the table, and though his wife had once been in St. Louis, and seen many fine things, it was clear she had seen nothing like this. At the front of the restaurant was a glass case, with a slot at one side for a coin, and on dropping a coin the violin in the case would begin to play. One hand held the bow, the other plucked the strings. As she was very fond of music he walked forward twice and played it for her.

At the end of this meal he told her what he had in mind. He described, pretty much in detail, what T. P. Luckett had told him, and how Calloway, inside of twenty years, would be a dead town. A man of his caliber, he said, quoting T. P. Luckett, had no business wasting his life in a jerkwater hotel. He had meant to say small, not jerkwater, but when he got there the word came out, and he saw that it made quite an impression on her. She had never seen the hotel, or the town, in quite that light before. Perhaps she hadn't thought of him, her husband, as a man of caliber. It made a lasting impression on her, and while they sat there a Mr. Tyler, the man who owned the restaurant, presented her, absolutely free, with a souvenir. This was a booklet describing the town of Murdock. There were thirty-two pages, every page with a picture, and at the back of the booklet was a table showing how all the real-estate values were shooting up. On the cover was the greeting:

In the Clearing

and while she glanced through it he walked back to play the magic violin again.

3

IN THE town of Murdock Will Brady bought a house with a room at the front, which he used to sleep in, and a room at the back where he ate his meals. Once a week, however, he would take his family to the Japanese restaurant, sit them in a booth, and give the boys coins to play for their mother the magic violin. His wife, Ethel, liked to sit where she could see the wax hand move the real bow. Will Brady took the seat facing the window where the yokels that stood along the curb would walk back and press their noses to the glass and peer in at them. He had never really thought much about these people, the kids off the farms and the old men still on them, until he sat there in the booth and saw their corn-fed faces grinning at him. Then

67

he knew that they were yokels, corn-fed hicks from the ground up.

That's what they were, but with the war coming on, things were looking up. Sometimes a farmer with six or seven kids would bring them into town, herd them into the restaurant, but leave his wife in the buggy until she had finished nursing the little one. Will Brady could see that buggy through the window, and it would be new, the spokes would be red, and there might be a new creaking set of harness on the old horse. The horse would toss his head to get the feed at the bottom of his new feed bag. And the woman in the buggy might have a new hat, a Sears Roebuck print dress, or the high button shoes that he could see when she lifted her skirts from the buggy wheel.

And at the edge of town, where there had once been weeds, or maybe nothing at all to speak of, there was now a field of grain or a new crop of beans. Every acre that would grow weeds had been plowed up. And it was no passing thing, people had to eat—hadn't Will Brady himself just read somewhere that the rich Missouri Valley was going to be the bread basket of the world? The world had to eat something, so it might as well be eggs. Fresh, day-old eggs if possible. Somewhere else he had read, or heard a man say, that there were more than four hundred million Chinamen who had never had a really square meal in their lives. Well, an up-and-coming man like Will Brady would give it to them. All that had to be done was to stop them eating rice, start them eating eggs.

In the old country this Kaiser fellow had done a lot of damage and killed a lot of people, but in the new country he seemed to be doing a lot of good. Will Brady could see it on the faces of the men who came into town. This war boom was about the finest thing that had happened to them. Some of the women might feel a little different, but it was hard to complain about a new buggy, a roof for the barn, and a machine that would separate the milk from the cream. And now and then a tired farm woman liked to eat out. She liked to see her new baby in the red high chairs that came along with the meal, like the cups and plates, and sit there at the table with her own two hands free to eat. Nothing in her lap but the folded napkin and the bones for the dog. Just a year or two before, this same woman came to town in the wagon, with the tailboard down, but now she rode in a tassel-fringed buggy with a spring seat. And having tasted the finer things in life, like Will Brady, she would go on wanting them.

4

THE HOUSE Will Brady bought had five other rooms besides those he ate and slept in, but he didn't have much to do with them. The house was usually dark in the morning when he left it, and again in the evening when he got home, and rather than fool around with the lamp, he undressed in the dark. The wick of the lamp was charred and left an oily smell in the air.

Was he all right? Once a week his wife, Ethel, asked him that. She spoke to him through the bedroom door, the lamp shadow at her feet. Yes, he was all right—just a little preoccupied. That was it, he was just a little preoccupied.

There was a window at the foot of his bed, but he kept the blind drawn because the street light, swinging over the corner, sometimes kept him awake. As the chairs were hard to see in the dark, he kept one of them in the corner, and the other at the side of the bed for his watch and coat. Sometimes he put his pants there too if he happened to think of it. Otherwise he dropped them on the floor, or folded them over the rail at the foot of the bed, with his collar and tie looped around the brass post. He slept in his socks, but that was not something new—he had always done that. It helped keep his feet warm and also saved quite a bit of time.

The room was always dark, but if he lay awake he could make out the calendar over the stovepipe hole, the white face of the clock, and the knobs on the dresser from Calloway. But the grain of the bird's-eye maple was lost on him. On the dresser was a bottle of cherry cough syrup, which he took when he had an upset stomach, a comb and a brush, and a very large Leghorn egg. This egg had three yolks, but he couldn't decide what to do with it. As it was ten days old, he would soon have to make up his mind. At the foot of the bed, in the cream-colored wall, he could see the door that he used twice a day, and on hot summer nights he left it open to start a cool draft. The rest of the time he kept it closed, with the key in the lock.

It might be going too far to say that Will Brady lived in this house, as he spent his time elsewhere and usually had other things on his mind. But he came back there every night, went away from there every morning, and something like that, if you keep at it, gets to mean something. There were always, for instance, clean shirts in the dresser drawer. There were always socks with the holes mended, and if they had just been washed this woman, his wife, first ran her hand into each one of them.

71

There were always collar studs in the cracked saucer beside the clock. When he was sick, or coughed in the night, or was found there in bed the following morning, the woman of the house came to the door of his room and knocked. She would give him hot lemonade and sound advice. The blinds would be raised to let in the sunshine, his coat and pants would be hung on the door, and she would ask him—after looking for them—for his socks. She always found it hard to believe that they were still on his feet.

The woman of the house lived at the back, in a large sunny room full of plants and flowers, but the children of the house seemed to live with the neighbors, or under the front porch. They went there to eat candy, drink strawberry pop, and divide up the money they took from his pockets on Sundays, holidays, and any other time he had to change his pants. In the evening Will Brady sometimes stopped to peer under the porch, and wonder about it, as nothing ever seemed to be there but the soft hot dust. The lawnmower and the wooden-runner sled were pushed far to the back.

Other evenings Will Brady might stop in the alley and look at the yard, the three white birch trees, and the house that had now been paid for, every cent of it. It looked quite a bit like the neighboring houses in most respects. It had a porch at the front, lightning rods, a peaked roof, panes of colored glass; and in the rooms where the lights were on, the blinds were always drawn. Homelike? Well, that was said to be the word for it. And after a certain hour all of the lights in the house would be out. The people in the house would do what they could to go to sleep. By some common agreement, since there was no law saying that they had to, they would turn out the lights, go to bed, and try to sleep. Or they would lie there making out the shape of things on the wall. Why did they do it? Well, it was simply how things were done. It was one of those habits that turned out to be pretty hard to break.

Will Brady often wondered—when he didn't sleep—what the man in the neighboring house was doing, if he slept well himself, or if he came home and undressed in the dark. This man was a prominent citizen. He had just installed a new marble fountain in his store. Revolving stools, on white enamel posts, sat in front of it. During the evening his daughter, a large pasty girl, would wipe off the counter and the marble-topped tables, and Mr. Kirby himself would walk around and push the wire-legged chairs back into place. A little stout, in his forties somewhere, Clyde Kirby always spoke to you by name, asked about the missus, and sent you one of his New Year calendars. Hard to say, offhand, whether he undressed in the dark or not. He had raised five sons and was old enough to have learned a thing or two.

Will Brady sometimes stood in the alley adjoining Clyde Kirby's house. The blinds were usually drawn, as they were in his own, but one evening the windows were up and he saw Clyde Kirby, with his sleeves rolled up, standing in the pantry door. He was crumbling hunks of cornbread into a tall drinking glass. He filled this glass to the top with cornbread, then he took a can of milk, punched two holes, and poured the heavy cream over the cornbread, filling the glass. With the handle of his spoon, like a soda boy, he slushed it up and down. He seemed to be in a hurry, for some reason, but before he could lift the spoon to his mouth he heard a noise in the house, a door at the front had opened and closed. And like a kid who had got into the jam pot, this Clyde Kirby, a leading citizen, took the glass of cornbread he was holding and hid it behind his back. He just stood there, as if he was thinking, while the woman of the house came out of the hallway and carefully drew the blinds clear around the living-room. One by one she drew down all of the blinds on that side of the house. Then she entered the kitchen, walking past Mr. Kirby like a propped-up ironing board, and drew the blinds around the kitchen, hooked the screen, then went back the way she had come. All of this without making a gesture, without saying a word. And Clyde Kirby stood there, the glass at his back, until he heard the door at the front snap closed, then he crossed the dark kitchen and stood at the sink. He poured more canned milk over the cornbread, slushed it up and down with the spoon, then stood there gulping it down as though he was starved to death.

If it was the man's business to eat in the kitchen, it seemed to be the woman's business to keep the blinds drawn, and to make out of what went on in the house a home. For good or bad, a man seemed to need a woman around the house. And if Will Brady was a father, then this woman he had married was a mother of sorts.

Concerning his fatherhood, Will Brady sometimes walked from the front of the house to the back, tapped on the door, and with a serious face then put in his head. This woman he had married would be sitting there, mending clothes. Will Brady would say what he had to say—something about the poisons in penny candy—and she would agree with him, this woman, that the poisons were there. But the pimples, if that's what he meant, didn't mean anything. All boys had them. And that was what he wanted to hear. The poisons in penny candy were a man's business, and when he spoke she respected him for it; but the pimples on the chin were a woman's business, and he respected her. And it was up to her to make, out of all of this business, something called a home.

Well, that was the woman's business, but what about his own? If you want to get the feel of the egg business you take an egg in your hand—that is, you take thousands of them—and from each egg you slowly chip off the hen spots with your thumb. It isn't really necessary to candle the egg or peer around inside. The necessary thing is to get the feel of an egg in your hand.

That's how it is with eggs, but chickens are something else. A few old hens in the yard are one thing, but when you take a thousand pullets, say several thousand Leghorn pullets, what you have on your hands is something else. To get the feel of something like that troubled a lot of men. No man would rein in his horse to look at one chicken, but there were sometimes four or five buggies, or a wagonful of kids, drawn off the road just east of the Brady chicken farm. On Sunday afternoons even the women would be there. Five thousand Leghorn pullets was something no man had been able to describe. There was nothing to do but put the family in the buggy, let them see it for themselves.

They were usually farm people for the most part, people who ought to be sick to death of chickens, but they would get in their buggies and ride for half a day just to look at them. Some of these families brought their lunches and made a picnic out of it. Monday morning the ditch grass would be short where the grazing horses had clipped it, and the road would be scarred where the buggy weights had dragged in the dust. As these people didn't know Will Brady from Adam, he was free to drive his own team right in among them, let his mares graze, and look on with the rest of them. Five thousand Leghorns, five acres of white feathers, if a man could speak in terms like that. And why not? Somehow he had to describe this thing. Or perhaps a sea of feathers, a lake of whitecaps, when the wind caught them from the back, fanning out their tails and blowing loose feathers along with the dust. Will Brady used the word, though of course he had never seen the sea. Nor had he ever seen a larger body of water than Carter Lake. It was simply that the word came to mind, and Will Brady often spoke of his sea of chickens the way other men would refer to a field of corn. If and when he saw the sea, very likely he would think it looked like that. He would gaze out on the water and see five thousand pullets that would soon be hens.

There were also some sheds, which seemed to float like so many small boats in the sea of feathers, and there was a bare clearing where he planned to erect a fine city house. But from the buggies men saw just the chickens, the high unpainted cable fence, and the green bank of the railroad like a dam to hold it all in. Different men, of course, saw different things, but perhaps the best way to describe it was a remark that T. P. Luckett let drop one day.

"How's your empire, Brady?" he said, and most people let it go at that.

5

ONCE a month he went to Omaha on business, what you might call a business investment, as he found he worked better if he got away from Murdock now and then. The life in the city seemed to stimulate him. He always took a room at the Wellington Hotel, where there were fine potted palms in the lobby, a large map on the wall, and where altogether he felt more or less at home. He would sit between the palms, facing the street, or he would swing the chair around and face the lobby, the elevator cage, and the cigar-counter girl. She would usually be rattling the dice in the leather cup, or kidding with the old men. Summer evenings he might walk out on the new bridge and look at the bluffs across the river, or at the swirling brown water, more like mud than water, that he saw below. T. P. Luckett had said that part of the state was washing away. Standing there on the bridge Will Brady could see the truth of that. On his walk back to the hotel he would pick up a jar of hard candy for the boys, and make arrangements for the flowers, the roses, he would take to his wife.

"Would the gentleman like to include a card?" the flower girl always said.

"No," he would say, "no, thank you—it's just for my wife."

If the weather was bad he would sit in the lobby facing the girl behind the cigar counter and observing the way she had learned to handle the men. These men were all older, by and large, being traveling men with a sharp sense of humor, but she had learned to talk right back to them without batting an eye. Most of the men played dice with her for cigars. The dice were held in a leather cup, where they made a hollow rattle like peas in a gourd, and after the rattle she would roll them out on a small green pad. The older men liked to do it, it seemed, whether they won or not. The girl would slide back the glass top to the case and the man would reach in, helping himself to a La Paloma or whatever brand he liked. At the side of the counter was a small lamp, in a hood to keep the flame from blowing, and on a chain was a knife with a blade for snipping off the tip of your cigar. They would then purse their lips like a fat hen's bottom as they moistened the tip. It seemed to give these men a great deal of satisfaction just to rattle the dice, win or lose, and to help themselves to a cigar from the glass case. The hollow sound of the dice could be heard in the lobby, and in his room on the second floor, if the transom was down, Will Brady could hear the game being played. The men usually laughed, a booming manly laugh, if the girl won.

Although he neither smoked nor gambled Will Brady seemed to like the sound of the dice, and something or other about the game seemed to interest him. Perhaps he had a yen to take the leather cup in his hand, shake it himself. To see if he could roll a seven, an eleven, or whatever it was. When the girl won, as she usually did, she would often wink at somebody in the lobby—at Will Brady if he happened to be sitting there. Although he didn't gamble, he would wink back at her. It was something she did with all the old men: it didn't mean anything. The day she spoke to him, for example, she was just playing the game with herself, she didn't trouble to wink, she just spoke to him right out of the blue.

"Come and have a game on me," she said.

"I don't play," he replied, but in a friendly manner.

"Come and play for a good cigar," she said, and rattled the dice. "Three," she said, "you can surely beat a three."

"Maybe," he said, "but I don't smoke."

"You don't what?" she said.

"I don't smoke," he replied.

The girl put down the leather cup she was holding and looked at him. "You're just kidding," she said, "what's your brand? I'll bet it's La Paloma for a man like you."

"Thank you very much," he said, "but I don't smoke." She looked at him for a while, and he looked back at her. She winked at him, but of course it didn't mean anything.

"You don't play either?" she said.

"No," he said, "I don't play."

She rattled the dice in the cup, then said: "You don't play, you don't smoke—what do you do?"

"I work," Will Brady replied, as if that explained everything, and maybe it did. He had never put it just that way before. "I work," he repeated, and smiled at the girl, but this time she didn't wink.

"If you don't smoke, why don't you smoke?" she said.

"I suppose I never started," he said; "if you don't start, maybe you don't want to."

"You really think so?"

"Well, I don't smoke," he said.

"I thought maybe you didn't smoke for your wife," she said. As he didn't get the point of that right away, Will Brady turned and looked at the lobby. When he got it, he said:

"I don't think my wife cares very much."

"I would," she said, "I would if I had any choice." Before he could think of an answer to that another man, about his own age, stepped up to the counter and pushed back the glass top to the case. He helped himself to a cigar, moistened the tip, then went off chewing on it. "You see what I mean?" the girl said, and made a face. When Will Brady didn't answer, she said: "Just imagine kissing something like that."

Turning to face the lobby Will Brady replied: "Well, I hear that some of them do."

"They don't if they have any choice," said the girl, and rattled the dice. He didn't have an answer to that, so she said: "—but I guess they don't have much choice. What choice do you have when some men never take a day off?"

"What would a man want to take a day off for?" he said.

"It's a good thing I don't take you men seriously," she replied.

As he wanted to be taken seriously, he said: "I've never had a day off in my life."

"You men!" she said, and made a clucking sound with her tongue.

"A day off—" he said, "what for?"

"I like men who wear red ties," she said.

He looked down at his new red tie, then he replied: "Not every man can take a day off, but there's some men who can if they want to. Men of a certain caliber are more or less free to do as they like."

"If they don't smoke," she said, "I suppose they've got to do something." She winked at him, and this time he winked back. "That's why I wish I was a man," she said; "a man can do as he likes, but a woman only has one day a week."

"What day is that?" he said, and looked her right in the eye.

"Friday," she said, looking right back at him, "I'm off every Friday at five o'clock." She rolled the dice out on the pad, and when it turned up a four and a three she said: "That means it's lucky for me. What kind of car does a man like you drive?"

Several years before, listening to T. P. Luckett, something of this sort had come over Will Brady, and he had become, overnight almost, a man of caliber. Now he became the owner of a car. An Overland roadster—one of the kind that a man like himself might drive.

He bought this car in Columbus, where he had to change trains, and the new Willys-Overland dealer had a fine big showroom facing the station and the tracks. In the window was the Overland roadster with the sporty wire wheels. They were red, and about the same color as his tie.

As he stood there listening to the powerful motor he let the owner of the shop persuade him that he might as well get into the car and drive it home. On west of Columbus it was wide-open country, there was nothing but horses to worry about, and the only way to learn to drive a car was to get in and drive. Once he got in, and got the car moving, he would find that the Overland drove itself, leaving nothing for the driver to do but sit there and shift the gears. At the railroad crossings he would get a lot of practice in.

He got in a lot of practice, all right, but some of

it was lost owing to the fact that he drove along, thirty miles or so, in second gear. The road was so bad that he didn't seem to notice it. Ten miles an hour was pretty good time over most of it. It was just getting dark when he came into Murdock, at the edge of the Chautauqua grounds, where he saw that several boys had built a bonfire near the tracks. One of them, a very spry little fellow, was hopping around. Now, boys often behave like that and he might not have thought anything of it if he hadn't noticed, in the light from the fire, that he had on no pants. He was hopping up and down, hollering and yelling, without his pants. When Will Brady saw who this spry boy was, and what it was they all seemed to be doing, his hand went forward, in spite of himself, and honked the horn. They jumped up like rabbits, every one of them, and ran for the trees. But not a single boy, and there were maybe ten of them, had on his pants. They ran off like madmen, hooting like Indians, through the scrubby willows along the tracks, and bringing up the rear, his bottom bright in the car lights, was Will Brady's son. Farther down the tracks they picked up their pants and ran along waving them, like banners, but there was not time, of course, to stop and put them on. Will Brady just sat there till he heard the motor running, and the hooting had passed.

Perhaps that was why he went to Omaha again the following week. He had it in mind to walk down lower Douglas, where he knew there were doctors "for men," and speak to one of these doctors about the strange behavior of the boys. He had often seen the signs that were painted on the windows on the second floor. So he walked along this street, he read the signs, but he couldn't seem to make up his mind how to describe what had happened, or whether Willy Brady, aged nine, was a man or not. These doctors for men might think that Will Brady was kidding them. He went back and took a seat in the lobby of the Wellington Hotel. It happened to be Saturday, not Friday, but the girl behind the counter had been thinking it over, and she wondered if Sunday wouldn't be a better time for him. Now that he had a car, and in case he really wanted to take the day off.

If there were people in Murdock who had picked up the notion that Will Brady liked other chickens as well as Leghorns, talk like that somehow never got around to him. It couldn't, as he seldom talked to anyone. Not that Will Brady wasn't friendly— everybody remarked how friendly he was—but he didn't have the time, or whatever it took, to make friends. Will Brady was what they called a go-getter, a man who not only was up and coming, but in a lot of things, the important things, had already arrived. Just north of town, for example, he had a chicken farm with five thousand Leghorns, and on a cold windy day some of the feathers even blew into town. And work had begun on his modern thirteen-room house. As illustrated in *Radnor's Ideal Homes,* Will Brady's house would have a three-story tower, and was listed under "Mansions," the finest section of the book. Not listed, but to be part of the house, were the diamond-shaped panes of colored glass, imported from Chicago like the marble in Clyde Kirby's new drugstore. As there were thirty-six windows in this house, including those in the basement and the tower, there would be nothing like it in either Murdock or Calloway. If there was light, it came through a panel of colored glass. If there was no light, as sometimes couldn't be helped, a lantern would be burning in the top of the tower, shining through a green porthole like the semaphore far down the tracks. A man out on the plains could get his bearings just by looking at it.

This fellow Brady was a comer, as everybody said, but not many people would have recognized him, or the girl along with him, on certain warm summer nights. Out in the Krug Amusement Park he would sit on a bench, holding her cone of spun sugar candy, while she rode the roller coaster and other up-and-down rides that made him sick. Early in the evening she would first go swimming, leaving him on the beach with her comb and her lipstick, or in the wicker chairs for parents on the balcony behind the diving board. Before diving she would turn and wave to him. Chased by boys, she liked to swim under water, and in his anxiety Will Brady would rise out of the chair and somebody would ask him to please sit down. There were other people who had children to account for, this man would say.

Elderly folks, both men and women, often drew up their chairs to speak to Will Brady, ask about his girl, and tell him what a fine-looking child she was. When he agreed, they would point out youngsters of their own. Most of them were plump, good-looking girls, squealing like pigs when the boys edged near them, and Will Brady could see that nearly all parents had the same concern. To be there to wave when the children dived, to tell them when they turned the soft blue color, and to shoo off the boys, like flies, when they sprawled out on the sand. Later would come the Ferris wheel, the Spook House, the balls thrown at something, and if it was hit he would carry the Kewpie doll. He would spend five dollars to win a fifty-cent Ouija board. In the ballroom, with these things in his lap, he would sit on a folding chair in the corner watching her dance with some young buck who had asked her to. A youngster who thought *he* was her father, naturally. And they would bring him a hot dog, a bottle of red pop, and stand there before him, trying to be friendly, looking over their shoulders at the young people who danced.

"Now, why don't you kids go and dance," he would say, and while they did he would eat the hot dog and look at the Ouija board, as the boy would be hugging her. But not too much, as he *was* her father, and after a while the boy would bring her back, shake Will Brady's hand, and try to leave a good impression with him.

"I'm very glad to have met you, sir," these boys would say.

But after the swimming, the riding, and the dancing, she would play with him. She would take him for several long rides on the Swanee River, that is. Will Brady found it spooky and unpleasant, the rocking of the boat troubled him, but on the whole he got along without getting sick. And in the dark part of the river, in the mossy wood, where the water splashed over the mill wheel, she would take his hands in her own and put them around her waist. There she would hold them, tight, until they reached the pier where the ride had ended, and everybody on the pier could see how it was with the pair in the boat. That this man with the straw hat was a good deal more than a father to her. He was her lover. A man to be pitied and envied, that is.

To make it perfectly clear who Will Brady was, she needed help with her clothes in lobbies and restaurants, and out on the street dust was always blowing into her eyes. She would have to press against him while he saw what the trouble was. In the aisles of big stores she liked to swoon, as the high-class ladies swooned in the movies, and to have him come with her while she shopped for stockings and underclothes. Nobody had taught her how to wear clothes so that she looked covered when she had them on, but she had learned from her mother how to go without them and look all right. Like swimming under water, it astonished and troubled him. Her mother was an actress on the vaudeville circuit, and her father was one of five men, in a ten-minute act, who entered the room and hid under the bed. Will Brady had once seen her mother, on a poster, on lower Douglas Street. Her daughter looked a good deal like her in most respects.

There was little resemblance, certainly, between this girl and sad-eyed Opal Mason, but at night he had the feeling Opal Mason would approve of her. Like Opal Mason, the girl liked to talk. Will Brady often had the feeling that he was there in bed for reasons he hadn't really looked into and were not at all the reasons that an outsider might think. He never said much himself, as he was too sleepy and felt he was there for fairly obvious reasons, but toward morning, without her saying anything, he would wake up. Why was that? It seemed to be because she wanted him to. He couldn't really do much for her, somehow, but one thing he could do was wake up in the morning, roll on his back, and lie there listening to her. Sometimes he wondered if this might be another form of loving, one that women needed, just as men seemed to need the more obvious kind. But he didn't really know, and the talking never cleared it up. As a matter of fact, the more she talked, the less he understood.

Sometimes this girl would begin with the morning and describe everything that had happened; she would describe, that is, every man who had troubled to follow her. She remembered and described these men so well that Will Brady, who saw very little, would recognize these men as the familiar fops he passed in the street. Every one of them useless, whore-chasing men, with a gold-toothed smile, light-tan button shoes, and a pin in his tie he could buy for fifteen cents. And they were all, she insisted, very fine gentlemen. When he scoffed at this she wanted to know what he would know about men like that, not knowing anybody, let alone classy people like that. Then she would go on—she always went on—to tell him that a lady knew a gentleman by the oil in his hair and the fancy silk socks that he wore. And the way that he would stand, in the better-class lobbies, shooting his cuffs.

Well, there were things that he might have said, but he would have to lie there, his mouth tight shut, as right there on the floor, at the side of the bed, were his own dirty socks. Or worse yet, they might still be on his feet, right there in the bed. What could he say—a man like that—about fine gentlemen? Nor could he even ask her where she had picked up such notions. He knew, for one thing—he knew she had smelled this hair at close quarters, snapped the cuff links herself, and praised the gentlemen's taste in socks. He knew, and it was the last thing in the world he cared to hear about.

If she liked these dandies, he had said, and he liked the word *dandy*, what in the world did she see in a man like him?

"Your hair," she had replied. Just like that. That had made him so mad he said what he had on his mind.

"And how are these dandies to sleep with?" he said.

"Oh," she said, "like anybody." But as he lay back she added: "But what's that to do with what I like?"

*　*　*

In the Clearing

As he drove into Omaha every Friday and home again on Sunday evening, he may have picked up the notion that it might go on indefinitely. Now and then he did wonder about the girl, and the five days a week he wasn't there to watch her, but he neither wondered nor worried about his wife. She lived in the sunny room at the back of the house, and when she heard him come in, on Sunday evening, she would call out: "Is that you, Will?" and he would answer: "Yes, Ethel," and hook the screen, turn out the light. Then he would walk through the dark house to his room at the front.

The night she didn't call out, his first thought was that she might be asleep. He didn't worry about it until he got into bed, when the quiet of the house, something or other about it, and the creaking street light seemed to keep him awake. The night, he thought, seemed quieter than usual. That might have been because of the noise of the city, where a street car passed right below the window, but it kept him awake like the lull that follows a wind. He sat up in bed at one point and looked out. He could see the gnats and hear the big fat June bugs strike the street light. Turning from the window he noticed the door that led from his room into the boy's, and on the chair in front of the door were his pants. On holidays, when he might sleep late, the boy would open the door and take some of the small change from his pants. Was that stealing? Neither of them had mentioned it.

It occurred to Will Brady that it had been some time since the boy had come in to swipe a little money, or since his father had opened the door to question the boy. Not since the week the boy had taken to drinking vinegar. He would take the big vinegar jug to his room, hiding it beneath the bed or inside of his pillow, and when the lights were out he would pull out the cork and take a swig. Later he would be sick and vomit over his Teddy bears. It had been a very strange thing to do—like the hooting and howling with his pants off—but Dr. Finley had said some boys would surprise you. And they certainly would.

At that time Will Brady had suggested that the door between their rooms might be left open, but the boy said his father's snoring kept him awake. Perhaps it did. So the door was closed again. But there was no more vinegar trouble and for a while everything seemed all right, until Will Brady came home one night and found the entire house lit up. The boy was propped up in bed with his bears, but his hair was shaved off. He had dipped his head, with all of his lovely curls, in a barrel of hot tar. Several men had been repairing the roof of the church, and while they were up there working on it, the boy had sneaked over and dipped his head in their barrel of tar. God knows how he had ever thought of something like that. A crazy thing to do, but he had done it, and the long silken curls that hung below his shoulders were thrown away with the stiff chunks of tar. The top of his small, narrow head had to be shaved. He looked like a bird that had just been hatched, and it upset Ethel, who was not his real mother, a good deal more than it did the boy. She took to bed for several days herself. It might be that Ethel, who already had a boy, had wanted a small pretty girl for a change, as she let his hair grow and liked to dress him in rompers and Fauntleroys. But the tar had put an end to that.

With his small head shaved Willy Brady was neither a boy nor a girl. In the evening his father would sometimes open the door and look into the room, where the lamp sat on the table, and the boy would be sitting there in bed with his three brown bears. One of them, the papa bear, almost as big as he was. And always reading, as *they* had just learned to read. As Will Brady didn't want to disturb them—the three bears had staring glass eyes—he would close the door without saying anything. Standing there in the dark, he would hear the boy whisper to one of them.

Although he had never done it before, he got out of bed, lit his lamp, and opened the door to the boy's room. He first thought the figure propped up in bed was the boy, with his eyes wide open, but it turned out to be the papa bear. The boy was not there in the bed at all. But pinned to the bear's woolly chest was a piece of note paper, torn from a pad, that seemed to be blank until he came forward with the lamp. It was not signed, nor did it say to whom it was addressed, but Will Brady recognized the writing well enough. His wife, Ethel, wrote a fine Spencerian hand.

Willy is with Mrs. Riddlemosher

it said, and that was all. That was all he ever heard from Ethel Czerny Bassett, his wife.

6

WITH a small pail of sand containing horsetail hairs that would turn to garter snakes when it rained on them, Will Brady and his son moved from the town of Murdock to the city of Omaha. They took a room on the mezzanine floor of the Wellington Hotel. The pail of sand was kept at the front of the lobby, behind the tub with the potted palm, so that Willy Brady, in case it rained, could run outside with it. Sometimes he did, other times he just let it rain.

In the morning the boy would be there in the lobby, sitting near one of the brass spittoons, where he was told he could whittle or spit the black licorice juice. Most of the time he just sat there, with his legs straight out. The women who worked in the hotel restaurant would stop and speak to him.

After lunch, with his friend Mr. Wherry, he would play four or five games of checkers, or a game of parcheesi with the cigar-counter girl. It might be that Mr. Wherry, who was fond of children, thought the girl behind the counter was the boy's sister, as he seemed to think they were both Will Brady's kids. He bought them bags of candy and took them down the street to the matinee. He was a fine old man, but a little hard of hearing; and something like that, a problem like that, was better left alone, as it might prove hard to explain.

If the boy wasn't there in the lobby he might be on the mezzanine, in the phone booth, having long conversations with the telephone girl. He would leave word with her to have his father call him when he came in.

"This is Willy Brady Jr.," the voice would say, with the confident tone of a Singer's midget, and somehow his father, Will Brady, was never prepared for it. He would stand there, and the boy would say: "Who is this speaking?"

"This is your father, son," Will Brady would say, in the sober voice of a father, but he never had the feeling that the boy was impressed. He didn't believe it any more than Willy Brady did himself.

Once a week, as a father should, he would borrow the boy from Mr. Wherry and take him to the places a boy would like to go. This was usually to see a man named Eddie Polo, whom they left in some pit, every week, as good as dead, only to come back the next week and find him big as life. The boy was also crazy about Charlie Chaplin, but he had seen everything a good many times, and made a nuisance of himself as he always got the hiccups when he laughed. He would have to be led back to the lobby, many times, for a drink. As Will Brady didn't care for Eddie Polo himself, any more than he did for the roller coaster, he would pass the time eating the popcorn or peanuts he bought for the boy. As he couldn't get his hand in the small-size bag, he had to buy the large-size ones, and near the middle of the movie he usually wanted a drink himself. They would both have a phosphate, usually cherry, at the drugstore when they got out.

Summer evenings, if it was still light after they had got out of the movie, he might walk the boy down Farnam Street to the Market Place. Will

Brady's place of business faced the west, and if it wasn't too late in the evening some light from the sky might be on the new sign he had at the front. This sign cost him three hundred dollars, and featured two roosters, drawn by hand, crowing over a large Leghorn egg. Through a misunderstanding both of the birds were Plymouth Rocks, as well as roosters—a point that troubled Will Brady, but the boy never noticed it. He didn't seem to care what color the eggs, or the chickens, were. On the wide glass window, lettered in gold, were the words:

WILL BRADY
EGGS

but the boy never seemed to realize that name was his own. That one day it would read WILL BRADY & SON. Any number of times, as they came around the corner, Will Brady meant to bring it up, but when they got there and stood facing the building, nothing was said. There seemed to be no connection. Perhaps that was it. There they were, Father & Son, looking through the window of their future—but it seemed to be Will Brady's, not the boy's. He never walked up and pressed his nose to the window, as most boys would do, and he didn't seem to care what went on behind the glass. If Will Brady said: "Now just a minute, son," and felt around in his pocket for the keys, the boy would stand out on the curbing while he went in. Sometimes he made quite a racket to attract attention, or stood in the candling-room, holding some eggs, but the boy never came back to see what was delaying him.

No, the only person that seemed to care, or wonder what it was he was doing, was the old man who sometimes slept in the back of the shop. A drifter, a wreck of a man with a dark bearded face, and one hand missing, he would sometimes get up from where he was lying and come peer at him. He would open the flap to the candling-room and put in his head. There he would be, a strange smile on his face, and perhaps a nail in one corner of his mouth, looking in on Will Brady as if he had called for him. Wagging his head, this old man would say: "Mr. Brady, how's that boy of yours?"

And it had turned out the old man had a boy of his own. Older, of course. Gone off somewhere, that is. A boy who had a mother who had also gone off somewhere. This old man probably didn't understand some of the words Will Brady fell to using, but he had been a father, and seemed to know the way of boys. He would wag his head as if it was all familiar to him. His own name he never mentioned, but a boy named Gregor, and a girl named Pearl, were very much like their mother, a woman named Belle. At the thought of her he would reach for the nail keg, put more nails in his mouth.

The old man kept the stub of his arm in his pocket, but speaking of war, which he knew at first hand, he would draw it out, like a sword, and point with it. The missing hand seemed to be something, like a glove, that he had left in his coat. He kept a small tin of water on top of the stove, to which he added, when he thought of it, coffee, drinking his own from the can but serving Will Brady in a green tin cup. When he stood near the stove the smell of wet gunny sacks steamed out from his clothes. By himself, he spit into the fire, cocking his head like a robin to hear the juice sizzle, but with Will Brady he would walk to the door, spit into the street. The blue knob of his wrist would wipe the brown stain from his lips. Coming back to the stove, he would take off his hat, look carefully into the crown, then use the stub of his arm to hone, tenderly, the soiled brim.

One evening in March, nearly the middle of March, Will Brady stopped the old man at the door to tell him that he could have the next day off. A holiday? Well yes, in a way it was. He, Will Brady, was taking himself another wife. Taking her, he added, before some other lucky fellow did. The old man seemed to think that was pretty sharp, pressing on his mouth to keep his chew in, and Will

Brady pressed a crisp new ten-dollar bill into his one hand. "Have yourself a good time," he said, but perhaps a man who had never had one, never bought one, anyhow, wasn't the man to bring the matter up. The old man stood there with the money, looking at it. Somehow it made Will Brady think of the boy, as when he didn't know what else to do he would give the boy money and say: "Go buy yourself something." The old man stood there, strangely preoccupied. Will Brady left him, but when he looked back he saw that the old man was still in the doorway, but his good arm was stretched across his front to his left side. He was trying to put the money in the pocket where he couldn't take it out. To get it out of that pocket, as he had once said, he had to take his coat off his back, which was not an easy thing for a one-armed man to do. Money put there was usually still there when he needed it.

Will Brady thought of that, oddly enough, when he reached across his front for the girl's small hand, and it may have been why he had a little trouble with the ring. They were married on the second floor of the City Hall. They stood in the anteroom of the Judge's office, facing the Judge himself and the green water-cooler, and the four or five people who were waiting to speak to him. A man who is married for the second time will probably look out the window, if one is handy, and think of the first time that such a thing had happened to him. It seemed, it all seemed, a good while ago. Thinking of that he turned from the window, where a ratty-tailed pigeon was strutting, and looked at the boy —a Western Union boy—who stood in the door. On his way somewhere, the boy had stopped to look in. Perhaps he had never seen a man married before. When he saw Will Brady, and Will Brady saw him, the boy took off his uniform cap, held it at his side, and ran his dirty fingers through his mussy hair. His eyes were wide, his lips were parted, and though there were other people in the room, what you call witnesses, it was only the boy who saw something. It was the boy that reminded Will Brady of what was happening to him. That taking a wife, as he had put it, was a serious affair.

He wanted to go out and speak to the boy, perhaps shake his hand, or give him some money, but all he did, of course, was stand there shaking hands with the Judge. The Judge turned from him to the water-cooler, tipping it forward as it was nearly empty, and had several long drinks from a soiled paper cup. Michael Long, his wife's father, crossed the room to shake Will Brady's hand and give him a wink, showing the gold caps on his teeth. Mr. Long was a dark-haired, rosy-cheeked man who had once been quite an actor, one of the five men, wearing spats, who tried to hide under a bed on the stage. A little old for that now, he had given it up, and come by bus from Kansas City to see the little girl finally hitched—as he said. Mrs. Long herself, a well-preserved woman, was still in considerable demand as the actress who lay in the bed with the men beneath it. This was why she had not been able to come. She was under contract to do three matinees a day.

Michael Long told Will Brady this as they stood in the lobby, but he left the impression with Will Brady that something else, of far greater importance, was on his mind. In the men's room, where they went to think it over, he explained himself. He wanted Will Brady to know, he said—holding his wig flat while he combed it—that he was making no mistake, no sireee, with this little girl. She was just like her mother, he said, who was as good now as she ever was, and by that he meant something better than thirty-five years. Every bit as good, Michael Long said, and put out his hands on something he saw before him, which might have been a stove, a radiator, or a woman's hips.

Mr. Long had told him that before the ceremony, in case he thought he might change his mind, but his hand was still sticky and smelled of hair oil when he shook Will Brady's hand. Will Brady dropped it and wiped his own on the side of his pants. He kissed an Aunt Lucille, who offered a cheek like a piece of saddle leather; then he led his wife down the wrought-iron stairway to the street. They had left the boy with Mr. Wherry, as he was a great stickler for details, knew all about weddings, and might object to one in the City Hall. As they entered the hotel and the smoke-filled lobby, the girl led him forward to meet the boy as if they had been lovers, *her* lovers, and now had to patch up their quarrel.

7

As HIS bride had never been west before, and as Will Brady wanted her to get the feel of the country, they left Omaha early in the morning on a fine spring day. Just west of Fremont he took the flapping side curtains off the car. In the West, as he told her—that is, he told them, as the boy had got to be quite a city kid—there were no wooded hills as there were along the river around Council Bluffs. It was not hilly country, and the rivers were apt to be wide, shallow affairs, as most of the water was somewhere underground. It was what men called open country, where you could see a good ways. When the sun was right—that is to say, behind you

—a man could see from town to town, and his bride, Gertrude Long, seemed to think that this was wonderful. She was so tired of being cooped up in the dirty city, she said. But when the sun was wrong—as it was when you were driving west, along toward evening—everything that you saw, if you cared to look at it, looked quite a bit alike. Pretty much like the same town, usually, with the same grain elevator along the tracks, and the same gas pump out in front of the same hay and feed store. Through the vibrating windshield, as the roads were pretty bad, the wide empty plain seemed to shimmer, and the telephone poles that slowly crawled past appeared to tremble and blur. The evening sun was like a locomotive headlight in their eyes. To get away from this sun the girl dozed off with her head bumping on Will Brady's shoulder, her mouth open, and her tongue black with the licorice she liked to eat. The boy sprawled with his feet on the seat, his head in her lap. A wad of Black Jack chewing gum was being saved on the bridge of his nose.

Will Brady drove mechanically, his fingers thick like those of the boy when he roller-skated, his hands gripping the wheel, his tired eyes fixed on the road. Once he stopped the car, as he had come to feel that one more mile would rattle him to pieces, but as he sat there, brooding, neither the boy nor the girl woke up. A cow tethered in the field near by turned to gaze at him. Her dung-heavy tail made a flapping sound like that of a loose board, wind-rattled, when it thumped, like a bell clapper, on her hollow frame. He returned her solemn gaze until she started to moo, when he drove on.

A little after sundown he drove into Murdock, an abandoned town on a Sunday evening, with no sign of life anywhere but the revolving barber pole. He drove on through the town, past the piles of cases that were stamped WILL BRADY—EGGS—MURDOCK, and that had been stacked under the shelter, ready for loading, on the station platform. He drove down the road that led, as they said, to the Brady Egg Empire. He had planned it that way, to arrive about sunset, so that the last rays of the sun, no longer touching the plains, might be seen on the tower of the new house. But from the bridge over the creek, which was just a mile or so from the farm, he saw the tower to the house and it struck him as higher than he thought it would be. And the house itself, the bulk of it, struck him as even larger than he had remembered, and a good deal stranger than it had appeared in *Ideal Homes*. Something was missing, but hard to say what it was. It was both larger than he had thought, the tower was higher than he had thought, and somehow or other he had expected a few trees. Perhaps he thought the trees came with the house. There had been a small grove around the house he had seen in the catalogue.

Still it was his own place, all right, as there in the fields were thousands of chickens, and on the new shingled roof were the lightning rods with the polished blue balls. He had asked for them, picked that color out himself. It was their place, but he drove on by, neither slowing down nor honking the horn nor doing anything that he figured might wake his family up.

What if they should ask him who in the world lived in a place like that? What if they should want to know, as they would, who in the world had been such a fool as to build, out here in the country, a fine city house. One that needed a green lawn, many fine big trees with a hammock or two swinging between them, and a birthday party going on clear around the run-around porch. What good was such a house without the city along with it? That's what they would ask him, laughing and hooting when they saw that he had no answer, so he drove on by, neither speaking to them nor shifting the gears. He followed one of the quiet, grass-covered roads back into town. When he drew up at the Cornland Hotel he just sat there for a while, with the motor running, reading the sign that asked guests with horses to leave them in the rear. Then he shut off the motor, and the sudden quiet woke them up.

He left them there in the car, the girl rubbing her eyes, while he stepped up to the counter of the hotel, where a Mr. Riddlemosher, once a neighbor, shook his hand. He asked about the boy as he handed Will Brady the counter pen. He watched Will Brady sign his name, then he twirled the ledger around to read for himself, over his glasses, just what it said. *Will Brady, wife & son*. That was what it said.

"Well," Mr. Riddlemosher said, "well, well—" then he looked up from the ledger to see the boy, his hands full of tinfoil, run into the lobby of the hotel. It was Mr. Riddlemosher who used to buy it from him at ten cents a pound.

8

TEN or twelve hours a day—when he wasn't eating, arguing with his family, or sleeping—Will Brady uncrated the furniture and drove it out to the farm. He had a freight car on the siding, full of it. While he did this he hired a man from Chapman, a farmer with two husky boys, to dig up some small shade trees and plant them in the yard. He wanted *something* to be there in the yard when he drove them out. Something besides chickens, that is, as even the full-grown Leghorn hens looked like so many pillow feathers blowing around a big empty house. They were fine big birds, but they looked awfully small. Everything did.

Now and then he would wake up at night with the notion that his strange house, like a caboose left on a siding, had somehow drifted away during the night. That he would drive out of town in the morning and find it gone. It was a wonderfully hopeful feeling—without it he might not have got up in the morning—but it made it that much worse when he saw that it was still there. Bigger than life. That was the hell of it.

With still half a car of furniture to unload, he had enough sofas for four or five houses, as they would not fit inside of the rooms he had bought them for. The doors opened wrong, or a window proved to be in the way. Some of the beds wouldn't fit in the rooms and he asked Mr. Sykes, his hired hand, if his wife might not care for one of them. What Mrs. Sykes didn't want they stored in the loft of the Sykes barn. It was Mrs. Sykes, of course, who asked him, when he came to the door of the kitchen, when he was going to get around to the kitchen stove. An honest man, Will Brady simply said he hadn't thought of it.

In the Clearing

It seemed hard to believe, a little weird in fact, that a man like Will Brady, born and raised in a soddy, had spent three thousand dollars without buying himself a kitchen stove. Had he come up too fast? Mrs. Sykes implied as much. She stood there looking at him, then said: "Well, it's up to the woman to think of the stove," and maybe it was. But not every woman. Not one like his wife.

He tried to explain, as they drove into town, that the reason his wife hadn't thought of the stove was that city-born girls, of a certain type, never cooked anything. They ate in restaurants. The food they ate was brought to them.

And who, Mrs. Sykes said, was going to bring her food to her in the country?

Well, that was one more thing he hadn't got around to thinking about. There had been too many things. There had also been restaurants where they could eat.

But he thought of that, among other things, as he watched Mrs. Sykes build a fire in the stove, breaking the stiff pine kindling between her strong hands and over her knee. Tough pieces she leaned on the leg of the stove, then stepped on them. She set the drafts on the pipes, then dipped a corncob into a pail of kerosene, lit it with a match, and used it like a torch to start the fire. As it roared up the chimney she said: "Well, I guess it draws all right."

111

Mrs. Sykes was an angular woman, a little blunt in her ways, and Will Brady felt right at home with her, as his own family treated him the same way. As a man, that is, who didn't seem to know anything. Not only in the woman's place, in the kitchen, but if Mrs. Sykes saw him out in the yard she would call to him, put a pail or a shovel into his hand. On a farm, she told him, something always needed to be done.

Would she happen to know a woman, he said, who would like a nice home in the country? A woman like herself, who would like to do the cooking, look after the house.

Mrs. Sykes wiped her hands and stiffened her back at the same time. She held her right hand to her face and picked at a splinter in the palm.

Did he know what it was like, she said, to keep a thirteen-room house?

Suppose they just closed off some of the upstairs rooms, he said. Would a woman like herself mind keeping a five- or six-room house?

Did he think, she replied, a woman would call that *keeping house*? That was what she said, leaving him there in the empty kitchen, with the fire burning, and the smell of the paint rising from the new stove. Then she was back—her head in the door but her face turned away from him. She said that she did know a woman, and if she happened to see her she might bring it up. But she wouldn't recommend it to any woman—not something like that. Then the door slammed behind her in a way that made it clear what she thought.

Four or five days later, a Saturday morning, Will Brady thought he saw Mrs. Sykes in the kitchen, but the woman who turned to face him had white hair. She was panning water from the bin on the range, the handle of the pan wrapped in her apron, and he had the feeling that she might be a little deaf. She didn't seem to be surprised to see him standing there. A tall heavy-bodied woman, with a dark skin, she didn't look any too well around the eyes, but to see her working, it was clear that she was strong enough.

"You're from Mrs. Sykes?" he said to her, raising his voice as she didn't seem to hear him. She stooped for some cobs, then settled the kettle over the plate hole.

"Mrs. Sykes said you could use a woman," she said.

"My wife is a city-bred girl," he said, which was true enough, but strange to hear him say it. "And city girls," he went on, "aren't really used to country ways."

That was strange kind of talk for him, but the woman seemed to follow it. It didn't seem to strike her, as it did Mrs. Sykes, that a city-bred girl was out of place in the country.

"To tell you the simple truth," he said, as he felt an urge to speak on this topic, "I suppose what I've tried to do is to bring the city out here." He gestured with his arm at the house, then added, "I wanted her to feel at home out here." Nor did this woman seem to see anything strange in that. "My name is Will Brady," he said, "and I'm very glad you've come to help us out. If the house is too big—" he waved his hand at the house, "we can shut some of it off."

"I'm getting on now," this woman said, "but I can still keep a house."

She didn't seem to feel it necessary to say any more than that. He stood there, and after a moment he realized that the sound that he heard, like a pole humming, was one that she made in her throat. A familiar hymn. She was humming it.

"If there's anything I can do," he said, "I want you to feel free to call on me." Then he coughed, took a drink of water, and hurried out. Where had he picked up such a fancy way of putting things? He turned back to the door and said: "If you want anything, let me know," but she seemed to be busy again and had her back to him. He crossed the yard to Mr. Sykes, who was mixing up a barrel of laying mash, but he stopped when Will Brady walked up to him.

"You happen to know this old lady's name?" he asked.

"Mason," Mr. Sykes said. "Anna Mason—she's a good sort."

"She strikes me as a pretty fine woman," Will Brady said.

"She's a good sort," Sykes said again.

But there was something about the woman that Will Brady felt needed some comment. "I'd say she was a woman a man could depend on," he said.

"Kept house for her brother," Sykes said, "going on about forty years. He died last year. Guess she misses him."

"She never married?" Will Brady asked.

"No, she never married," Sykes said; then he looked up and said: "She had her brother, one of her own people, to think of."

In April it was spring out in the yard, where the fat hens made nests in the dust heaps, but the winter still seemed to be trapped in the house. Mrs. Sykes had finally told him about the stove, but nobody had told him about the furnace, which was supposed to have been in the basement of the house. Now that the house was up, there was no longer any way of getting it there. The basement was a big whitewashed room, clean-smelling from the earth, and sometimes even sunny, so he put his desk in the basement and lived down there himself. It was handy to the yard, and getting in and out he didn't trouble anyone.

The boy and girl—that was what he called them —lived, with an oil stove, in the master bedroom on the second floor, where they had their meals unless he drove them into town to eat. During the day they played phonograph records on the machine he had ordered from Omaha, and when the windows were up he could often hear the music himself. The kind of music that they liked sounded very strange in the chicken yard.

Although there was always work to do, and not enough help on the place to do it, he sometimes found himself at the narrow basement windows, peering out. The window on the yard was about chest-high, with a deep sill that he could lean on, and he found that he could see out without Mrs. Sykes being able to see in. Twice a day the local train came down from the north, and even before the bell was ringing, Will Brady would be there at the window, peering out. He liked to watch the smoke pouring from the wide funnel stack. As she came around the curve, the bell wagging, the fireman would climb out of the cab and crawl back over the coal car to the water bin. She took water in Murdock, and he had to be there to pull the stack down. Will Brady would look on while all of this happened, seeing very little from where he stood, but knowing, as an old railroad man, what was taking place. He could hear, on certain days, the water pouring through the chute. He might be able to see a passenger or two get on or off. And all this time the bell would be ringing as there were no guard gates on the Burlington crossing, nothing but kids who would be standing on the cowcatcher, waiting for the brakeman to run up front and shoo them off.

Will Brady would stand there, maybe five or ten minutes, until the caboose finally disappeared, and he could hear the whistle, thin and wild, as if the train was calling for help. Was something wrong with him? Or was it just spring fever, or something like that. A tendency to let the team idle on the bridge, so that he could see, through the cracks, the clear water, or to let them graze in the sweet grass at the side of the road. Only flipping the reins now and then to keep the flies off their spanky rumps.

After several years of working day and night, perhaps Will Brady had begun to stop working, to stand as if thinking, as if great thoughts were troubling his mind. Mr. Sykes often had to repeat everything he said. It was not the proper state of

mind for a man who had around five thousand laying hens to think of, and who had often been asked
what he intended to do when one hen took sick.
Well, he didn't know. No, he didn't even know
that. Standing at the basement window he sometimes marveled at this strange fellow, Will Jennings
Brady, known all over the state as an up and coming man of caliber. A man who lived in the basement of his fine new thirteen-room house.

On a Sunday morning, on his way into town, he
found this woman Anna Mason walking down the
road, her skirts pinned up, and her long underwear
tucked into her high laced shoes. When he stopped
and spoke to her she said she was on her way to
church. A woman nearly seventy years of age,
heavy on her feet and not any too well, on her way
to a church that was a good three-mile walk.

"Now look here," he said, but she wouldn't listen to him. Nor would she get into the car and ride
in with him. She would go to church, she let him
know, just so long as she could get there; when
she couldn't get there any more, why, then she
wouldn't go. She would be dead then, she said, and
looked at him.

All right, he replied, but he would be there to
bring her home.

If he just happened to be there in the church,

she said, if he happened to be there, and she happened to see him, why, then she supposed he might as well bring her home.

He wondered if that was how it happened that most men went to church. There would be a woman there, too old to walk, who would like a ride home. A woman with white or gray hair, her long underwear tucked into her shoe tops, and spectacles that had got to be the color of flecked isinglass. She would be there in the pew, her hands in her lap, or pushing up to share with somebody her hymnbook, then singing, or humming, in a voice that made little boys wet their pants. He had done just that, anyway, many times. His mother had had such a voice, throbbing like an organ on the chorus, and this throb passed down through her arm into his hand, the one she was holding, and made the small hairs rise on his neck, and his knees rub. And when the hymn was over he usually found that his pants were wet.

Now he came late and took a seat near the door, where he had sat that Sunday that the boy had won a Bible, with his name stamped on it, and brought it up the aisle to him. Where, come to think of it, was that Bible now? He had driven them all—it was Ethel then—out to Nolan's Lake for the barbecue, the motorboat ride, and the hymn-singing after dark. The choir in their long white robes on the platform, the hissing red flares very good on the women, and in the dark like that, out in the open, he could sing himself. It was said that he had a fine baritone voice. Well, that night he had sung many hymns, the fires had made it seem like a gypsy encampment, and the boy, who had eaten too much, fell asleep in his lap. The new Bible, with the cover sticky, had dropped from his hand. Will Brady had picked it up and said: "Ethel, maybe you better take that Bible," and she had said yes, and that was the last he saw of it. Moving around, as they did, it was hard to keep track of things.

From where he sat at the back, beneath the limp flags, and with the stack of collection plates beside him, he thought he could pick out Anna Mason's voice. Anna Mason would have his mother's voice, and with it his mother's kind of religion, and a man with his voice, and his kind of religion, was not in her class. He didn't belong, if the truth were known, in the same church. But he was there now, he was sure, for a good Christian reason, and he had something like a religious feeling about the choir. They wore black gowns and sat under the golden organ pipes. They rose as one, the women at the front and the men, who were taller, lined up in back, and the sound of their robes was like the clearing of one great throat. They sang, and he closed his eyes and waited for the moment when they would stop and there would be nothing, nothing—till the first hymnbook closed. That moment always struck him as something like a prayer. He observed it, that is, as he did Memorial Day, and in that sense of the word he considered himself a religious man.

Then he would stand by the aisle, his hat in his hand, until Anna Mason came up and walked by him, and he would not step to her side until she reached the street. She was not a woman to stand out in front and talk with someone. But she did think it was pleasant to take a short buggy ride. Not in the car, which made her nervous—as she liked the horses out in front, where she could see them, not bottled up, like some sort of genie, under the hood. She liked it off the paving, along the streets where the buggy wheels ran quiet in the dust, and the reins made a soft, lapping sound on the rumps of the mares. As it just happened to be on their way, they usually passed the house where the blinds were drawn, and there were still three birches, a little larger now, there in the yard. He admitted to her that he had owned that house. He said owned advisedly, as the words *lived in* struck him as strange, and did not describe, as he remembered, what he had done in the house. But for several years he had come back and gone to bed there. It was in that house he had had erysipelas, a painful, contagious disease, and a woman, his wife at the time, had taken care of him. Lovingly, as the doctor had said. A very strange word, he thought, and he had marveled at it. She had made him well, she had kept him clean, and when he was fit to be seen again, he had made love to a plump cigar-counter girl. How was that? Time passed. Perhaps that was it. Every morning it was there on his hands, and had to be passed.

But if it was Anna Mason that got him to church, and kept him there while the choir was singing, it was a chicken—a sick chicken—that made him a religious man. It made a man wonder, and wonder makes a religious man. Some people might say that it was the girl, or the city house he had built out in the country, but he knew in his heart it was neither the house nor his family. It was the chicken. Nobody needed to tell him that.

Now, a sick chicken is always a problem, but when you put that chicken with five thousand others, all of them Leghorns, your problem is out of hand. The people in Murdock, you might say, had figured on that. They had all looked forward to it, and some men put their families into buggies and drove them out in the country so they could watch Will Brady's chickens die. All day long he could hear the buggy weights plop in the dust. Just by turning and looking at the buggies he could tell which way the wind was blowing, as they were always careful to park away from the smell. Others claimed they could smell it clear in town. He never knew, personally, as he never got out of the yard, and he slept in the basement where Anna Mason brought him his food. He couldn't have smelled very much anyhow, as he was covered with smells from head to foot, and dirty Leghorn feathers were said to be tangled in his hair. Even Anna Mason, a pioneer woman, kept out of his draft.

In the second week the big hens were dead before he picked them up. It was not necessary to cut their throats or to wring their necks. They were stiff, and yet they seemed very light when he scooped them up on the shovel, as if dying had taken a load off of them. During the third week three experts arrived, at his expense, from Chicago, and took most of one day to tell him there was nothing to be done. Then they went off, after carefully washing their hands.

Sometimes he stopped long enough to look out at the road, and the rows of buggies, where the women and the kids sat breathing through their handkerchiefs. That was something they had picked up during the war. When the flu came along, everyone had run around breathing through a handkerchief. In spite of the smell, they all liked to sit where they could keep their eyes on the house, and the upstairs room where the boy and girl were in quarantine. He had more or less ordered them to stay inside. Now and then he caught sight of the boy with his head at the window, peering at him, and one evening he thought he heard, blown to him, the music of their phonograph. Something about a lover who went away and did not come back.

Nothing that he did, or paid to have done, seemed to help. The hens he shipped off died on the railroad platform overnight. They were left in their crates and shipped back to him for burial. He was advised to keep his sick chickens to himself. Other men had chickens, and what he had started might sweep across the state, across the nation, right at the time that the state and the nation were doing pretty well.

And then it stopped—for no more apparent reason than it had begun. It left him with one hundred and twenty-seven pullets still alive. He sat around waiting for them to die, but somehow they went on living, they even grew fatter, and early every morning the three young roosters crowed. It was something like the first, and the last, sound that he had ever heard. When he heard them crow he would come to the window, facing the cold morning sky, and look at the young trees that he had planted at the edge of the yard. They were wired to the ground, which kept them, it was said, from blowing away.

It would soon be summer out in the yard, but when he went up the spiralling stairs to their room, he could smell the oil burner that they kept going day and night. They liked the smell of it better than the one out in the yard. There was music playing, and when he opened the door a man's clear voice, as if right there before him, came out of the horn that had the picture of the white dog stamped on it. The boy, the girl, and the dog were all listening to him. The man was singing of the time when the girl was a tulip, and he was a rose. This had been, he seemed to remember, her favorite song. As the man went on singing, the girl took hold of his hand, looking toward the horn where the needle was scratching, and he saw that she had no idea of what had happened to him. Not an inkling. Nor had the boy, who was sniffling through his adenoids. They had lived in this private world together, playing their records, caroms, and dominoes, and sometimes marveling at the strange things they saw in the yard. It seemed hard to believe, but somehow it didn't trouble him. When the music stopped he heard her say: "Will, you remember?"

"Why, yes," he said, his head nodding, and put a warm smile on his face. And when they both looked at him, waiting, he knew what he would say. He had come into the room not knowing, not having the vaguest idea, but now he knew, and he looked through the window as he spoke to them.

"How would you two like to go to Omaha?" he said.

IN THE MOONLIGHT

1

IN THE middle of life Will Brady bought a house with the roof on sideways, as the boy said, and a yard without grass that he could pay the boy to mow. Under the fenced-in porch were a lawnmower and a cracked garden hose. On the porch were a swing, a hammock rope, and between the stone pillars at the front two wire baskets of dead ferns. In the house were a new player piano and a large box of music rolls.

From the swing on the porch, since the ferns were dead, Will Brady could look down the street to the park, the end of the car line, and the health-giving mineral spring. At night, when the motorman changed the trolley, there would be a hot sizzling sound, and flashes of white light, like heat lightning, would fill the air. From where he sat on the porch Will Brady could see that the ferns were dead.

Beyond the mineral spring, said to be good for you, the green hills were trimmed by mowing machines, and men could be seen playing the new game of golf. They wore breeches quite a bit like those worn by the boy. The hitting of the ball took place near the spring, where the men would stop for a drink of the water while the boys went off with the bags of sticks to hunt for the ball. Will Brady bought the boy a set of the sticks, which he found around the front yard every evening, and a box of the balls, which he often heard rolling around the house. He couldn't seem to interest either the boy or the girl in the park. It was too big, too open, and too much like Murdock, they said.

Sunday afternoons, to be with his family, he would sit in the parlor with the player piano while the boy played some of the rolls backwards, others too fast. The girl would sit on the floor playing card games with herself. On the table at his side were the magazines, the *Youth's Companion* and *Boys' Life*, that came through the mail once a month for the boy to read. He read them himself, and ordered through the mail such things as the watch with the compass in the winder, and the Official Scout knife, with which a clever boy could do so many things. One of the watches he bought for the boy, the other for himself. In the dark candling-room he liked to take it from his pocket and watch the tiny needle waver toward the north, telling him, as nothing else would, about where he was.

On top of the magazines, perhaps to keep them from blowing, was a heavy glass ball with a castle inside, and when he took this ball and shook it, the castle would disappear. Quite a bit the way a farmhouse on the plains would disappear in a storm. He liked to sit there, holding this ball, until the storm had passed, the sky would clear, and he would see that the fairy castle with the waving red flags was still there.

Every morning, with the exception of Sunday, Will Brady would get out of bed at six thirty, fry himself two eggs, and eat them while standing on the fenced-in back porch, facing the yard. At that time in the morning a rabbit might be there. He would then leave some money on the kitchen table and drive through the town to his place of work, a long narrow building with a wooden awning out in front. As the owner of this business he wore a soiled jacket, with blue flaps on the pockets, and when he stood in the door there was usually a clipboard on his arm. On it he kept a record of the eggs that came in, the chickens that went out. He also wore a green visor and a sober preoccupied air. In the middle of life, with his best years before him, he seemed to have a firm grip on all serious matters, and a pretty young wife who called him once a day on the telephone. She called to let her husband know what movie his wife and son were at.

In the morning there was usually ice on the pail where the dung-spotted eggs were floating, and he could see his breath, as if he were smoking, in the candling-room. If he seemed to spend a good deal of time every day looking at one egg and scratching another, perhaps it was the price one had to pay for being a successful man. One whose life was still before him, but so much of it already behind him that it seemed that several lives—if that was the word for it—had already been lived. Had already gone into the limbo, as some men said.

He had his noon meal across the street, usually chicken-fried steak and hash-brown potatoes, or stuffed baked heart with a piece of banana cream pie. After eating this meal he would stand on the curbing out in front. As he neither smoked anything nor chewed, he would usually stand there chewing on a toothpick, and he seemed to have the time to listen to what you had to say. He seldom interrupted to say anything himself. He neither heard anything worth recounting nor said anything worth repeating, but he gave strangers the feeling that one of these days he might. He was highly respected and said to be wise in the ways of the world.

There were evenings that he sat at the desk in the office, with the Dun & Bradstreet open before him, and there were other evenings that he spent in the candling-room. He would take a seat on one of his egg cases, using the thick excelsior pad as a cushion, and the light from the candler would fall on the book he held in his hands. Dun & Bradstreet? No, this book was called a *Journey to the Moon*. Written by a foreigner who seemed to have been there. Will Brady's son had read this book, and then he had given it to his father, as he did all of his books, to return to the library. One day Will Brady wondered what it was the boy liked to read. So he had opened the book, read four or five pages himself. He had been standing there, at his candler, but after reading a few more pages he had seated himself on an egg case, adjusted the light. He had gone without his lunch, without food or drink, till he had finished it. The candling-room had turned cold, and when he stepped into the office it was dark outside.

That night Will Brady had tried to sleep—that is to say, he went to bed as usual—but something about having been to the moon kept him awake. He got out of the bed and stepped out on the porch for a look at it. The moon that he saw looked larger than usual, and nearer at hand. And the light from this moon cast a different light on the neighborhood. There before him lay the city—growing, it was said, by leaps and bounds since the last census —where many thousands of men, with no thought of the moon, lay asleep. He could cope with the moon, but somehow he couldn't cope with a thought like that. It seemed a curious arrangement, he felt, for God to make. By some foolish agreement, made long ago, men and women went into their houses and slept, or tried to sleep, right when there was the most to see.

Over the sleeping city the moon was rising, and there in the street were the shady elms, the flowering shrubs, and the sidewalks slippery with maple pods. On the porches were swings, limp, sagging hammocks, roller skates, and wire baskets of ferns, and in the houses the men and women lay asleep. It all seemed to Will Brady, there in the moonlight, a very strange thing. A warm summer night, the windows and the doors of most of the houses were open, and the air that he breathed went in and out of all of them. In and out of the lungs, and the lives, of the people who were asleep. They inhaled it deeply, snoring perhaps; then they blew it on its way again, and he seemed to feel himself sucked into the rooms, blown out again. Without carrying things too far, he felt himself made part of the lives of these people, even part of the dreams that they were having, lying there. Was that a very strange thing? Well, perhaps it was. Perhaps it was stranger, even, than a Journey to the Moon.

And the thought came to him—to Will Jennings Brady, a prominent dealer in eggs—that he was a traveler, something of an explorer, himself. That he did even stranger things than the men in books. It was one thing to go to the moon, like this foreigner, a writer of books, but did this man know the man or the woman across the street? Had he ever traveled into the neighbor's house? Did he know the woman who was there by the lamp, or the man sitting there in the shadow, a hat on his head as if at any moment he might go out? Could he explain why there were grass stains on the man's pants? That might be stranger, that might be harder to see, than the dark side of the moon.

Perhaps it was farther across the street, into that room where the lamp was burning, than it was to the moon, around the moon, and back to the earth. Where was there a traveler to take a voyage like that? Perhaps it was even farther than twenty thousand leagues under the sea. Men had been there, it was said, and made a thorough report of the matter, but where was the man who had traveled the length of his own house? Who knew the woman at the back—or the boy at the front who lay asleep?

How many moons away, how many worlds away, was a boy like that? On the moon a man might jump many feet, which might be interesting if you went there; but it was no mystery, a man could explain something like that. But what about the man who stood in the dark eating cornbread and milk? What about the rooms where the blinds were always drawn? If there were men who had been there and knew the answers, he would like to know them; if they had written about these things he would read the book. If they hadn't, perhaps he would write such a book himself.

What writer, what traveler, could explain the woman who rolled herself up in the sheet, like a mummy, or the man who came home every night and undressed in the dark? All one could say was that whatever it was it was there in the house, like a vapor, and it had drawn the blinds, like an invisible hand, when the lights came on. As a writer of books he would have to say that this vapor made the people yellow in color, gave them flabby bodies, and made their minds inert. As if they were poisoned, all of them, by the air they breathed. And such a writer would have to explain why this same air, so fresh and pure in the street, seemed to be poisoned by the people breathing it. So that in a way even stranger than the moon, they poisoned themselves.

In the Moonlight

Was it any wonder that men wrote books about other things? That they traveled to the moon, so to speak, to get away from themselves? Were they all nearer to the moon, the bottom of the sea, and such strange places than they were to their neighbors, or the woman there in the house? What the world needed, it seemed, was a traveler who would stay right there in the bedroom, or open the door and walk slowly about his own house. Who would sound a note, perhaps, on the piano, raise the blinds on the front-room windows, and walk with a candle into the room where the woman sleeps. A man who would recognize this woman, this stranger, as his wife.

But if books would put a man in touch with the moon, perhaps they would put him in touch with a boy—a very strange thing, but a lot of people owned up to them. Mothers and fathers alike seemed to be familiar with them. When he returned the *Journey to the Moon*, he spoke to Mrs. Giles, the librarian, and tried to phrase, for her, some of the thoughts that were troubling him. Had any man taken, he said, a journey around his own house?

Not for public perusal, Mrs. Giles said.

That would be a journey, he said, that he would like to take, or, for that matter, a journey around his own son.

That had been done, Mrs. Giles said, so he could just save himself the trouble. All kinds of men had already done just that.

Was that a fact? he said.

Hadn't he read *Tom Sawyer*? she said.

And who was Tom Sawyer? he said, so she brought him the book. She also brought him *Penrod*, by another man, and several books by Ralph Henry Barbour, that would give him a good idea, she said, of what was on a boy's mind. That was just what he wanted to know, he said, and went off with the books.

He read *Tom Sawyer*, in one sitting, in the candling-room. He took the tin bottom off the candler, so that it cast more light for him, and he used two of the excelsior egg pads to soften the seat. There was a much better light in the office, with a comfortable chair to sit in, but he had hired a girl to sit there at the desk and answer telephone calls. She might not understand a man of his age reading children's books.

He read *Tom Sawyer* during the morning, and reflected on it while he had his lunch; then he came back and read the book by Tarkington. By supper time a great load had been lifted from his mind. If he could believe what he read—which he found hard, but not too hard if he put his mind to it—boys were not at all as complicated as he had been led to believe. When all was said and done, so to speak, they were just boys. Full of boyish devilment and good clean fun. If neither this Penrod nor Tom Sawyer reminded him very much of Willy Brady, that might be explained in terms of how they lived. Penrod had brothers and sisters, many freckles and friends, and a very loving father and mother. Willy Brady didn't have all of these things. But if his father could believe what he read, all Willy Brady had on his mind was baseball, football, Honor, and something called track. In Ralph Henry Barbour's opinion, that of a man who really seemed to know, these were the things at the front and the back of a boy's mind. If he could believe what he read, and Will Brady did, it was coming from behind in the great mile race that made the difference between a boy and a man. But to lead all the way was to court disaster, as the book made clear.

One began with a fine healthy boy like Penrod, who had a real home, a loving father and mother, and perhaps an older sister who brought out the best in him. Then one day, overnight almost, his voice would change. Fuzz would grow on his lip, and his father would send him off to a boarding school. There he would live with other clean-cut boys like himself, eating good food, reading fine books, and talking over the problems of the coming Oglethorpe game. The walls of the room would be covered with banners from big Eastern schools. The window would open out on the field where he would throw the javelin, run the race, and pitch the last three innings with a pain in his arm. In the winter he would sit at his desk and study, or go home with his roommate over Christmas, whose father was a big corporation lawyer of some kind. His roommate's sister, a dark-haired girl who attended some private school in the East, would ask her brother, in a roundabout way, all about him. After that one thing would lead to another until he struck off somewhere on his own, or accepted a position with a promising future in her father's firm. The only problem would be how long he would have to wait for her.

Will Brady hoped it wouldn't be too long, thinking over his own experience, as once out of school, like that, life seemed harder to organize. There were many pressures, and not nearly so many lovely girls. Nor were there many things that a father could do to make sure that the boy picked the right one, when the boy still had neither fuzz on his lip nor a voice that had changed. He was twelve, but he looked more like nine or ten. The only hair on his body was there on the top of his head. But with this boy he did what he could—that is to say, on Sundays afternoons he would walk him through the park to the baseball diamond, and sit with him in the bleachers behind the sagging fence of chicken wire. Thanks to Ralph Henry Barbour, Will Brady knew the names of the players and the places, and he pointed out to the boy the pitcher's mound, and the batteries. In his own mind, of course, he saw the boy as a pitcher, pitching the last three innings with his arm sore, but the boy took an interest in the catcher as he wanted the mask. Nobody else on the field seemed to interest him. He wanted to wear what the catcher wore, and peer out through the mask. So he bought the boy a glove, a ball, and a mask, but he put off buying the rest of it until he had a long talk with the man in the Spalding store. This man, a Mr. Lockwood, seemed to take a personal interest in Will Brady's boy.

Mr. Lockwood had been a great athlete himself. As a student at the University of Nebraska he had run the mile in record time, the last thing you would think of, so to speak, when you looked at him. He didn't look any too well, as a matter of fact, and he had grown a little heavy for a man his age. In a separate compartment of his wallet, however, Mr. Lockwood had a bundle of press clippings, some of them with faded pictures showing how he looked at the time. The clippings were now yellow, and hard to read, but Will Brady could make out that

141

the man who stood before him had once run the mile, all the way, in 4:23. A mile, as Mr. Lockwood reminded him, was fourteen city blocks.

With Mr. Lockwood's expert help, Will Brady bought the boy shoes for running and jumping, shoes for baseball, special shoes for football, and rubber-soled shoes for doing things inside. He also bought him the shirts, pants, and socks to go along with all of these things. He might grow out of them at any time, but he would know the smell and the feel of a sweatshirt, and the smell was an important thing. As Mr. Lockwood said, it was a smell that he would never get out of his nose.

If there was something about Mr. Lockwood that had gone unmentioned in all of the books, perhaps it was because the author had had no need to bring it up. As a writer of books, Ralph Henry Barbour described what he saw in the newspaper clippings, and the young man that he saw, with his muscles bulging, breasting the tape. He was not concerned with the middle-aged man in the sporting-goods store. Everything Mr. Lockwood said about himself, and his wonderful college life at Nebraska, would lead one to believe that Ralph Henry Barbour was absolutely right. Everything that had happened to him, back then, had been wonderful. If he had been a writer, he would have written those books himself. Listening to Mr. Lockwood, and he liked to talk, Will Brady often came away with the feeling that Ralph Henry Barbour had given a modest picture of college life. Everything in the world, it seemed clear, had happened to Mr. Lockwood, the great mile runner, but nothing much had happened to the man in the sporting-goods store. Nothing much had happened since then, that is. He still had the smell of it all in his nose, and some people might say there was something like it, if not worse, on his breath. He reminded Will Brady, at times, of a man very much like himself. A man who might live in one of those houses across the street. He would probably have a wife named Gladys, who slept alone in the bedroom at the back, and a daughter named Mabel, or Eileen, who slept in the room at the front. And perhaps at this point people were saying how much the mother looked like the daughter, and talk like that would be scaring the girl to death. Or maybe it wouldn't. That would be hard to say. Perhaps it was her father she took after, having his light-brown hair, his pale-blue eyes, and perhaps the smile that he once had in the photographs. Before he began to die, that is. Before something began to poison him.

It was no help, of course, to say so, but the man in the sporting-goods store, the celebrated athlete, looked like a man who was being poisoned to death.

He smoked too much. Perhaps that was it. The man who was pictured in the press clippings did not smoke. Whatever this thing was, it seemed to be something that he had picked up later; it was not in the air on the college campus, nor what he breathed on the track. It was not something that Ralph Henry Barbour felt he had to describe. But something had happened. What had it been? The great mile runner, the baseball star, had accepted an offer from Spalding & Brothers to go out on the road and sell their guaranteed baseballs, their autographed bats. After a while he had married his childhood sweetheart, settled down. For a year or two he had kept his paper clippings just loose in his desk, where he could find them; then one day, one spring day more than likely, he took them out. After mulling them over he put them in his wallet —began to carry them around. Some time later maybe he noticed how dry and brittle they were getting, or maybe he didn't—maybe it was just a chance remark by his wife. Whatever it was, he made a little pile of the best of them. He put the best picture in the back of his watch, the best clipping in his vest. They were always with him, as if he couldn't part with them. Some writer of books might even say that these clippings poisoned him. That they were old, brittle, and fading, like the man himself. People will believe anything that they read, and if they happened to read, in a book some-where, that a man was poisoned by some newspaper clippings, why they would swallow it. And a writer of books might even say that these people were right.

But what would this man say of Will Brady's son? One that happened to be, as Will Brady seemed to think, the complicated type. A boy that once a week, while his father was shaving, would come to the door of the bathroom and wait for his father to turn from the mirror and look at him. The boy would be wearing his Official Boy Scout uniform. He seemed to wear the shirt more than the pants, as the shirt had faded to a washed-out color, and on his feet were the Official green, chrome leather shoes. They hurt his feet, badly, but he never complained. From his belt hung a flashlight, a compass, a metal canteen in a soft flan-nel cooler, a key ring with some keys, a medal for swimming, another medal for walking, one for not smoking, and a waterproof kit containing materials for building a fire. This was in case his waterproof matchbox got wet. On his back was a knapsack containing maps, a snake-bite cure, a day's balanced rations, and Dentyne gum, which he chewed for his teeth and to allay the thirst.

"Off for the woods, son?" Will Brady would say,

but sometimes the boy wasn't. No, strange to say, he might not be off for anywhere. He would just be prepared, in case he felt like being off. He would follow his father back to the bedroom and sit on the bed. He would sit there and watch his father dress, as if there was something very strange about it, or he would take out his maps and spread them on the bed.

"Where is the exact center of the U. S. A.?" the boy might ask. At one time Will Brady thought such a question was put to him. He didn't answer for the simple reason that he didn't know. But the boy was just talking to himself, as first he would put the question, then he would answer: "The geographical center of the United States is in Osborne County, Kansas." It was never necessary for Will Brady to say anything. Looking at Omaha the boy would say: "The metal smokestack at the smelting works is the highest metal smokestack in the world," or "Omaha spaghetti is now sold in Italy."

It was something of an education for Will Brady to listen to him. They seemed to be educating young people better nowadays. As for himself, he had eight years' schooling, but in so far as he could remember, no one had ever mentioned that Omaha spaghetti was sold in Italy. The boy said it was. And he always seemed to have the Gospel truth.

Right out of the blue, without any warning, the

boy once asked: "Why are you so different?" Will Brady had been facing the mirror in the men's room of the Paxton Hotel. He had taken the boy down there before they went to the show.

"Kid—" he had said, then hearing what he had said he turned the water on, let it run. After a bit he turned it off and said: "Yes, son?"

"I don't mind kid," the boy said, "if you want to call me kid that's all right with me."

"That was a slip, son," he said. "That was just a slip."

"The name I really like is Spud," the boy said. "I always say call me Spud but nobody does it."

"What's wrong with Willy, son?" he said.

"I've been Willy for a long time," the boy said, and Will Brady bent over, turned the hot water back on. What in God's name did the boy mean by that? With a paper towel Will Brady wiped the steaming mirror so that he could see the boy's sober face. His eyes, his mother's eyes, that is, were watching him. What did Will Brady feel? Not much of anything.

"All right, kid," he said, and that was just about that.

He would take them out to eat, where music was playing, and they would sit there together, in league against him, looking at him from a long way off. Very much as if he were an imposter. A father, one who didn't know what being a father was like, and a lover, one who didn't know much about love. More or less hopeless. For different reasons they both pitied him.

2

So HE would give them money, put them in a show, and drive downtown to his office, where he would take off his coat and sit at his new roll-top desk.

Some nights he did that, other nights he might walk around the streets, or out over the river, and on Saturday evenings he often stopped in at Browning King. It was Fred Conlen who had got him to wear the soft-collar shirt. In Fred Conlen's private fitting-room he would see himself in the three-way mirror, and it was there that he saw the new expression on his face. While he was talking— at no other time. While he talked this man in the mirror had a strange smile on his lips. This smile on his lips and a sly, knowing look about the eyes. Something shrewd he had said? Well, he never really seemed to say much. Just a good deal implied, so to speak, in what he did say.

"What about a pair of pants," he would say, "that a man never has to take off?" That was all.

What did he mean by a remark like that? Whatever he meant, Fred Conlen often thought it was pretty good.

"Brady," he would say, "you ought to be on the platform. You got a head."

"When I was a boy," Will Brady had said, "I had the biggest hat on the lowest peg. Seems to me the peg's lower every time I look at it."

"Bygod, Brady," Fred Conlen had said, "there you said something."

Had he? Well, nothing you could put your finger on. You needed mirrors, so to speak, to see a trick like that. To see a man with a big head, narrow shoulders, the new soft-collared shirt, and along with the toothpick that sly smile in the corner of his mouth. About to say something. And when he did, it would be pretty good.

"I notice these new twin beds are pretty popular now," he would say, and Fred Conlen, with the pins in his mouth, would turn to look at him.

Will Brady bought his clothes from Fred Conlen —Hart Schaffner & Marx, direct from Chicago— and his shoes from Lyman Bryce, who ran the Florsheim store. If he stopped by in the evening Lyman Bryce would take him to the back of the shop, pull up a stool, and show him what they were wearing in Palm Beach. Will Brady would sit there, his shoes off, and this fellow Bryce, a gray-haired man, would lace him into the latest thing in Palm Beach shoes. He would ask him to stand up and walk around in them. People in the street would come to the door and peer in. Bryce had a fine new home in Dundee, and a prominent place in the Ak-Sar-Ben parade, but what he really liked to do was sit there on a shoe stool and talk. He was a big fellow, like T. P. Luckett, but he was quite a bit different from Luckett in that he hinted that a good egg business was not the last word. Nor was the shoe business. Nor anything of that stripe. Lyman Bryce seemed to think that Will Brady was meant for more than that. "Forget about the money," Bryce would say, "I'll take care of the money." What he seemed to be looking for, as he said himself, was the right man.

What was being done, Bryce wanted to know, down in the deep South, or out in Texas? Wouldn't a little loose money start something really rolling out there? Couldn't a man with a few big tractors start plowing it up? Instead of fiddling with eggs— as Bryce called it—why didn't Will Brady take thirty thousand dollars, or fifty if he liked it, and go out there and start something? "God Almighty, Brady," he would say, "stop fiddling with eggs." He seemed to think the country was still wide open for a man with some cash.

In the Moonlight

When he talked with Lyman Bryce, Will Brady always had a smile on his face. Was he amused? No, there was more to his smile than that. It was more like the smile he had when he faced three mirrors with just one face. Or when he sat there with Bryce, and Bryce would say: "Now bygod, Brady, I'd like to have you home for dinner. But you know the little woman—the little woman is fussy as hell."

Did he know *the little woman?* From that smile on his face, you would think that he did. You might be led to think that some of these little women were pretty big.

Clark Lee, for example, had one of them. Lee ran the Gaiety, and he was one of the big show men in the state. He used *the little woman* to explain a good many things. "Geez, Brady," he would say, "I wouldn't want the little woman to get wind of this," or "Well, I'd better get along, Brady, if I'm going to keep the little woman in line." Now, both Lee and Bryce were pretty big men, Lee a notch or two above six feet, but the way they talked about these little women made them seem pretty small. You got the idea that *the little women* were all bigger than the men.

For example, the big thing in Clark Lee's life, besides the little woman, that is, was something that he called the *chalk line.* He often drew this line, with his finger, across his desk. Or if he was stand-

151

ing he would draw this line on the air. The little
woman expected him to walk that line, he said.
Perhaps he did, as this line always seemed to be with
him, either there on his desk, drawn on the thin
air, or like a pattern in the rug. A line drawn between Clark Lee and everything else. "With the
little woman," Lee would say, "I got to toe that
line!" and he would tap on it, putting out his feet
to where he saw something on the rug. It would be
wrong to say that this line was imaginary. It was
there in the lobby, in his office, in the sidewalk
when he stepped in the street, and it hung like an
invisible clothesline in the air. Ready to trip him
or support him, as the case might be. Big man
though he was, Clark Lee often seemed to lean
on it.

Perhaps *the little woman* was sometimes on Will
Brady's mind, those long summer evenings, when
he stopped in at the Paxton to see if Evelyn Fry
was there. She sold cigars, but she was no cigar-
counter girl. She knew the one Will Brady had
married—she was a married woman herself—and
she always asked him how his *kids* were getting
along. Sometimes Evelyn Fry like to go for a ride
where they could just sit and look at the river; other
times she would make him a cooling drink of something in her rooms. The fellow she had married
had left her a lot of furniture. There were tasseled

lamps, a grand piano with a shawl and some photographs, and sometimes there was a smell stronger than the incense she liked to burn. A cigar, but that was all right too. That was something they had both come to understand. These things didn't matter so much any more, and perhaps the thing they had in common was the knowledge of what things seemed to matter and what things did not. A cigar or two didn't. Which was why he was often there.

Sometimes he would sit there with the glass of beer she was sure he would like if he would just drink it—until the foam was gone, the beer was warm, and she would drink it herself. Other times he had grape juice with lumps of ice in it. He would suck on the ice while she played him records on the gramophone. Perhaps she thought he was homesick, lonely, or something like that. It probably meant she was sometimes lonely herself.

He liked to be with Evelyn Fry just to be with her, to sit there in the room, and to stir the ice in what he was drinking with one of her spoons. While the music played, nobody had to talk. He would sit facing the piano with the hanging shawl, the vase with the red paper flowers, and the picture of a gaunt-looking man in his underwear, rowing a boat. Her husband. He had left her, naturally. He had a stiff black beard and it had probably tickled her face.

"That song," she would say, putting on the record that he seemed to like, but never knew the name of, "what is it you like about it so much?" Did he ever answer? No, he never had to say. He had ice in his mouth, and perhaps he didn't know, anyhow.

That was how he liked to put in an evening—not too often, just now and then—when he had the need of a little woman for himself. Someone to pour him a drink, and ask him simple questions about his kids. And around ten o'clock he would leave, as he had to go and pick them up. If they were at the Empress, but not in the lobby, he would ask the manager, Mr. Youngblood, to run the slide advertising Will Brady's Chickens and Eggs. This would let them know that he was in the lobby waiting for them. But if they were at the World, or the Orpheum, where slides like that had gone out of fashion, he would just sit there in the lobby until they came out. People like Tom Mix, Hoot Gibson, and Wallace Reid they liked to see twice, which took a good deal of time if six acts of vaudeville came in between. In that case he would buy a bag of popcorn, and the usher would let him sit in the lobby as they had all got to know him and knew pretty well what his problem was.

But in August he found the boy in the lobby alone. As that usually meant that the girl was in the ladies' room for a moment, he sat down and waited while the boy finished eating a peanut bar. When the girl didn't come, he said: "Son, where is your mother?"

"She left," said the boy, "she left before the vaudeville."

"Your mother left?" he said.

"She went off with the Hawayan," said the boy. "He liked her and she's going to work for him."

"A Hawayan?" he repeated.

"She's going to dance for him," the boy said. "If I could dance I'd have gone to work for him, too."

IN THE LOBBY

1

IN THE suburbs Will Brady owned a fine house with a chain swing on the porch, a playroom in the basement, and a table in the kitchen where he left pocket money for the boy. But both the boy and the man did their living somewhere else. The boy did all of his living next door—that is to say, he added one more plate to the table that already numbered three on each side and one at the end. So it was the boy's plate that evened it up, as Mrs. Ward said.

When Will Brady walked over to discuss the matter, there was really nothing that remained to be said, as the boy had been living—Mrs. Ward said *living*—with them for some time. If he passed the night at home it was merely to make his father feel all right. Nobody liked to sleep in a big empty

159

house alone. All Will Brady could do, speaking up when he did, was recognize what had already happened and offer to pay, as he did, for the boy's board. It was agreed that he ate around five dollars' worth of food a week. He was small, but a small growing boy could somehow stow it away. It was also agreed that his father should continue to buy his clothes. These matters taken care of, Mrs. Ward agreed to let him see the boy, once or twice a week, and give him pocket money so long as it wasn't too much. She took away from him sums that she didn't think it wise for a boy to have. In case the boy got sick, or really needed something, or might, for some reason, just want to see his father, Mrs. Ward would leave a message for him at the Paxton Hotel. That was where Will Brady, for the time being, had taken a room.

When a man has lost something he would like to get back, say a wife, a boy, or an old set of habits, he can walk around the streets of the city looking for it. Or he can stand on a corner, nearly anywhere, and let it look for him. The boys and girls Will Brady found under the street lights, or playing around the posters in the theater lobbies, didn't know what he had lost but they had learned what he had to give. They could hear the coins that jingled in the pocket of his coat. If he stood on the corner, a well-lighted corner, sooner or later they would gather around him—just as the pigeons would gather around him when he sat in the park. They didn't know what he wanted, but they were willing to settle for what he had to give.

"Hello there, Harry," Will Brady would say, as he liked to call all of them Harry. As it was never their name, it gave them something to talk about.

"My name ain't Harry," they would reply, then: "Gimme three cents."

"What you going to do with three cents, Harry?"

"My name *isn't* Harry!" they would say; then, getting back: "if I had three cents I could go to a show."

"So you think you'd like to take in a show, Harry?" he would say.

"You gimme three cents an' I'll have ten."

They were smart, these kids, and so they would talk for quite a while. Sometimes it took quite a bit of handling—knowing when to stop calling them Harry—but with a pocket full of pennies a man like Will Brady could talk for an hour.

"Don't tell me, Harry," he would say, "I've got a grown-up boy of my own. I can tell you a thing or two about boys."

"What can you tell?" they would ask, and of course he couldn't tell them much of anything. Nothing but what he had read about this Tom

Sawyer, or this Penrod. They were the only boys, it seemed, that he knew very much about.

And as for girls, he knew even less—no, he didn't know a thing about girls until the one called Libby —Libby something—spoke to him. On 18th and Farnam, near the *Omaha Bee*, somebody ran out from the shadows toward him, and he assumed it was one of the boys, some skinny kid.

"Well, Harry," he had said, "is this a holdup?" and put his right hand into his pocket before he really knew—before he looked, that is—at the sharp freckled face. The girl was tall and thin, and the dress she had on was too small for her.

"Well, well," he repeated, "is this a holdup?"

"No, sir," she said, "it's not holdup," but he couldn't see her face as she stood between him and the light. He stepped to one side to look at his hand —in the palm of his hand were coins, most of them pennies—and she came around to lean over his arm, look at them too. She put her small head between him and the light. It was narrow, and the long black hair was in braids. The braids were hooked over her ears, like pulleys, and as she peered into his hand she tugged on them, slowly, tolling her head like a bell.

"That ain't enough," she said.

"For a show?" he said.

"For kisses," she said, "I'm sellin' kisses." When

he didn't speak right up, she said: "I'm not beggin' anything, I'm sellin'."

"I see," he said, and raised his head as if someone had called his name. He looked to the corner where swarms of bugs flew in and out of the street light. Passing beneath the light were a man and woman, the man with his coat folded over his arm, and the woman a step or two away from him, as if he were hot.

"Twenty-five cents is what I try and get," she said, "but if that's all you got, it's all you got," and with her dirty brown fingers she removed the coins from his hand. One at a time, pecking at his palm like a bird. When she had them all she stepped forward, putting up her face, rising on her toes, and gave him a noisy peck on the cheek. Then she stepped back, moving out of the light, to see if he was pleased.

"That wasn't so much," she said, "but it was fourteen cents' worth. Wasn't it?"

He agreed. "Oh yes," he said, and wagged his head.

"But I can do better," she said, and lifted her arms as if she were a dancer, letting her hands, the fingers parted, droop at the wrist. From a bench in the park Will Brady had seen little girls drop their jacks, or the doll they were holding, and throw up their arms, their heads back, as if they would fly.

Without warning, as if some voice had whispered to them. Sometimes it was pretty, other times it was like what he saw now. She leered at him over her left shoulder, her eyelids fluttering, and he knew he had seen it all less than an hour before. On the Orpheum billboards, where two beautiful girls were wrapped in gauze. Maybe he looked unhappy, for she said: "Did I take all your money?"

"Oh no," he said.

"I'll bet I took your carfare," she said, and looked at the coins in her hands. The dime she removed, held out to him.

"No, no," he said, "and besides, I walk. I like to walk on nights like this."

"Me too," she said, and danced around him, swinging her braids. Still dancing, she said: "And I know what you're thinking."

"What?" he said.

"That I'm not old enough. You're thinking I'm not old enough to take care of myself." He shook his head. "Well, that's what you're thinkin', you men."

"You're quite a big girl," he said.

"I am. I make my own livin'. I make up to five dollars a week. Isn't that good?"

"That's a very good living."

"It's more than my father makes," she said.

Still facing the light, he said: "What does your father do?"

"Nothing," she said, and sang that a bridge was falling down. She danced around him twice, singing, then she stopped singing, hopped up and down, and ran toward the corner, where she suddenly stopped. Her dress was too small, and she drew it down toward her sharp knees. Then she turned to wave at him, her long braids swinging, and was gone.

2

Two, sometimes three or four times a week, she "did business with him." It was strictly a business proposition, as she said herself. The fact that he seldom had the right amount of money didn't trouble her much. Sometimes she would have newspapers under her arms, usually old papers, which she would sell him, as she was in business, she told him, for herself. But kisses were a better proposition, as they cost her nothing. All she had to do was find somebody who wanted them.

On the week ends, when she specialized in kisses, she wore a large flowered hat with a flapping brim, and in the crown of the hat there were many flowers, some of them real. But what he smelled, as she always had to tell him, was her perfume. It was sometimes so strong that as she rose toward him he closed his eyes.

Inside her dress, these nights, she wore a brassiere, the pink cups folded over very neatly, and in the one on the right she kept all the money she made. It jingled as she ran off or stood hopping up and down. Week nights she had to be home early, but Saturday nights she had time to talk, if that was what he wanted, or a marshmallow sundae, if he wanted something like that. As her shoes hurt her feet, they usually had the sundae sitting down. In the ice-cream parlor she would take off her hat, as the veil on the hat tickled her face, and sometimes fell in the marshmallow sundae when she closed her eyes. She always closed her eyes, as ice cream tasted better that way. He would have a cherry phosphate, or a root beer, and when her mouth was full, and her eyes were closed, he would sit there looking at her sticky, freckled face.

Was he in love with her? That was what she wanted to know.

He said he wasn't sure. He said he didn't know.

He ought to make up his mind, she said, because if he was in love with her, really in love, he could kiss her without paying anything.

In the Lobby

Was she in love with him?

She didn't know. No, she didn't know, she said, a whole lot about love. She didn't know if what she felt was what she had heard, or if what she heard was what she felt about it. She didn't know if she had ever loved anybody or not. When she had a baby she would probably love it. Then she would know. Then she would know if what she felt for him was love or not.

Eating and talking also made her sleepy, and she would let him walk her home—to the corner, that is, where she kissed him for nothing. He could see the rooming house where she lived, the cracked yellow blinds, the old men on the porch, and watch the gas jets flutter when she closed the door at the end of the hall. Then he would go home, lying awake in the hot front room across from the boy, watching the flash in the night when the street-car trolley was switched around. When the last car for the night went back into town.

During the day he had eggs in his hands, things that he could pick up, that is, and put down, and tell what they were, good or bad, by holding them to the candler. But during the night there was nothing he could grasp like that with his hands. You can't take a notion into your hand, like a Leghorn egg, and judge the grade of it. You can't hold it to the light, give it a twist, and see that it is good. Nor is there any way to tell if it is what you are missing or not.

Could a man say, for instance, that what he really needed was a woman's hat? A cheap straw hat with a wide flapping brim, a long pin through the faded paper flowers on the crown. A hat made of yellow straw, shiny with varnish, with dried marshmallow stuck to the veil, and both dark and blond hairs tangled in it. All of its long life it had been just a hat, an inexpensive straw hat no longer in fashion, and then one day, in spite of itself, it was on a new head. It became, overnight almost, something more than a hat. It became a notion—something missing, that is, from a man's life.

So that when this girl Libby took off this hat and set it on the marble-topped table beside her, the man seated across from her might put out his fingers and touch the wide brim. He might sniff at the flowers, or take between his fingers a torn piece of the veil. Just as he had once, standing idle on the corner, let his hand rest for a moment on a boy's knobby head, or let his fingers tangle for a moment in the wild hair. But when this boy got away some man would say—some stranger, that is, would step up and say—"If you want to handle the kids, you better get 'em off the street."

And what do you say to that? Why, you say thank you, thank you very much. Maybe this stranger has what he calls your own interests at heart. Thinks that he is doing you a personal favor to speak like that. But a hat, after all, is just a hat, and if you want to lean over and sniff the paper flowers, or touch a piece of the veil, why that is perfectly all right. Very likely it was something you put up your own good money for.

But near the end of the summer he found the girl in a telephone booth at the back of the drugstore, and in the booth with her, sitting there hugging her, a fat blond boy. They had been to Krug's Park, and the boy's pink face was badly sunburned. On the lapel of his coat, like a lodge button, was a live chameleon. The boy said: "Howdy, Mr. Magee," as he naturally assumed Will Brady was the girl's father, but he stayed right there in the telephone booth, with one arm around the girl. She was giggling over the phone about boys to some other girl. Will Brady looked at his watch, put it away, advised them to have a nice time that evening, then walked out into the street before he noticed what he held clasped tight in one hand. A handful of coins: five pennies, two nickels, and one shiny new dime.

That was not the last he saw of the girl, but she no longer ran toward him out of the shadows, or wore on her birdlike head a wide flappy-brimmed hat. The braids were gone, and the dirt now showed

behind her large ears. He would see her in the battered front seats at the Empress, sitting there with
some boy, or some middle-aged man, the pale light
of the screen blinking on her powder-dirty face.
The large mouth open as if to help the eyes drink
it all in. And later, like a sleepwalker, she would
walk into the luminous glare of the lobby, where,
with one finger, she would loosen the wad of gum
from her front teeth. Facing, but not seeing him,
she would start chewing on it.

3

WELL, that was how it was, and if it sometimes
seemed strange, it was hardly any stranger than
anything else, and not so strange as the fact that
only in hotel lobbies was Will Brady at home.
Somehow or other he felt out of place almost everywhere else. In the houses that he bought, or in the
rooms that he rented, and even in the cities where
he lived. But in the lobby of a good hotel he felt
all right. He belonged, that is—there was something
about it that appealed to him.

He liked to sit in a big armchair at the front—in

a leather-covered chair if they happened to have one, and under a leafy potted palm, in case they had that. He also liked a good view of the cigar counter, and the desk. He liked the sound of the keys when they dropped on the counter, the sound of the mail dropping into the slots, and the sound of the dice—though he never gambled—in the stiff leather cup. God knows why, but there was something he liked about it. Hearing that sound he immediately felt at home.

A curious artificial place, when you think of it, glowing nightlike by day, and daylike by night, with no connection whatsoever with the busy life that went by in the street. And when a man came in through the revolving doors, it was the man that changed. The dim, shaded lights and the thick carpeted floors cast a spell over him. His walk, what you think of as his bearing, the way his arms moved or hung slack from his shoulders, all of these things were not at all what they had been in the street. He took on the air of a man who was being fitted for a new suit. A little bigger, wider, taller, and better-looking than he really was. And on his face the look of a man who sees himself in a three-way glass. In the three-way mirror he sees the smile on his face, he sees himself, you might say, both coming and going—a man, that is, who was from some place and was going somewhere. Not the man you saw, just a moment before, out there in the street.

A man comes into the world, you might say, when he steps into his first lobby, and something of this knowledge brings him there when he expects to depart. If something is missing, the lobby is where he will look for it.

And yet no two lobbies are exactly alike, there is a difference in the rugs, or the lighting, in the women at the desk, the price of the cigars, and the number of plants. There will sometimes be a difference in the men and women you find in them. There may also be a difference in the marble columns, their thickness through the middle, the height of the ceilings, and the quality of brass—if that is what it is—in the cuspidors. There will often be a difference in the service, the age of the bellhops, the location of the men's room, and the size of the carpets at the sagging side of the beds. But the figure in the carpet will be the same. Not merely in the carpet, but worn into the floor. A man seated on the bed could feel it through his socks, recognize it with his feet. All hotels are alike in this matter, and all the lobbies are more alike than they are different, in that the purpose of every lobby is the same. To be both in, that is, and out of this world.

The same things go along with lobbies that go

along with dreams, great and small love affairs, and other arrangements that never seem quite real. The lobby draws a chalk line around this unreal world, so to speak. It tips you off, as the closing of the hymnbooks tips you off in church that the song is finished and that it's time to get set for the prayer. It prepares you for a short flight from one world to a better one. From the real world, where nothing much ever happens, to the unreal world where anything might happen—and sometimes does. But there is no mystery about it. It is just a matter of rules. Just as there are hard and fast rules in the street that make it impossible for some things to happen, so there are rules in the lobby that make it possible. You can sense that as you come through the door. You can breathe it in the scented air, hear it in the women's voices, the creak of leather luggage, and the coin dropped on the counter for a good cigar.

And the name that is written there in the ledger? Take a look at it. Is it Will Brady, or is it William Jennings Brady, or is it perhaps just Will Jennings, as it doesn't really matter, for the time being?—you can be whom you like. And as for that young woman there at your side—is that your wife? You hope so. That is the gist of it. For it is the purpose of hotel lobbies to take you out of the life you are living, to a better life, or a braver, more interesting one. More in line with your own real powers, so to speak. The porter cries aloud a name in the lobby and you turn, for it might be yours, and perhaps you have never met this stranger before, your better self. You can see him in the eyes of those who turn and look at you. To size you up, to compare you with their own better selves. Just as there are men who are never lovers until they meet their wives in the lobby, there are women who have never been loved anywhere but in a hotel room. Only there does the lover meet the beloved. In the rented room is where men exceed themselves. Lovers and seducers, prosperous, carefree men of the world. What you find in the lobby, what you hear in the music, what you feel in the air as you saunter across it, is the other man and the other woman in your life. There in the lobby the other life is possible.

Perhaps that man at the counter, rolling the dice, is the one who made the Beautyrest mattress possible—but not the sleep. No, you can't have everything. You can't manufacture the good night's sleep and sell it with the bed. But, still, it is something to know that the sleep would be a good one, and that the man responsible for it is quite a bit like yourself. Middle-aged, paunchy, and often subject to lying awake.

And when you've lost something you would like to get back, the lobby is where you can look for it, sit waiting for it, or, if you know what you want, you can advertise. As you probably know, it is smart to advertise. Adam Brady did it when he wanted a wife, Will Brady did it when he wanted an egg, as the only problem is in knowing what you want. Knowing, that is, how to put it in ten or twelve words. But that can be quite a stickler. Take something like this:

> FATHER AND SON seek matronly woman take charge modest home in suburbs.

Was that what he wanted? Well, he thought it was. But he would have to wait and see what an ad like that turned up. If what he said, so to speak, had covered the ground. On the advice of the girl in the office, he ran that ad in the "Personal" column, as he was looking for something rather special, as she said. He gave his address, of course, as the Paxton Hotel. The lobby would be just the place for a meeting like that. It would not be necessary for him to inquire what such a woman had in mind, as it was there in the ad, and all the woman had to do was answer it. That was what he thought, this fellow Brady, when he took his seat at the front of the lobby, wearing the look of a man who was the father of a homeless boy. That was what he was thinking when a Miss Miriam Ross asked to speak to him.

"Hello," she said to him as he came forward. "Where'll we park?"

With the hat that he held, Will Brady gestured toward the back.

"Okey-dokey," she said, and walked ahead of him with her shoulders back, her hips thrown forward, with the motion of a woman going down a flight of stairs or a steep ramp. From the back Will Brady could see the rolled tops of her stockings, the red jewel clasps, and when she sat down—dropped down—he saw them at the front. He had never seen a flapper before. Not up close, that is. He wondered if, over the years, he had fallen out of touch with the motherly type.

Miriam Ross lay in the lobby chair, her arms wide, her legs spread as if the room was too hot, and smoked cigarettes while peering at him dreamily as he talked. What did he say? Something about himself and a homeless boy. Every now and then he fanned the blue smoke away from his face. Now and then the girl sighed, as if tired, or tipped her head to blow the smoke in her lap, or make little cries, like a puppy, while dusting her cigarette. Later she leaned forward, on her sharp knees, to powder her face. On a piece of gum wrapper she wrote her name, her address, and her telephone number, then she slunk along before him, coughing softly, toward the door. "Be seeing you, daddy," she said, and patted him gently on the chest.

When you know what you want, perhaps you still have to learn how to ask for it.

> FATHER seeks large matronly
> woman to mother homeless boy.

Was that too plain? He would drop the *large*. Somehow, when he was a boy, matronly women were all large.

> FATHER seeks matronly woman
> as companion growing boy.

Perhaps it was best to keep the father out of it. He let a week pass, then he ran this ad in both the Des Moines and the Omaha papers, and in the following week he received eighteen replies. He made appointments with a Miss Lily Schumann, a Miss Vivien Throop, a Bella Hess, and a Mrs. Callie Horst. Mrs. Horst's letter to him had been very brief:

> *I sometimes get so sick and tired of all of them.*
> *How old is yours?*

Mrs. Horst also lived on a farm and didn't know whether she could get to town within the month or not. But his first appointment was with Miss

Schumann, who would be wearing, as she said, white feathers, a fur muff, and a red handbag. She also described herself as stylish stout.

He found Miss Schumann seated near the phone booths, asleep. She was well dressed, her hands in a fur muff, and her corset hugged her body so that it seemed to prop her upright, like a barrel. Now and then she burped, putting out a pink tongue to lick the film from her lips. She was rather short, with small hands and feet, and from time to time her brows arched up, her face flushed, and her small white teeth would bite down on her lip. She seemed to be digesting, and enjoying it very much. Without opening her eyes she removed from her handbag a small handkerchief, with blue tatting, and wiped her full lips, both inside and out, like a baby's mouth. Later she dropped a green mint on her tongue. Her small hand, with the fat fingers, rested on her muff like a picked bird, and when she sighed, her breath was scented with wintergreen. He let her sleep. She was still there in the lobby, blowing softly, when he met Miss Throop.

Miss Throop lowered herself—she did not sit down, nor drop down, she lowered herself—as her glasses, on a cord from her throat, swung back and forth beneath her large bust. "Throoooop," she

was saying, "old English," and when she was lowered, her legs crossed at the ankles, she felt about
on her front where her glasses had once been. This
was on the top of her bust, rather than beneath.
"Throoooop," she repeated, and found her glasses
in her lap.

Miss Throop had spent the best years of her life
as a tutor to the Countess Moroni, companion and
tutor to her three lovely children and the Countess
herself. This was of course in Italy. During the
morning she and the children spoke only Italian
and French, during the afternoon they spoke English and American. American was the hardest—she
had been away so long. It bored her to death—were
they seated in a draft? She stood up, wheeling, and
backed herself against the radiator. Did he mind a
woman standing, she asked, and spread her full
skirts to catch the heat. She simply felt *better* standing—that was what years of lecturing did. As the
heat billowed her skirts, she fluffed them out, let
them fall, and the sweetish sour smell hung over
the lobby, the smell of soiled clothes. She was getting warm, and the bangs of her wig, a crisp amber
color, stuck to her forehead when she raised her
hand, patted them down.

"And now tell me," she said, with her fingers on
her eyelids, "about your son."

While Will Brady talked, Miss Throop inhaled her own rich smell. She stood with one hand at her back, the other raised to her damp forehead, with the tip of the thumb and the first finger on her lidded eyes. Her glasses had made deep blue bruises at the bridge of her nose. Under her arms the colors had run, the dress snaps had parted, and there in the open were the shiny spears of her corset stays. When he stopped talking, for a moment, she turned to look at the rain.

"Rain, rain, rain, rain, rain, rain," she said, and gave her skirts a toss, like a dancer; then as they drooped she felt around once more on the top of her bust. But it was not for her glasses. Smiling, she said:

"You mind if I smoke?"

Bella Hess said no, no thank you, she'd just as soon stand up and talk, and looked about her as if the lobby chairs were so many beds, the pillows rumpled and the covers thrown back. Bella Hess had worked for years in Cedar Rapids, and she handed him a letter, several pages long, describing the cooking, the washing, and the hundred extra things Bella Hess had done. She had along with her a small bag of hard rolls, another letter of recommendation, and a wicker case with an umbrella strapped to the side. Will Brady just stood there, holding the letter, until Bella Hess picked up her bag, took the letter from his hands, and walked through the swinging doors into the street.

The next woman he met did not even trouble to answer the ad. She just happened to be standing in the lobby when he was speaking to Bella Hess, and while he stood there, wondering, she came up and spoke to him. She had a powder-stained face, bleached hair; but there was something familiar about her—about the walk, and about the way she rolled her eyes. Like the weighted, rolling eyes of a sleeping doll.

"You lookin' for somebody, daddy?" she said, and stepped so close to him that she touched him, with her head tipped back as if there was something caught in her eye—something that he, with the corner of his hanky, would have to remove.

"I am interviewing housekeepers," he said. God knows why, but he said it, and saw that her teeth no longer looked cold in her red mouth.

"You're doin' what, daddy?" she said, and pressed so close to him that he could see the pores in her nose. They had always been large. Yes, he remembered that. "I'm not so good at keeping house, daddy," she said, "but there's other things I can tend to," and she took his coat by the lapels, drew him down toward her lips. He was unable to move, or to speak, and when he saw her tongue wagging in her mouth, like a piece of live bait, he closed his eyes and put one hand to his face. At the front of the lobby someone rattled the dice, and he saw, as if cupped in his hand, the face of the girl behind the cigar counter at the Wellington. She had rocked the leather cup and said: "Come have a game on me."

"You sick, daddy?" she said.

"No," he said, "no, I'm all right," and opened his eyes and looked at this strange missing woman, his wife.

IN THE CLOUDLAND

1

AFTER putting his wife to bed, Will Brady came downstairs and took a seat in the lobby, facing a railroad poster of a palm-fringed island in a soft blue sea. A glass-bottomed boat, with many bright flags flying, the deck crowded with happy men and women, sailed from a white pier—so it seemed to Will Brady—toward happiness. The island of waving palms seemed to float in the blue —the pale blue of the sky, the deep blue of the sea —and to be nothing more than what men were inclined to call a mirage. But the name of this place was Catalina, and it was said to be real. It could be found, like the town of Omaha, on a map somewhere. And according to the message on the poster, this island was just two days away—just two days and three nights from where he sat in the Paxton

Hotel. Out of this world, and yet said to be in it at the same time.

In Will Brady's mind what the girl needed, what this strange woman, his wife, needed, was what he had often heard described as a change. It was linked in his mind with white Palm Beach suits, the shoes that Lyman Bryce wanted him to wear, gay beach umbrellas, and a wide view of the sea. Off there, if anywhere, the grease and paint would wash from the girl's stained face, her dyed hair would grow dark, and in time he would recognize her. And in the meantime he would go through a change himself—hard to say in advance just what it would be —but they would both begin, as he had read in books, their life over again. So he let it be known that Will Brady and his wife would be away several weeks. That seemed to be the time that it took to effect a real change. Then he stepped up and ordered, from the clerk at the desk, two round-trip tickets to California, with a passage to that island advertised on the poster—if there was such a place.

But two long days and three nights on a train can seem quite a while. He hadn't seen this girl, his wife, for some time, but after one good meal in the diner it seemed that he had run out of things to talk about. There was a good deal to see out the wide diner windows, and a good deal to eat, sitting there, but when you run out of talk the long days seem to drag. Fast as they were traveling, even the view was slow to change.

Was it twelve or fourteen telephone poles to the mile? Watching the poles file past like wickets, he thought of that. The red and white road markers were faded now, and the bleak frame houses, like bumps on the land, looked as lonely and forgotten as an abandoned caboose. It reminded him of something. He had traveled west with this woman before. At that time the painted bands on the poles were new, the winter wheat in the shimmering fields was new, and the girl and the boy, there in the seat beside him, were new as well. In a certain way, he must have been fairly new himself. A second-hand label might have looked strange on any of them. But now that new coat of paint was gone, the white band on the poles had faded, and he didn't have to look at himself to know other things had faded as well. Nor did he have to be told that the town down the tracks would be Calloway, a whistle stop now. He saw the fine City Hall was like a birthday cake without the frosting, and a strip of tattered flag was flapping from the stilts on the water tank. The word DOMINOES had been painted on the window of the Merchant's Hotel. Down the spur of weedy track he saw the lumber mill, with a few weathered boards in the yard, and beyond it the frame house with the clapboards peeling, the windows smashed. He remembered there had been a creaking flight of stairs on the east side. Now they were gone, the lantern was gone, but the rust-colored scar, like a gash, was there, with the tattered, blowing strips of a Hagenbeck & Wallace circus poster. The mouth of the rhinoceros, like a great hole in the wall, was still there.

The good will prevail, Anna Mason had said, but sometimes a man was led to wonder. Was it possible that a man died just to be dead? The answer was no—if you had to answer a question like that. Will Brady's father had died, his mother had died, and around five thousand leghorn chickens had died, but certainly not for nothing. No, they died to give him a piece of advice. What was it? Well, it seemed to have faded a bit as well. Something or other about how, in the long run, the good would prevail.

Hadn't he, for example, found his wife? After a change and a rest wouldn't she be as good as new? If he sometimes lay awake at night just to look at her face while she was sleeping, it was merely because she looked more like her old self that way. During the day he found it better not to look at her. He didn't know the face. The woman he saw looked like somebody else.

For a while it did him good to see her eat—the

rest and the food would do her good, he thought—but watching her eat, his own appetite began to fall off. He stopped eating. He settled for a cup of coffee now and then. As this meant there was food left on his plate, she would reach for the toast he didn't eat at breakfast, dip it into his egg, and then finish off his marmalade. She poured his cream into her own coffee, asked for more of it. In the last swallow or two of her coffee she liked to dip the lump sugar, suck out the coffee, then leave a heavy syrup in the cup and on her lips. Between meals she ordered sandwiches from the porter, and if the train stopped at a station she would lean out the window to buy candy bars and fruit. She couldn't seem to eat enough, sleep enough, or even see enough out the wide windows, as if every moment that passed might be her last. In the evening he read to her from some movie magazine.

In the window that he faced he could see her tongue coming and going as she washed her teeth, explored her gums, or found bits of food in her mouth that she had stored away. There were little pads of fat, like sideburns, in her puffy cheeks. Stage make-up had coarsened her skin and there was a deep-blue stain, like a bruise, that would not wash out from beneath her eyes. It was part of her face, like the distracted baby-roll of her eyes. She used the white tongue to pick her teeth, and every now and then, facing the window, she would stick it out and have a look at it.

At night she slept with her mouth open, which was normal enough in some ways, except for the change that it brought to her face. Her body, all of this time, remained the same. There seemed to be no connection between this body and the face. This may have been why she could eat all day long and half the night, feeding her face, without her body showing any signs of it. The face had gone off, was going off, that is, somewhere on its own. But the body was faithful—put it like that. The body was faithful even though the face seemed to find the world too complicated, the going too rough, and the living too sick at heart.

From the Biltmore Hotel, in Los Angeles, in the big red cars chartered for that purpose, they rode down to the sea where there were piers, crowds of people, and amusement parks. Facing the sea there were benches, and seated in the sun, wearing the dark glasses, Will Brady would read from the guide-book to her. He kept himself posted in order to point out the interesting things. From a glass-bottomed boat they peered into the sea at schools of fish, drifting like birds, and in the evening they would sit on a terrace somewhere, watching young people dance. Now, however, no young man came forward and spoke to her. It seemed to be clear that the woman at his side was not his child. Out on the dark sea were the lights of boats, pleasure craft as some people called them, and across the water, sparkling like stars, were the lights of the shore. Very much as if the sky—or the world they were now in—was upside down. Which was not at all strange as that was how this world really was.

There were people who told him that the City of Angels was an unreal city, a glittering mirage, and that the people were as strange, as rootless, and as false as the city itself. That the whole thing was a show, another mammoth production soon to be featured in the movie houses, and that one fine day, like the movie itself, it would disappear. Will Brady couldn't tell you whether that talk was true or not. But he could tell you that part of the description was real enough. This unreal city, this mammoth production full of strange, wacky people like himself, was an accurate description of a place Will Brady recognized. Here, bigger than life, was Paradise on the American Plan. A hotel lobby, that is, as big as the great out-of-doors.

Every morning they rode off to look at something described in the guidebook or pictured on the cards, or they sat in the lobby, where other people came to look at them. Or they rode out in buses to watch the great lover, John Gilbert, make love. They saw him kneel, one knee on the floor, and make love to the woman whose eyes looked bruised and whose armpits were sore where she had just been shaved. In the sun a small boy walked an aging lion about the streets. Over a cardboard sea great towers fell, and men leaped from the windows of burning buildings to fall into nets held aloft on wooden spears. Half-naked women, in skirts of straw, lay about on a floor sprinkled with sand, their bodies wet from the heat of great smoking lamps. Thick custard pies, suspended on wires, made their way around corners, and curved around poles to catch the man—the villain, that is—full in the face. Beyond, the mountains rose up to be seen from the valley, and the valley dropped down to be seen from the mountains, and so that nothing might remain unseen the dry air was clear. And one went to bed, in this unreal world, but not to sleep. The eyes were closed, it seemed, the better to look at onself.

All that Will Brady saw he kept to himself, perhaps lacking the words for it, but what the girl saw when her eyes were closed kept her awake. Lying there in the dark, as she had years before, she would talk. Once it had been men that troubled her sleep, but now it was herself. During the day he sometimes wondered if she saw anything very clearly, but during the night she seemed to have eyes like a cat. She saw everything. Even stranger, she had the words for it.

There was a Mr. Pulaski—or so she said—who took her for long buggy rides in the country, where he would fish, with a pole, while she played at rowing the boat. In the afternoon he took naps, lying with the newspaper over his face, and she ate chocolates and shooed the flies off his big hands. They were red on the back, with knobby knuckles, and the nails of one hand were blue from how he had worked in Poland, the old country. He napped with his hands lying at his side, like a dead man. He was good with horses, and they would run without his whipping them. Every week he gave her a five-dollar bill, saying: "Now you go and buy yourself something," but that wasn't what she wanted to do. He kept giving her money for something she didn't want to sell. He was very nice, but she stopped seeing him.

There was a Hazel Roebuck, who was head cashier at the Moon. Hazel Roebuck knew in advance when Wallace Reid or Francis X. Bushman was coming, and she would give her tickets for the mezzanine seats free. Hazel Roebuck had a nice room at the Paxton Hotel and she liked to have help while trying her clothes on, taking a bath, or doing any number of things. There wasn't anything that she liked to do alone. She liked to let down her long hair and let someone do it up, or leave it long and try on broad-brimmed summer hats. She showed her what ice would do to the nipples of her breasts. Hazel Roebuck did not give her money, but she left her with the feeling that what she got, she got for nothing, so to speak. As she didn't want it for nothing, she stopped seeing her.

There was a Mr. Marshall, who was head floor-walker for Burgess & Nash. He wore expensive clothes like an actor, a paper flower on his coat, and, under his vest, buttons that held his shirt pulled down. As he was the last man out of the building, they could use the ladies' lounge, or the men's dressing-room on the second floor. He would sit on a chair and patiently watch her take off her clothes. He liked her to undress so that all of her clothes fell in a puddle at her feet, except her black stockings, which he liked her to leave on. Then he would give her all new clothes to put back on. He never once put his hand on her, said anything nasty, or giggled, and everything that she could wear out of the store she could have. In the winter that was quite a bit. He was very shy, and the first man ever to call her Miss Long. He didn't give her money, or tickets, but when she had all of the clothes she could wear, summer and winter, she had stopped seeing him.

Did she *like* him? he had asked. He had interrupted her to ask her that.

Like him? she had said. Oh, she had liked him all right.

Did she feel any *love* for him—that was what he meant to say.

No, she had replied, she hadn't felt anything like that. It was Francis X. Bushman who had awakened her to love.

When she recognized it for what it was she sat in the movies eight hours every day, loving him and hating the women that he kissed. That was love. A woman only felt like that just once.

What about—he said—what about himself?

Whatever it was, she said, it was not love at first sight. Maybe it was not what she would call love at all. She might not have even looked at him if it hadn't been for the way he looked, and the way he didn't seem to know what to do with himself. He just sat there in the lobby. Or he got up and went for long walks. All the other men she had ever known were able to talk, to smoke, or do something, but he just sat there without doing anything. He had money, wavy brown hair, and strong white teeth like Mr. Pulaski, but the first time she saw him she simply didn't feel anything. The second time maybe she felt sorry for him. Then one day, God knows why, she saw what was wrong. She saw that Will Brady knew how to give, like Mr. Marshall and Mr. Pulaski, but what he didn't know was how to receive anything. Maybe what she felt was love the day that she saw that. Maybe she really loved him, that is, the day that she saw that he was hopeless—or maybe what she felt was something else.

Getting back—he said—getting back to other men besides himself, just what was it that she felt for them?

For *them?* she said.

The other men in her life. What did she feel for the other men in her life?

Sorry, she said, she felt sorry for them.

Just what did she mean by that, he said, what did she mean by feeling sorry?

They were moths, she said, that flew away from the flame.

And where, he had asked her, where in the world had she picked up *that?*

It was a line in one of her plays, she said. In this play she would climb out of the bed, or if she was out she would climb in it, and the man in the bed or the room would run away. She would call to him that he was a moth afraid of the flame. Everybody would laugh. Why did they laugh?

It was the way of men to laugh, he said. That was their way.

Was he different, then, she said, from other men?

Was he? Did she mean that he had been burned? Did she mean that he, Will Brady, had not run away from the flame? Did she mean that all the other men had got out of the bed or hid beneath it, or did she mean that all the other men were part of the play? She liked this play? he asked.

She liked the view from the stage.

The *what?* he said.

She liked the view. From the stage she had a good view of all of them.

Them—? he said.

The men, she said. It was like a new show for her every night. They came to see her, they paid their good money, but the light from the stage was on their faces and she didn't have to pay a cent to see all of them. And they didn't care—they all wanted her to look at them. So she made it a point, lying there in the bed, to look at each man in every row, and if the town was big and the house was full this took time. It might take her two or three weeks to see all of them. If the show had a long run, as it often did in the larger places, sooner or later she saw most of the men in town. Five or ten thousand men, some of them single, some of them married with wives and children, some of them rich, some of them poor, some of them good and some of them bad, but every living one of them there to be seen, and to look at her. She knew them all, and all of them knew her. But they were all moths, she said, that flew away from the flame.

It made him smile, lying there, to hear her talking in terms like that, and to think that of all these men she had picked him out to be burned. When she had held the flame up to him, he hadn't run. Some people would say that he hadn't even sense enough to do that.

But he didn't laugh, as he might have, or ask her if she thought he was such a fool as to believe the only men in her life had been under her bed. No, he didn't ask her. He didn't even bring it up. The longer he lived the easier he could believe wild talk like that. He didn't find it hard to believe at night, and it didn't strike him as silly in the morning when he took a seat, with the other old men, on a bench in the park. In the unreal world, talk like that seemed real enough.

On the one hand you would say that the old men in the park had either lost or given up something, like the ratty-tailed pigeons that paced up and down on the walk. They had given up the notion of being some fancier kind of bird. They were no longer ashamed to let their feathers drag on the walk. On the one hand you could see they had given it up, on the other hand there was a man

called Teapot. That was the only name that he had
—where had he picked it up? Every morning, like
the sun itself, he entered the park. To the casual
passer-by it might appear that this fellow Teapot
had some kind of trouble, bodily trouble, that
forced him to walk along with one hand on his
hip, the other raised in the air. But those who knew
better knew that this fellow Teapot had become a
new thing. No longer merely a man, he was a Teapot. He was meant to be poured.

"Brother, pour me!" Teapot would say, and the
brother would take Teapot by the arm, as you
would kettle, and tip him forward till he poured.
Whatever Teapot contained would flow out the
long spout of his arm. "Thank you, brother," he
would say, and proceed across the square. Later in
the day, several times, he would need to be poured
again. Now, there were people who would class
Teapot as odd, or even downright wacky, but Will
Brady had acquired a different feeling about such
men. Put it this way: he felt right at home with
them.

Every day Will Brady saw, on the bench near
the fountain, an old man with brown bare feet, his
soiled pants legs rolled, and three or four wiry hairs,
like watch springs, on his flat, leathery chest. He
passed most of the day with a newspaper spread
over his face. Morning and evening he fed the

pigeons, wetting the hard dry bread in his mouth, rolling it into a ball, then feeding this spittle to the birds. Some of the old men in the park sat and wagged their heads over something like that. But not Will Brady. No, he felt very much at home.

Was there any man, Will Brady asked himself, who didn't understand something like that? Who wouldn't like, that is, to be fed to the birds himself? Well, there were several men who said the old fool with the bare feet had a brain that was soft. Sitting in the sun, they said, had done that to him. The old man's hands, lying in his lap, had got to be the color of walnut stain, and if he napped sitting up, the pigeons roosted on his shoulders, dirtied his front. It soon dried in the sun and he chipped it off later, absently. The way Will Brady would chip the hen spots off a Leghorn egg. In one pocket of his coat the old man kept reading matter, in another pocket eating matter, and every hour or so he got himself up and took a long drink. He would peer through the palm trees at the clock to see how much time he had passed.

Was this an example of what the sun would do to a man? Perhaps it was, as Will Brady passed the time that way himself. The great problem in life, as any old fool could tell you, was not so much about love, or the man and the flame, nor did it have much to do, in the long run, as to who it was that was burned. No, the real problem was nothing more than how to pass the time. Every day it was there, somehow it had to be passed. The really great problem in life was merely how to get out of the bed in the morning and put in the time until you went to bed again. The girl solved this problem by lying awake at night, having breakfast in bed, and trying to sleep during the day. Will Brady got up and sat on a bench in the park.

In the early evening the girl would get up and they would go out some place for dinner, but one evening, after his walk, she was not there. Neither in the lobby nor up in the room. That usually meant she would be in the ladies' room, and he took a seat near by in the lobby, across from a tall flat girl who stood in the door chewing gum. This girl seemed to take an interest in him. On the seat beside him was a magazine open at a picture of Pola Negri, but Will Brady couldn't keep his mind on what he read. The girl in the door kept staring and smacking the gum. So he put the magazine back on the seat, took time to look at his watch, but when he walked across the lobby the girl followed him. Before he could make a getaway she said: "You lookin' for somebody, daddy?"

"I am waiting for my wife," he replied.

"Adds up to the same thing," she said, and when

he looked at her face she smacked the gum she was chewing, sucked in on it. "You got a nice long wait," she said, and when he didn't answer that, she added: "I'd just as soon sit down, daddy," and then she pushed through the swinging door and walked into the street. He followed her. She was wearing the kind of clothes that the girl liked to wear. A shabby fox fur hung from her shoulders, and the shriveled grinning head, with its glassy eyes, bounced on her hip. He walked behind her to the corner, where she turned and said: "This be all right, daddy?" and nodded her head toward the corner drugstore. As they went in she called to the waitress: "Make it a double chock-Coke, honey," and as they sat down at the back she took her gum from her mouth, stuck it to the seat.

"You have seen my wife?" Will Brady said.

"Not any too good," she said, "she was on the floor, and it was hard to see her." He stared at her, and she said: "Daddy, you want me to begin at the first?"

"Why, yes," he said, and felt his head nodding. When the girl brought the Coke he asked her for a cup of coffee, black.

"First you get a bottle, daddy," she said, "then you lock yourself up in a nice pay toilet, then you empty the bottle, and then after while you fall off the seat. When you fall off the seat I come along and pick you up."

"Thank you," he said, "very much."

"Oh, I'm paid for it," she said, and tapped a cigarette on her thumbnail. "I'm paid," she said, "but God knows I've done it for nothin' enough." She lit the cigarette and blew the smoke in his face.

"She's all right, then?"

"Daddy," she said, and closed her eyes. With her eyes closed she let the smoke drift through her nose. "Daddy," she went on, "a nice man like you makes a bad girl like me feel better. You owe it to a girl—where'd she pick you up?"

"Miss—" Will Brady began.

"Clinton," she said, "Flora Clinton."

"Miss Clinton," he said, "if you have seen my wife—"

"You a Mr. Metaxas?"

"Brady," he said, "Will Brady."

"Next time you pick up a little girl," she said, "say you look in her handbag and see who she is. Say you find out whether you're a Mr. Metaxas or not." He looked at her, and she said: "Well, daddy, you asked for it."

He turned from Flora Clinton and looked at the Palms in Pershing Square. The old man with bare feet was feeding the pigeons from a paper bag. He wet the food in his mouth, then spit it out and fed it to them. The flapping of their wings stirred the stringy hair at the back of his head.

"You mind a personal question?"

"No," he said, and wagged his head slowly.

"Where'd she ever find you?"

"Omaha."

"Where is that?"

"It's a town on the Missouri," he said, and saying that, he saw it there before him, a town on the bluffs. He saw the muddy river and the new toll bridge they had put over it.

"That must be a great place," she said, "Omaha, I'll remember that," and took from her purse a small card, wrote a number on it. She handed it to him and said: "Next time you feel like a little girl, daddy—"

"This woman is my wife," he said.

"That makes it even worse, daddy," she said, and finished her Coke. There was ice in the glass, and she tipped her head back till it spilled into her mouth. Then she patted his arm and said: "I've got to run along now, daddy," and stood up from the table, smoothed the wrinkled front of her dress. "You say this kid was your wife?" she said.

"This woman is my wife," Will Brady replied.

"I don't get it," Flora Clinton said, "I don't see why she didn't talk." She looked at her face in the mirror, then said: "When people don't talk they think they're in love. Maybe she was so drunk she thought that she was." That made her smile, sucking in the air from the side of her mouth, where a tooth was missing. "Well, bye now, daddy," she said, and he watched her walk away.

From the corner, where he stood at the curb, Will Brady watched the old fool who was feeding the pigeons, and saw on his face the rapt gaze of a holy man. A circling flock of pigeons hovered above him, flapping their wings. On the old man's face was the look that Will Brady had seen, many years before, on one of the calendars at the foot of his mother's bed. A religious man, it was said, who fed himself to the birds. So it was not a new notion. No, it was a notion of the oldest kind. Very likely this old fool let himself think that in just such a manner he might fly himself, grow wings like an angel, and escape from the city and the world. As the spirit is said to escape from the body, when the body dies. Perhaps he thought that—or perhaps all he was doing was making love. There were many ways to make it, after all, and perhaps that was one of them.

No voice had ever spoken to Will Brady before —or even whispered to him, for that matter—but now from out of the sky, above the noise of the pigeons, one spoke to him.

"Old man," this voice said, "so you think you are a lover?"

Did Will Brady smile? No, he kept a sober face.

"Speaking of heaven," the voice went on, though of course they had not been speaking of heaven, "I suppose you know there are no lovers in heaven. I suppose you know that?"

"No lovers in heaven?" Will Brady replied, but the voice did not answer. Will Brady thought he heard it sigh, but it might have been the wind. "Then why go to heaven?" Will Brady said.

"I don't know," said the voice, "I've often wondered." Then it added: "But I suppose the small lovers like it. They like it up here."

"And the great lovers?" Will Brady said.

"There's no need," said the voice, "for great lovers in heaven. Pity is the great lover, and the great lovers are all on earth."

That was all, that was all that was said, but somehow Will Brady was left with the feeling that this creature in heaven, somehow, envied every old fool on earth. That something was missing in heaven, oddly enough. As it had never occurred to Will Brady that something might be missing in heaven, he turned to watch the pigeons wheeling over the park. They were rising, and filled the sky with the sound of their wings. On Will Brady's face, strangely enough, was the rapt, happy gaze of a holy man, like the old fool who stood barefooted in the park. Together they watched the pigeons wheeling until they were gone, the sky was void, and the old man suddenly threw into the air his flabby brown arms. Over his head, for a moment, floated the empty paper bag.

IN THE WASTELAND

1

H<small>E HAD</small> asked the porter to wake him out of
Cheyenne. That was not necessary, how-
ever, as he was wide awake, his eyes were open,
when the porter rattled the curtains of his berth.
With his pajama sleeve he wiped a small hole in
the frosted glass. A new fall of snow, like a frozen
sea, covered the earth. In the spring and the fall,
through the wide diner windows, a man who had
felt hemmed in by the city, or who had had, as he
thought, enough of people, might find relief in the
vast emptiness of the plains. He might feel what
some men felt when they came on the sea. In the
winter, however, there was no haze to soften the
sky, blur the far horizon, or lead a man to think
that he might, out there, make a go of it. Everything visible had the air of being left there, dropped

perhaps. Every mound or post had the look of cattle frozen upright. Will Brady, for example, had seen such things as a boy. It was strange to find them, after so many years, still vivid in his mind.

He could see the winter dawn, a clear ice color, and far out on the desolate plain, like the roof of the world, were two or three swinging lights. He could make out the dry bed of the river, and as the train was stopping for water, he could hear, down the tracks, the beat of the crossing-bell. The rapid throbbing of this bell, at such a godforsaken and empty corner, seemed to emphasize that this scene, the birthplace of Will Brady, was as remote, and as dead, as a crater on the moon.

As the train slowly braked to a stop, he could see the frame of the cattle loader, and then, suddenly, the station along the tracks. A lamp, with a green glass shade, hung inside. It threw an arc of light on the wide desk, the pads of yellow paper, and the hand of the man who sat there, a visor shading his face. The fingers of this hand were poised over the telegraph key. His head was bare, getting bald, and the green celluloid of the visor cast a shadow the color of illness on his face. He was staring, absently, into the windows of the passing cars. On the table before him lay a bamboo rod, curved at one end like a plant flowering, and a sheet of folded paper was inserted at the curved end. Will Brady saw all of this as if it were a picture on a calendar. Nothing moved, every detail was clear. He could smell the odor of stale tobacco, and the man's coat, wet with snow, gave off the stench of a wet gunny sack. He could see the wood stove, just back from the light, and he thought he could hear, out there in the silence, the iron ring of the ground where a brakeman stamped his feet. In the man's dark vest were several red-capped pencils, and as Will Brady gazed at his face he raised his head, suddenly, as if a voice had spoken to him. He gazed into the darkness where Will Brady lay on the berth. And Will Brady fell back, he held his breath, and as his hands gripped the side of the berth he heard again the mechanical throbbing of the crossing-bell. He seemed to see, out there on the horizon, the snout-like mound of the buried soddy, where he had been, even then, the last man in the world.

He closed his eyes, and when the morning light came though the window he drew the blind to keep it from his face. He did not rise on his elbow to look at Murdock, or Calloway. Nor did he get off at Omaha, although that was his destination, and the conductor came back through the car to speak to him. Where was he going? Well, he hadn't made up his mind. He was going where the train was going, and when that turned out to be

Chicago, he implied that that was all right with him. All the roads seemed to lead to Chicago, so there was no reason why Will Brady, who followed the roads, shouldn't go where they led.

2

To GET to Menomonee Street in Chicago you take a Clark Street car in the Loop and ride north, twenty minutes or so, to Lincoln Park. If you want to get the feel of the city, or if you like to see where it is you're going, you can stand at the front of the car with the motorman. On certain days you might find Will Brady standing there. Not that he cared where he was going, but he liked the look of the street, the clang of the bell, and the smell of the track sand that came up through the floor. He liked to stand with his hands grasping the rail at the motorman's back.. At certain intersections he liked to turn and look—when the door at the front opened—down the streets to the east where the world seemed to end. It didn't, of course, but perhaps he liked to think that it might. When it did, as one day it would, he wanted to be there. On up the street he could see the park, and in the winter, when the trees were bare, he could make out the giant brooding figure of Abraham Lincoln himself. Soft green, like the color of cheap Christmas jewelry, or the fine copper gutters on the homes of the rich.

Lincoln Park was right there where the street angled. He could see the Moody Bible Tabernacle, and at the next stop Will Brady would step forward and get off. Menomonee was the street that went off like an alley to the west. To get to 218 on this street he would follow the curb on the north side to where this number was nailed on the first door on his right. The second door was the entrance to Plinski's delicatessen store. The first door was usually kept shut, even in the summer, to make the rats from the store go around and use the stairs at the rear. But the second door was open until ten or later every night. There was a sign on the door saying as much, but anyone who lived in the room overhead, and who tried to sleep there, didn't need to be told.

Will Brady lived in the room at the front, over the screen door that slammed with a bang, in a room that was said to be suitable for Light Housekeeping. To get to this room he walked up the stairs, along the bright-green runner of roach powder, and at the top of the stairs he took the door on his left. It opened on a small room with two windows on Menomonee Street. The window on the left was cut off by the bed, but over the years and through many tenants one window on the street had proved to be more than enough. On a winter afternoon it might even be warm, as the slanting winter sun got at it, and by leaning far out one could look down the street and see the park. An ore boat might be honking, or the sounds of the ice breaking up on the lake.

Inside the room was a small gas plate on a marble-topped washstand, a cracked china bowl, a table, two chairs, a chest of drawers, an armless rocker, an imitation fireplace, and an iron frame bed. Over the fireplace was a mirror showing the head of the bed and the yellow folding doors. The bed was in the shape of a shallow pan with a pouring spout at one side, and beneath this spout, as if poured there, a frazzled hole in the rug.

To get from the stove to the sink it was better to drop the leaf on the table and then lean forward over the back of the rocking-chair. On the shelf over the sink were four plates, three cups and one saucer, a glass sugarbowl, two metal forks, and one bone-handled spoon. On the mantlepiece was a shaving mug with the word SWEETHEART in silver, blue, chipped red, and gold. In the mug were three buttons, a roller-skate key, a needle with a burned point for opening pimples, an Omaha street-car token, and a medal for buying Buster Brown shoes.

In the Wasteland

At the back of the room were the folding doors that would not quite close.

To get to the bathroom, the old man who lived in this room would open these doors, greet Mrs. Plinski, then proceed to the back of the house. Mrs. Plinski was usually there in a rocker, nursing her twins. In the bathroom, seated on the stool, was her oldest boy, Manny Plinski, watching his baby turtles swim around in the tub. Manny Plinski was seventeen years old and had the long narrow face of a goat, big wet eyes, and a crown of silky, corn-yellow hair. This hair grew forward over his face and he stroked it forward, with a raking motion, as if there was something tangled in it that would not comb out. When he was displeased, Manny Plinski would make a sound like priming a pump. Mrs. Plinski would put down the twin she was nursing and wet her fingers under the tap, then sprinkle Manny Plinski as if she was dampening clothes. That would make him all right, and he would just sit there, staring at his turtles, or he could be led out in case you wanted the bathroom to yourself.

That wasn't very often, as the old man had got to be fond of the turtles, nor did he seem to mind Manny Plinski just sitting there. He would wink at the boy while the lather was thick on his face. Manny Plinski never laughed, but if he was pleased he would take one of the turtles, one that he liked, and slip it into the pocket of the old man's pants. The old man, somehow, never seemed to catch on to this. Later, of course, he would find it there and cry out for help. For a man so fond of turtles it was strange how they nearly scared him to death.

Leaving the bathroom, he would come back through the house, nod to Mrs. Plinski, then pass through the folding doors without closing them. He would let them stand open, as if his room was part of the house. He could see out, or any Plinski that cared to could see in. If a turtle was missing, this would be Manny Plinski, raking his hair in an excited manner; otherwise it might be Mrs. Plinski herself. What did she want? Well, the old man in the room had spoken to her. He had called out, perhaps, to ask if she had ever heard the likes of this. A clipping of some kind, or a passage from a letter spread out in his lap. So she would get herself up, this woman, in spite of the twin she was nursing, and brace herself, as she often seemed tired, between the folding doors. One heavy arm she would prop on the door, as if it weighed on her. The old man himself, seated at the table, would have the long sleeves of his underwear rolled, as otherwise they dragged in the food on his plate. He would be eating; that is, he had been eating, but he had stopped eating in order to examine, as the writing was fading, the letter in his lap. Two sheets of yellow paper, each sheet with widely spaced green stripes. The top sheet spotted with grease like a popcorn bag. The old man had spread the letter in his lap as his own fingers might be greasy, or in order to open, with the bent prong of a fork, the plugged hole in a milk can.

The letter was not new, it was cracked at the folds, and there were coffee stains in the margins, but it described in considerable detail an unusual event. How a snake, taken sick at the stomach, threw up a live frog. It described how the boy, the writer of the letter, picked this snake up by the tail, twirled him like a rope, and then watched him whoop up this poor frog. Not many city people would be familiar with anything like that. Mrs. Sigismund Plinski, for example, who had lived for forty-six years in Chicago, had heard the letter many times but couldn't seem to get enough of it. She would just stand there, wagging her head, as she did when the world was too much for her, and listen to the old man read parts of it aloud. Sometimes he just read the last of it, which he thought was particularly clever, and then went on to read how the boy had signed his name.

Your son—Willy Brady Jr.

that was what it said.

"You would think," the old man would say, putting the milk can down on the table, "that a boy who could write a letter like that would write a little oftener." Not that he meant it, of course, as a smart boy like that had things on his mind. It was enough for him to know that his father was sometimes one of them.

"Oh, how he must love you!" Mrs. Plinski would say. "Oh, how he must love you!" and that would be all. In some respects that was about all that she ever said. Then she would wag her big head, with the loose flesh on it, and roll the little eyes that were too small for her face. "Oh, how he must love you!" she would go on, and before Will Brady went on with the letter, or read the passage over, he would blow on the coffee that was already cold in his cup. It was never hot, but it seemed to do him good to blow on it.

"Mrs. Plinski," he would say, "now you know how boys are," and indeed Mrs. Plinski did. Both men and boys. If she knew anything, that is, this woman knew that.

"How he must love you!" she would repeat, and shift her great weight as her feet were tired, and whichever twin it was, astride her haunch like a saddle, would be asleep.

Once a year this boy wrote to his father, and maybe ten or fifteen times a year Will Brady wrote, but somehow never mailed, a postcard to his son. It would have a picture of the park or the wide blue lake on it. But every month Will Brady expected to move into larger, more homelike quarters, and when he moved—the very day that he moved—he would mail that card. It was there in his pocket, already stamped and addressed. All he had to do was put his own new address on it. This address would be—as he told everybody—over facing the park. There would be trees and grass when the boy walked to the window and looked out. There would always be a cool summer breeze blowing off the blue lake. Every year he had to write this card many times as the writing would get smudgy from the dirt in his pocket, or even the picture on the front of the card would begin to fade. So he would buy a new one, in the hotel lobby, and seated at the table where the pens were chained, he would write on the back in such a manner that it also showed on the front. It had got so the message was more or less the same. It was always spring on this card, the same robin always caught the same worm.

DEAR SON—

Have moved. Have nice little place of our own now, two-plate gas. Warm sun in windows every morning, nice view of park. Plan to get new Console radio soon now, let you pick it out. Plan to pick up car so we can drive out in country, get out in air. Turning over in my mind plan to send you to Harvard, send you to Yale. Saw robin in park this morning. Saw him catch worm.

Sometimes he said radio, sometimes he said coupe, every now and then he put Princeton instead of Yale, but he always held out for a place of their own, a nice view of the park. He always insisted that the robin caught the worm. Perhaps that was why, after three years, he was still in the room over the delicatessen, and why that postcard with the view of the park had not been mailed.

It might be wrong to say that Will Brady, an old man in yellow underwear with the sleeves rolled, lived in this room any more than he lived anywhere else. He slept there, or tried to sleep there, and that was enough. It gave him certain habits that he found very hard to break. All during the day the screen door slammed, strange children ran in and out of the hallway, and the old man who sold snails seemed to sell most of them right in one spot. Will Brady would lie there, listening to the strange cry that he made. He could hear the snails scooped out of the tub, hear the man put his hand in the striped popcorn bags, and then hear the shells when the little boys stepped on them with their heels. A powdered sound, like the track sand, but without the fresh flinty smell.

The room in which he lay had folding doors that would not quite close. The boy named Manny Plinski often stood there peering in. He was said to be a mute, that is to say that he couldn't speak in the usual manner, nor understand very much, nor do very well at the other boys' games. But the old man in the bed seemed to understand him pretty well. They had found there was very little that needed talking about. Once a week, in the good weather, the old man and the yellow-haired boy might be seen in the zoo, facing one of the cages of monkeys, bears, or strange exotic birds that looked and sounded like Manny Plinski himself. If there was a difference it was not in the feathers, nor in the cage. The man who came to feed them never stopped to sprinkle water on them.

In Will Brady's room was an iron bed, several chairs, and what a man might need to do a little housekeeping, but these things were not, strictly speaking, inhabitants. Like Brady himself, they might easily be taken away. One morning Mrs. Plinski might peer in and find them gone. But while the room was there, there would always be the smell. It was there in the floor, in the plastered walls, in the draft that stirred but never departed, in the idle curtains, and in whatever clothes hung on the back of the door. Day in and day out, winter and summer, this smell was there. A stranger might refer to this smell as a stink, as some of the lodgers were loose in their habits, and another might notice the odor of the grease, and the stale coffee grounds. But only Will Brady knew this smell for what it was. It was the smell of man. And there was something that he liked about it.

This smell was in the lining of the brown coat that both the sun and sweat had faded, and everything in the pockets, old or new, had picked up the scent. The money in the wallet, and the letter even before it was read. Once opened, and read, the letter might be said to be full of it. The message might fade, but with every reading the smell increased.

"Just listen to this," Will Brady would say to Bessie Muller, the waitress at the Athens, and read her that part about the boy and the frog-sick snake. She was a farm girl herself, but she had never seen a snake carry on like that. Or get sick at his tummy just like she did.

"You would think he liked his father," Will Brady would say, "to sit down and write him a long letter like that," and Bessie Muller would agree to that, naturally. She would even point out that nobody—*no*body—was writing letters to her.

"That kid sure likes his daddy," she would say,

and take one of the bobby pins from her hair, clean her nails with it, and then bend the point between her chipped front teeth.

If the night was warm Will Brady would walk past the moss-green statue of Abraham Lincoln, then on across the tennis courts with their sagging nets and the blurred chalk lines. There would be men with their shoes off padding around in the grass. There might be women with white arms in the shadows, fussing with their hair. Under the sheets of newspaper, with what was left of the food, some child would lie asleep.

If there was a moon, or a cool breeze off the lake, Will Brady would walk through the park to the water, where he would stroll along the pilings, or under the trees on the cinder bridle path. He had walked on cinders, he seemed to remember, somewhere before. As he had in the past, he would have to sit down and tap them out of his shoes. In the dusk there would be lights on the Wrigley tower, an airplane beacon would sweep the sky, and at Oak Street beach people would be lying in the warm sand. The drinking fountain would give off a strong chlorine smell. He would wet his face at the fountain, then take his seat among those people who had come to the beach but didn't care to take off their clothes; who had been hot in their rooms, and perhaps lonely in their minds. In the dark they could speak what they had on their minds without troubling about their faces, the sound of their voices, or who their neighbor was. Will Brady was their neighbor. He sat with his coat folded in his lap, his shirtsleeves rolled.

All over the wide beach he could see the white legs of the men, the white arms of the women, and the half-empty milk bottles propped up in the sand. Matches would flare, cigarettes would glow like fireflies. He could hear someone wading, and see the water foam at their feet. When the excursion boat left the North Pier there would be a lull in the beach murmur, and men would rise on their elbows, as if awakened, to watch it go by. They would crane their necks as if they feared to miss something. The red and green boat lights would swing on the water, the music blow in, then out again, and later the long white wave would draw a line on the beach. And after the wave, if there was a breeze, the music again.

"I see by the paper," Will Brady would say, and smooth the sleeve of the coat he was holding, "that it was over a hundred in western Kansas today."

To whom was he talking? Perhaps the murmuring air. It had come, one might say, from Kansas itself. Many things had. Perhaps the old man seated there on his left.

"Bygod, now that's hot!" this old man says, and rubs the balls of his eyes with his knuckles, as if he could see—could look back to Kansas and see for himself. He stares at the night, cranes his head, then makes a blowing noise and says: "Kansas—what part of Kansas you from?"

"I'm from Nebraska," Will Brady says, "I'm a Nebraska boy myself"—though God only knows why he calls himself a boy. An old man more or less at the end of his run. "Born and bred in Nebraska," he says, as if talk like that would revive him. "Got a boy out there now. He writes me that it's pretty hot."

"You don't say," the old man replies, and wets his lips. It would probably turn out that he had a boy somewhere himself. Or if he didn't, that he was small-town boy himself. Nearly everybody was. Where else was there to be coming from? It might surprise you how many men are small-town boys at heart, and how many small towns it takes to make a big one. Make it go, that is.

"The city's no place for a boy," Will Brady says, and gets to his feet as if that would end it. As if he didn't want to hear what the place for a boy was. "No, the city's no place for a boy," he would say, and then he would turn, look at the clock on the tower, and see that it was time for one old man to get back to work.

Another day he might not walk in the park at all, or even stop in at the Athens to see Bessie Muller, but he would go down Clark Street to the Gold Coast Café. He would sit at the counter and order one of their chicken-fried steaks.

"And how is your boy?" Mildred Weigall would say as she poured him a glass of water; she took it for granted that he would always order a chicken-fried steak. "Is he feeling his oats yet?" she would say, as she liked to think that he probably was, for she was young and feeling her oats herself.

"He's the outdoor type," Will Brady would reply, though it was hard to say what he meant by that. Did he mean that outdoor types didn't feel their oats? Probably not. Hard to say what he meant. It just so happened that one day Will Brady had sat there, reading a letter, when a snapshot of the boy had dropped out of the letter onto his plate. Mildred Weigall had wanted to know, naturally, who in the world it was. "Just a snap of the boy," Will Brady had said, and showed her that snapshot of the boy, without a stitch on, holding up one end of a canoe. But he was turned from the camera, so it didn't matter very much.

"Why, he's a nice-lookin' kid," Mildred Weigall had said. "Why don't you bring him around?"

"You think I'd try an' raise a boy like that back here?" Will Brady had said, and waved his hand, with the letter he was holding, toward the street. It had been snowing that day, and the street was full of slush.

"Not on your tintype," he had said; "kid's out in the country where he belongs."

"He's a nice-lookin' kid," Mildred Weigall had said, "he's got nice legs."

"Got his father's brains," Will Brady had replied, "and his mother's looks." That was pretty good. Somehow, it was always good for a laugh. "Thought I might bring him back," he had said, "just to show him what this place is like. But he wouldn't like it. He likes nature. Just take a look at this—" Then he would head her that piece about the frog and the snake. Like Mrs. Plinski, Mildred Weigall couldn't seem to get enough of it.

"He's a nice-lookin' kid," she had said. "when he comes, you bring him around."

On the left side of Clark Street, near Division, he passed a small movie house. Sometimes, just in idling by, he would see through the lobby doors, through the darkness behind, to the glowing silver screen. As if there was a crack in his world and he could see into another one. For a moment he might see, as if in a dream, men leaping from trains, trains leaping from bridges, lovers embracing, or the flash of guns in a battle scene. Or he might hear a song —hear it, that is, from the lover's lips. One night he had stopped, turning like a man who had been softly tapped on the shoulder, to hear the love song that came through the crack in the lobby door. A love song, and a pagan lover was singing it. This was something new, and, an old lover himself, he surrendered to it. He became a young man more or less without clothes, his strong tanned legs washed by South Sea water, and with the sunset behind him he sang this love song to his mate. *"Come with me,"* the pagan lover would sing, and Will Brady would, he came gladly, transporting himself to the land of White Shadows, to the land of true love. There he stood ankle-deep in the warm green water, sometimes spearing fish, sometimes singing love songs, and sometimes, on the palm-fringed islands, making pagan love. What kind of love was it? The doors usually closed before he found out. He might have bought a ticket, but perhaps he didn't want to know. It was enough for him to know that the young lover was there, still doing what he could.

Sometimes, standing there in the street, Will Brady felt that perhaps he had died, but the man in charge of him, the man this side of heaven, had not closed his eyes. So he stood there, a dead man in most ways, but with his eyes looking out. Eyes that seemed to look backwards and forwards at the same time. An old sorter of waybills and a pagan lover at the same time.

Was he—or was that just a way of putting things? Perhaps he was in his mind, the one place that was more or less his own. For instance, just a block or so up the street was a library, with a desk near the door, and a friendly gray-haired woman sat there in charge of things. He had walked up to this woman and said: "What I have in mind is something on education, something on leading colleges, institutes of learning—"

"You have something in mind?" she replied.

"I have a boy," he said.

"Well now," she said, "that makes it interesting."

"The place to raise a boy," he had said, to show her he had thought quite a little about it, "is in the West, but the place to educate him is in the East." Now, that was sharp. He had read that in a book that she had given him. "Boy is also quite a writer for his age," he told her; "think he might become a writer of books himself."

"In that case," she had said, "he will need the very best this country affords," and that statement had come to mean a good deal to him. He had never really thought about it before, in just that way.

"That's just what I figure," he had said. "Right now I'm thinking of Harvard, thinking of Yale. Boy has a mind of his own, but I guess his father can think of these things."

"Yes, indeedy," this woman had said, which was a favorite expression of hers, and a sign that maybe she ought to get back to work.

He went without dessert at the Gold Coast Café in order to stop for a bite at Thompson's, where the coffee was good and there was a wider range of pie. The chimes would ring when he pulled his check from the checking machine. Mrs. Beach, the cashier, would smile at him, and if she was not too busy counting change, she would swing her chair around so they could talk while he had a bite to eat.

"And how is *our* boy?" Mrs. Beach would say, as she was a mother with four boys of her own, so there was nothing you needed to tell her about boys. When a picture of the boy had stuck to one of his bills—he carried it in the wallet along with his money—Mrs. Beach had insisted on knowing who this fine-looking boy was. Luckily, it was not the picture of the boy without his clothes. It was just his head, showing his mother's wavy black hair.

"Boy takes after his mother," Will Brady would say, and to that Mrs. Beach always answered:

"She must have been a very lovely girl—she certainly was that."

"Out of this world," Will Brady would say, and turn to blow on his hot cup of coffee. He would sip it, then add: "Died no sooner than the boy was born."

"You don't mean to say," Mrs. Beach would reply, "that that boy of yours has never had a mother?"

"Just me and the kid," Will Brady would say, and blow on his cup.

"Why, I just think you've done wonders, Mr. Brady," and it was clear that Mrs. Beach did. She couldn't imagine a boy without a mother like herself. "I just wish," she would sometimes say, "that she could come back for just an hour, just be with us for an hour, to see what a wonderful father you have been to him."

When she got around to that, Will Brady would turn to his pie. It was hard for him to straighten out the many things he thought. Rather than get into all of that, which might require quite an explanation, he would go back to the counter for another cup of coffee, drink it standing up. There were things that a mother like Mrs. Beach might find it hard to understand.

* * *

From Thompson's he went on down to Chicago, and some nights, there at the end of the street, he found the drawbridge rising on the sky, like a wall. The guard bell would be clanging, and the red lights blinking at the top of the span. In the bridge tower room, on warm summer nights, the man in the tower might lean out the window, the visor shadow on his face, and his shirtsleeves rolled on his thin white arms. He liked to spit in the street, and use a tenpenny nail to tamp down his pipe.

If the span was up, Will Brady would stop in LaMonica's Lunch. At that time in the evening Mrs. LaMonica would be cleaning up. On a sultry summer night she might be out in front, sitting there on a chair with her little girl Sophie, or in the back of the store cooking up tomorrow's hamburgers. She left the front door open as the back of the store would get pretty hot.

When he asked for coffee, Mr. LaMonica would say: "What the hell'd we do without a hot cup of Java?" and Will Brady, for the life of him, never seemed to knew. It seemed a simple question, but he never had an answer to it. Into his own cup of Java he would pour some of the cream from the milk can on the counter, a small can with two holes punched in the top, and the picture of a cow on the side. But Mrs. LaMonica, who had never seen a cow, liked her coffee black.

"When you know what I know," Mrs. LaMonica would say, rolling her eyes to think about it, "when you know what I know, you drink your coffee black." No doubt she knew a good deal, but it was never clear what she had against cows. She had never seen one. Perhaps that was it. But she had often lain awake at night and heard the moos they made going by in the trucks, and she smelled the empty trucks the next morning, on their way back. It was enough, anyhow, to make her drink her coffee black.

"Maybe a new prideswinna?" Mrs. LaMonica would say, and all because Will Brady, having nothing else to do, happened to mention that the boy had won a prize.

"Oh, nothing much," Will Brady had said, and showed Mrs. LaMonica the picture of the boy that had appeared in the *Omaha Bee*. The name was clear, but his face didn't come out very well. "*Tech student writes prizewinning letter*," it read. "You would think," he said to Mrs. LaMonica, "that a boy who can write prizewinning letters would find the time to write a few more of them to his dad."

"They're all of them no goddam good," Mr.

LaMonica said. He stopped frying hamburgers to say: "You start out all alone, and that's how you end up. You live long enough and bygod you're right back where you start up from."

"They're a comfort at the breast," Mrs. La-Monica said.

"A lotta good that does a man," Mr. LaMonica said, and slapped himself on the chest. "A hell of a lotta good!"

"A prideswinna is a comfort!" she had said, and there was no use in arguing the matter. Mr. La-Monica had tried. It was better to fry hamburgers.

"Well, I better get to work," Will Brady would say, "Or I'll never get him to college."

"Oh, Mike!" Mrs. LaMonica would say. "Col-litch—you hear?"

"If you and I were college men," Will Brady would say, when Mr. LaMonica turned to admire him, "we wouldn't be here. No sir, we'd be over on the Gold Coast."

"Now bygod you're right," Mr. LaMonica would say, and look to the east, where it was said to be.

Will Brady would take a toothpick from the bowl and say: "If the kid's going to do better than his dad, he's going to need the best this country affords. He's going to need the finest education money can buy."

"You hear that, Mike?" Mrs. LaMonica would say, but before Mike would answer Will Brady would get up, drop his nickel on the counter, and walk out into the street. Talk like that always made him excited, and he would be out on the bridge, over the water, looking down at scum, wide and green as a meadow, before he knew where he was. But the sight of all of that, and the smell of it, would cool him down. Something about that smell was like a good whiff of salts, the way it cleared his mind. But like the salts, it left him a little wobbly, walking along with his head in the air, and he usually tripped as he crossed the tracks in the cinder-covered yard. It would remind him to put away the letter, or the snapshot, that he still held in his hand.

3

IF THE old man who sorted waybills in the freight yards felt himself more alive there than anywhere else, it had something to do with the tower room where he worked. On one side of the room was a large bay window that faced the east. A man standing at this window—like the man on the canal who let the drawbridge up and down—felt himself in charge of the flow of traffic, of the city itself. All that he saw seemed to be in his province, under his control. He stood above the sprawling freight yards, the sluggish canal, the three or four bridges that sometimes crossed it, and he could look beyond all of these things, beyond the city itself, toward the lake. He couldn't see this lake, of course, but he knew that it was there. And when the window stood open he thought he could detect the smell of it.

Between Will Brady and this lake were thousands of people, what one might call a city in itself; people lived there, that is, without the need of living anywhere else. They were born there, and sooner or later they died. Mrs. LaMonica had lived there for forty-eight years, hating all cows and loving pagan lovers, nor had she ever found it necessary to go anywhere else. It was only necessary to have the money and to pay the price.

The bay window in the tower room was a frame around this picture. It hung there on the wall. The man in the room could stand there, at his leisure, and examine it. He would come to know, after a time, just what bulbs were out in which electric signs, and how the shadow of the bridge, like a cloud, moved up and down the street. If he was more alive there than anywhere else—if he seemed to come to life when he faced this picture—it had something to do with the fact that he was cut off from it. Which was a very strange thing, since what the tower room made him feel was part of it.

During the long day there were trains in the yard, and a great coming and going over the bridges; whistles were blown, and the tower room trembled when a train went past. But at night this old man, Will Brady, was alone in it. When the drawbridge went up he was on an island, cut off from the shore. Without carrying things too far it might be said that this tower was the old man's castle, that the canal was his moat, and that at night he defended it against the world. That is to say, that he felt himself the last man in the world. He was back—sometimes he felt that he was back— where he had started from.

In the windows along the canal the blinds were usually drawn, and behind the blinds, when the lights came on, he could see the people in the rooms moving around. Nearly all of them ate at the back of the house, then moved to the front. There they would talk, or sit and play cards, or wander about from room to room until it was time, as the saying goes, to go to bed. Then the front lights would go off, other lights come on. A woman would stand facing the mirror, and a man, scratching himself, would sit on the edge of a sagging bed, holding one shoe. Peering into it as if his foot was still there. Or letting it fall so that it was heard in the room below.

In all of this there was nothing unusual—every night it happened everywhere—except that the people in these rooms were not alone. The old man in the tower, the waybills in his hand, was there with them. He had his meals with them in the back, wandered with all of them to the front, listened to the talk, and then saw by his watch what time it was. With them all he made his way through the house to bed. He sat there on the edge, looking at his feet or the hole in the rug.

It seemed to Will Brady that he knew these people, that he had lived in these rooms behind the windows, and that he could walk about in the dark as if the house was his own. The life and habits of the house were not strange to him. No stranger, you might say, than that house down the tracks in Calloway, where a man named Schultz was said to have lived with a city girl. To have lost her, that was the gist of it. Quite a bit like what another old man, Will Brady, had done himself. As so many men seem to do—to have won, that is, and lost something—and to end up sitting at the edge of a bed, holding one shoe. Or to lie awake until the shoe upstairs has dropped.

From the tower room Will Brady could see all these people at their work, what they called their play, and the hours that they spent at what they called their sleep. Lying sprawled on wrinkled sheets on hot summer nights. Thinking. What else was it that charged the night air? That gave it that hum, that flinty smell like the sand crushed under the car wheels, until he felt that the lid to the city was about to blow off. And that the city itself, with a puff of sound, would disappear.

And then there were times—there were times toward morning when the city itself was as real as a picture, but the people who had lived in the city all seemed to be gone. Every man, woman, and child had disappeared. The lights still burned, the curtains still moved in the draft at the bedroom windows, and here and there, like a young cock crowing, an alarm went off. But there was something or other missing from the damp night air. The smell of man—as Will Brady could tell you—was gone from it.

What had happened? It seemed that the inhabitants had up and fled during the night. As if a new Pied Piper, or some such wonder, had passed in the street. Hearing this sound, they had rolled out of bed, or raised on one elbow as if the siren, the voice of the city, had leaned in the window and spoken to them. Beckoned, whispered to them, that the time had come. Nor were they surprised, as every man knew that it would. So they had risen, soundlessly, and gone into the streets.

Still there on the floor were their socks and shoes,

on the bedpost their ties, on the chair their pants, and on the dresser, still ticking, the watches they could do without. Time—that kind of time—they could now do without. They had marched off in the manner of sleepwalkers—and perhaps they were. They had moved in a procession, with the strong helping the weak, the old the younger, and what they saw—or thought they saw—out on the water, cast a spell over them. Perhaps it had been the bright lights on a steamer, or the white flash of a sail. But whatever it was, whether true or false, whether in their mind's eye or far out on the water, they had followed this Piper, followed him into the water, and disappeared. They had waded through the cool morning sand still littered with cigarettes, pop bottles, and rubbish, and without hesitation, like sea creatures, they disappeared. Nor was there any sound, none but the water lapping their feet.

So it was with those who had the faith; but there were others, even thousands of them, who wanted to leave, but they wanted to take the world along. They had brought along with them everything they would leave behind: magazines and newspapers, chewing gum and tobacco, radios and phonographs, small tins of aspirin, laxative chocolate, and rubber exercisers to strengthen the grip. Decks of playing cards, and devices to promote birth control. They had brought these things along, but the water would not put up with them. As they entered, it washed them back upon the sand. There it all lay, body and booty, like the wreckage of the world they had been departing, as if a great flood had washed it down to the sea ahead of them. In the pale morning light their bodies looked blue, as if they had been long dead, though living, and a child walked among them spreading sheets of newspaper over each face. As if that much, but no more, could be done for them. How live in this world? They simply hadn't figured it out. Nor how to leave it and go to live in another one.

Sunday morning Will Brady would walk through these streets, marveling at the empty houses, and gaze at the lake where the faithful had disappeared. He was not one of them, but it was a thing he could understand. He had his own way for departing one world, entering another one.

On these Sunday mornings he wore his Florsheim shoes, his Stetson hat with the sewn brim, and both the pants and coat to his Hart Schaffner & Marx suit. He did not walk in the sand, but in the grass at the edge of the bridle path. The Stetson hat, level on his head, he would tip to the ladies on the well-bred horses, their long tails braided, and a sudsy white lather between their hams. The ladies in turn would tip their heads, or lift their leather riding crops in a friendly gesture, as any man out for a walk, at that time in the morning, was one of themselves. One who preferred to walk rather than ride, but who was up like them to breathe the morning air before three million other people were breathing it. A thing reserved, by and large, for successful men. Men who hadn't the time, during the busy week, to idle and play like normal people, but who could make the time early Sunday morning, while normal people slept. Most of these men liked to ride, but there were others, like Will Brady, who were known to walk.

Both these men and women came down from the north, in the big cars with the very small seats, or they lived in the apartments overlooking the lake, along the Gold Coast. In these windows the blinds were always drawn against the morning sun. Uniformed men stood at the doors to these apartments, as they did before the fancy theater lobbies, but a man with Florsheim shoes, and the pants to go with them, could walk past. A man who knew when to à-la-carte, when to table-d'hôte. Such a man could walk into these lobbies, seat himself in a chair, examine the potted plants, or step to the desk and ask to speak to Mr. So-and-so. Will Brady usually inquired if a certain Will Jennings Brady was there. A big egg man from Texas, friendly, rather elderly.

In the Wasteland

So he would take a comfy seat in the lobby while the bellhop, or the secretary, or the manager himself would see that this matter was looked into. When he wore his Stetson hat, his soft leather gloves, and the hair combed back from his high forehead, quite a fuss might be made as to who this Will Jennings Brady might be. He would be paged in the lobby, and his name would stop the music in the dining-room. Words would be exchanged between himself and the management. Important gray-haired men, with their young wives, or perhaps it was their lovely flaxen-haired daughters, would pass in front of him with their thoroughbred dogs on a leash. Some of these dogs would stop and sniff at Will Brady's feet. They knew, these dogs, but they said nothing. Between the old man and the dogs there was quite an understanding, and they both needed it.

Sometimes Will Brady's fine voice would be heard in the lobby, also his laugh, perhaps a little strained, and that habit he had, when laughing, of cuffing himself on the knee, as if nailing that leg to the floor. Quite a performance, when you consider who this old man was. An old fool with one suit of underwear to his name. Just one pair of pants that he could cross at the knee like that. Naturally, Will Jennings Brady was never on hand, but one day an Ivy Brady, from South Carolina, spoke to him

over the house phone and asked him to come right up. Hell, a Brady is a Brady, Ivy Brady said. But Will Brady asked to be excused as he had, he said, an important engagement with a big out-of-town man in the Loop.

But all of this took time—the sitting and the waiting, the patting of other people's dogs in strange lobbies, and the reading of papers left on the bench along the walk. The morning traffic would flow toward the city from the north, white sails would appear on the lake, and in the park life would begin all over again. Candy and peanuts were sold, men would roll the sleeves on white arms, put away for the winter, and women would sit fanning the flies away from baskets of food. Games would be played, young men would run and fall, others would stand in a row behind chicken-wire fences, and others would run toward Will Brady himself, waving him away. Crying that he should look up, or down, asking if he had eyes in his head. So he would make his way north, careful to avoid the deceptive clearing, where the unseen might be falling, or the games of young men who would suddenly turn and chase him away. The papers he found here and there he carried under his arm. It gave him the feeling that along with other people there was something in the park for him to do; also, he could sit on them in some places, in

others he could read. It seemed to be the thing to do while waiting for the zoo to open up.

Later he would find himself a seat facing the strange big birds, or the melancholy bears, with an elderly man, about his own age, seated on his right. Not on his left, as that side of his face didn't feel right. There was an opening there that talking wouldn't fill up. He would take this seat, sighing, then say: "Kid writes me that there's bear where he is in the woods. Hardly a day, I guess, he doesn't stumble on a bear of some kind."

"You don't say!" That was what this man at his side would say. If he didn't, Will Brady would get up, sighing again, and try another bench. Sooner or later he would find a man who knew what was what.

"Only thing that worries me," Will Brady would go on, "is how a kid like that, a boy who loves nature, is going to like it in some place like Harvard or Yale. How he's going to like it in some quiet place like that."

It might surprise you how many men knew all about Harvard and Yale. Had a definite opinion, one way or another, on a subject like that. Had a boy there themselves, or a friend, or the son of a friend, or a brother, or some member of the family who had passed through there, going somewhere else. Who had seen it anyhow and knew what it

was like. Nine out of ten men, you might say, seemed to have given either Harvard or Yale, or both of them together, more thought than Will Brady managed to. Their opinions, anyhow, were stronger than his own. They were either all for Harvard, without a quibble, or all for Yale. None of these men had been to college themselves—being tied up at the time with something or other—but they seemed to have a clear idea what they were talking about. They were glad to advise a man who hadn't quite made up his mind. Who had a boy who wasn't tangled up, as yet, with some damn girl. The general consensus seemed to be, in so far as Will Brady could order the matter, that great scholars went to Harvard and great athletes went to Yale. Albie Booth, for instance, he was going to Yale right now. But what about a boy who was showing signs of being both of them, an athlete and a great letter-writer at the same time? The first in his class, if it hadn't been for five or six girls. The place for a boy like that, one man told him in a confidential manner, was neither Harvard nor was it a place like Yale. It was Princeton, a place he had seen himself. He was a big man, with a beard, reduced to selling flags on pins for a living, but who nevertheless spoke with authority. As a boy he had passed— and he remembered it well—within a few miles of the place.

In the Wasteland

But it all took time—the life of the mind seemed to take as much time as a real one—and it would be midafternoon and the air would be hot when he started for the house. He would carry his coat folded over his arm and walk in the grass. His collar would be open and the Stetson hat pushed back on his head. Wherever tennis was being played he would sometimes stop and watch it, as the boy was said to be a coming tennis man. It helped him to see with his own eyes what the boy was. If one of the white balls came his way he would stop it, pounce on it, then hurry to where he could toss it to the players underhand. He had never learned to throw anything the other way. Tossing the ball, he would say: "I've got a boy who plays for Harvard," and then he might stand, if they would let him, close to the net. Some of them played very well, but it was clear that they were no match for the boy.

Sunday afternoons snails were sold on Menomonee Street. They were sold by a man who drove a small wagon, wearing on his own head nothing at all, but with three, sometimes four straw hats on the head of his horse. This was to make, as he said himself, the children laugh. He was a sad man and never laughed himself. He kept the snails in large tubs of water, and when he counted them into the bags, they made a sound like lead coins dropped on a slab. It was hard to tell the good snails from the bad. Most of them were bought by Nino Scarlatti, a boy with wild eyes and a curling harelip, and by Manny Plinski, who stood there with his money in his mouth. He would keep it there until he held the snails in his own hand.

After eating the snails, Manny Plinski liked to put the empty shells back in the bag, twist it at the top, and then make a fool out of somebody. That was always Will Brady, who would buy it for five cents. He would make himself a fool at the foot of the stairs, where the whole world could see him, and Manny Plinski would cry like a bird for his mother to come and look. So Mrs. Plinski would come, leaning over the railing, and Will Brady would stand there, a smile on his face, and with the nickel Manny Plinski would buy himself another bag of snails. "Oh, how he will love you!" Mrs. Plinski would say, and wag her big head.

On a hot summer day a big woman like that would not have much on. She would be in her bathrobe, or maybe her slip, with a damp towel thrown around her big shoulders, and she might have to stand there with her bosom gathered in her arms. In the winter she would be in the bone corset that made her arms stand out, as if she was crowing, and made it hard for her to scratch her back, pick her teeth, or get a comb into her hair. And in the corset she would always stand up rather than risk sitting down. She would stand between the folding doors, as if propped there, with her arms half raised.

"A new letter?" she would say. "A new winner?" And the old man there in the room, with his elbows on the table, would hold up the sheet of paper that he held in one hand. New? Well, hardly—the pages were torn at the folds. The light came through where bacon grease had been dropped on it.

"I was just wondering," the old man would go on, "what a boy like that"—he would wave the letter—"what a boy like that is going to do in a place like Harvard, or Yale?"

"Oh, how he will love you!" she would say, which it was hard, offhand, to picture the boy doing. But Mrs. Plinski was like that. A big, friendly woman who knew how it was.

4

IN THE papers that he found in the park on Sunday mornings, Will Brady always read the want ads, as a man who wasn't quite sure what it was he wanted might find it there. Perhaps somebody, some man or woman, was looking for him. Perhaps a man like Insull had a position for him to fill. Perhaps—anyhow, Will Brady read the ads. And one Sunday morning—a cool November morning—he came on something that made him chuckle, made him put down the paper, rub his eyes with his knuckles, and wag his head. He looked around for someone to share it with, but he was alone on the bench. "Well, well," he said aloud, as he did with Mrs. Plinski; then he read it again.

MAN wanted for Santa Claus.

Now, that made him smile—he could feel the tightness at the corners of his mouth. It was enough to make him wonder, an ad like that—but he tore it out. He slipped it in with the letter and the photographs he had from the boy. Having it there in his pocket, as well as on his mind, he naturally showed it to Mrs. Plinski, asking her if she knew where they might dig up a good Santa Claus. Where Montgomery Ward—for that was who it was—could lay their hands on a man like that: a man big enough, fat enough, and of course out of this world. And then, just by way of a joke, asking her what she thought of a man like himself—a man like himself, that is, as Santa Claus. But this woman would surprise you. This woman didn't think it was a joke at all.

"How they will love you!" was all she said, as she seemed to have the idea that something like that was all you needed for a Santa Claus. It didn't seem to cross her mind that his cheeks, for one thing, weren't rosy enough.

As he had that ad right there in his pocket, he also showed it to Bessie Muller, asking her if she thought he was jolly enough for a Santa Claus. As a joke, of course, but she didn't take it that way.

"Why, you'd make a honey of a Santa Claus, pop." That was what she said.

"I don't know as I'm plump enough," he said.

"Oh, they put a pillow in you," said Bessie Muller, "you'd be all right. You'd make a honey of a Santa Claus."

Mildred Weigall thought the same thing. He didn't even show her the ad, he just happened to say that the one thing he missed, around Christmas time, was the right kind of Santa Claus. One that was, so to speak, really fond of the kids. Mildred Weigall had interrupted to say that she had known of kids, friends of hers, who had been pinched while they were sitting on the lap of Santa Claus. By the old bastard himself. That was what she said.

"If you don't like kids—" Will Brady had begun.

"You'd make a good Santa Claus," she had said.

"What they need is a man like yourself for Santa Claus."

Mrs. Beach said, holding the want ad close to her face, as she was nearsighted: "Why, Mr. Brady, all you need is just a touch of color on your cheeks." Then she looked at him as if she was the person to put it there. When Mr. Beach was alive, she went on, there was not a single Christmas that passed, in those happy days, that Mr. Beach himself wasn't Santa Claus. A big man—perhaps a little too big—he was especially good with other people's children, his own, of course, knowing him just too well.

He had been turning it over, Will Brady said, just turning it over in his mind, that he might at least stop by and look into it. He was alone pretty much, and it would give him something to do. It would at least be better than being alone at Christmas time.

"I think you'll find," Mrs. Beach said, "that they don't pay much."

"I just thought I'd ask," Will Brady said, and then put some toothpicks in his vest before going on to say that the pay wasn't what he had in mind. He had a job. The pay wasn't so important to him. "I just thought I'd inquire," he said, as, if the honest truth were known, it hadn't crossed his mind that a man would be paid for something like that. Was it possible they paid a man to be Santa Claus? Perhaps it was. It seemed that anything was possible. His first thought had been that he would have to pay for that himself.

"It just so happens," Will Brady said, "that I'm more or less alone at Christmas."

"I can understand that," Mrs. Beach replied, as her own children were gone and seldom came around, as they all had children of their own. Nor was there any chance of her, plump as she was, of pretending she was Santa Claus. She was simply not the type—whatever that might be.

The retail store of Montgomery Ward & Co., where they were looking for a Santa Claus, was right where the drawbridge crossed the sewage canal. So it was not any trouble for Will Brady to just stop by, as he said. To inquire what it was they had in mind for a Santa Claus. But as he entered the store the main aisle was obstructed by ten or twelve people, gathered in an arc, facing a corner with a well-lighted display. There was a comfortable chair, of the reclining type, several lamps with large aluminum shades, and a young man with taffy-colored hair and a deeply tanned face. He wore a clean white jacket of the type Will Brady had seen on dentists and doctors, and held in his tanned right hand a long wand. With this wand, as he talked, he pointed at the statements on a large poster, which included a detailed, cut-away picture of one of the lamps. The name of the lamp was NU-VITA, which meant new life.

The voice of the young man was pleasant, and he had that healthy outdoor look that city people, like Will Brady himself, liked to gaze upon. It might be that Will Brady was reminded of his son. Not that there was any particular resemblance— this boy was older, larger, and blond—but Will Brady saw the boy whenever he saw the outdoor type. The athlete who still wore his study glasses, so to speak. As the young man talked, in his persuasive voice, Will Brady read the statements on the poster and discovered that the lamp he saw on the platform was a marvelous thing, a lamp that trapped the sun, so to speak. That gave off the same life-giving rays of light. These rays gave plants the color of green, and man the life-giving coat of tan. The city dweller, the young man was saying, lived little better than the life of a mole, but science had now discovered how to bring the sun right into his room. Right into his attic, if that was where he lived. With this wonderful lamp he could sit at home—reading a book, or just resting with his clothes off—and absorb the mysterious life-giving rays of the sun. Without the sun there would be nothing on earth—nothing but cold rocks and fish-less seas. But with the sun there was light, plants, and creatures like themselves. And with this lamp a man could have the sun with him anywhere.

Perhaps it was the sun-tanned face of the young man—the very picture of life, if Will Brady had ever seen it—that led the old man in the aisle to gaze at him in a certain way. Perhaps it was this gaze, somehow, that attracted the young man. Whatever it was, he suddenly stopped talking, turned the wand he was holding from the poster, and pointed it over the heads of those who stood at the front. Pointed it, that is, at Will Brady himself.

"Will the gentleman," the young man said, "be so kind as to please step forward? Will the gentleman allow me, without cost or the slightest obligation, to demonstrate?"

It would be wrong to say that Will Brady followed all of this. He saw the pointer, he heard the young man's voice, he felt the eyes of those assembled upon him, and when those at the front made way, why, he stepped to the front. He took a seat in the reclining chair that was prepared for him. A white bib, like a barber's cloth, was placed upon his front. Then his head was raised—through it all he heard the clear, calm voice of the attendant —and a pair of dark glasses was placed over his eyes, tied at the back. For a moment he saw all before him darkly, as if submerged in muddy water; then he was tipped back, and as his head went down, his feet went up. Over his head appeared the wide shade, he watched the adjustment of the black carbons, heard the hum of the current, then the crackling as the flame leaped the arc. A burning smell, perhaps the breath of life itself, made him wrinkle his nose.

"If the gentleman will kindly lid his eyes," said the voice, and as the crackling spread into a glow, Will Brady felt himself in a warm, colorless bath of light. The odor of the carbon was strong in his nose, and the flavor in his mouth. But he felt no fear; in the words of the voice, now disembodied, that he heard above him, he felt himself "cleansed of pollutions and invigorated from head to toe." The life-giving rays, as the voice went on to say, were mingling with his blood.

He felt suspended—out of this world, as he described it to Bessie Muller—and then, just as he was reborn, the power went off. For a moment he felt that his own worldly system had come to a stop. He made as if to rise, he gasped for air, but the young man's firm hand pressed him back, removed the white cloth, and then slipped the glasses from his head. As he sat up, blinking, the young man said: "You will notice the healthy touch of color

that the life-giving rays have given to the gentleman's face."

And so they did, as he saw them nodding, their
eyes filled with wonder, as they gazed on what it
had done to him. For himself, he could feel the
tightness in his cheeks. "That was but a moment,"
the young man was saying. "If the gentleman could
spare me more of his time—just a few moments a
day—he would soon be as sun-tanned as myself."
So saying, he rolled up his sleeve, showed the
brown arm. He smiled, showing in his dark face
the firm white teeth. Then he assisted Will Brady
to his feet, putting into his right hand, as he did so,
a wide selection of charts concerned with what
the Nu-Vita would do for him. It could also be
purchased, as he pointed out, on the easy-payment
plan. His own brown hand on Will Brady's shoulder, he called everyone's attention to his fine,
healthy look, and asked him, when he found the
time, to drop by again. A few more treatments, as
he said, and he wouldn't recognize himself.

In this rejuvenated condition Will Brady found
himself in the aisle, and he wandered about, from
counter to counter, for some time. He seemed to
have forgotten why he had entered the store. He
stopped to gaze, wherever it was reflected, at his
own new face. It was different. There was no doubt
about that. Around the eyes he was whiter, but the

warm cheeks were pink. Rosy? Well, there was even a touch of that. His own yellow teeth seemed to look whiter when he smiled. In this condition he sought out the man at the back of the store—a Mr. Nash—and inquired of him what they had in mind for Santa Claus. Mr. Nash, looking at him soberly, begged him to have a seat.

What they had in mind, Mr. Nash said, speaking to him very frankly, was no monkey business. They had to be sure of that. While he was on the job he had to be Santa Claus, nobody else. Having said this, Mr. Nash looked at him, and what he saw in the new pink face before him seemed to be what he wanted, seemed to be a Santa Claus that he could trust. One that he could turn over, as he said, their reputation to. He had on file other applications, but if Will Brady wanted the job he would take him upstairs and show him the setup, give him the suit. All that he would have to dig up himself was a kid to blow the balloons.

"To blow what?" Will Brady said.

He would need a kid to blow the balloons. He would give away balloons, but he would need some kid to blow them up. The kid sat under the throne, under the seat, that is, where Santa Claus would be sitting, and after blowing up the balloon he would pass it between his legs. That was how they did it. He would have to find the kid to do that himself.

Will Brady said that he would think it over—if he could find the right boy, he would surely think it over—and on his way through the store he passed a new crowd of people around the sun lamp. The young man with the pointer, seeing him pass, waved the wand at him.

"There goes a satisfied user, right there," he said, "it has made that gentleman look years younger," and everyone in the crowd, half the people in the aisle, turned to look at him. He smiled, he felt the strain of trying to throw his shoulders back. He reached the street, he crossed the bridge, he made his way through the freight yards and into the tower room, before he noticed that he still held the literature in his hand.

"Plug in at home or office," it said, and he read that the small model in question, meant to sit on a table, could be had for just four dollars a month.

On the first Monday in December, following another successful free trial, Will Brady purchased a desk-model sun lamp, carrying it along with him, in its carton, as he left the store. The warm glow of the lamp, in the crisp night air, was still there on his face. Mrs. Plinski had remarked the new look to his face, which she thought was due to the brisk fall weather, and after thinking it over he decided to let it go at that. Woman that she was, she might find it hard to understand something like the Nu-Vita, a marvel that brought the sun, so to speak, right into the house. And along with it the crackling sound, and the crisp frying smell. As he could plug it in either at home or at the office, he decided on the office as he could be alone, day or night, in the tower room. He could give himself a treatment, as it was called, any time that he got around to it, which turned out to be two or three times a night. Once when he arrived, as a rule, and then again when he left. He would clear one corner of the table of waybills, take off his vest, his tie, and his shirt, then open his underwear so that some of the rays fell on his chest. The only problem he faced was in keeping the time, as it passed very fast. Five to seven minutes were supposed to be enough. But seated there in the glow, like a warm bath, it was hard to keep from dozing off, or thinking thoughts that he could time or bring to a stop. With the dark glasses on he found it hard to read his watch. So he may have slipped over now and then, but not that it mattered, as he had only five days to prepare himself as Santa Claus.

As Santa Claus he wore a red cotton flannel suit, loose in the seat and very long in the arms, a pair of black rubber boots, and a soiled, strong-smelling beard. He sat on a throne, which in turn was on a platform, between two large cardboard reindeer, one of them with electric eyes that sparked on and off. At the back of the throne was the room where he dressed, hung up his clothes, and walked out on the fire escape, now and then, for a breath of fresh air. Under the throne was Manny Plinski, seated on a stool. In his lap he held a large bag of Christmas balloons, and at his side, in a glass jar, the baby turtles he had brought along to keep him company.

When Santa Claus wanted a balloon he would tap with his heel on the throne, and Manny Plinski would blow one up and pass it to him. Sometimes, however, he handed Santa Claus a baby turtle instead. As you can't risk passing out live turtles to little city boys who had never seen one, Santa Claus would have to slip these turtles into the pocket of his coat. Toward the end of the day he might have more than his pockets would hold. He would have to get up and take out the sign reading:

MAKING DELIVERY
Santa Claus Back Soon

and go through the side door and speak to Manny Plinski, personally. There were times when Manny Plinski was ashamed and took it all right. There were other times when he giggled, ran his hands like a rake through his yellow hair, and passed up another turtle as soon as he laid his hands on one.

These times Santa Claus would have to rap his knuckles, or sprinkle him with some water from the empty turtle jug on the floor. That sometimes did it; other times it didn't work out too well. He would blow up balloons and sit there popping them with his teeth.

Another thing that Manny Plinski liked to do was take the brown tweed suit that belonged to Will Brady and fill the pockets with turtles and balloons. He seemed to like the brown suit better than he liked Santa Claus. He liked to take the brown suit and go off alone somewhere and sit with it. Santa Claus would have to stop and hunt him down, as he couldn't blow balloons for himself, but this wasn't too often, and Manny Plinski was never far. He was usually out on the fire escape, just sitting there. He like to watch the trains shifting around in the freight yards, and the boats on the canal. He would blow Christmas balloons, like bubbles, and let them drift away.

Not that it seemed to matter, as there were plenty of balloons, plenty of time to stop and look for him, and the old man in the Santa Claus suit seemed to like his work. He would have paid Montgomery Ward & Co. in order to carry on with it. Out on the street an old man cannot hold hands with children, bounce them on his knee, or tell them lies that he will not be responsible for. Nor can he bend his head and let them whisper into his ear. Very much as if he, this old man, could do something for them. Very much as if he knew, like the children before him, that there was only one man in this world—one man still living—who was prepared to do certain things. To live in this world, so to speak, and yet somehow be out of it. To be himself without children, without friends or relations, without a woman of his own or a past or a future, and yet to be mortal, and immortal, at the same time. Only one man in the world could answer an ad worded like that. Only one man, that is, and get away with it. For in the world it is evil for an old man to act like that. There is a law against it—unless the old man is Santa Claus. But for this old man these things are all right, they are recognized to be the things that count; and the children, as they do in such cases, all believe in him. Some men will put up with a good deal, from certain quarters, for a job like that.

"Oh, how they will love you!" Mrs. Plinski said, and every day his cheeks seemed a little redder, his smile a little brighter, and the face in the mirror no longer his own. It had become, it seemed to him, the face of Santa Claus. Only the eyes, with the white circles around them, were still his own. They were there because of the goggles, and the darker his face seemed to get, the redder his cheeks, the more pale and sallow his eyes. So he began to move the goggles up and down, first to one side, then to the other, and one evening he tried it without the goggles for a little bit. It wouldn't matter, he felt sure, if he kept his eyes closed. Nothing came of that, so the next evening he tried it a little longer, and was pleased to find that the white cricles were getting pink. They began to blend in, a little more, with the rest of his face. So he tried it again, this time a little longer, as it was past the middle of December, and Santa Claus had before him only one more week.

That was the morning of December 19, but it was late in the afternoon, the daylight gone, before his eyes began to smart. They watered a little, and the lids were red when he looked at them. He had to buy a handkerchief in the store and keep dabbing at his eyes when he stopped for supper, and he noticed that the boy, Manny Plinski, kept staring at him. Sometimes he would whimper as if he wasn't feeling good. In the evening the lights seemed to make it worse, and he had to stop, every half hour or so, to step back behind the curtain where it was dark and press the lids shut. When he did that, he found it hard to open them. The salty liquid that kept running seemed to make them stick. Something in the lids seemed to draw them closed, so that he had to stare to hold them open, but all the time, without letup, the tears ran down his face. Around his red, peeling nose the skin was very tender, smarting when he wiped his cheeks, and he thought he detected in the handkerchief the burned-carbon smell. As if the rays that had soaked into him were now sweating out.

Later he put up the sign; he found it hard to recognize the little boys from the girls, and to open his eyes he had to use his fingers, separate the lids. The inside of the lids was bright red, like the gills of a fish. When he removed his fingers, the lower lids would roll up, as a curtain rolls. Nothing he could do, even with his fingers, would put a stop to this. For air, for fresh cool air, as that in the room seemed to blow hot on his eyeballs, he walked to the back and opened the door to the fire escape. It was snowing a little, and the sharp, cold pricks felt good on his face. He opened the door and stepped out on the landing, facing the freight yards, the sluggish canal, and the blinking traffic that passed on Halsted Street. The water in the canal looked like pig iron poured out to cool. Rising from the water, like a dark-red planet, was the lantern on the drawbridge, and beyond the arc of the bridge he could see the tower room. The light was on. He had probably forgotten it. Beyond the bridge, and the sluggish water, were the smoke and steel of the freight yards, where a brakeman, waving his lantern, walked along the cars. Beyond this, as if a fire was raging, there was a bright glow over the street, and from these flames there arose, along with the din, a penetrating smell. He could breathe it, like the carbon, he could taste it on his lips. It was like the grating sound of steel, a blend of the sour air and the track sound, of the gas from the traffic, and the sweetish smell of powdered Christmas balloons. All of the juices of the city were there on the fire, and brought to a boil. All the damp air of the chill rooms that were empty, the warm soiled air of the rooms that were lived in, blown to him, so it seemed, by the bellows of hell. An acrid stench, an odor so bad that it discolored paint, corroded metal, and shortened the life of every living being that breathed it in. But the old man on the landing inhaled it deeply, like the breath of life. He leaned there on the railing, his eyes closed, but on his face the look of a man who was feeding the birds. When the lantern dropped down, and the traffic flowed, he went down the turning stairs toward the water, toward the great stench as if he would grasp it, make it his own, before it could blow away from him. Or as if he heard above the sound of the traffic, the tune of that Pied Piper—who had drawn him, time and time again, to where a rope, a rope with a knotted end, heavy with ice, hung to where it swept the water.

In the Wasteland

There was no one on the stairs, nor any boat on the water, and only Manny Plinski, with a brown tweed coat, was there on the landing when they came to look for Santa Claus. In the pockets there were turtles and a postcard to his son that had not been mailed.

THE
HUGE
SEASON

For

HENRY ALLEN MOE

rainmaker

to many huge seasons

Those who lay naked in the huge season arise all together and cry

    that this world is mad!

    For us who were there, we forced on the frontiers exceptional accidents, and pushing ourselves in our actions to the end of our strength, our joy amongst you was a very great joy....

—ST. JOHN PERSE: *Anabasis*

THE CAPTIVITY: I

They tell me that my father, a Latin teacher, would place his silver watch, with the Phi Beta key dangling, on the right-hand corner of the desk in his Vergil class. When he was not lecturing, the students would hear the loud tick. The watch had been given to him by his father when he became a Cum Laude Latin scholar, and the inscription *Incipit Vita Nova* had been engraved on the back. A very punctual man, my father wound the watch when he heard the first bell ring in the morning, then he would place it, with the fob dangling, on the corner of his desk. Time, for my father, seemed to be contained in the watch. It did not skip a beat, fly away, or merely vanish, as it does for me. So long as he remembered to wind the watch Time would not run out. There was no indication that he found his subject a dead or dying language, or the times, for a man of his temperament, out of joint. He died the winter of the flu epidemic during the First World War.

I never heard my father lecture, but I have his silver watch here in my pocket, still keeping very good time. It is his watch, but my own Phi Beta key now dangles from it. I have the habit of looking at the watch without seeing the time. I teach, among other things, my father's subject, but it seems to me the times *are* out of joint, and that the language is not merely dying, but dead. It was still alive—or I was more alive—when my father, for cultural reasons, spoke it at the table more than thirty years ago. The dining room was always dark, even in the morning, and the Latin my father passed to me with the toast seemed as good a language to start the day with as anything else. Our house was on Byron Street, in Chicago, just a five-minute walk, as my father timed it, from his room on the third floor of the Lakewood High School. That part of Chicago, even today, might be in Terre Haute, Des Moines, or Ann Arbor, or any other town with a fairly large residential area. It is why I feel at home, as we say, in any town where the houses have lawns and front porches, and something of a stranger where the living has moved around to the back.

We had a brown frame house, more or less like the neighbors', with the gable at the front and the back, the front porch open, but the porch at the rear closed in with screens. A piece of sagging wire went around the small patch of grass at the front. In the spring my father would put in a little grass, then tie strips of rag, like ribbons, to the wire, so the neighbors' kids would not trip on it in the dark. A broad flight of steps led up to the porch, where my mother, between supper and the dishes, would sit in the swing behind the wire baskets of fern. She would sit there because her kitchen apron was still on. My father would sit on the fourth step from the bottom, sprinkling the grass. The best stand of grass was there near the steps, where the water dripped from the leaky nozzle, and the third step from the bottom had warped so badly it had worked loose. It was one of the things my father always intended to fix. My mother had warned him that some member of the family was sure to break his neck. But my father died in bed of the flu, and my mother, for reasons of her own, preferred to go up and down the rickety stairs at the back of the house. I lived in it long enough to go off to college, and some years later the house was sold. The loose step was still there when I walked past the house eight or nine years ago.

My room was at the front of the house, under the gable, where the ceiling sloped down over my bed and the window at the foot of the bed opened out on the roof of the porch. The street light came through that window, and in the spring and summer the sounds of the street. A block to the west, then a block north, the Ashland Avenue cars reached the end of their run, and when the trolley was switched there would be a white flash, like lightning, on the sky. Both summer and winter this white flash would light up my room. Where the ceiling sloped down over my head I once wrote out the declensions of my Latin verbs, and on the warm summer nights I would lie there on my back, memorizing them. I would wait for the flash of the trolley wire to check on what I had learned. Later I began to pin up certain pictures—Bebe Daniels was there at one time, beside Sappho—and, for all I know, a picture of Charles Lindbergh may still be there. It showed him in the cockpit of the *Spirit of St. Louis,* about to take off. It was a picture you have probably seen, but I doubt if you ever saw, or heard of, Charles Lawrence, the tennis player. I took his picture down when we moved, and I still have it somewhere.

Lawrence was quite a tennis player at one time, and the picture I have, although it is faded, gives you some idea of his tennis form. His back is to the camera, and he is about to serve the ball. You can see the ball at the top left corner, you can even read the label stamped on it. All the other details in the picture tend to be a little blurred: the wire screen at the back, the row of white bleacher faces with deep eye shadows so that they look like pansies, and the racket itself a blurred current of air approaching the ball. It is not, by modern standards, a good photograph. They do that sort of thing much better these days. They don't play better tennis, however, and the one thing that comes out clear in the print, blurred though it is, is the way the player goes after the ball. You can see that he takes the game seriously. I do not mean that he takes it professionally. A stranger to the game might feel that this was not the picture of a game at all, or that the blurred figure was preparing to strike nothing more than a ball. That kind of seriousness—I almost said deadly seriousness—has gone out of it. On the other hand, the stranger might not notice it at all. It might strike him as not much more than a poor photograph. If you think that great champions are made by eating Wheaties, that great songs can be written on commission, you will be inclined to feel that I am reading something into this photograph. In that sense you will be right, as I am reading into it most of my life.

My mother believed that true breeding, like crime, would sooner or later appear on the surface, but she was thinking of the Nielsons, the Vikings whose course she had charted for nine generations, across continents and oceans, to a grand anticlimax in me. Of my father's country breeding she did not speak. A self-made scholar, born in South Dakota long before true breeding or my mother got there, my father could give me little, she believed, beyond parenthood. His Greek translations rather than his Irish background appealed to her. At Oberlin, happily, he met my mother, which assured me the breeding I might have lacked, and an eye on the future as well as the past. From Oberlin my father went to Colton in California, where he was known as something of a classics scholar, but my mother didn't think there was much of a future for the classics in the West. They came back to Chicago, and while they waited for an opening that would open into the future, the war came along, and near the end of the war, the flu.

I was not quite nine years old when my father died. As I had been when he lived, I was sent to bed early, where I studied the verbs I had written on the ceiling, with the understanding that one day I would take my father's place. Lying there on the bed, summer and winter, I relied on my ears more than my eyes, and put great store in all the neighborhood noises. On summer afternoons I could hear the crowd roar over at Wrigley Field. Later I would read that Hack Wilson had hit a home run. In the winter I could hear the boom and the crack of the ice on the lake. Many years later, in France, where I should have been homesick, I felt more or less at home because the grass below my window was cut with a mower that had been made in South Bend. I knew the sound, even though it was cutting French grass.

Our house was like a tunnel in some respects, the daylight glowing at the front and back, but the blinds drawn at the dark windows on both sides. Our neighbors, in my mother's opinion, were too neighborly. In the summer, when these windows were open, we could smell what the Millers were cooking, and hear how well they liked it when they sat down to eat. After the meal the Miller boy would run the player rolls through the piano backwards, or the Miller girl, Arlene, would turn up the radio so she could hear Guy Lombardo while she sat out in front of the house with her date. He was, as I remember, almost a young man, with cuts on his face to indicate he was shaving, and a Scripps-Booth roadster with Northwestern pennants on the windshield. I saw only his face, for he never got out of the car. I remember the ah-oooga of his horn, and the glow, after it was dark, of the red and green gems in the nickel-plated dashboard light. Later he took her to dances when Wayne King was over at the Aragon. Arlene was nearsighted without her glasses and thought she was dancing under the stars—the boy didn't tell her that the clouds were on the ceiling rather than the sky. But that is not so unusual. He might not have noticed it himself.

I didn't have the time for girls, but I took in a movie on Saturday night. They were featuring some pretty good bands, at the time, on the stage. The band leader acted as a sort of master of ceremonies. I usually went early, if the show was in the Loop; it gave me time to maneuver from a seat at the back to one nearer the front. During the intermission the organ played, rising out of the pit like a car for a grease job, and we all sang the songs the projector flashed on the screen. There often was a glowworm hopping from word to word. I didn't sing, not having much of a voice, but after the show I would walk along the river, where the Wrigley Tower was reflected in the water, and hum to myself the tunes I particularly liked. "If I Could Be with You

One Hour Tonight" was one of my favorites. I first heard "Yes Sir, That's My Baby" at the State, where they had a fiddle player no bigger than his bass fiddle, and he could hardly be seen until he started thumping it.

My mother was usually out on the porch when I got home. We had a radio of our own, but the dry-cell batteries were usually dead, so my mother would listen to whatever was on the Miller set. The Millers usually watered their lawn in the evening, when the water pressure was up, and Mr. Miller liked to water the lower limbs of the trees. Long after he had stopped, the leaves dripped water on the walk. The night would be quiet, with the groan gone from the hydrant, except when the motorman, over on Ashland, walked through his car, turning over the seats for the trip back. We could hear the Miller dog skid on the kitchen linoleum. Mr. Miller usually commented that now he had sprinkled it would probably rain, and Mrs. Miller would ask him to bring in the chair cushions from the porch. When it was finally quiet my mother would offer me a penny for my thoughts.

At the end of the war, to make a little money, my mother decided to take in a roomer, a Mrs. Josephare who taught History of Art, Spanish, and French. We spoke nothing but Spanish and French at our meals. One summer Mrs. Josephare went to Seville, but as she was going just for the summer she left her books and box of wide-brimmed hats in my father's room. She never came back, and we never heard from her. My mother kept the box of hats in the attic; Mrs. Josephare, who was very frugal, had often complained, in both Spanish and French, about the things Americans threw away.

I was brought up with the understanding that I would go to Oberlin, like my parents, and I had my father's Oberlin pennants on the walls of my room. I spent a weekend on the campus to pick up impressions, and I was impressed. But my mother, in order to avoid putting all my educational eggs in one basket, also applied for a scholarship in California, where my father had taught. Thanks to his reputation, I received a four-year scholarship. That was two years better than the Oberlin offer, and my mother reasoned that the thing for me to do was start at Colton and finish at Oberlin. That way my education would be accounted for. The turning point in my life, if it had one, lay in the decision to go to Colton first, for it was there I met Charles Lawrence, the tennis player. He was there because one member of his family had endowed the school. The endowment would help fill certain unusual gaps in his scholarship. We were both freshmen, and we shared a suite of rooms with two other freshmen, Jesse Proctor and Ed Lundgren, so that Lawrence had his captive public right from the start. I remember thinking, at the time, that we were like the iron filings in the field of a magnet that Lundgren liked to play with at his desk. But that was not it. Or rather, it was more than that. All that does is give a name to the magnet— it doesn't explain the lines of force, or why it was that Lawrence, who was the magnet, became a captive himself. So there we were, the four of us, in a strange captivity.

PETER FOLEY: 1

Early morning, the 5th of May, 1952.
The man in the bed, a professor named Foley, lay listening to the mournful cawing of the crows. They cruised directly overhead, or hovered like vultures in the tulip trees. Cawing at the house, the cat in the house, and the man in the bed. Blackbirds hammered at the seedpods in the gutters, starlings strutted in the grass beneath his window, and on the chicken wire spread across the top of the chimney a robin built her nest. Now and then a rain of soot or a sprinkling of twigs, pipe cleaners, and string dropped down the chimney, spattering the yellow pages of a manuscript lying in the fireplace. Thrown there to be burned by the author himself, the man in the bed.

The manuscript was entitled "The Strange Captivity." The author had worked at the book, off and on, for fifteen years. He knew everything about it, that is, but how to finish it. Now he knew that, but the knowledge had come too late. You couldn't call a man a captive who had lost all interest in his escape.

The morning of the day before, the 4th of May, the professor had got up to let out his cat and found the Sunday paper lying on the porch. The name of Mrs. Hermann Schurz, his landlady, was scrawled across the top left corner. Foley picked the paper up, glanced at

the headlines. They were not happy. He returned the
paper to the porch. Then he stooped over, propped on
his knees, to examine a head that looked familiar—the
back of the head, for that was all that showed in the
photograph. This man sat at a table, facing the micro-
phones, and the questioner faced him and the cameras.
Beneath the picture the caption read:

UNMASKS VOICE OF AMERICA

"Well, I'll be goddamned!" Foley said aloud, as if
unmasked himself. He knew the head of this man, even
without the face. He knew the unmasked voice as well
as he knew his own. Better, perhaps. Eyes closed, he
heard this voice say, "There's a bull in this story, Foley.
But he's a nice bull. He don't shit in the bullring."

There was always a bull in one of Proctor's stories,
and this one, Foley felt, would be no exception. He
grinned. With good-humored admiration he wagged
his head. Then he stooped over, smiling, to read the
article.

> The last-named witness, J. Lasky Proctor, created
> a stir at the proceedings with the frankness with
> which he collaborated with the senators. Asked
> if he had once been a member of the Party he re-
> plied, Well, in a sense—
> What did he mean, "in a sense"?
> Back at that time, he replied, he had been a very
> good American. A good American had to believe in
> something good. The Party had been it. It had been
> something in which a man could believe.
> Did he mean to say he was no longer a good
> American?
> If he was, he answered, he wouldn't be here.
> In Russia, perhaps?
> No, just in jail, he had replied.

And everybody had laughed. Foley also laughed, thinking to himself how much it sounded like Proctor, and how little, in more than twenty years, he seemed to have changed. It was twelve years since Foley had spoken to him; in the city—in New York, that is—bending over one of the toothbrush bowls in the lavatory of the YMCA's Sloane House, the grape-colored bruise still showing on the foot where he had shot himself.

"I'll be goddamned!" Foley repeated and, still smiling, entered the house. He walked to where the percolator rocked on the stove, poured himself a cup of coffee but did not drink it. Unsmiling, he stood at the window, smoking cigarettes. The morning breeze was strong with the scent of the rotting ginko pods. He faced it, he hardly remarked it, for the mist was rising from the pond, revealing what Mrs. Hermann Schurz described as a sight for sore eyes. A small flock, a covey of water birds, unidentified. Ducks of some kind, looking like freshly painted decoys. A sight that Mrs. Schurz loved, but she never ceased fearing for their lives. They were innocent ducks, like Peter Foley, J. Lasky Proctor, and other birds of that type. Sitting ducks, seemingly unaware of the facts of life. The patriotic marksmen of the penny arcade would soon pop them off. And that book, that thing Foley was writing, what was it but the "Sitting Duck Hunter's Manual"— a guide to the look, the diet, and the habitat of all sitting ducks? Dead ducks as of Sunday, the 4th of May, 1952.

Foley had walked down the hall to his study, scooped the pile of yellow sheets from the canned-milk carton, crossed the room to the fireplace, and thrown them into the grate. He had stooped to scratch a match on the hearth, but in the quiet, his head in the fireplace, he could hear the birds nesting at the top of the chimney. The match had burned down, and he had gone back to bed.

Everything in Foley's life dated from something—his father's watch, his mother's death, the characters and events of his first two years in college—but his real life dated from J. Lasky Proctor, and they both dated from Lawrence. Charles Gans Lawrence, heir to the barbed-wire empire, once well known for his tennis game without ground strokes, his bullfighting without sword strokes, and now remembered, if at all, for his early death in the afternoon. Known to the world as Lawrence; to Proctor as the man in whom the sun rose and set. They had all risen with it, perhaps, but they dated, like fashions, from the moment it set. The 5th of May, 1929. Other suns had set that particular year, few of them in a blaze of glory, but with the passing of Lawrence a constellation had blacked out. Gone. One seldom, if ever, heard from such bright suns as Proctor and Lou Baker, such satellites as Lundgren, Livingston, and Peter Foley himself. Snuffed out, leaving no trace, casting no light, emitting no radiation, no blaze of worlds in collision, but still circling in their orbits, in their appointed places, after twenty-three years.

On the 3rd of May—the date was certain in his mind as he had kept the stubs of two lottery tickets—on the 3rd he had spent his first night in Paris, kissed his first girl, and all but had his tongue bitten out of his mouth. Near the Etoile. In the shelter of a bus stop on the avenue Hoche. Girl known as Montana—Montana Lou

Baker—and the morning of the 5th she woke him up to tell him that Charles Lawrence, the man in whom the sun rose, had shot himself.

That had been the end—but not officially. Officially, the survivors had gone on to die off piecemeal, as play-boys or professors, or reappear as fossils, taken alive, on the nationwide patriotic TV programs featuring the good, as well as the bad, Americans. The good brought forward, like a painless extraction, to smile at the world through all-American bridgework and speak with the filtered, uncontaminated voice of America.

That had made it official. That made it clear the jig was up. What had taken more than twenty years to die was now dead. The Lone Eagles were now a covey of Sitting Ducks. Dead, or good as dead, like the striking resemblance that Peter Nielson Foley once bore to Charles A. Lindbergh, another fossil from the great Age of Flight. The lemming-like un-American drive of young Americans to be somewhere else.

"Foley," Proctor had once said, "you self-effacing bastard, who the hell are you?"

Well, who the hell was he?

From the mirror that he faced, twenty-five years later, there came no reply. The blue eyes were now gray, the cleft chin was now double, the sandy hair had receded, the nose and ears protruded, but the self, that fossil-haunted self, was still effaced. Name being with-held until kith and kin had been notified. Remains bore close resemblance to Nordic (maternal) side of the family, strongly given to notion that the Vikings found, then lost, America. Bachelor, professor of lan-guages of no practical value, well known on quiet cal-

cified campus for lifelike impersonations of Buster
Keaton and a record of Hoagy Carmichael singing
"Hong Kong Blues."

"A penny," his mother used to say, "a penny for your
thoughts."

God knows why. He really never had thoughts. But
that was how his mother had faced the problem of silence, and when Lou Baker had been snuggled in his
lap, before she had bitten him, such a silence had to be
faced.

So he had said to Montana Lou Baker, "A penny for
your thoughts."

A mistake. One of the turning points in his life. For
Montana Lou Baker, Bryn Mawr '27, had thoughts—
but not her own.

"Give me the penny," she had said, and he had
fished out a small French coin. She grabbed it, raised her
head, and intoned, "There's more crap talked about
this town than any other goddam place in the world."

"Is that *your* thought?" he asked knowing that it
wasn't.

"It's his," she said, "but I agree with it."

" 'Crap' doesn't sound much like him," he said.

"He didn't say crap," she said, "he said bullshit," and
when the word came out, although he had been prepared, he recoiled.

"Didums nasty word hurtums?" Lou Baker said.

"I guess I don't like to hear a woman swear," he replied.

"You know the three ages of man?" she asked, and he
neither did, nor did he want to, but she sat up straight,
her fingers spread, to count them off. "There's the age
of stone, when you throw rocks at each other; then

there's the age of steel, when you throw that at each other; then there's the age of bullshit, when you throw—" and he clamped his hand over her mouth. He held it there till she squirmed, then he removed it, and she said, "My mother used to wash my mouth out with Fels-Naptha. She made me bite it. You want to wash my mouth out?" and then she turned and stuck her red tongue right in his face. He almost got it, but she was too quick for him. She slipped off his lap, where she had been curled up in the ankle-length camel's hair coat she was wearing, and ran down the street to the *pension* where she lived. But her coat was heavy, and he soon caught up with her. He grabbed the belt across the back, swung her around, took a grip on her short hair as they did in the movies, and with her head tipped back he kissed her on the mouth. She returned it—then clamped down on his tongue. The pain was so bad his eyes filled with tears, and he covered his mouth. She ran down the street, laughing and hooting, the flat-soled huaraches slapping on the pavement, and before he could catch her she had got the door open, then closed again. From an upper-floor window she pelted him with pennies, as if he were an organ grinder.

He had walked three or four miles, through the Paris night. Above the trees along the Champs Elysées the morning sky was reflected in the curtained windows, and the gray stone buildings had a bluish cast, as if dipped in the sky. When a taxi driver hailed him he would signal that he wanted to walk. He was ashamed to try to speak any French with his swollen tongue. From the corner of the Tuileries, looking back, he watched the sun rise on the Eiffel Tower, come down the tower, that is, like a lift making all the stops.

Foley's life—such life as he possessed—seemed to have begun with one Jesse Proctor and to have ended when *that* Proctor had given up. The Laureate of the Age of Bullshit, as Proctor had prophesied himself, had survived the stone and steel, but the manure had been too much for him. The single shot that killed Lawrence had crippled all of them. That shot had been fired on a warm spring morning, like the one Foley could see from his bathroom window, a mist over the pond as there had been over the Seine. When Foley had crossed the Pont des Arts a bum of some sort had been seated right beneath it, rubbing a thick, soapy lather into the curls of a high-bred dog. The dog's fine collar and leash, with a clean towel for drying, lay at his side. Twenty-four hours later Lawrence was dead, and almost twenty-three years later, to the day, one J. Lasky Proctor was burning at the stake. One manuscript, ready for burning, lay in the grate.

On his lidded eyes Foley rested a forefinger, a thumb. Like a bouncing ball, or the glowworm hopping from word to word, he saw the legendary headlines, exploding like fireworks:

LINDBERGH LANDS IN PARIS

EDERLE SWIMS CHANNEL

LOEB & LEOPOLD CONVICTED

RUTH MAKES IT SIXTY

And larger still, like a backdrop against which the fireworks were displayed, the mural-size photograph of a tennis player serving the ball. This photograph was printed on the cover of a book, with the player's signature at the bottom, and across the top the Spanish word

QUERENCIA

Querencia? That part of the ring, the bullring, where the bull felt at home. The book was a novel about a tennis player who, when injured, had made himself a great bullfighter. The author's name appeared on neither the cover nor the title page. It was *in* the book, rather than on it, turning up in the dedication, which read:

For
JESSE PROCTOR
Without whom this book
would not have been
written

A hoax, the neatest trick of the decade; published without its concluding chapter, the author's name unmentioned except on the dedication page. The morning it was published, May 5th, Peter Foley was awakened by Montana Lou Baker, who told him that Charles Lawrence, the subject of the book, had shot himself.

Only one man knew whether Lawrence had ever set eyes on the book. Richard Livingston the III, the practical joker, the man who had published the book in ten copies, knew that, of course, but nobody knew Richard Livingston. Not that well. Not after Lawrence had shot himself. But whether Lawrence had seen it or not he was dead; Jesse Proctor, the novelist, had been blighted; and Peter Foley, the witness, still had an unfinished book on his hands. Not to mention Lou Baker, the haunted siren, with a blighted masterpiece of her own that filled to overflowing two Campbell-soup cartons. It was Foley who had kept her at work on it.

Knowing all the time it would never be finished—no more than his own. Unfinished, these books gave purpose and direction to their lives. There was always a page, a scene, or a chapter to be modified. New material, or new light on old material, was always turning up. Now there was more of it. A chapter on J. Lasky Proctor, ex-novelist, salvage expert, and importer of Jews.

Montana Lou Baker had been a little haggard, a bony, legend-haunted Garbo, the last time Foley had seen her in New York. They had gone over to Chumley's, where the walls were lined with the jackets of books other people had written, a few people had read, and everybody had forgotten—except Lou Baker. She knew the authors. She had read and remembered the books. She lived a life as bygone, and as dated, as the characters. In the Chumley museum of jackets and blurbs she was at home. La Grande Baker, in her turtleneck sweater, a few stringy wisps of hair stuck to her forehead, forever picking the crumbs of badly rolled cigarettes from her lips.

"Oh, Christ, Foley," she had said, and after a while he had put in, "A penny for your thoughts." He *would*. He had blurted it right out.

And Lou Baker, naturally, had said, "There's the age of stone, when you throw rocks at each other; then the age of steel, when you throw that at each other; and then—"

Then came the age they were living in now. The age of—the blighted Laureate. Jesse Proctor become J. Lasky, the suspect Voice of America. In twenty-three years Foley had spoken to him just once.

Year of the Fair—the World's Fair out in Flushing. Foley had gone into town, taken a room at Sloane

House for the night. Slept late, and had the barracks-size bathroom almost to himself. He stropped his razor, lathered his face, then noticed—reflected in the mirror—the legs of the man at the toothbrush bowl at his back. Had a towel around his waist, head bent over the bowl, and very fine legs. Foley knew them, both legs and feet, in particular the foot with the bruise on it, about the size and color of a smoky Concord grape. That was where Jesse L. Proctor had shot himself. Shot himself with a Colt .38 or whatever, while crossing the Mojave in the seat of Lawrence's sports coupe. It had put him on crutches for at least eight months. Up until that moment he had been a quarter-miler, and not much else. But after shooting himself it had been necessary for him to take stock, as the saying goes, and while his foot had healed he had begun to write stuff that was pretty good. He had never run again. From that point on he had done nothing but write.

So Foley turned, his face lathered, and said—no, he didn't say it, it was not necessary, for Proctor turned from the toothbrush bowl and said, "How are you, old man?"

Just the same? Almost, but not quite. The blue-edged barbed-wire scar was still like a bone in Proctor's face. And the face was more—well, it was more Jewish, whatever that was. Head thrust forward, cocked a bit to the right. Foley finished shaving, and Proctor led him back to the room he shared with two other fellows, but they were gone all day, so it was like an office, he said, all to himself. There he showed Foley letters, at least five of them, on the letterheads of important business houses, giving him large orders for a new, patented World's Fair cane. It was not at all new, and not yet

patented, but it was designed to wholesale for three
cents, and was stained and grooved to resemble a piece
of rustic wood. With a banner and a tin-plate tip on the
point, it would cost five. The cane would retail at the
Fair for fifteen or a quarter, and in the letters on hand
Proctor said he had requests for two hundred fifty to
around three hundred twenty thousand canes. His cut,
per cane, would run about one-half cent, but if he could
place orders for two hundred thousand with a firm he
knew in South Carolina the cost would be reduced and
his profit would run a good full cent. When you figured
in the hundred thousands, that added up.

Then Foley took him to Childs for breakfast, since
Proctor was a little short of cash at the moment, although his credit, not to mention his prospects, was
extremely good.

"I'll give you a blast, old man!" he said, rushing off
to a sales appointment, and Foley noticed that he
still had his limp.

Hearing the cries of the birds, hearing them coming
nearer, Foley closed the slats of the venetian blinds,
stood with his back to the window as the cat, with his
escort, passed. Routine maneuver. No crisis, as yet.
Peace did not reign, but it was being observed in the
northeast corner of God's half acre. Mrs. Hermann
Schurz, in bed over Foley's head, would have her ear to
it.

He left the bathroom, took a seat on the bed, put on
his socks. He put a shoe on, then slipped it off, thinking now was the time for his narrow-cuff flannels.
French seat, English flannel, dating from the spring that
Ivar Kreuger, the match king, shot himself in Paris, and

Bruno Richard Hauptmann, paroled ex-convict, kidnaped Charles Augustus Lindbergh, Jr. No one would ever believe he wore a pair of pants that old. Or that his gabardine jacket, trimmed with chamois, dated from the contract negotiations, successfully concluded, for a prospective Foley book. Book now lying in grate of fireplace, jacket now hanging on imported hanger. Would have looked good on Lawrence, man from whom Foley took his cues. Lawrence had been the model, but it had taken Foley, on what was described as his salary, all of twenty years to assemble the parts. And in those twenty years the world had gone on to other things. Leaving Foley with a style, an air of distinction, that he otherwise might not have had. He seemed to represent the finer things of a better day. In the twenties the rich spent their money on feathers and established standards that were hard to follow, but in the forties the rich made the old cars do and wore the old clothes. Foley was not rich, but he had something of the patina. In the lobby of a building on Fifty-seventh Street, on his way to somebody's water-color show, he had been stopped by a woman, a woman of breeding, with the well-preserved sheen of good saddle leather, and she had wanted to know, she simply had to know, where he had got his shoes. The shoes on Foley's feet that day were more than twelve years old. They might well have been the last pair of such shoes in the world. Foley couldn't tell her that, or that he had bought the shoes back when she might have been in college, but he could tell her that he had bought them in Vienna, he had forgotten just where. He didn't tell her this was back before Herr Dollfuss was Chancellor. The style had come back, in the last few years, but not the men

who patented it. In such shoes there were feet, but not
those of Proctor, and in such jackets there were arms,
but not those of Lawrence. With the exception of Foley.
He still wore the same shoes, the same pants, the
same coat. But he was not, of course, the same man
himself. Not after twenty-two years, three hundred and
sixty-four days. The night Montana Lou Baker had bit
him a waiter at the Café des Deux Magots had congratu-
lated her on being with such a handsome young man.
Foley made him think of Le Grand Charles Lindbergh,
he had said. Lou Baker had smiled. She had resembled
La Grande Garbo that night herself.

A dull thud, characteristic and familiar, communi-
cated to Foley through the boards in the floor, announced that the cat had come in the pantry window.
In with a bird, that is. If he had no bird he was willing
to use the door. With bird, however, he used the pantry
window, dropping from the high shelf with a thud, then
depositing the bird either in, or on, the sack of Bermuda onions in the vegetable bin. If *in,* it might not
be discovered for some time.

That made it three birds in five days, and Foley sat
quiet, his eyes lidded, listening for the telltale scrunch
of the onion bag. It came. It seemed to come with the
draft from the fireplace. Foley opened one eye—closed
it when he saw the pages of the manuscript. Relief.
Almost sickening sense of relief. What would he do, in
God's name what *would* he do, without his own captivity? As if it mattered if these captive ducks were
dead. *His* ducks. Dead or alive, what mattered was that
they were *his.* Foley's lifelike decoys. He would make
them look so real nobody would know it—not even the
ducks.

He crossed the room to take the sheets from the grate, but as he kneeled on the hearth something splattered on the top sheet. Bird dung. Asterisk indicating the chapter left out. "Always let it dry, old man," Proctor had said, "then chip it off."

He left it there to dry, finished dressing, checked his pockets for money, keys, and Lou Baker's phone numbers, leaped the gap in the hallway the rug did not cover, and let the door slam behind him, rattling the bottles with the note that said "No milk until tomorrow," and under a cloud of cat-yawping birds he began to run. Across God's half acre, around the edge of the pond to where the two strange birds, unidentified, were napping, but suddenly arose, water dripping from their feet, and flapped away. There he turned and looked back, glanced rather, for in the window directly over his study he could see the figure, massive and yet suspended, of Mrs. Schurz in a cloud of gray flannel, made by herself when she learned that ladies' nightwear, in her size, came only in pink.

He walked on, across the empty pike as strange as the vacant morning aisles of Macy's, then cut around the supermarket, the entranceway full of bucking broncos, jet-propelled rockets, and cans of Miracle-Gro plant food, across the acre or more of blacktop staked out with posts, and diagramed for parking, then up the flight of steps to the local platform and down the tracks to the east. As he went along the platform he passed an old man stretched out on a bench. A hat was tipped on his face, and his head rested on an overcoat tied up with a rope. A man of fifty-five, maybe sixty, an old-style tramp rather than a bum. Foley had seen him around the neighborhood for five or six years. The old man often used the gents' facilities in the college dormitories. He attended the spring track meets, the home ballgames, lolled at his ease on the slopes around the pond, and was sometimes observed listening to the long Field Day speeches with a critical air. Foley had seen him as far as Paoli down the line. Always walking. He never hailed anybody for a ride. In the summer he was often seated on the big sandboxes of the Highway Department, swinging his feet like a kid and whistling softly as he watched the Main Line traffic flow by. He recognized Foley, for they exchanged greetings from time to time. The old man puzzled Foley because he hardly seemed aware that he was a bum. He might have passed as any local character, somewhat seedy, who pushed a mop in the diners or swept out the drugstores, if he had just given up carrying his winter coat tied up in a rope. That troubled Foley. The man seemed to have no pride. Otherwise he seemed to have what he needed—enough money for the food he ate out of paper bags, and paper cartons of milk that, when empty, he carefully deposited in the bins for trash. He did not smoke, was not known to drink, and chewed on nothing more offensive than the row of toothpicks he kept in the band of his hat.

One day Foley saw him in the gay deck chair of the new laundromat that had opened near the college, watching most of his clothes swill around behind the glass of the machine he faced. He had taken off his shirt, socks, and underwear, but not his pants and coat. He sat at his ease, a toothpick in his mouth, watching the clever, almost-human machine wash, rinse, and spin-dry his clothes. A ladies' wrestling match on a TV screen couldn't have absorbed him more. It was clear that he was pleased, but not overly impressed. He seemed to be, like his rope-tied bundle, nearly self-contained. Fussing all round him were a dozen rattled women, their eyes scanning some page, their fingers plucking at their hair, but even the pitiless stare of their spoiled children failed to penetrate him. For one spring, and all of one summer, Foley had hated the old man's guts, but now he walked in an arc, at the edge of the gravel, to keep from troubling his sleep. The sweat-stained felt hat with the toothpicks in the band remained flat on his face.

Looking south, beyond the pike and the market, Foley could see the green, parklike gap of the campus and the tops of the drooping willows that surrounded the pond. An island. Not a piece of the main. The world passed it by like the stream of traffic on the pike. One morning, from where he now stood, he had watched the blue heron that summered on the pond appear above the trees, the great wings flapping, water dripping from the feet like wet and trailing kite tails, and cruise over his head like some unnamed bird from the lost world behind the trees. A symbol of the college. A symbol of Foley himself. But the heron could fly, Foley could not, and the heron had other, wilder rendezvous, where the world along the pike was as passing strange as a crazed bat's dream.

The tramp sleeping in the station, the heron on the pond, and Foley teaching Pindar to the Quaker freshmen were three examples of the prehistoric present, the persistence of the past. But the heron and the tramp had the better of it. The past that persisted in them had less compromise. Compared with the heron and the apple-cheeked tramp, Peter Foley was as ancient

as the coelacanth, that steel-blue fish, long reputed
dead, that had somehow refused to give up, and shared
with J. Lasky Proctor the news spotlight and the Com-
mittee nets.

Foley stepped back from the edge of the platform as
the local pulled in. He started up the steps, backed
down, as a passenger, the image of his father, and a
Latin teacher at a boy's school near the campus, was
getting off.

"Morning, Peter," he said, raised his gobbler's
neck from the raddled rim of his collar, and passed,
with a glance, judgment on Peter Foley, playing hookey
from his academic duties.

"Morning, Allen," Foley muttered, let the old man
get off, then walked through the empty train to the
smoker. He dropped down in a seat where a morning
paper had been left. A New York paper, with a two-
column photo on the front page. The Senator from
Wisconsin, his back to the camera, was wagging his
finger at a man with a saintly, that is, almost silly, smile
on his face. A bone-white scar showed in the dark beard
along his chin. His hair was clipped like that of a
monk, and though he faced the inquisitor his gaze was
like that of the marble heads in Foley's Latin books.
The stone eyes open wide, polished and smoothed, but
not drilled for the pupils, so that the vacant, dreamy
gaze was turned inward rather than out. Very much like
the gaze of a tennis player well known in the twenties,
and a flyer whose picture Foley had pinned to the ceiling of his room. But this was J. Lasky Proctor, unmasked Voice of America. Foley recognized the scar,
and perhaps the gaze was due in part to the flashbulbs
that were popping—or was it also due, in part, to the

persistence of the past? Jesse L. Proctor, of Brooklyn, Avenue J, shown wearing the expression popular in the twenties, once worn by Lindbergh, by Lawrence, and known as the Lone Eagle gaze.

"Christ!" Foley said aloud, which was what he had exclaimed when he had bumped into Proctor, or Proctor into him, in the Hoffritz lobby near Forty-third Street.

"Sorry, old man," Proctor had replied, "not Him, just one of His humble servants," then he had turned and limped off, still favoring that foot where he had shot himself.

THE CAPTIVITY: II

But I go too fast. Before going to college I stayed out of school and worked for a year. I worked for Mr. Conklin, an insurance broker, and my job was to open and close the windows, put the bottled water on the water cooler, deliver signed checks, and put the stamps on the outgoing mail. Mr. Conklin was a big man in the business, but after signing checks most of the morning there was sometimes not much to do in the afternoon. He would step out of his office to see what I was doing, and if I wasn't doing very much he would say that he would like to have a word with me. We always had it in his office, where the chairs were more comfortable. He would first ask me how I liked my work, and I would say I liked it all right. Then he would ask me if I planned to lick stamps the rest of my life. I usually said I didn't think I'd like it very much. Then he would ask me what I expected to do with my life. What did I intend to make, he would say, of myself?

It had never occurred to me that I had much choice. My father had been a classics scholar, and I was following in my father's footsteps, but when I told Mr. Conklin that, he would slowly wag his head. He kept a glass of sharpened pencils on his desk, and when he heard that I was following in my father's footsteps, he would lean forward, take one of the pencils, and use the point to pick his teeth. It was what he did when he feared that he might be led to influence me. He didn't believe in that. He believed that every young man should decide for himself. Should decide, that is, to make something of himself.

That was the spring of 1927, and as an example of what he had in mind Mr. Conklin often mentioned Charles A. Lindbergh, a young aviator. He was making plans to fly from New York to Paris, entirely on his own. Mr. Conklin read the papers every morning, coming down from his home in Winnetka, and he would clip out everything pertaining to Lindbergh and read it to me. He felt I should plan to do something of that order myself. I wouldn't have to fly, just so it was something that had never been done. Mr. Conklin himself, when he was no more than a boy, had come to Chicago from Ladysmith, Wisconsin, and lied about his age to get a man's job with Commonwealth Edison. The rest was history. If there had been planes to fly, or if, as it turned out, he had just been born ten or twenty years later, Mr. Conklin implied that Charles A. Lindbergh would have been too late. Since he liked to talk, and I was paid to listen, we would sit in his mahogany-paneled office and go over what he said life in America was offering me.

The windows of his office were over Clark Street. One June morning, when I opened the windows, half the people in Chicago seemed to be on Clark Street, or in the windows of the office buildings that lined both sides. That morning Charles A. Lindbergh came to Chicago, and Mr. Conklin held both of my legs at the window while I emptied our wastebaskets over the hero when he passed below.

I didn't see much of Lindbergh through the clouds of paper, but Mr. Conklin had placed a large bet on him, and with some of that money he bought me a large signed photograph. I pinned it to the sloping ceiling over my bed. According to Mr. Conklin, I resembled the Lone Eagle quite a bit. I was tall and slender, self-effacing, and said very little. I had no plan to fly to Paris, or anywhere else, but I let him know that my mind was not closed and announced my intention of going to college in the fall. If I should ever need money, Mr. Conklin told me, for the big hop to Paris, or anywhere else, I should let him know, and he gave my mother two shares of his stock to put away for me.

If you remember the college movies of the twenties, the healthy sun-bronzed boys, the long-limbed girls, the football field green as the grass around a Maypole, the cloudless sky, the great eucalyptus trees, the orange groves like the labels on the ends of fruit boxes —if you remember these things you would recognize them when you saw Colton. The scenic props were all there; nothing had to come down or be put up. The Sugar Bowl, the Model T Fords, the ivy-covered buildings and the red-roofed dormitories with the view of the mountains that the prop man must have had in mind. The barren desert that glared in my father's photographs had disappeared. Hundreds of blackbirds, their eyes like hatpins, walked around under the cloudy mist of the sprinklers, preening and worming the green lawns.

When I arrived there was no one on the campus but the birds. An old man, a Mexican, watered the shrubs along the walk. The pits dug around the trees had

been filled with water, the sandy earth soaked dark. I
could hear water running between the shrubs, and see
it moving, under a film of dust, between the trees in the
orchards, or running clear in the channels where the
earth was packed hard. A thin stream of it darkened
the asphalt at the edge of the street. Water was everywhere, the sprinklers spit and hissed, but the cloud of
mist low over the campus left no smell of morning fresh-
ness in the air. It was there, like smoke, and then just
as quickly it was gone.

A young man with a hose was wetting down the
gravel near the freshman dorm. I told him who I was,
where I was going, and he squirted his hose in the direction of my room. Then he turned it aside, into the
bushes, so I could go along the walk.

Our suite was on the top floor of the dorm, a long
narrow room with bedrooms at each corner, and in one
of them, sprawled out on the bed, was a young man. He
lay on it rather than in it, and wore only the tops of his
pajamas. I made a racket coming in, but he didn't seem
to notice it. Room B, at my end of the suite, was full
of luggage covered with steamer labels, and four or
five tennis rackets, in heavy wooden frames, were
thrown on the bed. The bed had been slept in the night
before and the covers thrown back. On the desk in the
room, the lid up, was a portable phonograph.

I unpacked my bag, hung up my clothes, then walked
down the hall to the shower room, where I sat on the
floor, in a cloud of steam, and washed the cinders and
soot out of my hair. Then I took a cold shower and
stood at the window, wiping it off. The window faced
the east, the sun was still low and hot on the roofs of
the nearby buildings and the leaves, dark and dust-

coated, of a few old oaks. Beyond the oaks a green field, smoking with sprinklers, then the football field with the cinder track around it, and still farther beyond, white and glaring, a battery of tennis courts. A yellow sports roadster was parked in the gravel near the first court.

On the court the player threw up a ball, hit it, and as he threw the second ball up and hit it, the sound of the first, like a cork popping, came along on the breeze. The player went on serving as if each one was an ace, or out of the court. None of the balls he hit into the opposite court came back. I couldn't see that court—the scoreboard at the end of the football field blocked it off—but the player went on serving, hitting each ball hard. When he ran out of balls he picked up the green wastebasket he had brought them out in and walked slowly around the court, picking them up. There was no one else on the court. I couldn't see too well, but I could see that he was out there by himself. He wore a band around his head, and his wrists appeared to be taped. The rest of the courts, ten or twelve of them, were all empty. On beyond were orange groves, then a hot strip of desert, then the loaf-shaped foothills like folds of drapery, then the haze on the mountains and the milky haze on the colorless sky. Nothing moved, between the mountains and the campus, but the tennis player. Waves of heat blurred the yellow hood of his car, and I could see the white sweater spread on the seat to keep the leather from getting too hot. Nothing stirred or seemed alive that morning but the balls that made a sound like a cork popping and the white-banded wrists of the lonely tennis player. His name was Lawrence. I had seen it on the steamer trunk

in the hall and the racket presses lying on his bed.
Charles Lawrence, of Troy, Indiana, the dean had notified my mother, would be in Room B—the room, that
is, right across from mine.

When I came back to the room the fellow sprawled
on the bed had rolled over on his back. His long legs
were brown, with crisp golden hairs, and his feet stuck
through the posts at the foot of the bed. One arm
slanted across his face to keep off the sun.

I dressed, put on one pair of my new two-pants suit,
hung up one pair, and put back on the shoes I had worn
out on the train to take off the new look. Then I went
off to look for something to eat. The young man watering the shrubs pointed out the mess hall, one of the
new buildings on the campus, with the court plowed
up where they were planting olive trees. I walked
around the court to keep the sand and gravel out of my
shoes. The mess hall, a big, pitched-roof building, was
part of the new unit of dorms, and there were men on
ladders up in the gables, painting the trim. When I
stepped inside I saw four or five students, in white
aprons and jackets, seated at one of the tables, eating
off the trays they had just brought from the cafeteria
line. I picked up a tray and some silver, went down the
line myself. I went the full length of the line without
choosing anything. The woman serving the coffee told
me to go back and come down again. I didn't know the
rules, and there was so much food I couldn't make up
my mind. I ended up with orange juice, bacon and eggs,
hot biscuits, a coffee cake I saw after I had the biscuits,
marmalade, a bottle of milk, a bowl of hot cereal, and
coffee. The woman serving the coffee didn't bat an
eye. I took a seat at one of the empty tables near the

door. I could tell a freshman when he arrived, because each one looked around for an empty table, or they came in awkward, gawking gangs, like a bunch of kids. I could see how much good the year out of school had done for me. I didn't have too much of a beard—I hadn't had to shave since I left Chicago—but, after sizing me up, these freshmen moved off and sat somewhere else. That would never have happened if I hadn't had a year of high finance.

I sat there till eighty or ninety of the freshmen had arrived. I thought Charles Lawrence or the tall fellow on the bed might turn up. They didn't, however. One of the upperclassmen, a sun-tanned fellow with a numeral sweater, rapped his spoon on his empty milk bottle and said he would like our undivided attention. All freshmen would meet in the olive court, he said, at ten o'clock. At that time they would be driven into the mountains in upperclass cars. No freshmen cars, under any circumstances, would be allowed to go up. We would all go up in the old jalopies belonging to the upperclassmen, he said, and have a wonderful time even though we were freshmen, so to speak. That didn't get a laugh when he paused, so he repeated it. I didn't laugh, although I knew it was funny. I was sitting off by myself, and I could see that some freshmen thought I must be upperclass and driving one of the cars. The upperclassman repeated the time and the place, went over the rules about campus smoking, and said that there would be no smoking in the mountains because of the fires. In the fall of the year the mountains were very dry. If we smelled something burning it would probably be a freshman who had not got a card off to his mother.

I sat around till most of the freshmen had gone off. Then I walked back to the dorm, passing the jalopies with their upperclass drivers and the yellow sports roadster with disk wheels that had been parked near the tennis court. It was a foreign-make car I had never seen before. In the seat of the car was the green wastebasket, full of tennis balls that had been new that morning, for the boxes were crumpled on the floor. When I got upstairs I could see that someone else had taken a shower. I thought that would be Lawrence, because the wet tracks went down the hall and into our suite, but when I opened the door the fellow with the brown legs was drying himself. He was standing in the sun at the window, fanning the air with a towel. He was tall, about six two or three, on the lean side but not quite skinny, with a good even tan but a bad complexion on his face and back. He had athlete's foot, and he had painted his toes with mercurochrome. When I opened the door the curtain at the window blew the other way, pressing on the screen, but he went on fanning himself as if he hadn't noticed anything.

"Pardon me," I said, "are you Proctor?"

He bent over and spread two of his toes. Using the towel, he dried the spot carefully, then looked at the mercurochrome stain on the corner. Without looking at me he said, "Who?"

"Proctor," I said, "Jesse Proctor. I understand he's in one of these rooms."

"Maybe that's it," he said.

"What?" I said.

"If Proctor's here, that must be Gamble." He snapped his towel at the luggage at my end of the room, the leather bags and steamer trunks covered with foreign labels.

"I think that's Lawrence," I said. "There's a Lawrence in Room B."

"Lawrence who?"

"Charles Lawrence," I said.

"Jesus Christ and little apples!" he said and stared at me. Then he walked past me to the door of Lawrence's room. He looked at the rackets piled on the bed and leaned in to see the record on the record player. "Well, fan my brow," he said.

"You know him?"

"You kidding?"

"All I know is that his name is Charles Lawrence."

"Walk on water," he said very softly. "Think of that." From a pack of cigarettes on the edge of the table he took one and tapped it several times on his thumbnail. He used that nail to strike a match, lit the cigarette, and blew out a cloud of smoke. All this time all he had on was his tan, not another stitch.

"My name is Foley," I said, "Peter Foley," for I still didn't know who he was.

"Lundgren," he said, "Edward A., Long Beach, Palm Beach, Rex Beach, and Jack London."

He didn't step forward or put out his hand, and because of the way he looked I didn't either. I had never shaken hands with anybody in the nude.

"I don't think I know much about Lawrence," I said as he stood there staring at the luggage.

"You know what barbed wire is?" he asked. When I nodded he said, "Well, they sell it for money. A lot of people buy it. It makes a nice business."

"They make it?" I said.

"His old man invented it," Lundgren said. While I thought that over he added, "If not his old man, his old man's old man. It's in the family. Goddam barbed wire clear around the world." He hadn't finished his cigarette, but he stepped into Lawrence's room, looked around for a tray, then stubbed the cigarette on the corner of the desk. "Saint Cloud," he said, reading one of the labels. "Where the hell is that?"

"San Cloo?" I said. "I think San Cloo is just outside of Paris."

He did not turn to face me. "You been there?"

"I've done a little reading in French."

"That's nice," he said. "That's awfully nice, baby. That means you two will have something in common. Zan Klooo! Well, I'll be a sonuvabitch."

Lundgren had had smallpox at some time, and the lower part of his face was pockmarked. His head was big, but very knobby at the back, like the head of a kid.

"What a lovely goddam year I'm going to have, baby," he said and smiled.

"I guess Lawrence goes in for tennis." I nodded at the bed covered with framed rackets and several cartons of new balls on the floor at the foot of the bed.

"You ever hear of the Davis Cup, baby?" he asked.

I had heard of it, but I didn't know much about it.

"Well, they talk about this kid and the Davis Cup, baby," he said. Lundgren was six foot two, which was pretty tall, but I was pushing five feet eleven myself, and I wondered if he called everybody baby or just his friends.

"He was out on the courts this morning," I said, but I didn't say he had been out there alone.

"Probably why they sent him here, baby," said Lundgren. "Here he can just play tennis day and night. All he needs is just a pinch of that barbed-wire dough for the rackets and the balls."

He turned and left the room, crossed to his own, and sprawled out on the bed the way I had first seen him. "What a lovely goddam year this is going to be, baby," he said and groaned.

"Before I forget it," I said, "all freshmen are supposed to go up to the mountains. We meet in the olive court and go up in the upperclass cars."

Lundgren didn't answer. The draft through his window stirred the crisp golden hairs on his arms and legs. He was brown all over, except for the band where his swimming jock crossed his buttocks and the mercurochrome stains between his toes and the big pimples on his back. I went into my room, took off my suit pants, put on the khaki pants the dean had recommended, a shirt with short sleeves, and tennis sneakers with suction-grip soles. Then I took my new sweater and wore it with the sleeves tied around my waist.

It was half-past nine, and I stood at my window, looking through the tangle of vines at the campus, the grass dry now that the sprinklers had been turned off. Students were lying on it as if it had never been wet. In the street below my window were the upperclass cars, the yellow foreign sports car of Lawrence, and an Express baggage truck that had been backed up close to the door. Near the front end of the truck I could see the fake stickers on my own trunk. I had never been to Marquette, Illinois, or Northwestern, but I had found a store that would sell me the stickers and a bottle of shellac to keep them from peeling off. But I didn't

want to be in the room when the Express men brought
it up.

From the door of the suite I said, "You want to
tell Lawrence we're all going to the mountains?"

"I'll tell him, baby," Lundgren said. He had rolled
over on his back, his head propped on a pillow, so he
could lie there and smoke.

On my way down the stairs, between the first floor
and the second, I had to press flat against the wall to
let two of the baggage men pass with a trunk. I could
read the small type on the French spa stickers as they
passed my face. Behind the trunk, carrying three tennis
rackets, the sleeves of his sweater looped around his
neck, was the young man I had seen on the tennis court.
For a tennis player he struck me as a little short, but he
was wide in the shoulders and had very good arms. His
hair was blond but cut so close to his head that it was
like the fur lining of a helmet worn inside out. The
cropped hair seemed to begin at his eyebrows, with
hardly any gap for his forehead, the lower part of his
face being the most prominent. The jaw was long,
squared off at the bottom, and seemed to be out in front
of his face, but that might have been due to the way he
held his head. As he came up the stairs his right hand
rested lightly on his hip. His elbow brushed against
me, as if he hadn't noticed I was there, and one of the
sleeves of my sweater slipped up and over his brown
arm. I went on down to the bottom, from where I
looked up and watched them make the turn at the top.
I could hear him give the men directions in a very low-
keyed voice. I think he tipped them pretty well—the
first man down was smiling and his hat was still off
when he stepped through the door into the sun.

We went up the mountain a little after ten o'clock. The frat cabins were above the timber line, but this particular mountain went up so fast, and the road along with it, that it was less than nine miles from the center of the campus and the olive court. There were about twenty cars with about five or six of us to a car. The car with Lundgren and Lawrence was an old Packard touring, with a smooth, oil-burning, twelve-cylinder engine, two extra seats in the back, and I could see Lundgren high on one of them. Lawrence was at the front, his right arm holding a bag on the running board. I was in the rumble seat of a Ford coupe with a boy named George, from Seattle, who had a small hole in his forehead to drain a sinus that was very bad. He talked most of the way, but I didn't hear anything. The wind was on my side and blew whatever he said back into his mouth.

We went up the wide, dry bed of a river full of boulders washed down in the floods, and big rocks that were scored where boulders and trees had dragged over them. We went up fast to a place called Baldy, where there were overnight cabins, hotdog stands, and clear mountain water spilling over the dam just above the bridge. There we began to pass the cars with boys who had got carsick. They would walk down the road, behind the cars, and bend over as if they had lost something. The altitude and the winding road were too much for them. Although we had been at the end of the line we passed every car except the Packard and arrived at the frat cabins at the same time. They had a very sick fat boy in the Packard, but they had let him be sick rather than stop, and he was still on the floor of the car, stretched out, when Lundgren got out. Not counting the sick boy, there were seven of us. Two upperclassmen, who were driving, myself and George, Lundgren and Lawrence, and the fellow named Proctor, who had been sick for a spell but held out. That ride made it clear who would run the freshman class. We sat around in the shade, on the pine needles, looking at the haze that concealed the valley and listening to Proctor and the upperclassmen talk. Neither Lawrence, Lundgren, nor I said much of anything.

So Lawrence and I were never formally introduced. I knew who he was, of course, but he had no way of knowing about me. Not that it mattered, since he referred to all of us as "old man." I mean he referred to the three of us, Lundgren, myself, and Proctor, as "old man," but the rest of the class he referred to, when he had to, as "old boy." There was a nice distinction there, but to get it you had to hear his voice.

For the mountains he had taken off his tennis shoes, his white flannels, and his crew-necked sweater, and put on gray flannels without cuffs, a tweed jacket with chamois leather patches on the elbows, and a dirty pair of white buckskin shoes with red rubber soles. He hadn't troubled to tie the laces of his shoes or pull up his socks. Under the tweed coat he wore a turtleneck green jersey with the laundry tag showing on the collar. It was not what I'd expected of an heir to great wealth. He lay on his back, his hands cupped behind his head, where the brown pine needles made a carpet on the slope, one of the needles in his mouth while he listened to Proctor talk. I had always been under the impression that commanding personalities had high foreheads, but Charles Lawrence seemed to have no forehead at all. From the eyes up he looked more like a bird. His forehead seemed to slope back just that fast. As his eyes were not particularly friendly, the part of his face you looked at, when he was talking, was the wide mouth and the lantern jaw. He may have looked a little odd, though I think he looked better lying down.

All this time this fellow Proctor sat there and talked. When the upperclassman asked him where he was from, he said the Jewish Alps. I didn't know at the time that he meant the Catskills above New York. I didn't have to know that to think it was funny, but I didn't know how to take it, for it was clear that Proctor was a Jew himself. I had never met a Jew who talked like that about himself. Proctor told one story after another, most of them pretty funny, but nearly all of them having something to do with comical Jews. Some of these stories were good, but neither Lawrence nor Lundgren laughed. Once or twice I laughed because I couldn't help myself. Proctor was about average in size, with thick curly hair that he liked to run his hands through, a big expressive mouth, and friendly, sheepish eyes. He sat on the ground with his legs folded under, like a girl. Oddly enough, he was dressed quite a bit like Lawrence, with leather patches on his jacket elbows, dirty white shoes, a faded red turtleneck jersey, and dirty sweat socks. That much was similar, but the effect was not the same. Lawrence didn't seem to care about his clothes, as if he found it too much trouble to tie his shoelaces, and Proctor didn't care either—but something about it didn't quite come off. If you wanted your white shoes to look good dirty, they had to be the best sort of shoes in the first place, and the patches on your elbows weren't supposed to be there to cover up holes.

We sat there on the slope for an hour or more, until

the last car pulled up. While we sat around eating our
box lunches we learned and sang the traditional songs,
and were tipped off on how you could tell a Colton
man, and why you couldn't tell him much. In the afternoon we were free to mill around and get acquainted,
form teams to hunt for firewood, sleep, or go for a walk.
Lawrence, Lundgren, Proctor, and I hiked up to the
falls. On the way to the falls Proctor did a little sprint-
ing up and down the road, whenever we crossed it,
and Lundgren commented that he like the way Proctor used his arms. Proctor said he wished he could say
as much about his legs. He was a quarter-miler, and
couldn't run the quarter on his hands. Lundgren asked
him what his best quarter had been, and Proctor said he
had run a fifty-one flat on a two-curve track, soggy as a
mattress, and in the teeth of a driving rain. Lundgren
said Proctor ought to run a fifty flat on the springy
California tracks. He said he had had the same sort of
trouble in Alaska, where he had tried to pole-vault off
a grass runway, the pole too short, and had landed on
his back in a piece of plowed field. Proctor said he had
seen many fine pole vaulters in Madison Square Garden
and elsewhere, but he had never seen a man who had
a better build for it than Lundgren had. Would Lundgren mind saying just how high he had gone? Lundgren
said he wouln't mind if it was understood that he had
had to do his vaulting in a goddam pasture, dodge the
cowpies, and with a pole that was something for prop-
ping up a clothesline. If that was kept in mind, he would
say he had twice vaulted eleven feet. Proctor said if
Lundgren didn't vault twelve feet, maybe higher than
that, before the first year was over—well, if he didn't
do that they could ship him, Proctor, back to the Jew-

ish Alps. We said the hell with that, and then Proctor wanted to know what my line was, because I looked like a miler, but I said no, that in the way of sports I hadn't got around to doing much of anything. Lundgren said you had to choose, and any man who spoke French, and knew French history as well as I did, could not waste his goddam time out on a track, running around and around. Then Lundgren said to Proctor, "Baby, you ever hear of a man named Lawrence?"

"Lawrence?" said Proctor, coming to a stop. "Don't tell me! Let me guess!" He thought for a while, his hand over his eyes, then he lowered that hand and wiped it on his pants, stepped up to Lawrence, looked him in the eyes, and offered his hand.

Lawrence took it, squeezed it, let it drop again. "Glad to meet you, old man," Lawrence said.

"What'll I do with this now?" Proctor said and held up his hand, the fingers glued together like a fin.

"Have a cast made of it, baby," said Lundgren. "Plaster cast. This hand shook by Lawrence."

"*E pluribus unum,*" Proctor said, prying apart his fingers and pretending to read that inscription where his high-school ring had dug into the flesh. We all laughed at that, and Lawrence made a low bow.

We could see the falls from where we were standing, and on our way back, on the slope above the cabins, we could see smoke from the fires and hear the twang of a ukulele string.

"It's going to be a lovely goddam year, baby," Lundgren said and slapped his hand on my back.

In the evening we gathered in the main lodge, around the fireplace. We sang over all the songs we had learned

and heard a few words from Stan Lowell, a football
man, who told us that he had some very big news for
all of us. He had stumbled on it himself by the purest
chance. He had just happened to run his eye down the
list of the freshman class. On that list was the name of
a man who was internationally known, and he was going to ask that man to step forward at this time. Then
he asked for quiet, and asked Charles Lawrence please
to stand up.

Lawrence, Proctor, and I were sitting on a ping-pong
table at the back. Lundgren was standing, leaning back
against the wall. When Lawrence slid quietly off the
table and just stood there, saying nothing, some of the
frosh thought it must be Lundgren that was meant.
Beside him, Lawrence looked a little small. He just
stood there, waiting, until Stan Lowell asked him to
step up to the front. So Lawrence walked up and stood
beside him, his back to the fire.

I couldn't see his face, with the light behind him, but
against the fire he looked like a dancer; there was something nearly feminine, something a little insolent, in
his pose. He stood with the weight on the balls of his
feet, his hands balanced on his hips. Stan Lowell led
the applause, then he said that it was hardly necessary
to tell us that Charles Lawrence was considered one of
the hopefuls for the Davis Cup. He for one, Stan said,
would like to shake his hand, and he offered his hand,
Lawrence shook it, and right at that solemn moment
Proctor cried out, "Have a cast made of it, Stan!"

That brought the house down, naturally. We were all
just a little tense till he made that remark. There was
nothing particularly relaxed about Lawrence, and he
made me think, the way he stood there, of a firecracker

that had been lit but not gone off. He was so quiet, so intact, it made you tense just to look at him. Proctor's remark put an end to that, and when Stan Lowell called for class nominations, and then for quiet, I heard Proctor's voice. As luck would have it, he said, he knew just the man for the post. One who was quiet, self-effacing, but with a background of travel and experience that peculiarly fitted him for leading a class. He went on in this vein, then he paused and mentioned my name. Everyone applauded, and he raised my right hand in the air. Stan asked if there were any further nominations, then moved that the nominations be closed, and I was elected by unanimous consent. Called upon to say a few words, I said that I would gladly accept the post, since I knew that my old friend Jesse Proctor would do all the work. That went over very well, and Proctor was elected class secretary. Stan Lowell then said that the sergeant at arms should be a man big enough to keep our meetings in order, and half the frosh in the room turned and pointed at Lundgren, who was leaning on the wall. No official vote was taken. And that was how we wrapped it all up.

We topped the meeting off with doughnuts and cider, sang "Hail Colton, Alma Mater," then organized in five teams to see that all the fires were out. Lawrence, Lundgren, Proctor, and I went down the mountain in the Packard with Stan Lowell. We took it easy. We didn't use the motor all the way. Proctor said the road was like a ribbon of moonlight, and when we got below the fire area Stan Lowell and Lundgren lit up cigarettes. With the motor dead we could hear the whine of the suction tires. The dry bed of the river looked wet in the moonlight, and when we were alone, with no

frosh cars behind us, Stan Lowell switched the head-
lights off. The blacktop road curved along the white
river, the straps holding the top creaked like buggy
harness, and far below, bobbing like lanterns, we could
see the lights of the upperclass cars and the moonlight
on the boys who had gone into the mountains with
their pith helmets.

FOLEY: 2

        In the Philadelphia station, changing
trains, Foley looked to see if the *Times* carried the
story, and saw a photograph of Proctor with "a faded
blond companion" on the front page. Her faded blond
hair showed, but not her face, because she had hid behind her handbag as the flashbulbs popped. Something
in the gesture seemed a little old-fashioned, like the
camera dodging of Greta Garbo, and indicated that this
woman was perhaps more faded than she looked. A
fossil of some sort, like Proctor himself. Fished up from
the past, the murky depths, in the haul of the Commit-
tee nets.

The year the banks closed Foley had a letter from
Jesse Proctor, the first in several years, asking if he
could visit Foley and spend a night or two in his room.
Foley thought Proctor might be thinking of going back
to school. Taking the degree, he would need to do a
little teaching or get a better job. Foley said sure, and
a week or so later Proctor appeared. He had spent the
day hitch-hiking down from New York and arrived
wearing army-store dungarees, Sears, Roebuck work-
shoes that blistered his feet, and a soiled khaki shirt
with a leather, gas-station-type bow tie. A paper bag of
fig newtons bulged out the front of his shirt.

Although he had only one suit of clothes himself,
Foley felt tainted with capitalism, a white-collar serf
living off the fat of the poor man's land. During

Proctor's stay he hid his carton of cork-tipped cigarettes. He wore soiled white sneakers with loose crepe
soles that flapped. Proctor did not attend any of Foley's
classes, nor had he come with the idea of going back to
college. He came down to use, as he said, the facilities.
The chairs in the mess hall, the bumpers of cars, the
steps of any building where the students gathered,
served Jesse Proctor as a suitable podium. He closed
every discussion—as he termed his lectures—with an
invitation to spend the evening, and the night too,
going into matters further in Foley's room. Seven to
ten students, as a rule, put in the full night. Foley lay
on the bed near the window, listening, night after night,
to the theme and variations Proctor played on one
word. *Disinherited*. Proctor was. Had been, literally,
since Lawrence. So it made sense enough for Proctor.
But why did it make sense for the others? Thousands
of them. The word, in Proctor's mouth, seemed to cast
a spell. They had all wondered what they were, and
now they saw. They were disinherited.

Proctor's work—for the time being—had been cut
out for him. He slept in frat rooms, the back of campus
cars, on porches, in parks, and sometimes in guest rooms
where the change of linen he always needed was put
out for him. He made, understandably, quite a name
for himself. His educated feet learned to walk in his
proletarian shoes. Foley saw snapshots of him, in his
homespun beard, crouched on his haunches like a hill-
billy, photogenically dangling or chewing on a spear of
long-stemmed grass. The disinherited, it turned out,
were everywhere. In Omaha, in Cedar Rapids, and in
the shrubs of those penthouse gardens where, it would
seem, they had inherited everything. In Walla Walla he

recruited a corps of Seventh-Day Adventists. The Gospel according to Marx was his text but not, strictly speaking, his subject. His subject, for the time being, seemed to be himself.

A year or two later, for the time being, Foley often saw Proctor's name in the list of rally speakers, or his face in the choir surrounding Eleanor Roosevelt. A pale, secular monk, camera-conscious, his barbed-wire scar luminous in the flashbulbs, clearly destined to be one of the boys in the nation's back room. And then— then came the bombing of Guernica. Before Foley knew that he had gone (Lou Baker, that year, had been convalescing), Proctor had entered the Spanish war— and made his exit from it. A grenade had gone off in his hand—one he had caught when it was thrown at him—and he had buried the two dangling fingers, like lovers, in Spanish soil. Weeks later, from Madrid, Foley received a postcard of a Spanish whore, her blouse unbuttoned on the hand-painted nipples of her breasts. On the back:

> *For the time being, old man, I'm a casualty in your little allegorical war. We arranged to keep it in scale so you cool boys could study the pattern. Act One, as they say, in the Spanish theater. Spring here. How is the dogwood at Valley Forge?*

The dogwood, as a matter of fact, was beautiful. Foley drove out there to read the letter, the first one in months from Lou Baker, that brought him up to date on such things as Proctor and the Spanish war. Proctor a live hero—for the time being—but two fingers gone. And then, a year later, he stopped fellow-traveling —one of the rats, Lou Baker said—equipped with radar —long before the disciples, swooning and lovelorn, left

the ship. Where did he go? For the time being no one
knew. But on, it turned out, to another belief. The
choir boy whose voice would not settle down. Pushing
forty, but his voice still changing, a fresh, cocky, cham-
ber-of-commerce note the summer Foley stumbled on
him in the Sloane House john. Up to his ears—for the
time being—in World's Fair canes.

And then? One day Foley spied him on Fifth
Avenue—and avoided him. With him, there on the
corner, a boy in a low-crowned, wide-brimmed hat,
holding a bundle of clothes tied with a string. Dark
ringlets of hair, braided, framed his solemn, flour-white
face. Foley thought he was Amish—but no. A ghetto
Jew. He held fast, like a child, to Proctor's three-
fingered hand. They stood there together till a uniformed chauffeur picked them up.

Foley called Lou Baker, and from her he learned
that Proctor was in the import business. The impor-
tation of Jews, for the time being, a specialty. Flown
in from Spain, Portugal, Mexico, and South America—
in his own planes. And in New York they were condi-
tioned, as in an air chamber, to a different climate of
existence, then flown on to relatives, friends, spas, or
out of the country again. And the ghetto boys? Proctor
called them his dividends. With every five that could
pay, one such boy was thrown in free. That was the
story, as Lou Baker told it, but the imports dwindled
with the rise of Zion, and Proctor, for the time being,
took up something else. The Voice, now unmasked,
of America.

"Christ!" Foley said again, folded the paper, and
walked through the train to the smoker at the front,

where one of the trainmen sat in a seat across the aisle. He was carefully smoothing out the pages of a Washington paper he had found in the car. Foley watched him, remained standing until the trainman had worked through the paper to the front and passed a heavy hand over the smiling face of Proctor, now unmasked. Expression of a man given up for lost, miraculously found alive.

Foley took a seat, wiped from the window the hair oil of the man who had been leaning on it, and saw that the world was more or less as he remembered it. Wide, sluggish bend of the Schuylkill, spire of an unnamed church, acropolis hulk of the Art Museum, and the trees along the river lush and dark green under the pale English water-color sky. Opening the paper, he read:

WITNESS CITED FOR CONTEMPT
When Asked What He Was Doing,
Says He Was Eroding

"I was eroding," the witness had said, and that was how he looked. All the soft gentile topsoil, the non-furrowed regular guy, the comical Jewish clown, had eroded away. Leaving bedrock. A flood-scored Jewish bedrock showing beneath. Foley remembered the first joke Proctor had told them—might have been the first thing he said—about the house full of Semitic baroque in the Jewish Alps. That was gone. That had eroded, leaving no trace. A white scar across the jowl indicating where the anchor might have dragged.

Foley took a penknife from his pocket and with the nail scissors attached snipped out the picture of Proctor on the front page of the *Times*. Lou Baker might like to see it. Just the picture. Not the interview. She had prophesied—in one of her recurrent Delphic traumas she had prophesied—that Jesse Proctor, self-styled Jewish clown, would return to the faith of his people. Had he? There was just a suggestion that he might have gone back farther than that. Not so much a prophet now as a martyr. Showing his wounds. Throwing open his shirt front to show the public his wounds.

The clipping safe in his pocket, Foley trimmed his nails. The blades of the shears were not what they used to be. Like everything else. He had had the knife for twenty-three years. On the blade he examined the fading trademark, the pair of Henckels twins, Solingen. The best. None too good for the Lawrences. The knife had turned up in the fine tweed jacket that hung in one of the Lawrence guest rooms, and Mrs. Lawrence had suggested that Foley should take both the jacket and the knife. Some Lawrence—she didn't know which one—had left them there. There had been dozens of well-groomed, wealthy young men in and out of that room.

Foley had been neither well groomed nor wealthy that summer, but he had come back from France with the body of Lawrence, who had died, it was said, of a lovely cornada, a horn wound. That was almost true, and might have been true if it had been anybody but Lawrence, for he had been badly horned in an amateur bullfight in Pamplona. Peter Foley had been asked to bring the body back to Troy, Indiana, Lawrence's home town. He had been put in the guest room at the end of the hall, in a house that was like an empty dormitory, and in the closet of that room he had come upon

the jacket and the knife. His own clothes were soiled,
so he had worn the jacket while he was there. It fit
him well—as Proctor would have said, it did something
for him. They were closing up the house, and Mrs.
Lawrence had insisted that he take it along. Foley had
worn the jacket back to Chicago, where his mother saw
the chamois leather patches on the elbows and said
that he could wear a patched coat in the house but
not out on the street. His mother did not know that
was what the boys were wearing at Princeton and Yale.
She didn't know that leather patches were a sign of
class, just like very dirty white buckskin shoes or the
old Pierce-Arrow that Mrs. Lawrence preferred to all
the new cars. His mother didn't know that life had
taken a turn and that Mrs. Lawrence, in her old clothes
and cars, was already anticipating the age of the vulgar
nouveau riche. People who could buy *anything,* that
is, but the class that went along with an old Pierce-
Arrow or the feet that went into a pair of Lawrence's
shoes. Proctor had known it, however, and he had been
the first to pick it up. But his position, from the start,
had been ambivalent. There was a point in Abercrom-
bie & Fitch, as there was in sex and the Ten Command-
ments, which he could see beyond but beyond which he
could not go. "The rich are different from us" was
said by one who really knew. Peter Foley had known
it the day he put that coat on. They had more money,
but having more money was not at all the same as
being rich; only the truly rich knew how to enjoy the
money they had. Which was why Peter Foley had put
that jacket away for nearly ten years. He had not worn
it once at Chicago, where he took his degree; nor at
Columbia, where he did some graduate work. When the

moths had eaten it so badly that the patches on the pockets made it look real, he began to wear it, as a sort of smoking jacket, around his own room.

The Lawrence family, so far as Foley knew, still had their home place in Indiana, but the family had dispersed, and he had heard them mentioned all over the world. Troy had been a sort of park, a memorial almost, to the legendary head of the family, the old man who had invented barbed wire and stretched it around the world. Back in the twenties the members of the family, far flung as a rule, and trained professional gadders, would come back to Troy for a few weeks every summer, some of them with new children, old guests, or new brides, to drink the fountain of youth as it was dispensed by Grandfather Gans. The man who had invented, so long ago it seemed childish, a way of twisting two straight wires together so that a few barbs, headless nails, were held fast in it. Other men had thought of it too, dozens of them, but the man whose barbed wire took the field was Colonel Clayton Gans, founder of the barbed-wire empire.

Out in back of the mansion, in a sort of arbor, was a stretch of barbed wire about fifty feet long, with the wires at one end fastened to the hub of an old grindstone. Using that grindstone, pedaling the treadwheel, Colonel Gans had twisted his first piece of wire, and between the wires, every foot or so, he had inserted a nail. Later he had gone along and snipped off the heads. That piece of wire and the nails were still there: still well enough preserved to illustrate the idea. The strength and twist of that wire showed in old Colonel Gans, in the sinews of certain members of the family, but it had come through clean, without a flaw, in

Charles Lawrence, the old man's favorite grandson.
The one who had made up his mind to be a tennis player.

Lawrence had been called home from school that
year to see the old man die. Since it had been at
Christmas he had asked Foley to come along. And
Foley had gone because he liked Lawrence. That is,
he admired him.

The big thing Foley admired in Lawrence was the
thing that didn't show much. His money. Foley thought
it was very nice to have it but ill advised to work for it.
Part of Lawrence's charm was that he already had what
most people thought they wanted, without the ill effects
that came from having to work for it. Foley's charm,
for Lawrence, was that he openly admitted it.

They went back on the train because blizzards were
reported in the Middle West. Foley put in his time on
his outside reading, and Lawrence played a game of
solitaire at which he cheated in the morning, but in the
afternoon he played it straight.

"Well, I'm cheating now, Foley," he would say and
ask Foley to watch him. Not that he cared about the
game so much, but he didn't want to cheat himself cov-
ertly.

They came into the town of Troy from the north-
west. There had evidently been two railroads in the
town at one time, for they crossed a railbed buried in
the snow and passed a signal tower with the lights shot
out of the semaphores. A narrow country road without
a track of any kind ran along beside the train. The
whistle scared up a rabbit, and he raced along in the
ditch that bordered the tracks. The coach shadows
were on that side, and the rabbit paced the train, stay-

ing within the shadow, running up to the bright edge,
then darting back, the way a big jack would stay within
the lanes of the car lights till the road made a turn.

They came into the town like a wagon train, on a
level with the road. They came in easy, the bell clanging, through the empty backyards of the big houses,
the coach windows flashing when they passed close to
the sheds and the barns. The dark smoke fanned out
through the trees of the park, and they came up and
went by several crossing bells, but the roads were
empty, and nobody's children had made tracks in the
park. Nobody else got on or off the train when it
stopped. Down the street snow was banked on a no
longer revolving barberpole.

They stood in the clean snow on the platform till
the train pulled out. As the last coach passed they
looked into the park at the snow-covered cannons, the
swings and teeter-totters, and the bandstand where the
shingles were black on the slope facing the sun. On
the far side of the street an old air-cooled Franklin was
parked at the curb. The motor was running, and the
chauffeur sat erect, gripping the wheel. Lawrence
raised his hand, waving it at him, but the old man held
the wheel like the reins of a team that might, at any
strange sound, bolt away from him.

"This is Peter Foley, Hawley!" Lawrence yelled,
but the old man didn't seem to catch it. He wore a cane
hat, like a train conductor, with a hackdriver's license
fastened to the front, and as he eased out the clutch he
sucked in his cheeks, then puffed them out. "Hawley
came out with Grandfather, old man," Lawrence said,
then they went back in the tracks the chauffeur had

made coming down, the straps that held the top on snapping like wires in the cold air.

They went around the park, then turned into a drive that was lined with snow-covered cars: out-of-state cars, with a wide assortment of license plates—Connecticut, New York, Wisconsin, Illinois, and a car from Florida without a top. The snow lay thick on the lap robes that had been left in the seat. The house sat in a grove of big trees, at the back, and as the car moved around behind it Foley saw that the blinds were drawn at the windows on the second floor.

They entered through a door near the kitchen, where the smell of coffee was strong in the hall. Foley caught the smell of ether and burning logs that came through the double doors they passed, and the sound of a spoon rocking in a glass. An elephant's foot, like a huge leather bucket, served as a post for the railing on the stairs, and someone had drawn faces, with red lipstick, on the toenails. They had started up the stairs when a voice cried out, "Where the hell is everybody?"

It came from the room where the log fire was crackling. A woman's voice said, "Now is that the way to talk?"

"Where the hell *is* everybody?" the voice replied, and a glass rattled on the table beside the bed.

"They're asleep," the woman answered, "but they won't be if you make a noise like that," and Foley heard her hand slap the pillow and then smooth down the sheet.

"This way, old man," Lawrence said and led Foley to the second floor. Rows of stuffed animal heads, some of them with antlers, all of them wearing hats,

woolen scarfs, and driving goggles, lined both sides
of the long hall. They seemed to lean out of the transoms above the doors and roll their glass eyes at Foley
as he walked by. "Hope you don't mind a little bullshit, old man," Lawrence said and led Foley to the last
room on the left, where a giant teddy bear, with eyes
that bugged, sat up in bed. He was wearing horn-
rimmed glasses, a Princeton dink, and a brown-derby
button that said "I'm for Al."

Foley took a shower, using a bar of soap that
was wound up tightly in long strands of blond hair,
and wiped himself with a towel that had lipstick on
one corner of it. Then he stood at the window, looking
down the driveway at the row of parked cars. Where
the hell *was* everybody? Asleep, the woman had replied.
Under the new fall of snow that also seemed to be true
of the town. Nothing moved anywhere. Time seemed
to have stopped. Foley did not hear the steps in the
hall, but he knew, before he turned, that he would find
somebody standing in the door. She carried a tray with
two steaming cups of coffee, the steam rising from the
cups clouding her glasses.

"Dickie!" she cried. "Dickie!" And the tray she was
holding tipped toward Foley. The spoons, then the
cups and saucers, began to slide. He lunged toward
her, but too late. One of the cups bounced on the rug,
but the other fell against a chair leg, caromed against
the baseboard, and rolled under the bed.

"Mother!" Lawrence cried, coming up behind her,
and took the empty tray out of her hands.

"It's not Dickie?" she said.

"It's Peter Foley, Mother."

"I wondered what had come over him," she said,

then dropped down on her knees, like a girl, and felt around for the cup under the bed. She was a very small, slender woman, the type Foley's mother described as mousy, meaning they were quick and nimble, not slow and easygoing, as she was herself.

"Let me get this coffee," Lawrence said. Some of it had splattered on Foley's pants, and one of the spoons had flipped into the cuff. "It's a feather in your cap, old man," Lawrence said. "Mother only spills things on people she likes." He used his handkerchief to wipe off Foley's shoes, then he passed it to his mother, who was reaching for it.

"This floor needs waxing, Charles," she said, and crawled around on her knees, sopping up the spilled coffee. She found a hairpin, which she filed in her hair, an Indian penny, which she handed to Foley; then she went into the bathroom, filled the bowl with hot water, washed the handkerchief, and spread it to dry on the mirror. What Foley's mother might have done, but she would not have done it in her bathrobe, the tassel dragging, while a boy in his second year of college stood watching her.

Coming back into the room, she said, "Charles is like his Grandfather, Peter"—as if the thought had just come to her.

"She means Grandfather thinks he knows everything," Lawrence said.

"He does not know how to die," she said and hung the wet napkin over the towel bar.

"Mother!"

"Well, he doesn't," she said, and then she noticed the box of face powder on the bureau. "What in the world—?"

"Dickie," said Lawrence.

"Your grandfather was asking about him," she said and placed the lid back on the powder, pressed it down, and fanned at the cloud of dust that had squeezed out.

"Mother," Charles said, "if Grandfather is so—"

"Go tell him you are here, Charles." She put the empty tray in his hands, the box of powder on it, and Charles left the room.

Mrs. Lawrence went back into the bathroom to rinse her hands. From there she said, "I don't really see how you can stand him, Peter," which was what Foley's mother would have said if he had brought Lawrence home and she had got him alone. Then she would have waited for Lawrence to say how marvelous he was.

"Charles is not so bad, Mrs. Lawrence," he said, because she gave him the impression she knew her son pretty well. She didn't answer that but drew the blinds at the window to keep the sun off the green bedspread.

"Sometimes, Peter, I just wish he would break both of them." She was facing the window, gazing down the drive at the roofs of the snow-covered cars, and Foley thought she must be seeing whatever it was she wished Lawrence had broken. He looked, but he saw nothing to break.

"Both of what, Mrs. Lawrence?" he asked, but her mind seemed to have moved on to something else. She lowered her eyes and ran her hands into the loose sleeves of her robe. Foley thought she might be cold, in the draft from the window, but she did not move away from it.

"I might have known it," she said.

"What is that, Mrs. Lawrence?"

"He didn't tell you," she said. "I might have known he wouldn't tell you," and suddenly pushed back the sleeves of her robe, rubbing her hands on the arms and wrists that were more like those of a girl. She thrust out her right arm, the small fist clenched, and flexed it at the elbow, slowly, as if it hurt her. When she did that Foley understood.

"He broke it?" he said, and could see Lawrence's arm, the one he never flexed, poised on his hip, like a dancer's.

"They said he'd never be good at anything," she said. "He can't throw with it. He can't even bend it," and she doubled up her own arm, the fist close to her face, to show him what she meant.

"I don't see how he ever did it," Foley said.

"Skiing," she replied. "He did it skiing."

But that was not what Foley meant. What he meant was that he didn't see how Lawrence got away with it. How with one bad arm he played such marvelous tennis, and how with one good arm he shaved, brushed his teeth, combed his hair, and gave the impression that he wasn't really trying.

"He can do whatever he has a mind to," she said. "It doesn't seem to matter if he kills himself trying."

Foley believed that himself. He knew Lawrence well enough to see the truth in that. But he thought she must be worried about Lawrence and Proctor, because it was Proctor, just the year before, who had almost killed himself with Lawrence's gun, while riding in his car.

"Mrs. Lawrence," he said, to put her mind at ease, "you'll never catch Lawrence shooting himself."

"Not unless he has a mind to, Peter," she said and

lowered the blind another notch at the window. She said it so calmly, so matter-of-factly, that Foley heard it, but it did not penetrate. "His Grandfather would shoot anything," she said, "and he is worse than his Grandfather." Then she turned from the window, for someone in the hall was calling her.

"Mother!" Charles called from the landing on the stairs. "Oh, Mother—it's Grandfather!"

"Excuse me, Peter," she said and left the room.

As she hurried down the hall Foley could hear her knocking on all the doors. "Hurry, please!" she said each time she knocked. "It's your grandfather!"

But that was not it. Almost, but not quite. He had a stroke, he lost the sight of one eye, but four days later the crisis had passed, and the snow-covered cars parked in the driveway drove off. They went off, Foley remembered, crowded with the clever people he had never met, like a caravan of Princeton cars leaving the Yale bowl after a defeat. The following day he and Lawrence took the train back to school.

"This seat taken?" the woman said, took it, then leaned over Foley to tap on the window, wave at the child, the dog, and the man on the leash. The train jolted, she sat down, then arose to take from the seat the front section of the *Times* and smooth out the wrinkles she had ironed into Proctor's smiling face.

THE CAPTIVITY: III

One of those tarnished mirrors they hang on walls to cover up cracked plaster or peeling paper hung on the wall in the middle of our suite of rooms. Thanks to that mirror, I came to know Proctor's room as well as my own. If he was seated at his desk, or lying on his bed, it reflected him. If he wasn't there I saw his desk, with the pair of chipped Lonely Indian bookends, or his bed with the blanket from the Brooklyn YMCA. Over the towel rack on his door he had towels from the La Fonda, in Santa Fe. He kept his two pairs of shoes under the bed, on trees he made out of wire coat hangers, and in one drawer of his desk he kept a green metal cashbox with a padlock and key.

The rest of us had suitcases in our rooms, or mailing cartons we shipped our laundry home in, but Proctor said he couldn't stand to have his room all cluttered up. He did his own laundry, and he had learned to travel light, with just his typewriter case. The typewriter meant a lot to him; he would oil it with a feather whenever he used it and put it under his pillow when he was gone long from his room.

He kept a pad of yellow paper in a drawer of his desk, and in the water glass he took from the bathroom he kept eight or ten pencils, with their sharpened points sticking up. He sharpened the pencils with a knife shaped like a woman's leg and honed down the points on a piece of fine-grain sandpaper. Proctor majored in English, with a minor in French, spent four hours a day washing dishes in the mess hall, and did what studying he had to late at night. Between the Lonely Indians on his desk he had four books. *The Story of Philosophy* and *The Sun Also Rises* had library numbers on the spine, but *Peter Whiffle* and the other one might have been his. That one had no spine, but Proctor had printed his name on the flyleaf as if he were the author of *This Side of Paradise*. They were books I hadn't read, but I planned to when I got the time.

Lundgren's room was usually full of a strong yellow light. He liked to sleep late and kept the yellow blind at his window down. He liked to wear army shoes, with army pants, shirts, and socks, and when whatever he was wearing got dirty he took off the shoes, stepped into the shower, and washed the pants, shirt, and socks right on his body. He took them off to wring them out, then put them back on to dry. That way he didn't lose, he said, any of the body heat he liked to conserve.

Under his bed a wooden locker with a screw-down lid, the letters US ARMY stenciled on the ends, held his extra army shirts, socks, and several years' supply of mercurochrome. On his desk he kept a magnet, a tin pie tray with steel shavings that responded to the magnet, a large magnifying glass, a dissecting kit, a small geologist's pick with a sharp-pointed end, and a Kraft cheese box in which he kept rock specimens. *The Field Book of the Skies,* with the maps marked off by the ribbons he had won pole-vaulting, was usually on the chair, with his Lucky Strikes, beside the bed. The sky charts in the book were easier to study when he was lying down.

If Lundgren was in his room he was usually on the bed, his feet through the iron rails at the end, his head propped on the pillow, and the air full of smoke. If he was not in the bed the room looked unoccupied. *The Field Book of the Skies,* the small pick, and the magnifying glass would be gone. The tin plate with the metal shavings looked like something left by the cleaning woman. He never used an ashtray because he didn't like the smell of stale cigarettes. When he was down to a butt he removed the bit of paper, rolled it into a small wad, and dropped the tobacco on the floor. It was like sawdust in a bar, he said, and kept the dust down. He worked out on the track from two to four, in the mess hall from five to seven, and did most of his studying in the library over at the Physics Lab. He took a straight science major with ROTC instead of Physical Ed.

Whenever I walked out of my room I faced Lawrence's. He left one trunk in his closet, and several of the bags were under his bed. The trunk was a wardrobe, and he left his clothes in it, as if he couldn't bother to unpack them, and one of the larger steamer trunks we set up in the center room. That was Proctor's idea; he thought the steamer labels helped the atmosphere. The trunk contained racket frames, each one in a press, and the presses screwed into special racks so that the frames wouldn't rattle when the trunk was tossed around. Some of his bags had held nothing but cartons of English tennis balls.

Lawrence had no pennants on his walls either, but in October, from New York, he received a big carton

full of Hudson Bay blankets, football robes, canes with
Ivy League pennants, and a half-dozen pillows that he
asked us to distribute around the room. He didn't want
them on his bed, and they gave our big room a very nice
touch. He came supplied with gray flannels, white
flannels, dozens of shirts, several jock straps with silk
mesh pouches, made in France, but he didn't have a
tie of any kind and had to borrow one of mine. In the
evening, at dinner, we all had to wear coats, ties, and
buttoned shirts. I let him have my good tie, saying, at
the time, that I thought it was a pretty infantile custom,
but he said, "When in Rome, old man, you know—"
and gave me that smile. At first I thought he might
have braces on his teeth. I had seen girls with braces
smile like that.

I may have looked for the braces, for he said, "Just a
small chip, old man, but the cold air, you know—" and
showed me a very small chipped edge on a front tooth.

"I didn't even notice it," I said.

"Came down on the ten-foot board," he said, slipping
my tie around his neck. "Notice it as soon as the air gets
a little cool."

Lawrence had no pennants on his walls, but there
were two photographs on his desk. One was Cochet, the
French Davis Cup player, crouching for a low volley at
the net, and the other showed a young man with a
nude woman seated on his lap. He wore a stiff straw
hat and was sitting on a wire-backed drugstore chair.
We all took a good look at this picture because we
thought it must be faked. The woman had her back to
the camera, and the young man was leering over her
shoulder. The strap marks from the bra the woman
had taken off showed up very well. A pair of long

black sheer stockings had been left on. The picture had been taken somewhere in France, for there was French dialogue painted on the backdrop, but most of the words were not in my Larousse. It was signed "Love and kisses from us both, Dickie," and there was no indication that it had been faked.

Between the two photographs Lawrence had an onyx pen and pencil set, a glass paperweight containing a seahorse, and a small traveling clock, in a leather case, with an alarm. The alarm went off every morning at six o'clock. He would get up, brush his teeth, then fill the green wastebasket with balls, take along several rackets, and drive out to the tennis courts. He would practice by himself till seven-thirty, then come back and take his shower, have his breakfast, and go along with Proctor to his nine o'clock class. Three times a week, from three to five, a pro from Pasadena would come over and slam drives at him or try to lob over his head. Lawrence would hit everything, or try to, before the ball bounced. He would volley from the baseline as well as from the center of the court. All kinds of tennis were new to me, but this was new to the old tennis players, who found that his razzle-dazzle game more or less unbalanced their own. Lawrence either netted the ball, hit it out, or put it away. It was more like badminton than tennis—as if all the ground strokes had been ruled out. But you couldn't talk to Lawrence. That is, you couldn't tell him anything. Lawrence was on his own, but the coach let it be known that a kid named Crewes, who played for Southern Cal, would pin his ears back in the spring.

As he had lived all over Europe, Lawrence took his major in languages. He spoke French very well, and

while living in France he had been tutored in German
and English. The name of his tutor was Richard Olney
Livingston. Livingston had gone to Oxford, was now at
Princeton, and turned out to be the Dickie on the photograph, the leering young man with the French moll
on his lap. Lawrence would have gone to Princeton himself, if Princeton had been in California, on the Riviera,
or anyplace where he could play tennis most of the
time. He had come out to California because the California game was fast.

On my own desk was a snapshot of my mother holding one of Arlene Miller's new Belgian hares, one of
the few that the male had not eaten out of the last batch.
Between my father's bookends, two chunks of marble
said to be part of the Acropolis, I had his set of Rabe-
lais, in cracked morocco, and his *Oxford Book of Greek
Verse,* with the translations he had written in the margins forty years ago. I would get up when I heard Lawrence's alarm, work on some vocabulary until breakfast, then walk with Lundgren or Proctor to our first
class. After class we would end up together in the aisle
or on the concrete steps out in front, quite a bit like the
filings in Lundgren's magnetic experiments. Lawrence
was the magnet, but I doubt very much if we'd often
have got together, or stayed together, if Proctor hadn't
manipulated it. He was drawn, of course, but he didn't
want to do it all by himself. That was true of all of us,
but it took Proctor to figure it out; he wasn't afraid, as
we were, of making a fool of himself. He didn't seem to
mind if he wasn't left holding the bag alone. He would
yell, "Hey, Foley! Here's Lawrence!" just as if I'd been
looking for him; or say to Lundgren, "Hey there, bean-
pole! Here's Foley," although Lundgren never had any-

thing to say to me. But I don't remember any of us holding off or pointing that out. We were all feeling the pull, and Proctor just gave us the excuse.

I know that when we walked together other groups of frosh would step to the side. We gave the impression of being a pretty solid outfit, I think. One reason we gave this impression was that we let Proctor do all the talking and stood around listening, as if giving him support. We would go along abreast, around the big Lab buildings, then out on to College, where the whole student body, after the nine o'clock classes, would wait for Chapel in Smiley Hall. We weren't really that solid at all, which may have been why, at the start, Proctor had to carry the ball and keep up a line of talk. I think he felt if he didn't we might just walk away from him.

The steps were reserved for the upperclassmen, and the big crowd of frosh, the frosh that mattered, were between the rails that went along the sidewalk at the front. Proctor would sit on this rail, and the rest of us would stand facing it. Looking up the street, up the lane of trees that made a green tunnel toward the mountains, I could see the tawny fire break that went along the ridge to the big Colton C. In November some of the frosh went up with shovels and rakes and cleaned it off. On a clear day it seemed to rise above the campus like the bright green dink Lundgren was wearing, and wherever you saw Lundgren, in the morning, you would find the rest of us.

There were more girls than boys at Colton, but somehow they didn't cut any ice with us. The Colton girls were in the big dormitories or the sorority houses I could see from my study window, and about two hundred Phipps girls were on the new campus a few blocks north. The Phipps school was more or less new, with a Maxfield Parrish campus and some smart girls, but the Humanities program didn't give them too much free time. The Colton boys, as Proctor said, had a pretty wide choice. The Colton girls were mostly of the type that might have come from homes like mine, but Phipps featured girls of a different type. They had more, as a rule, of what Proctor referred to as "class." When the Colton women threw a dance in the gym there was a band at one end, down under the basket, with something like a no-man's land out on the floor. The Colton stags, over on the north side, would stand facing the Colton fillies near the door, with two or three sophomores running around clipping the lambs. There was very little of that sort of thing at Phipps. The Phipps girls had more know-how, and if the music stopped when you were dancing with a Phipps girl she didn't act as if she was being compromised, as Proctor pointed out. I didn't dance that year, but I could see the point in what he said.

On the weekends Proctor would go up to Phipps, Lundgren would look around for a Garbo movie, Lawrence would go to bed, and I would work at my desk. If my window was open I could hear the two bands playing at once. The Phipps band was better, with a crooner out from Los Angeles. A little after midnight they would break up, since some of the boys had to get back to Cal Tech. I would see the lights of their cars up on Foothill Boulevard. The local boys would come down through the orange groves, smoking their cigarettes. Some of the upperclassmen, with the upperclass girls who had taken out two o'clocks, would ride over into the wash to do a little necking, or go for a ride. Proctor would sit on the floor in the shower and sing "Sometimes I'm Happy." I was not indifferent to girls, myself, but I was a full-time scholarship student and had my father's reputation, as Proctor put it, around my neck. I was interested in making an agreeable impression, as my mother said. What I had seen of Colton I liked, and it had crossed my mind that Oberlin, where my mother had gone, would not be quite the same. It snowed back there. It would never suit Lawrence's fast type of game.

FOLEY: 3

A scene in hell, a cloud of sulphurous smoke dense and powdery as a pill dissolving, shot through with orange flames, burning like flares, and the dark suspended shell of the Pulaski Skyway. Along the train bank through the marsh grass a fringe of vomit-green froth, a signboard advertising clothes for fat boys, and a gray film of sewage on the surface of a river of pitted lead. The coach lights came on, the windows darkened; in the glass, as in a mirror, Foley saw His reflection—the Devil's horned profile and his leering smile of good fellowship. As the pressure built up in Foley's ears he closed his eyes, swallowed hard, and said, *"Lasciate ogni speranza, voi ch'entrate"*—then let the cool, dank air at the bottom of the tube blow into his face. As the train began to climb he stood up in the aisle, slipped into his coat.

On the track level at Penn Station he went along the platform to the escalator, rose one level, then blocked the stream of traffic till he sighted an empty phone booth, headed for it. Inside the booth, facing the eye-level sign that always left him confused, if he troubled to read it, he waited for the wobbly needle of his compass to settle, straighten him out. Then he closed the door, and in the dim light he examined the list of Lou Baker's phone numbers, decided on the last one, and dropped his nickel into the slot. Heard it clink through the machine like a loose part, and then nothing. Took time now to read the sign and read all calls were ten cents. He found another nickel, tried that.

While waiting for her voice Foley usually reflected that there was a book, of some sort, in Lou Baker, perhaps a better book than the one she had written herself. For more than twenty years, to a wide range of people who had never heard or set eyes on one another, Lou Baker was a legend as well as a link in a curious chain. Twenty years ago, for the time being—every move Lou Baker made was *for the time being*—she had accepted a position, for the summer only, of tutoring the child of a big theater man. That was the beginning, the opening chord, of a sort of tone poem that had no climax but endless variations on the same haunting, plucked-string theme. A tutor, a governess, a traveling companion, the anonymous author of well-read memoirs, and the companion of ladies, characters, and assorted, as well as unsorted, gentlemen. Always for the time being. Always a makeshift in the interests of *her work*. It happened to be, as Foley finally observed, the well-wrought urn of her own special gifts, the mobile salon of culture in the machine age, the free-lance Mme. de Sévigné, who held her séance wherever she happened to be working or boarding, opened and closed a romance in a five-day crossing, and somehow kept intact, however labeled and battered, the girl who had been the first one Foley had kissed. Over the years, and now there were many, hundreds of devotees had been exposed to the performance, most of whom fancied they saw through it, and all of them—except Foley and Proctor—had been glad to ring the curtain down, *finis,* and wonder who the hell it was that Lou Baker was currently stringing along. And all the time there was this book, a suitcase full of it, opened up and re-examined in dozens of apartments, spread over card tables and chairs in a score of attics, arranged and rearranged, long, fermenting evenings, in the drafty summer houses left vacant for the winter, turned over to Lou Baker and the gemlike flame of her art. It seemed impossible that so much concerted effort would not produce a book. That it would not, like other such labors, come to honor all the strangers who appeared in the foreword, up to that moment unaware of one another, but without whose money, whose attic or summer cottage, without whose wife and, on occasion, her husband, this book would not have been, as the foreword would say, as good as it was. For what was good, thank her friends; for what was not good, blame Lou Baker, the humble author. That was Montana Lou, the girl with short, cropped hair and the profile of a consumptive English poet, husky tobacco voice, radiant smile, and an air of the breed so obvious and rewarding that publishers took her to lunch, or chipped in further advances, not because they still believed that a book was forthcoming but because Lou Baker had the ring of gold in an age of brass.

And when that phase had passed, when it was more or less clear that no book of any kind was really forthcoming, there were several hundred people, maybe thousands, who would settle for the real thing. *The raw material,* as Lou Baker described herself. There were always a few, but not too many, Lou Bakers, and the market for the *real* product was enormous. Only the best agencies paid the highest fees for her wares. She had sat on Swiss balconies, like Hans Castorp, listening to people with real and imaginary troubles; and she had sailed around the world, been involved and uninvolved, but if involved it usually left her so exhausted she would have to take a trip and a rest cure somewhere, herself. At such a time, right out of the blue, Foley might receive a card from Taxco or Juan les Pins, informing him that she was suffering from scar tissue around the heart. Their little game, their little code, and Foley would sit down and rush off a letter, all in all the finest things he had ever written, summing up all of the world's known cures for scar tissue. She had never answered one of these letters, not by a line, but he knew that she kept them. He had run into people who had heard passages. The next word, for such it would be, would come around Christmas, or New Year's, the operator asking him to please hold the wire, that Santa Fe, Monterey, or Bermuda was calling, and then the voice of Lou Baker, husky, coughy, and a little bit tight.

"This Foley?" she would say, and then, "This Lou Baker, Foley's chick."

But now she said, "Yes?" and he heard something fall as she turned on the bed.

"This Foley," he said. "This Foley's chick?"

"Oh, God!" she said. She meant it, she had actually gasped it, and he said nothing. She said, "Is this *Friday?*" Friday was the day Foley usually called her.

"Monday, Lou," he said, wetting his lips, and when she did not reply he said, "You see the paper?"

She coughed, creaking the bed. Somehow he knew that she had.

"Who's the faded blond accomplice you suppose?" he said, to cheer her up. Faded blondes always cheered her.

"Who you think?" she said.

"No idea," he said. "I'm not a member of the Party," then forced a laugh to indicate how he meant that.

"That's too bad, Foley," she said. "We need members, and I'm the kid's faded blond accomplice."

He opened the door of the booth; a little fresh air might help. In the glass panel of the door he saw the shine of sweat on his face. "How is he, Lou?" he said. "How's Proctor?"

"He's here in bed. You want me to ask him?"

Foley did not breathe. He kicked the door with his foot to get more air. He wanted time to run out on the call, and the coin to clink—but nothing happened. He heard the smothered twanging of the springs.

"Who in Christ's name is it?" the voice said. Hoarse from talking.

"Him," she said, as if they had been waiting. As if they had gone to bed with his name on their tongues and knew that he would call. He heard the padded phone base drop on the floor, then the drag of the cord across the bedclothes.

"That you, Proctor?" said Foley.

"Good morning," said the voice, falsetto and sunny, "Goldberg's Spa and Breast Developer on the Boardwalk."

"How are you?" said Foley.

"Shit to the eyelids."

So he was all right then. Same old Proctor. "That's fine," said Foley. "I mean, it's good to hear your voice."

"I have several," Proctor said. "Which one you like me to use?" Foley did not reply. Proctor cleared his throat and in another voice said, "What brings you to Elsinore, old man?"

Foley tried to think, thought of something, and said, "You know what day it is, Proctor?"

"Hmmmmm," Proctor said, "Mother's Day perhaps?"

"Anniversary," said Foley, standing by. "What anniversary it is?"

"This woman here in bed your wife maybe?" said Proctor.

The phone clicked, the operator signaled that his time was up.

"Look, old man," said Proctor, "why don't you come over? Why don't you get a bottle and come on over?"

"You still—I mean, she's still—"

"Same old stand," said Proctor. "Same apples. Say you let us get some shut-eye, then come on over."

The operator cut him off. He stood there in the booth listening to the buzz. He was free, he realized, to let the matter drop or to show up later. He was not committed. A state of mind that came to him naturally. He sat there in the booth, the door open, listening to the man in the adjoining booth drum his fingers on the glass panel of the door. Voice of party on the line like that of Lou Baker, Montana 1907, Sorbonne '29, free-lance pagan-Christian and girl about town, paranoid, Anglo-Irish, troubled in mind, Freudian before cocktails, Jungian when tight, sometimes drawn toward Schweitzer, then Eva Perón, rude to waitresses, salesgirls, and artists with beards, but great promoter of old and new masses, attracted to male Jews, hairy young men with good legal training, preferably Harvard, physical type prone to peanuts and growing bald early, something of

Helen, more of Cassandra, strong sense of guilt and opportunities wasted, fond of Leslie Howard, Joel McCrea, tin-roof sundaes, Peter Foley, but at the moment in bed with J. Lasky Proctor, very old friend and importer of Jews.

"All right, go to hell then," the male voice said, kicked the booth door open, and stepped out to smile at Foley. Short, square man, corseted waist, double-breasted suit with kerchief sewn to the pocket, topcoat hanging open so he could hook four fingers into pockets of coat. Effect of broad shoulders, trim waist. Habitat —usually seen around phone booths in Sun Ray Drug departments and United Cigar stores. "The two-timing little bitch," he said, pocketing the paper matches Foley had passed him, and walked off smartly on not quite invisible Adler Elevators. So he could be taller than she was—but perhaps he was not. Seeing man approach vacant booth, Foley snapped his door closed, sealed himself off.

Why hadn't Lou Baker married?

Not thought to be the marrying type. Why hadn't Foley married her?

When he had the impulse there hadn't been the time, and when there had been the time he lacked the impulse. Besides—besides, she wouldn't have married him. She didn't like to wake up with a man who still had things on his mind.

Why hadn't she married Dickie? Might be that she had never been asked. Back at that time, and place, marriage like long underwear on a chorus girl. Old-fashioned protection for troubles she was paid to suffer from. Through the glass in the door, the panel smudged by a child who had licked it while waiting, ogle-eyed,

for his mother, Foley could see the Métro station at
Raspail and Montparnasse. Where he had first seen
Lou Baker and Richard *Dickie* Livingston.

That had been his first night in Paris, just eight or
nine hours before Lou Baker bit him, and he was standing there smoking his first Caporal Jaune. He heard
them, talking English, come up the Métro stairs.
Through the railing he saw the smart fellow with a girl
on each arm. The girl on his left wore her hair in
braids, like the tails of well-bred horses, and the girl
on his right had her hair in a pompadour, like a man.
She wore an oversize, dirty camel's-hair coat and a pair
of soiled Mexican huaraches on her bare, dirty feet. The
coat was too long, too wide in the shoulders, and she
wore the collar turned up high on her neck. Something
new, Foley recognized, in the way of class. They
crossed the street to a table at the Dôme, back under
the awning, and Foley found a seat with a front-on
view of the girl with the braids. She had a fine skin,
small, close-set ears, a way of showing the tip of her
tongue when she talked, but Foley found it hard to picture a man roughing her up. He caught her eye, just
once.

She turned to the young man and said, "Honey, you
like to take the rap for me?"

"Love it, chick," he said, sizing up the situation. He
stalked up to Foley. "Livingston speaking. Would it be
Stanley?"

"No, it would be Foley," Foley replied.

Livingston screwed his neck around to leer at the
girls, then suddenly stopped as if he had cracked it.

"How is Lawrence, Livingston?" Foley went on, fol-

lowing up his advantage, but Livingston let him wait
till what advantage he had had passed.

Screwing his neck around slowly, Livingston said,
"I got an extra chick on my hands, old boy. Montana
born aus Bryn Mawr chick," and led Foley over to the
table and introduced him to the girls. The braided
number was Pamela Crowley, Lawrence's fiancée, and
the chick aus Bryn Mawr was Lou Baker, Montana for
short.

"Foley knows Lawrence, you chicks," Dickie said.

"Does he know that he's crazy?" Pamela asked.

They looked at Foley, and he said, "I lived with Lawrence for two years."

"You're in," said Dickie and took a pair of castanets
from his pocket, clacked them. He ordered an amer
picon for Foley and a second mandarin curaçao for himself.

Everything would have been fine if Foley had just
kept his mouth shut. It should not have been hard. He
had nothing to say. But that was his first night in Paris,
his first apéritif out on the sidewalk, and *being* in—he
wanted to show how far in he was. So he casually said
that he hoped Lawrence's car wasn't ruined.

"Why should it be?" Lou Baker had said.

"According to Proctor," Foley said, "he was hurt in
his Novillada—"

"Oh, my God!" Pamela said and pulled off one of her
gloves. While she twirled the rings on her fingers nobody said anything. Then she put the glove back on,
and Dickie said, "A novillada is a sort of bullfight, old
sport."

"Oh," Foley said and looked at the sweat on the
palms of his hands.

"If you want to be a bullfighter, old man," said Dickie, "what you do is arrange for a novillada. If you have money you can arrange it."

"What the hell is so wrong?" Lou Baker said. "Why the hell should he know about a novillada?"

"He might want to own one," Dickie said. "A twelve-cylinder Novillada."

Pamela laughed. "Excuse me," she said.

"So he was hurt by a bull?" Foley said.

"He was punctured," said Dickie. "A very lovely cornada."

"A cornada is a horn wound," said Lou Baker.

"A horn wound in the groin, dear," said Dickie.

"I'm awfully goddam sick of these distinctions," Lou Baker said.

"Was he hurt badly?" Foley put in.

"Truly, he was not hurt goodly," Lou Baker replied. "For him it was bad, but for the bull it was good. The bull loves to gore good."

"Very amusing," Dickie said.

"Dickie does not like my talk, Mr. Foley," she said. "It is not good. It reflects his latest reading. It is bad to be so influenced by one's reading. It is good to be influenced by one's environment only."

Pamela said, "Ha!" then covered her mouth as if she had been warned about that. "If I'm rude," she said, "it's because I'm faint with hunger." She took a compact from her purse, looked at her face, and smoothed out the lines that formed when she smirked.

Someone kicked Foley under the table, and when he looked up he saw it was Dickie.

"Like to wash up a bit, old boy?" Dickie said, and Foley followed him back between the tables, around the bar, and down the stairs to the men's room. As the door swung behind them Dickie took out his billfold, checked over the notes, and made an equal division. He passed them to Foley. "Take her to Voisin's, old man. Take her to Duval's. Take her anywhere she likes."

"Take *who?*" Foley said.

"Take your pick."

"Look—"

"I got to feed these chicks, old boy, but they won't slobber out of the same trough. Lou Baker doesn't seem to like the upperclass type of bitch."

"I'm not much for that type myself," Foley said.

"She's yours!" Dickie spat on the palm of his hand, then took Foley's hand and shook it.

"Who?"

"Lou Baker."

"Look—"

"Don't let the Bryn Mawr slouch fool you, old boy. Awfully nice kid."

"I'm not thinking of the slouch," Foley said.

"We'll go over it later." Dickie felt around in his pocket and took out a key. He gave it to Foley. "Make yourself at home."

"I'm at the Pension Lussaud," Foley said.

"What for?" Dickie said, and he was gone. He pushed through the doors and left Foley standing there, the money in his hand. So Foley had washed his hands, combed his hair, and allowed time for Dickie to make the division; then he went back upstairs, hoping to God they would all be gone. But Lou Baker was seated on a stool at the bar. She had a tall glass in her hand and a tired smile on her face.

When Foley stepped up to her she said, "I was wondering if you'd make it," and gave him the package of Caporal Jaunes he had left behind.

"Make what?" he said and tried to look surprised.

"Up your mind," Lou Baker said and blew a cloud of smoke into his face. Then she slipped from the stool and hooked her arm through the one he offered her.

"Nobody goes to the Café d'Harcourt any more," she said. "We're nobody. Suppose we go there?"

So that was where they had gone. And that was where, and when, it all began.

In the phone booth Foley noticed the air was bad. He opened the door, stepped outside, and let the momentum of the crowd carry him forward—or was it backward?—to where he stood with others in a line. With the others he rose, on the escalator, toward the opening looming like a cave's mouth, toward the morning stars singing together in the galaxy of neon signs.

THE CAPTIVITY: IV

In November we began to get fog in the morning, and around six o'clock, when Lawrence got up, the dormitory was like a freighter anchored at sea. The mountains, the campus, even the trees below the windows, had disappeared. Although the fog was very bad for his rackets, and so thick he couldn't see the lines on the court, Lawrence practiced his serve, fog or no fog, as usual. He would stretch clean towels along the net cord and put up a music stand, with a coat draped on it, to indicate the player in the opposite court.

I'd wake up when I heard Lawrence's alarm, but in November, if it was foggy, I might lie in bed for another half-hour till the heat came on. It would be another hour or two before Proctor or Lundgren got up.

One morning Lawrence was a little late—he had opened his trunk to get a new pair of rackets—and I heard Proctor say, "Like to give a new man a few pointers, Lawrence?"

I thought he was kidding. Some joke he'd stayed awake long enough to pull. Lawrence stopped twirling the screws on his press, but he said nothing.

"Seriously," said Proctor, "you think I'm too old to pick up the game?"

"Not at all, old man," Lawrence said, "but I'm too old to give you any pointers."

"I was just kiddin'," said Proctor, "but, as a matter of fact, I'm thinking of tryin' a little tennis. What the hell can I do with the quarter mile when I get out of school? Can't take the track along with me. Like to pick up something I can do out of school."

"I think they do it in the YMCA," said Lawrence.

"Not me," Proctor said. "I'm no bald-headed quarter-miler. What I'd like is a game I can play with my friends. Play with my wife, kids, et cetera. I won't be like *you*, anyhow. I won't be too good to play with my wife."

"Helen Wills strokes a nice tennis ball," said Lawrence.

"Don't see her as my wife," Proctor said. "Ever notice her muscles? Why don't I just pick up a few pointers myself?"

Lawrence didn't answer.

"You waste an awful lot of time out there," said Proctor, "pickin' up the balls after you hit 'em. Why don't you let me do that? Why don't I stand over there and hit 'em back?"

"Old man—" said Lawrence after a bit.

"I know just what you're going to say," said Proctor. "You're going to say I can't keep my big mouth shut. I swear to God I won't say a word, not a word—even if I'm hit!"

"You ever play the game?" Lawrence said.

"I know how to keep the score. Look," he said, "let me do it just once. If you don't like it you just say so. I swear to God I won't go near a tennis court again."

When Lawrence didn't answer I heard Proctor bounce out of bed.

"Got a racket," he said. "Borrowed a racket. You wouldn't happen to have an extra pair of shoes, would you?"

"What size, old man?" said Lawrence.

"I wear any size," said Proctor.

Lawrence went back into his room, opened a bag, tossed one shoe at a time across the room.

"Right with you," said Proctor. "Just a sec. How the hell'd I know I'd be takin' up tennis? Christ, man, these fit me like the eighteenth century!"

"You ready, old man?" said Lawrence, and they left.

As they went down the stairs I heard the frame creak on Lundgren's bed. He rolled over on his back and said, "Like to give me a few pointers on whoring, Foley? Like to take up something I can do at the office. Christ, man, you can't pole-vault at the office. Like to take up something I can do with my wife, your wife, or even one that ain't even married."

"You think he's serious?" I said.

"Dead serious," said Lundgren. "What to do after school is a very serious problem. I was thinking of not doing anything—but how the hell you do that? Takes practice." I didn't answer. "Point is, baby, that all we're doin' is just thinkin', but our little friend here is busy doin'. He just goes ahead and does what poor suckers like you and me just think."

"I wasn't thinking of taking up the game," I said.

"Don't be a goddam boob," Lundgren said. "He's not takin' up tennis, he's takin' up Lawrence. The only pointers he wants are on a piece of barbed wire."

I didn't reply to that, and Lundgren intoned:

"JESSE PROCTOR
Vice-prexy in charge of
LAWRENCE
BARBED-WIRE EMPIRE OF AMERICA."

"I don't know as I'd want that job," I said.

"Baby," said Lundgren, "that's exactly why Proctor is going to get it. He isn't squeamish. He isn't afraid of his own thoughts. If something needs running, he's the man to run it. You notice how nice and smooth he's runnin' all of us?"

"Well, if somebody has to do it," I said.

"I didn't think anybody could do it to Lawrence. I thought that kid could wipe his own arse."

"I'm not too sure he can't," I said.

"Mark my words, baby," said Lundgren, "today marks a change in the barbed-wire empire. If you're thinking of taking up tennis yourself, the man to get your pointers from is Proctor, not Lawrence."

I got out of bed, to get away from Lundgren, and took my towel and my toothbrush into the bathroom. I had once left my toothbrush in the rack for them on the wall. We all had. It was Lundgren who said he had found his own toothbrush wet in the morning, with the spearmint flavor Proctor so much admired. I didn't believe that, but I now kept my toothbrush in my room. I didn't seem to know, that is, what I really believed. I brushed my teeth, using my Dr. Lyons powder, and faced the billowing streamers of fog that shut off the mountains and hung low over the football field. I could not make out the scoreboard or the curve of the cinder track. I could not see the tennis courts or Lawrence's yellow car, but when I stopped brushing my teeth I could hear the fog-smothered, cork-popping sound of the racket on the ball. There were no voices at all, and the popping came at the usual intervals.

The following morning the drumming of the shower in the bathroom woke me up. I thought it must be Lawrence and that I'd slept right through his alarm. But Lawrence usually took his shower later, after he'd put in an hour or two of practice, and I was wondering about this when I heard his desk alarm go off. He was still in his bed—I heard him roll over and shut it off. Then I heard Proctor's wet feet cross the floor. He called out a cheery "Good morning!" to Lawrence, and while Lawrence was getting up I could hear Proctor bouncing a ball on the floor. When Lawrence was ready to go Proctor said, "Hope these foggy mornings don't warp your rackets, old man," but Lawrence did not reply, and they went silently down the stairs.

When they were gone Lundgren said, "I do hope, sir, these damp mornings don't shrink your imported jock straps!" and snapped the elastic band at his pajama waist.

I didn't want to lie there thinking about it, so I got up, went over to the mess hall, and did a little reading till the cafeteria line opened up.

All that week the fog rolled in from the sea and hung around the treetops until late in the morning, when the warm clothes you'd put on early in the morning were suddenly too hot. One morning Lawrence's car wouldn't start. He and Proctor had to walk the half mile to the courts and then walk back. A day or two later, late at night, one of Lawrence's strung-up frames split open, making a sharp, twanging sound like a broken piano string. Lawrence got out of bed to see what had happened, then went back. In the morning he was up again at six, and Proctor, with the racket he had borrowed, stood out in the hall, fanning it at the air, and waiting for him.

Then we had a short spell of dry wind off the desert, a high brown haze screening off the mountains, and a fine film of dust, like face powder, on everything in the rooms. The glare was bad, and, sitting in the classes, we would turn our eyes from the windows or wear the dark sunglasses they were selling cut-rate in the Co-op. The first morning of the wind, from the bathroom window, I could see the tennis courts and Lawrence's car, but I couldn't see Proctor anywhere on the court. I thought he might be in the wash, looking for a ball that had bounced out. Then I saw him. But he was not on the court. At the number one court they had put up some bleachers to seat about thirty or forty people, and Proctor was seated on the plank at the top. He was leaning forward, on his knees, watching Lawrence serve. Back in the seat of the car I could see his borrowed racket, strung, as Lundgren said, with butcher's twine, and Lawrence's white sweater tossed over the steering wheel. Lawrence went on serving until he ran out of balls, then Proctor picked them up.

Over the weekend it was foggy again, and I went to see a night football game with Proctor; the high punts would disappear in the fog and made the game interesting. After the game we walked back across the campus to the Sugar Bowl. Proctor usually liked the

girls better than football, and when he'd asked me to go
to the game I'd thought I'd better go. I knew there was
something on his mind. We sat in a booth at the back
of the room where the upperclass dates were dancing,
and we could hear the music through the backside of
the radio.

Proctor wanted to know if I had noticed anything. I
said I had noticed that he'd taken up tennis. He didn't
mean that, he said, and neither did he mean the usual
sort of gossip, but he just wondered if I happened to
have noticed anything. About what? I said. About Lawrence, he replied. I said the only thing I'd noticed about
Lawrence was that he really minded his own business.
I guess that does for me then, Proctor said. I said I
didn't mean any more by that than what I'd said. The
trouble with a bloke like himself, Proctor said, was that
he talked so goddam much all the time that when he
finally had something to say, something important, nobody would listen to him. I said I thought there might
be a touch of truth in that. Proctor said that what he
had to say dealt with Lawrence, and he had picked up
the idea that I sort of liked Lawrence.

I said I admired him very much.

That wasn't what he meant, Proctor said. Any goddam fool could admire Lawrence, but *liking* Lawrence
was something else again. He did. He had the sneaking
notion I did too.

Well, I wouldn't say that I *disliked* Lawrence, I said.

Let's take a walk, old man, Proctor said, and then I
let him pay for my hot chocolate. I knew he was currently sensitive on that point.

The fog was not rain, but the mist was so heavy that
it gathered in drops on the leaves, then fell like rain on

the gravel along the walk. Where the path cut in between the orange trees on the campus Proctor stopped. "You mind if I smoke, old man?"

"Not at all," I said, but right up to that point I didn't know that he smoked. A quarter-miler who expected to run a fifty flat shouldn't smoke.

"I don't inhale, old man," he said, "and I don't smoke unless I really have to." He took a single cigarette from the pocket of his shirt, a pack of paper matches, and lit it. When the match flared up I thought his face looked sweaty, but it might have been the fog.

"Old man," he said, blowing out the smoke, "couple mornings ago we were out on the court—*he* was out on the court, and I was sittin' in the bleachers, watchin' him." He stopped, then said, "I found it was better to get clean off the court while he was serving, then go in and pick up the balls when he was through."

"I see," I said.

"Well, I was sittin' there waitin' to do just that. He threw up a ball, caught it, then said, 'Old man, perhaps I better tell you.' 'Tell me what?' I said. 'My right arm, old man, is a bit longer than my left one.' I didn't know what in the hell to say, so I said, 'So what?' 'It's from the tennis, old man,' he said, 'the right arm is a bit overdeveloped.' He put his palms together, out in front, and showed me how his right arm was about an inch longer. 'Well, I'll be goddamned,' I said. 'I'm a little touchy about it, old man,' he said, 'so I rest the hand on my hip. You've probably noticed that,' he said. 'Hell no,' I said, 'never noticed it at all.' "

"I think you do notice it," I said.

"Hell yes," Proctor said, "but I wasn't going to say so." He threw the cigarette away and spat out the tobacco crumbs. "You see, Foley?" he said. "You see what I mean?"

"Sure," I said, although I didn't.

"It was me that made him do it, old man," he said. "Me out there sittin' and starin' at him. If it hadn't been for me he might not have noticed it."

"I wouldn't say that," I said.

"I'll swear to God," he said, "he's never told another human being. I'll swear to God I'm the only man he ever told."

"You couldn't help that," I said.

"The hell I couldn't," he said. "If I hadn't been there he'd never have said it. If I'd shut my goddam big horsy mouth he'd never said a word."

I didn't deny it.

"I feel like hell," he said. "I guess I just had to tell someone."

"I know how you feel," I said and raised my right hand toward his shoulder, but whether he saw that or not he pulled off. I dropped my hand. "Well, I don't think anybody else needs to know it."

"What I want," said Proctor, "what I want is for *him* to feel that way."

"I think he probably does."

"Jesus Christ, old man—isn't he wonderful?"

"He's quite a character," I said. I'd heard somebody call him that.

"He's got *it*," said Proctor. "He's really got *it*."

When I didn't reply to that he said, "Goddam it, Foley, I don't mean money. I don't mean all that goddam barbed wire."

"I know you don't," I said.

"I just wish to Christ I thought so," he said and suddenly bolted off, running, and I heard his shoes crunch in the wet gravel.

The cigarette he had dropped was still alive in the path. As we were out of bounds for freshman smoking I stepped on it. Not far ahead he stepped off in the grass, where I couldn't hear him running, and I stood there in the fog, listening to the leaves drip on the walk. When I got near the dormitory I could hear music blowing down from the dance at Phipps and see the car lights on Foothill barely creeping along in the fog. Proctor was in the shower, singing, when I got to the top of the stairs.

FOLEY: 4

Above the pyramid of oranges, grapefruit, and bananas interlarded with sheets of tissue paper and tinfoil, the hands of the clock said 10:17. Foley took out his father's watch, saw it was three minutes fast, said, "Ahhhh," and returned it to his pocket.

"Black coffee, right?" said the clerk.

"Right," said Foley.

Clerk smiled and winked. Foley returned it. Big, rawboned Swede, three kids out in Queens, always asked Foley how things were growing in the country. Seemed to have picked up the idea that Foley was some sort of country gentleman.

"How's the country?" he said.

"Little warm," said Foley. "How's it in Queens?"

"Hot," he said. "Plain Danish, right?"

"Right," Foley replied and watched him turn and flip tongs, flip plate to go under Danish, turn and flip fork before spearing chip of butter, flip knife before placing it on counter. As if trying its weight, dipped, then raised coffee cup beneath spout of coffee, spilled some into the saucer, emptied saucer into drain, spilled a little more from cup sliding it down the counter, followed by cup of sugar cubes that caromed off menu rack. Waste motion? No. Male lead in the Schrafft's midmorning ballet.

Into his coffee Foley dropped one cube, stirred, then

crunched it with his spoon. Three lumps of wrapped
sugar he dropped into the coin pocket of his coat. Habit
formed during war. Needed it himself. Single man
and bachelor expected to give his sugar coupons to
faculty wives with sweet-starved babies. Faculty men
lost weight, fattened wives explained by sharp starch
rise to get same food value. On the raw end of the Danish he had sliced Foley spread the butter, took a bite.
Turned over in his mind, while chewing, the problem
of a lonely lunch. Lou Baker was out. Proctor was out.
(They were in bed, that is, together.) Which left
Richard Dickie Livingston or Allen Blake. Dickie
Livingston had money, time, and excellent taste but
required a rather strong palate. The last time Foley
had called him, at his New York place, his wife's Fili-
pino had answered, Foley had given his name, then
heard the voice of Dickie.

"Finkel's Fortifying Leechbake on the Hudson, good
morning! Patrick O'Casey speaking."

"Look—" Foley had said.

"Fear of sex and Semitism," Dickie had continued,
"allergic symptom nine-oh-nine! Refer you to Glossary,
New and Revised Edition of 'Livingston's Manual
Modern Semitic Warfare.' There you will find that
Livingston is a bastard, Lou Baker is a bitch, Foley a
spineless egghead, but Jesse L. Proctor is a long-suffering, wall-weeping Jew. He cannot be a bastard, an egghead, or a bitch, because that would be anti-Semitic.
All men are brothers, saith Saint Gide, except those
who are really fond of each other."

"You through?" Foley said.

"Sonny," Dickie said, "I'm the only man you know
without a trace of concealed anti-Semitism. All out in

the open. Clear and sunny as a day at Jones Beach. Where'll we eat lunch?"

They went to Town and Country, where Foley liked the popovers, and Dickie talked for an hour or more about this guy Proctor. He couldn't leave him alone. He couldn't leave him alone because Proctor had never struck back. Not a blow. As much as any man might, Dickie Livingston had shot another man down, like a bird in flight, clipping him in a way that left him living but without use of his wings. And what had Proctor done? Nothing. He had not struck back or taken another shot at himself. He had become, after twenty years, J. Lasky Proctor, importer. So Livingston's prank, the neatest trick of the decade, had proved to be the trauma of two lives. Life seemed to have stopped, for prankster and victim, right at that point.

Dickie had proved to be a very durable playboy, gray at the temples and the liver, yet a boy at heart; but it had always been the 4th of May, 1929. The night before the big prank, like the rally before the big game. But now something had happened, the obscure Jew was in the eye of the TV camera, and the revenge he had put off for twenty-three years was there in his lap. All he had to do was mention, no more, the name of Richard Livingston. The Park Avenue playboy, sometime husband of Pamela Crowley, the tin-can heiress, who had had her pretty hands in all the good causes long, long long ago. Just mention the name, that was all, and leave the rest to the Senator from Wisconsin. But J. Lasky Proctor mentioned no name but his own. Was he protecting Lou Baker, Dickie—or his own buried past? The one that they had waited, for nearly twenty years now, to sprout. Foley didn't know, he had no idea, but with the pictures of Proctor in the morning papers he would not be having lunch with Richard Livingston.

That left Allen Blake, Foley's publisher. There was a time when Foley called Allen Blake fairly regularly. Just about as regularly, Blake took him to lunch. They usually went to Cherio's, where they would see other editors and authors, including Max Perkins, who might be sitting on a stool at the bar, alone. Blake was something of a kidder and liked to say that he had brought Foley there at a certain risk, what with Perkins and the boys on the look for new talent and that sort of thing. That was pure baloney, but Foley loved the smell of it. He often saw some of the big shots of the literary world, heard the latest gossip that was being circulated, and came away with raw material that he could polish up for the faculty teas. Foley was the only man on the campus with a book that anybody had a corner on, or could give you the impression of how a certain author struck him, personally. But after several years of this it began to taper off. Foley went on calling, of course, and Blake was always simply dying to see him, but right at the moment, as a rule, he was all sewed up. So Foley stopped calling, and in the past few years Blake stopped sending him that Christmas book, or special Christmas card, that the house mailed to their authors every year.

Foley hadn't called Blake in four or five years, but he had never forgotten the number, and he seldom came to town without its crossing his mind that he *might* give him a ring. He had even gone so far as to work out in advance what he would say. He had gone even farther— he had worked out what he thought Blake would say.

He would call, get Blake's secretary, and casually tell her that Peter Foley was calling.

Then he would hear Blake's voice, and he would say, "Allen, this Foley."

"Well!" Blake would say. "Well, well, Foley. Speaking of the devil, I was just talking with Lewis here about you. You remember Lewis?"

"That a fact?" he would say, not remembering Lewis.

"Lewis was saying good deal nostalgia right now. Good deal fresh interest in the twenties. Said we ought to get busy and set a fire under you."

"Well!" Foley would say, then he would clear his throat and say, "As a matter of fact, Allen, started a sort of little fire of my own several weeks ago. May be part of this feeling. Some sort of spontaneous combustion. Anyhow, I'd say it was going along pretty well right now—"

"Well, I've never heard sweeter music," Blake would say. "I'd say that's the best news I've heard in weeks."

"Ought to have it in hand next month or so. Last chapter pretty important. Whole goddam book sort of hangs on it. Without the right summing up might wonder what the hell the book's all about."

"I remember your pointing that out," Blake would say.

"Well, I think I'm on the right track now," he would answer.

"That's the greatest goddam news I've heard in months," Blake would say. Then he would add, "Just glancing here at my schedule. See that I'm sewed up as hell right at this point. Big Fall List conference coming up this week. You picked a hell of a week."

"Understand that," Foley would say. "Just thought I'd give you a buzz and tell you how things were going."

"Best goddam news I've heard in years," Blake would say.

"Well, be seeing you, Allen," Foley would say, then hang up quick before something spoiled it, or Blake might ask him just what day the ms. would come in.

This conversation often seemed so real—if he was sitting in a bar or at the back of a movie—that Foley sometimes thought it had actually taken place. He might take the train back with the idea that he was all set to get to work. On that last chapter. The one, that is, that would sew the book up. A book that would go down in literary history as the one that really threw light on the twenties, on the forces, that is, that gave the life and art of the twenties their form. The force behind Hemingway, Fitzgerald, and Lawrence, behind Lou Baker, Proctor, and even Dickie, and behind— perhaps a little far behind—Peter Foley himself. The flickering rites of spring that sputtered in Foley but burned with a gemlike flame in Lawrence. The buttered Danish on his lips, Foley paused, murmured:

> "Young men are a corn dance, a rite of spring, and every generation must write its own music, and if these notes have a sequence the age has a style."

Who said that?

Peter Nielson Foley.

Where could it be found?

Near top of last, or next to last, page of manuscript now lying in grate of his fireplace, unpublished, unfinished, and tentatively titled "The Strange Captivity."

Above statement led up to the following:

> The great style, the habit of perfection, united George Herman Ruth and Charles A. Lindbergh, Albie Booth and Jack Dempsey, Juan Belmonte and Jay Gatsby, and every man, anywhere, who stood alone with his own symbolic bull. He had his gesture, his moment of truth, or his early death in the afternoon.

Foley his own matador. The graduate seminar his arena. The yellow pages in the fireplace his moment of truth.

Into his Schrafft's paper napkin, folded, he blew his nose. He stuffed the napkin into his cup, placed a dime on the counter, and as his right hand fumbled for the check his left hand snitched five more sugar cubes from the bowl beside his water glass. Easy did it. Dropped cubes into left-hand pocket of his jacket as he asked cashier for paper matches. Outside, in the basket near curbing, he tossed cellophane wrapper of his second panatella on the face of J. Lasky Proctor, smiling up at him. *Times* photo. Deeply eroded profile, dialectical gaze. An elderly man, in torn seersucker jacket, casual as a dog passing fire hydrant, reached into trash bin and swished paper from beneath his gaze. Folded it neatly, like train conductor, and slipped it into his pocket for later perusal. Clock at the front of the station read 10:49. Foley turned, without lighting his cigar, and walked to the north.

On Fifth Avenue, near Lord & Taylor, spirit of the city of New York touched Foley, and he walked against the windstream of oncoming traffic with long strides. Sky soft cobalt blue through filter of traffic gas, slight smarting of the eyes. Often walked into people, friends and enemies, hadn't seen for years. Girl from Vienna, big, strong kid with piano legs, cornhusker's hands, callused from pulling the weights and the parallel bars; hadn't seen her since the days of his ex-change conversations at the Studenten Klub, on Schot-tengasse. One day *Colonel* Lundgren—high on a double-decker bus, wearing transparent raincoat over his chest of medals, firm, set expression of man who was beaten but would not give up. Cropped, sunburned hair, pocked, windburned face, with fingers of brown hand drumming on lid of his hat. Another day Jill Rote, girl at Phipps, who had dated Proctor but talked about Lawrence, name on masthead of *Life,* hoped that *he* was doing something interesting. She meant *also.* Air of Girl Scout leader with ink-stained finger on pulse of the world. Every day some Tom Buchanan, modern version, man whose last big moment had been in the backfield, shoulders hunched from invisible goalposts he had never put down.

One's own kind. Other animals strangely invisible. According to Lou Baker, world was an ark with all the animals on their proper levels, and these were the spec-imens, naturally, that one met. Any day now, soon, the youngsters he had spoon-fed the culture-pabulum. See in their eyes, stronger than their own shame, pity for Foley and his unpublished future.

Very thought of that made him pull into a lobby, stare at the ranks of shoes. Hand-crafted, hand-boned, hand-oiled and polished, urban-suburban casuals, masculine loafers, for indoor-outdoor athlete who did not read the seed catalogues. Bench-made by old cobbler in mural-size photo, flashbulb shining on his mussy white hair, honest sweat on his forehead from honest toil, tight-lipped smile due to nails in his mouth, and frank, folksy glint in his steel-rimmed eyes, old Yankee stock, sleeves rolled on white arms showing sailing ship, a clipper, leaving ever-snug harbor, thumbnail black on hand holding leather laces, craft-soiled apron with two pockets for nails, loops and hooks for tools of his craft, but on his own tired, arch-cracked feet machine-made shoes, made very poorly, with hand-crafted egg-shaped hole to exhibit homegrown corn.

Attached to photograph blown-up statement from Paid Advertisement in *Life*. Foley tipped forward, as if bidden by guide, to note eight cardinal points of bench-made shoe. Sacred-profane power of printed word. Thou shalt not kill nor live through the winter without enriched bread, homogenized milk, and new scientific filter that took out of smoking everything but the cost. Through shoe-store window, looking north, Foley saw Allen Blake, hatless and hope-borne, crossing street against light with his hand on the shoulder of up-and-coming author featured in last week's Sunday *Times*. Flight. He went out side entrance, back from where he had come.

Walked south on Sixth Avenue to Fortieth Street, headed back toward Fifth. Morning sun was warm and pleasant on freshly sand-blasted front of the library and on walnut-stained head of old man with a white beard. Venerable, high-domed, bum and sage, cane crossed on lap, right leg crossed on left, brown cotton sock showing through hole in sole of the shoe. Out of cradle endlessly rocking, comradely and phony sage of the open road. Pigeon feeder and urban conscience of passing captains of industry, wondering what he knew,

wondering what he read, wondering, by God, if the
old fool was right. Old man's flabby body tolerably
nourished by Salvation Army and Sisters of Mercy,
but his soul powerfully sustained by envious, troubled
glances of passers-by. Age could not wither nor custom
stale time-honored mask of venerable senility. Bearded
saints over curtain in high-school auditorium, hail!
Longfellow, Whittier, Smith Brothers Cough Drops,
and Father Time, all hail! Take that story of Lou
Baker, a child in Billings, Montana, taken by mother
to Salt Lake City, where she saw, near Mormon
Tabernacle, old man with long beard.

"Mother, there's God!" she cried. And no joke. Any
old white beard, in rags, meditating, is where He sits.
Eye of heavenly needle has leakproof valve to keep out
beardless giants like Hearst and Baruch.

Patriarchs, circuit riders, wagon trains headed west-
ward, tablets of the Law broken and unbroken, Found-
ing Fathers, Old Granddad, Socrates and Moses, lice-
ridden old men with thatches of white hair, socks that
do not match, bird-dappled shoulders, hair growing
from ears like Old Saint Stieglitz, all procreant spirit-
ual heirs of Ouspensky, Blavatsky, and Mary Baker
Eddy, Kahlil Gibran and the United Nations, deduct-
ible but ineluctable modality of the visible.

Coldness of the stone where he sat made Foley think
of piles. He arose. Had been warned by his mother
not to sit on curbing, never doubted its truth. He
watched a southbound bus, panting at the curb, take
on a boy and girl in for a day in the city. The boy's flannel trousers wrinkled from the long morning ride with
the girl in his lap. While the boy paid the fare the girl
went to upper deck and took a seat at the front, hat in

her lap, hair blowing, plain face and brown freckled arms. As boy dropped into the seat at her side he slipped an arm along the back of it. Plain freckled face, but not in his eyes, and no matter that her lips were chapped when he kissed her.

No matter? No, not in such eyes. It was Peter Foley who had laid down the law for it. Known as Foley's Mystical Law. When the world went up in smoke, the smoke would have this peculiar property. It would not, because of such eyes, be what it seemed. According to Foley's Law, what had been loved or created would be part of it.

He had told them. He had told them when they asked for it. They had asked the usual question, and, gazing at their pleasant, vacant faces, he had told them that nothing of any importance was decided by a vote. A judgment. On their goddam majority attitude. Their eyes had bugged, baiting him, and one had said, wasn't it by a vote that works of art were judged? Wasn't it by a vote of informed opinion that they were kept alive? Foley had taken out his father's watch, gazed at its face. They waited. They knew that he would now make a fool of himself. Then, in a luminous calm, he had told them that one hundred million votes, or five hundred million votes, or a solid vote of all the voters in the world, would not change, by a comma, the nature of a work of art. One man alone, the artist, determined that. Whether it was good or bad, mortal or immortal, was up to him. Artists, not votes, were responsible for works of art.

That was all very well, one had replied, that was all very well in the world of art, but what about the world in which they lived? What if the voters decided to burn all these immortal works? As they had in the past. As they well might decide again.

Foley had been aware that a froth had formed on his dry lips. Like a madman. Very likely how he had looked. Like a madman, nothing would shut him up. Once a work of art existed, he had told them, once it had been imagined, truly created, it was beyond the reach of vandalism. *They* were not, *he* was not, the un-created world itself was not, but what had been hammered out on the forge of art could be hammered to pieces, burned, bombed, or ignored, but it could not be destroyed. The outward form could be shattered, become smoke and ashes, but the inward form was radio-active, and the act of disappearance was the transformation of the dark into the light. Metamorphosis. The divine power of art. So it was meaningless for them to talk, as they did, of the lost plays of this man or that, because whatever art had touched, and made quick, was never truly lost. In the order that mattered, *their* order, they were there with those that had survived. Out of their reach, but not out of their lives. When the world went up in smoke, as everyone predicted, the creations of the human imagination would be in that smoke and give it a peculiar property. Light. Bomb-strewn seeds of immortality.

Foley looked up to see the light change, the bus jerk forward, the girl rock to the east, the boy to the west, as if something had suddenly gone wrong with gravity. The girl's brown hair swept the boy's flushed face, and he pointed, with a wagging finger, at the old fool seated on the bench in front of the library. Sun gleaming on the book lying open in his lap, shimmering halo of white hair. Struck the boy as funny, the girl as sad.

A swirl of traffic gas and wind combed her hair over her face, and the boy tipped her head back, as if he would kiss her, and her eyes were closed, her lips parted—but no—no, not yet, and with her head resting on his arm she opened her eyes and saw his finger pointing at the Empire State.

THE CAPTIVITY: V

The day after Thanksgiving we had a blow with a sleetlike rain that slapped on the windows, and when the sky cleared there was snow on the mountains to the north. All the frosh on the campus who had never seen snow took the day off. But it was gone before they got up to it, unless they drove all the way to Baldy, where the Cucamonga range cast a shadow that kept the sun off the slopes. We had all seen snow, in our suite, and smiled with good humor at those who hadn't, or who had seen it but couldn't wait to get their hands in it.

As a matter of fact, the snow looked different up there on the mountains than it did in Chicago, and some of those who knew snow went along just to check up on it. In the afternoon it got hot, we all took sunbaths on the football field, and watched the snow line on the mountains edge up toward the top. With Lawrence's glasses, which Proctor had borrowed, we could see the dark spots where the snow had melted and the steam, rising like smoke, where the rocks were hot. We didn't see any frosh, but we saw some wheel tracks along the ice-house road.

I was taking a shower back in the dorm when the phone rang. When I answered, the voice asked for me. Would I be able to stop by the dean's office immediately? I said yes, yes, I would, then stood in my room, facing the window, wondering which mid-semester exam I had failed. On my way over to the dean's office I tried to think of the best way, if there was a best way, to let my mother in on the bad news.

The dean had two doors to his office, one at the front where he let you in and one at the back, a sort of arbor, where he let you out. Nobody going in wanted to face those coming out. He came to the door himself and asked me in. The dean was a short, businesslike man, with nearly white hair at the temples, but so black on top the story went around that he wore a wig. He was very kind, asked me about Chicago, said how much he had personally liked my father, and how pleased they all were that I was preparing to take his place. Then he took off his glasses and placed his fingers on the bruised bridge of his nose. He was obliged, he said, to take me into his confidence. He didn't at all like to do this, it placed a great strain on the incoming student, but in the circumstances he felt it was unavoidable. He would have to pledge me, of course, to the utmost secrecy.

He looked to see if I agreed to that, then said that he had selected me, rather than my other roommates, because my record, so far, was impeccable. All of my teachers had spoken of this fact. But one of my roommates, unhappily, seemed to be having considerable trouble, which was probably due to the newness of college life.

The dean stopped there, and I waited for him to mention Proctor's name. I had often wondered when he found the time to do his work. He never missed a dance, and he washed dishes four hours a day. It was a very serious matter, the dean continued. Charles Lawrence came from a distinguished family, and it was well known that he had a very unusual mind. But he seemed to find it hard to put it to work. There was tennis, of course, but it seemed to be more than that. There was also the fact that Raymond Gans, an uncle of Charles, was a trustee of the college and personally responsible for the sprinkler system and the night lights around the football field. The problem needed to be handled, the dean said, with a great deal of tact.

"Just what is the problem, Mr. Nichols?" I said.

The dean opened his desk drawer, took out several theme papers, and passed me the one on top. The sheet was folded in the regulation manner, with Lawrence's name on the outside. On the inside there were two or three lines at the top of the page. The topic was:

REGARDS BERTRAND RUSSELL

and said:

> The works of Bertrand Russell give nice expression to lucid, forward-looking, remarkably shallow mind.

That was all.

"Does it sound like him?" said the dean.

"Not particularly."

"That seems to be our problem," said the dean.

I read the statement over, then I looked through the window of the dean's study at the frosh dormitory, the blind drawn at the window of Lawrence's room. Behind the blind sat his desk, his onyx pen-and-pencil set, his seahorse in the heavy paperweight, and the photograph of Dickie leering over the shoulder of the nude on his lap. It sounded like Dickie. I knew that without knowing how he would sound.

"The English papers are quite brilliant, but different," said the dean. "They seem to be concerned with his boyhood in Brooklyn. Remarkably well done"—he waved one in the air—"but—"

"You don't think he grew up in Brooklyn?" I said.

"There is no mention of it in the transcript."

"Lawrence has lived all over the world, Mr. Nichols, and he may have got to know somebody from Brooklyn."

"I'm glad to have you presenting the other side of it, Peter," the dean said.

"I know that Lawrence has had a very broad background, Mr. Nichols."

"We are anxious to do what we can, Peter, but we feel that we need something more to go on." He waved his hand at the paper I was holding.

"Lawrence is not an easy man to figure out," I said.

"We were wondering if you found that true," said the dean, and I thought he looked relieved. He reached for the paper I was holding, read the statement over, placed it with the others. "A brilliant mind, Peter," he said, "but extremely unorthodox."

"I'll see what I can do," I said.

"In strictest confidence, Peter, I'm afraid Lawrence intimidates Miss Loucheim. She doesn't feel that she's equipped to deal with him. We all feel that one of his friends, one mature enough to understand the situation—" The buzzer under the dean's desk sounded, and he stood up. "As soon as things quiet down a little, Peter," he said, "Mrs. Nichols and I plan to have you over. Mrs. Nichols knew your father. You are here for the holidays?"

I said that I was. Going back to Chicago, I said, was too great an expense. The dean said he thought I was very wise to look at it so sensibly, not to mention the free, undistracted time it would give me to work. He placed his hand on my shoulder as I went out the door. I went back across the campus and around behind the dorm to the football field. Four or five cross-country men were jogging around the track. I took a seat in the grandstand on the south side, facing the foothills and the mountains, the snow gone now except for the cap on Baldy's peak. The bright whiteness of the peak made the sky seem colorless. The foothills were nearly purple in the slanting light, spring green in spots from the heavy rain, and the shadows moved on the slopes like the hands of a clock. I sat there until I heard the supper bell ring in the dorm.

On the way to the mess hall I met Lawrence, walking along with his hands in his pockets, the chewed-off ends of his untied laces slapping on the walk. I waited for him to catch up, then we walked along together, under the new trees in the olive court, to where he opened the door to the mess hall and said, "After you, old man."

The next morning, following breakfast, I had to come back to the rooms for my books, and I was on my way out when Proctor came up the stairs. He came all the way up two at a time, and there was sweat on his face.

I waited till he got his wind, then he said, "This something I wouldn't tell anybody."

"Then why tell me?"

"I got to tell somebody."

"Which arm is it this time?" I said.

"He's takin' me with him," he said.

"With him?"

"Home for the holidays, old man. Home for Christmas. He's asked me to go along."

He watched my face to see how I was taking that. In his own face I could see that he didn't know how to take it. He wanted to know. He watched me for a cue.

"That ought to be mighty nice," I said.

"You think it's all right, old man?"

"I don't know why not."

He knew why not and said, "If his family didn't like Jews, would he ask me?"

"Of course not," I said.

"You really think so, old man?"

"Just so long as he asked *you*," I said.

"Christ's sake, old man, you think I'd ask him?"

I didn't answer.

"He asked me what I had in mind over Christmas, and I said I didn't have anything in mind. I didn't. So he asked me how I'd like to come home with him. I said, 'Lawrence, stop your kiddin'.' He said, 'I'm serious, old man.' I said, 'Look, where is it?' 'Back in southern Indiana, old man.' 'And how do we get there?' I said. 'I drive it in about three days, old man.' Then he said, 'Well—' so I naturally said yes."

"Well, that's that," I said.

"I can't believe it," Proctor said.

"They probably have a very nice place," I said.

"You think I'm just a crazy bastard, old man?"

"I'd have gone if he'd asked me," I said.

"Why don't I put it to him?" he said. "Why the hell not? More the merrier."

"I've been asked to meet the dean and his wife," I said. "Guess the dean knew my father. They've asked me to drop in on them during the holidays."

"That ought to be pretty nice too," said Proctor.

I agreed.

Then he said, "Foley, old man—"

"What's on your mind?"

"If you're going to be stickin' around," he said, "if you don't think you'll need that second pair of pants—"

"I'm pretty sure I won't," I said and went back to the door of my closet. I took the new pair off of the hanger, the pair I'd never worn, and tossed them to him. "I still got a pair," I said. "What the hell I need with two pair?"

"I tell you what we do," said Proctor, "we'll swap. You loan me the pants, I loan you my typewriter."

"I don't typewrite much," I said.

"Now's your chance to learn, old man," he said. "You got three weeks. You got three weeks to practice." He went off with my pants, came back with his typewriter. "The ribbon may be a little old," he said and opened the lid, peered at the ribbon. The bottom half was so chewed you could see the yellow sheet on the roller through it.

"I probably won't get around to it," I said, "but if I do I'll pick up a ribbon."

"I got to run," he said, ran, then stopped and said, "Keep it under the bed or somewhere, old man, would you?" I said that I would. Then I heard him go down the stairs, about four at a time, and out the front door.

I had my Phys. Ed. class in the afternoon, and on my way to the gym I passed Lundgren on his way to the field with his track shoes and vaulting pole. He was wearing his Long Beach High sweat pants and eating a Sportsman's Chocolate Bracer.

"Well, son," he said to me, "think you can bear up?"

"Under what?"

"Proctor's leaving us, baby. He's got a moral obligation. He's got a feeling that Lawrence needs him at Christmas. He feels that you an' me might make it alone, but Lawrence is a lonely cuss."

"He told you this?" I said.

"No, baby—just everybody else on the campus." He balanced the pole in his hand, tossed off the candy wrapper. "Lawrence ever mention any sisters?" he said.

I didn't answer.

"How you think it sounds better, baby," he said, "Lawrence and Proctor, or Proctor and Lawrence? Proctor and Lawrence sounds more natural, don't you think?"

I didn't know what to think, and in the spell-down drill with the Indian clubs I dropped out very early, which was not like me, and sat on the mats near the door from where I could see the snow cap on Baldy and the legs of Lundgren when he came down the runway and rose into the air. There was something on his mind, too, for he dropped out around ten feet.

Proctor and Lawrence got off after dinner on Wednesday night. That was a day early, strictly speaking, but they had about two thousand miles to drive, and by leaving at night they would cross the desert while it was cool. Driving day and night they would be in Indiana on the third day. A frosh named Crowell went along as far as Tulsa, and Proctor, to occupy his mind when he wasn't at the wheel, took along his copy of *The Story of Philosophy*.

Lundgren and I had one meal a day at the Sugar Bowl. On the way back to the dorm we would come up through the campus orange trees. The new crop of Valencias were dropping on the ground, and if they hadn't dropped, they would with a little shaking. We ate a couple dozen a day between us, and we both had a touch of the hives. Lundgren had it worse because there was wool in his socks and his army uniform.

We had the place to ourselves, but it took time to grow on us. During the day we might hear some of the maids mopping up the showers or the hallways, or the suction wheeze of the pump that was cleaning out the swimming pool. At night we'd hear the whine of the traffic on Foothill, and later, on the foggy mornings, the honking of the big electric cars.

Christmas Eve, Lundgren offered me one of his cigarettes. He had opened a fresh pack of Luckies and held it out toward me.

I took one, put it between my lips, and said, "What do you do?"

"Light it and suck on it like a titty," he said.

After Luckies I tried Melachrinos, for the flags that came in the box. To start the New Year I bought a pipe and a four-ounce tin of Three Nuns tobacco, and Lundgren bought a sack of Bull Durham, to roll his own.

I read all the books on my spring assignment, then I started on the books on Proctor's desk, but he had them pretty badly marked up and underlined. *This Side of Paradise* had pages I couldn't make out. Whenever Amory Blaine made a clever remark it was underlined. If Proctor had found it clever the second time around he had underlined it again. I recognized quite a few remarks he had made himself. His favorite word seemed to be "touché," which he put in the margins of all the pages, usually followed by a row of exclamation marks. At the top or the bottom he would jot down what he thought of the characters.

I finished *Peter Whiffle* on New Year's Eve, and I was still in bed, mulling it over, when Lundgren asked me how about a little hike. What he had in mind was getting up in the foothills, he said. Up there we would have a fine view of the valley, the signs of the zodiac, and any meteor shower, shooting stars, or comets that might turn up. We took along tobacco, hotdogs, coffee, and a supply of Sportsman's Bracers.

We got up to what they called the Summer House just before sundown. The house was gone, burned off in a grass fire, but the concrete foundation was still there, and the fireplace that had been at the east end of the club room. We watched the shadows, like an ebb tide, slowly cover everything in the valley, till there was nothing but the broomlike tops of the palms sticking out. Then they went under, the hills went under, and we sat with our backs to the fire, eating hotdogs and smoking our own brand of cigarettes.

Lundgren pointed out the planets, the constellations, the narrow band of the sky that the planets whirled in, and indicated about where the two of us were in the shape of it. I could see that talking did him good. In the glow from the fire it even seemed to me he had a good face. I wasn't struck by the pockmarks that covered it. I wondered how long it would take a girl, one of the smart girls at Phipps, to look at Lundgren, as I did, and

see only his fine points—his good teeth, his sky-blue
eyes, the way he could slouch like Gary Cooper—without troubling to notice that his complexion was not so
good. I had reached that point myself. I could be with
Lundgren without keeping my eyes off him. I wondered if Proctor, spending Christmas with Lawrence,
would forget that Lawrence's right arm was overdeveloped, or if that was why Lawrence had taken Proctor
home with him. To get used to it. To feel that Proctor
had stopped seeing it. So he could be with Proctor the
way I could be with Lundgren, sit and listen to him
talk, watch him roll his cigarettes, without thinking
what a shame it was that he had such a pockmarked
face. And as for himself, he might forget to notice
that Proctor was a Jew.

I let him finish with the sky, then I said, "Why are
you so down on Proctor, old man?"

"Et tu?" he said.

"Et tu what?" I said.

"This *old man* crap, baby."

"I don't see a hell of a lot of difference," I said, "between the *old man* crap and *baby*." I think that hurt
him. Besides, I didn't often swear. When I swore it
may have sounded stronger than I meant. "I know he
looks pretty bad," I said, "but he's not so bad as he
looks."

"Maybe I just don't like him," Lundgren said.

"I happen to know," I said, "that he's doing a lot for
Lawrence."

"We supposed to be doing something for Lawrence?"

"I didn't mean it like that," I said.

"Suppose we skip it."

"I happen to know," I said, "that Proctor is doing some of his papers."

He let some of the tobacco he was holding in the paper spill into his lap. "I'll be a sonuvabitch," he said.

"This is between you and me," I said, "and besides, I don't think it means much to Lawrence. It isn't like cheating. It's like Proctor's picking up his tennis balls."

"Jesus!" Lundgren said, and I could see that it made an impression on him. He rubbed his arms and legs as if he suddenly felt cold, and pulled me up. We kicked some loose dirt on the fire, wet it down a little with the last of the coffee, then made our way back in the tracks we had made coming up. On Foothill Boulevard the traffic was heavy, with snow on the cars returning from the mountains, and a car with chains had stopped along the road to take them off. They had a radio with them, and Guy Lombardo was playing one of Proctor's favorite numbers.

" 'A cup of coffee, a sandwich, and you, baby,' " Lundgren said and whistled it.

Proctor and Lawrence pulled in about sunrise that same night. We saw Lawrence right away, but not Proctor. He had shot a hole in his left foot with a big Colt revolver that he had been holding between his knees. He had been shooting at the rabbits that popped up and ran between the lights. That had been near Needles. Lawrence had driven it in two hours and a half. The hole went right through Proctor's foot, his rubber-soled buck shoes, and then through the floorboard. Lawrence had driven to the infirmary and carried him in. Then he had driven into town with the Colt revolver and reported the accident to the police, who called me up at the dorm—he gave my name as reference. They held him till it seemed reasonably certain that Proctor had shot himself, and not been shot by Lawrence, then they fined him for possessing an illegal weapon and turned him loose. Lundgren and I drove over and picked him up.

In the mail that morning we got the postcard that Proctor had dropped in the box at El Paso, showing a giant grasshopper and saying that they were having a hell of a time.

FOLEY: 5

Escorted by a coach-and-four advertising chocolates, Foley crossed to the shady side of the street, left arm brushing elbow of a woman in cloud of night-scented stock. Lou Baker's fragrance. Foley knew it well. Young man on her other elbow in charcoal flannels, patent-leather oxfords, chap at corners of his mouth, expression of comedian paid not to smile. Fayum portrait gaze of living on far side of the grave. Hand cupped to her elbow, wheeling her slowly, like Seeing-Eye dog. Walked her briskly, confidently, into air-cooled draft, along corridor between windows of cut flowers, inspirational pamphlets, and latest flood of how-to-do-it books. *How to Stop Smoking* on top. "How to Stop Letching" next big thing. At front of window, beneath advertising clipping, what looked like a compass, individually boxed. Foley stooped to read:

RECORDING ROSARY
Work & Pray
$2. P.paid.
(Auto clamp extra)
KEEPS TABS ON MYSTERY
Arrow points to bead to be prayed.
Car
Pocket or
Purse!
FATIMA ROSARY

Foley straightened with a sigh, loosened topcoat
button, walked away. Going north on Madison, left
the curb and walked in the street. Stopped at lights,
avoided fireplugs, made way for those who saw less
than he did, without actually seeing the things he
passed. Operating on his electric eye. Like passing cab
drivers with their eye on the ballgame at Ebbetts Field.

At Fifty-ninth, turning west, he could see the green
gap over the park. A policeman mounted on a horse,
a child with spindly legs holding up shreds of grass to
the policeman's horse. Also balloons, a bright cluster,
that seemed to suspend the peddler above the street
and beyond the balloons. Three horse-drawn cabs lined
up at the curb. Helping a young woman into first of
the cabs was tall, graying man with more courage than
Foley. About Foley's age. Old enough to know what he
was doing, that is. Courage to rent a horse-drawn cab
and take young woman for a spin in the park. Proctor
had taken Lou Baker. Lawrence had ridden down the
avenue by himself.

Once in his life Foley might have done it. Spring he
had signed the contract for his book. Had advance
royalties check in his pocket, rain-making impulse in
his heart. In the doughnut shop on the corner he had
called up Lou Baker, the corn-dance maiden, but the
phone had not answered, and his coin had dropped,
clinking, into the slot. Foley had sat there in the phone
booth watching other gallants go for the ride. Lacked
the guts, as it turned out, to go it alone. Lacked the
know-how, as it turned out, to make rain in the book.

Nearing the middle of the block, he stepped into
stale draft full of music. Fugue from Franck "Prélude,
Choral and Fugue," blowing from bookstore stacked

with remainders. But softly. Soothing savage breast
for possible sales. Walls hung with modern conversation
pieces, air full of transcribed classical pollen. Culture
by pollination. Painless. Dehydrated or sanforized.
As he dawdled between counters to the back, caught
sight of *Hound and Horn.* Single copy. Lou Baker, for
a year or two, had worked on the staff. Published
excerpt tautly titled "Disinherited." Now dated. What
did he mean, *dated?* Sense of having been—*having been
taken in.* Price on magazine forty-nine cents, so he
slipped it under several books on the counter, where he
might find it if he changed his mind on way back.
Turned to see clerk with saddle-leather tie pin eying
him. Button-down, too tight collar dating from odds
and ends sale at De Pinna's.

"Getting warm," Foley said and took out a
Schrafft's napkin, wiped his face. Clerk knew that.
Wearing Mexican ring hand-crafted in the Village, and
in spite of the heat cable-stitched pullover sweater. Living in windowless room where he let tap drip over
wilted head of lettuce in bowl in the bathtub. Argyle
socks drying on the faucet handles. Two liqueur glasses
from sale at Plummer's. As Foley idled toward the
front, clerk cruised around the counter to the back.
Foley watched him tilt over, shift pile of books, find
copy of magazine he had left there, and thumb through
rapidly for erotic illustrations he had missed. Returned
magazine to center of table, under Toulouse-Lautrec.
Take it home with him later, go over it carefully
while he sat on the john. Foley stepped outside, turned
as if name was called, but voice came from cab waiting
at the curbing. Yankee Stadium. Batteries for the afternoon game. In background Foley could hear sound of

foul ball slapping on screen of pressbox. Cab driver, noting he was listening, flipped up the flag on his meter, slowly drifted away.

When Foley talked about the good life in the city he didn't mean the city, he meant Central Park, and all he wanted of the park was a narrow green gap he could view from the window of a gray stone mansion. Below the window small trees, like celery stalks, wearing collars of garden hose and leashes of wire, as if taken in at night but curbed in the morning, like a good dog. Shaded street would be wet, with moist scent of early morning watering. Parked at the curb would be a wagon-wheeled electric, with flowers in the vases screwed to the doorposts, or an old Pierce-Arrow with the popeyed look of the fender lights. A chauffeur brightening up the brass with a cloth that smelled like an O-Cedar mop.

Foley's Fossil Diorama. Property of Peter Foley, born 1909: died 1929: corpse planted on the campus of quiet Quaker college, where it did not sprout. Spirit known to hover over scene of diorama, whimpering at night. Gatsby's dream, Proctor's trauma, like peignoir thrown to Foley as he soaked in the tub at St. Cloud, the night after Lawrence's death. Smelling strongly of girls, of the bags of sachet found in all the drawers of the guest rooms, smelling of caste, class, and coats of arms, Yardley soap, saddle-leather luggage, and the pollen-laden air over the olive court at Phipps. Lawrence laundry tag sewed onto the tail of it. Foley had slipped it on, easy enough, but couldn't slip it off. Had left it on, worn it wet and smelling, tails gathered in a bulging wad around his middle, under the linen coat and the pongee shirt all the way across Paris to his room. Swiped it, that is, in the American manner, like a piece of the Cross, Lincoln's ax or log cabin, or pocket said to be torn from Babe Ruth's pants. An object of magic, a pollen seeder, a hollow gourd full of the stuff that when rattled made the corn flower, the ghosts dance, and the dragon's teeth sprout like the rites of spring.

As if a finger had tapped him on the shoulder, Foley turned. Thought he had heard, would have sworn he had heard, some word spoken. No one stood behind him, but a small child, wearing a reindeer harness, peered at him through the bars of a playground, as from a cage. Gazed into Foley's eyes as if they were holes bored into his head. Poor damn kid, he thought, and smiled. But child did not smile. For a moment he stood fixed, powerless to act, like a specimen pinned to the wall, until the child's nurse picked up reins of his harness and pulled him away. Calmly, casually, Foley glanced at his watch, still keeping his father's time, then he ran for bus held up by corner light.

THE CAPTIVITY: VI

We had it nip and tuck with Proctor for four or five weeks. The shock was bad, and after the shock there was a run of blood poisoning, but that setback, as it turned out, may have saved his foot. They figured he was too weak at the time for them to amputate it. So he came through with his foot, but it would never run the quarter in fifty flat. The slug had smashed all the fine bones across the instep, and when they took the drain from the hole it looked as if he had been nailed to the cross.

That was the end of the great quarter-miler, and the new track shoes Lawrence had given him for Christmas hung by their laces at the foot of his bed like the small boxing gloves dangling on the windshields of taxicabs.

I had never seen him run without his sweat pants, or noticed him particularly in the shower, so I was surprised to see what beautiful legs he had. It made me wonder if a woman appreciated them. He had no arms to speak of, nor shoulders, but his legs were very nicely turned in the calves and like a good trotting horse where they met at the crotch. That explained why he made the racket he did when he wore corduroys. In a run much longer than the quarter mile he would need to be greased up between the thighs, like the well-bred horses I had seen in Chicago on the bridle paths.

When he was not so depressed he began to read and catch up on his work. He gave his papers to me or Lawrence to deliver, depending on the class. During the spell that he was sick, or depressed, I wrote the English and Civics papers for Lawrence—nothing was coming through from Princeton at that point that was fit to use. I wrote about Chicago more or less in the vein Proctor had written about Brooklyn, but much more acceptably, since it was known that Lawrence had a Chicago background. I had a note from the dean congratulating me on the good work. Proctor and I never discussed it, but when it was clear that I was doing so well, Proctor suggested that maybe I should keep it up. His own papers might get us into trouble; they were too bright. He was writing poems now as well as stories, most of them dealing with love, all of them with sad endings, but none of them reminding you of Lawrence. My papers reminded the dean of Lawrence quite a bit. They indicated, he said, that Lawrence was becoming more aware of himself.

Proctor and I never discussed certain details, but we worked out a program that would keep Lawrence in school. It called for handling some of Lawrence's mail. Every two or three weeks, as a rule, he would receive a big envelope from Princeton—he would, that is, unless Proctor or I headed it off. The envelope was full of papers Dickie Livingston had collected from his girls. They were usually from Vassar, Smith, or Barnard, but he also had a very smart number at Goucher, who would turn him out a fine paper to order, on anything. Lawrence would throw them into one of the bags under his bed. When he needed a paper he would take one out, retype the first page and put his name on it, then go through the paper making spelling corrections in his own green ink. It was a system of sorts but not very well worked out. It might have worked pretty well at USC, Illinois, or one of the big factories, but Colton was so small you couldn't get away with something like that. Proctor had seen that early in the fall, when he collected the mail. The only thing he could do was start writing the papers himself. Lawrence didn't seem to care where they came from, who wrote them, or even who saw through it. He left Vassar and Smith term papers in the seat of his car; they might turn up in the pocket of his coat, or anywhere. There had been nothing for Proctor to do but see that he didn't get more of them, and to do that he had to censor Lawrence's mail. That had not been hard, for Lawrence didn't seem to care about that either.

While Proctor was in bed I had to take care of that myself. As a matter of precaution I went through his car, cleaning out all the stuff I found in the rumble and taking out the front seat to get at the papers that had fallen behind. There were plenty. Some of them dated from 1924. I went so far as to clear out the top drawer of his desk. He sometimes left a paper there after he had finished retyping part of it. He didn't seem to give a damn. He had just forgotten that they were there. Except for French Survey, which he took up at Phipps, we had him pretty well organized by mid-February; a week or two, that is, before the freshmen took their physical exams. Right after the exams would come the first semester finals, which Lawrence would flunk, but his papers would be so good, we were sure, that he wouldn't fail the courses. So we had it all figured, we had it down as pat as you can have something like Lawrence, right up to the night that Lundgren tapped on the door of my room.

When I opened it he said, "Baby, how about you and me taking a little walk?"

I figured that some griped, pimply-chinned frosh had let the cat out of the bag. He had probably been smart and waited till he knew he had us all involved. That's what I was thinking, and as we headed for the wash, a sort of necking preserve behind the football field, I was trying to decide if I should write and break the story to my mother *first*. We poked along through the dark till we came to the Greek Theater. We came out on the stage, facing the curve of seats, and there was just moonlight enough to see the pairs of upperclass neckers, high at the back, under the blue and white Colton laprobes. Where we stood on the stage, just left of center, there were two rustic tables and several benches, left over from the Glee Club's holiday performance of *Robin Hood*. Lundgren dragged a bench up to one of the tables, and we sat down on it. He put his Bull Durham sack on the table, his papers, and about two-thirds of a Sportsman's Bracer he had started on the way over but decided to save. I've often wondered what the upperclass spooners thought of us. The moon was rising, and in the cold white light I couldn't see much of Lundgren's face but the blond top of his head and the white sweater he was wearing were very bright. In a clear voice he said that he had brought me out there to tell me the truth. I could hear the planks creak under the lovers who sat up to catch an earful of it.

He had been sitting in his room, playing with his magnet, when he turned and saw Lawrence standing in the door. Lawrence hadn't knocked, or spoken up, but just stood there with his right hand poised on hip.

"What's on your mind, Lawrence?" Lundgren had said. For certain reasons he never called him "baby." He admired Lawrence, but he reserved "baby" for people he liked.

"I'm in a bit of a jam, old man," Lawrence had said.

Lundgren said that he knew that so well he had agreed with it. He had nodded his head, and Lawrence had stepped into his room.

"I can't take it, old man."

Lundgren had naturally thought he meant the pace. In particular, the final exams that were coming up. "Oh, I don't know," he had said. "Aren't you in the upper bracket?"

"I mean the physical. I can't take it."

"The phys?" Lundgren had replied. "Why not?"

"Old man," Lawrence had said, putting his hand into his pocket, "I'll have to take you into my confidence."

Lundgren had just sat there, and Lawrence had gazed at the wall where Lundgren had drawn a target on the plaster. There were small holes in the plaster where Lundgren had stuck his compass, then drawn it out.

"What's the trouble?" he had said.

"Old man," Lawrence had said, "I got a dose of the clap."

"Christ!" Lundgren had jumped out of his chair as if Lawrence was so sick he might need it. But Lawrence didn't need it, so he had sat down again.

"Nothing urgent," Lawrence had said. "Responding to treatment. Got a little careless in the Latin Quarter.

Well under control, but there's still a little scar tissue."

"Christ almighty!"

"But I'm afraid an examination, old man—" he had said, and Lundgren had said, "Good God no, baby!" He had felt friendly toward Lawrence the moment he admitted to something like that. Lawrence had gone on to say that he didn't tell Proctor because he was young and it might sort of shock him, and he didn't tell me because he wasn't sure I was the type. But he thought Lundgren was more acquainted with the facts of life and was not the sort of man who would get excited when he heard the word clap. Lundgren had replied that he knew there were people with so little experience that they *did* get excited, but thank God *he* didn't, and then he asked Lawrence what he intended to do.

"I was thinking of shooting myself," Lawrence had replied.

The way he said it had made Lundgren's blood run cold. He had probably looked it, for Lawrence had gone on, "Not seriously, old man, just a small wound that would put me on the sick list for a short time." Then he had put his left hand into the air and said, "I hardly use this hand."

"Look!" Lundgren had said, but it had been sometime before he could speak. First of all, what the hell could he say? Finally he had cooled down and said that two accidental shootings in the same frosh suite might lead some people to wonder what the hell. They might think everybody in the suite was crazy, or something like that.

"I can see your point, old man," Lawrence had said, but he had just stood there looking down at his feet, in particular the foot that Proctor had drilled with the .45. Lundgren said it had given him the willies just to look at him.

"Look, baby," he had said, "suppose we think it over?" And Lawrence had said, much obliged, old man, just as if Lundgren had been the one with the clap and had to make up his mind. It had been too much of a problem for Lundgren to keep to himself. The more he had thought about it the less he knew what the hell to think.

"Christ made little apples," I said, to indicate what I thought about it, then I sat there and watched Lundgren roll a cigarette. It took him quite some time; his hands were so nervous the tobacco spilled.

"The crazy goddam booby-drawers, baby!" he said, and I could see that he was nearly overcome with admiration. He never cursed out anything he didn't admire a lot. He had something like a feeling of reverence for a man who could catch the clap. "The crazy sieve-brained romantic bastard!" he said in a voice you could have heard back on the campus. "He probably caught it from one of them goddam French whores!"

From the edge of the stage he flipped his cigarette into the dark side of the pit, turned on his heel and walked back into the wash, with me following him. There was not a peep, not a sound, from the lovers we left in the stands. It didn't seem at all strange, out there in the moonlight, that a man who played tennis without any ground strokes should naturally catch the clap, or something worse, from the Latin Quarter whores. It was just one of the chances that a man of that type would take. We walked back through the wash without any more talk, coming in from the back, across the football field, from where we could see the lights that were burning in the frosh dorms. But Lawrence, clap and all, had gone to bed. There was no light in his window, and it crossed my mind, as we went up the stairs, that now every one of us had something on Lawrence, good or bad. But it was drawing us together right when I thought we were falling apart. Now he had the clap, or at least scar tissue, and while he slept we would lie awake, wondering where the hell he got it and what it was like. He didn't seem to give a damn somehow, but we did.

"The hopeless goddam bastard," Lundgren said, but no more than a whisper, under his breath, because we could see the door to the room he slept in was ajar. We undressed and went to bed without turning on the lights.

On Washington's birthday, two days later, Lawrence disappeared. He got up from his desk, early in the evening, and I heard him speak to Lundgren, and Lundgren asked him if he would mind bringing back some hamburgers from Ma Slade's. He said he would, and we sat up waiting for them, but he didn't come back. When we got up in the morning we saw his unslept-in bed. He didn't show up all that day, so Lundgren called up the dean in the evening, pointing out the fact that Lawrence's car was gone and he was not in his room. The dean asked to speak to me, and I said that Lawrence had been feeling a little pressure, like everybody else, with the final exams coming up. That was all until Sunday evening, when an orange grower, over in the next county, found Lawrence's car parked under one of his orange trees. Everything that would come off or unscrew had been taken off it. The cops even found the holes that Proctor had shot in the turned-back top. The next morning the frosh physicals began, and in the evening papers there were pictures of Lawrence, with stories to the effect that he had probably been kidnaped. The police, however, said it looked like amnesia—they had stopped believing in kidnaping after Sister Aimee had *not* been kidnaped two years before. The Tuesday papers were full of more pictures, described the great wealth of the Lawrence family, and on Wednesday morning Mr. Raymond Gans, Lawrence's uncle, arrived on the campus. He brought along four or five Pinkerton men from Chicago. They spent one day picking up campus gossip, one day driving around and looking at the country, then they sat in our rooms playing pinochle and filing their reports. Mr. Gans called every hour from his room at the Ambassador in Los Angeles.

By Friday all the frosh physicals were over, and early Saturday morning, according to the papers, a half-starved, dazed college student, nearly crazy from lack of water and food, stumbled out of the sagebrush about a mile outside of Twenty-nine Palms. It was Lawrence, and he was in all the papers that evening. We had him back at school Sunday morning—we had him in the infirmary, that is, occupying the room right across the hall from Proctor. According to the papers, he was suffering from shock, but I couldn't see much of a change in him myself. If you didn't know Lawrence very well you might call it shock.

The story was that a couple of sailors, after thumbing a ride from Lawrence, had hit him over the head with a tire iron they found on the floor. Then they had taken his watch, his money, and stripped down the

car. The only part of the story that made much
sense was that he had been hit by a tire iron, and
around at the back, where he couldn't have hit himself.
He had been hit so hard he may have been out cold
several hours or more. Lundgren and I came to the
conclusion that he hired some thug to hit him over the
head, and that the thug thought he was crazy, and may
have stripped down the car. But there were also quite
a few holes in a story like that. When you were dealing
with a person like Lawrence you couldn't draw a line
around what might have happened, or say, as they
did, that he couldn't have kayoed himself. Monday
morning his uncle came out from L.A., and he was
there in the infirmary when Dr. Lynes checked Lawrence's heart, his lungs, and the bump on the back of
his head. Then he asked him to stand up and take the
test for hernia. He took it all right, and the doctor
gave him a clean bill of health.

FOLEY: 6

As the bus crossed Fifty-seventh Street the driver, swollen with a sense of power, malice, and adventure, ran past three stops, clipping one red light, and the swaying of the bus produced in Foley same effect as early morning coffee on an empty stomach. This sensation followed by lowered center of gravity in his bowels. About time. He had expected it earlier. Looked up at the familiar aspect of the street, suddenly transformed by the needs of the moment. Forty-ninth Street. Where would be nearest facilities? The great city of New York specialized in consumption but turned a prudish shoulder on evacuation. Streets of New York, unlike those of Paris, were not decorated with the pissoir kiosks, where the legs of men could be seen facing the facts of life.

Over the years—Foley rose from the seat, then braced himself at the hiss of the air-brakes—over the years he had given the problem considerable thought. The solution, a tentative solution, had come along with other relevant blessings when he became an author on a midtown publisher's list. Allen Blake's office was on the fourth floor, with the facilities right off the stairwell, so Foley could reach them without disturbing anyone. Girl at the desk, at the time, recognized him as one of "their authors." When this girl disappeared, and the one that took her place cast a cold and knowing

143

eye on Foley, he had resorted to a clever subterfuge. He took the elevator to the fifth floor, where there was no phone girl to spy on him, then walked down the stairs to the Blake facilities. As time passed, however, his sense of guilt increased. What he always feared might happen had happened, naturally. He had walked right into Blake standing there smoking a cigarette. It would not have been so bad if he hadn't caught Blake just standing there, like any office loafer, without the slightest suggestion of the literary life emanating from him. He looked played out. The shirt he was wearing had a tear in the back. It proved to be a faux pas, all around. Foley had to tell a big lie quickly, saying that he had stopped by on the chance that Blake might be in. So Blake had to lie, turning up with the whopper that he was there in the john brooding on a big problem, with the author in question waiting for an answer right at his desk. It had been so bad that Foley hadn't gone back for more than a year.

And then, as luck would have it, he had run into Blake washing his hands. Blake had seen him in the mirror, where Foley had seen Blake, and Foley had grimaced, as had Blake, then he had hurried on by and entered one of the booths.

As he had stepped inside he had heard Blake say, "In town for the day, Foley?"

"Yep," Foley had said, and that was all. It had been enough, as it turned out, and they each accepted the situation. The Foley in the john was no longer the author of an unpublished book. He was a professor, a tourist, trapped in the city for a day.

Passing Forty-ninth Street, Foley gave a sharp jerk on the cord. He wanted Forty-sixth, but the driver kept him on till Forty-fifth. There, because the light had changed, he let him off. Foley went across to Madison, where he paused to examine, in pipe-store window, imported English pipe knife in leather case. Reduced from three times its value to a little more than twice what it was worth. Foley had three pipe tools, but he had always wanted a knife.

As the light changed, walking east, found himself once more escorted by coach and four, hemmed in by big fellow with freshly powdered face, strong barbershop smell. To companion Foley could not see he said, "Why the hell is *free* love the most expensive?" Foley moved in close to catch the answer, but none was made.

They went south on the opposite corner, Foley went north. In the tiled lobby of the publisher's building Foley walked to the back, near side entrance to a bar, where he could duck in case Blake stepped out of the lift. He didn't, however, and Foley rode to the fifth, passed the offices of Tay-Koff, the miracle reducer, then padded down the stairs to the door that was blocked with a piece of wood. He stood a moment listening for sound of flushed john or crumpled paper towel. Hearing nothing, he entered, crossed the dim-lit room with his reflection bright in the mirror, and entered the booth beneath the ventilating fan. Latched the door, removed his two coats as one, hung them on the hook, and as he lowered to the stool thought he noticed spot move on the floor. Tobacco color. Staring, saw it move again. Go along the wall to where he saw the feelers waving. Saw it was a roach.

La cucaracha, voracious, nocturnal, and, in spite of the insecticides, immortal. Foley watched it cruise along woodwork, confident as a dog out for an airing.

But when it headed for the open, the no-man's land of cracked tile, he shooed it back. In God's name why? *J. Lasky Proctor, Salvage Operations.* Was that why? Dated from first cockroach Foley had ever known, personally. Chicago. Ludlow Terrace. Afternoon he had spent in Proctor's rented room. Foley had cut his hand on a metal ashtray, and Proctor had led him into the bathroom to rinse it off. Big room, small dirty sink in far corner, and Foley had sat on the stool, holding his hand under the water. Strong smell of chlorine and whiffs from coated piece of Lifebuoy soap. Bulb in ceiling as dim as glowworm trapped in a dirty glass. There were rings around the tub, like the banked turns on a track, but Proctor had his eye on something that was trapped there, something that moved. Foley watched him unroll several yards of toilet paper and lay down a ramp at the back of the tub, and the cockroach trapped in the tub ran up the paper ramp as if trained. It came up so fast that it nearly spilled over when it reached the top. Then it went around the wall side, skidding a little, because the game leg it had was dragging, and the room was so quiet Foley heard the drag of that leg. It went on to the soapdish, climbed in and out, then went up the wall to the ledge directly above it, along this ledge to a deep crack in the plaster, where it disappeared. Proctor rolled up the toilet paper he had put down, placed it back on the roll.

"Proctor Salvage Operations," he had said. "One poor goddam cockroach salvaged."

Kith and kin, perhaps, of the one Foley had just shooed into the dark. Another cockroach saved, another un-American act. FOLEY UNMASKED. *Sides with Red Roach against Common Man.* Behind a cigarette butt, its barricade, the roach turned to check up on Foley, and Foley strained to catch the glint in its eye. As its feelers waved, Foley intoned:

> "FOLEY AND PROCTOR SALVAGE OPERATIONS
> *Vermin a Specialty.*"

The door swung wide, a blast of hall air rocked the cigarette butt, startled the cockroach, and, feeling the cool draft blowing on his legs, Foley arose.

THE CAPTIVITY: VII

March was fairly quiet, except for Proctor's plaster cast going up and down the stairs. He proved to be about as pig-headed as Lawrence; he wouldn't lean on your arm, let you carry his books, or ride across the campus if he had the time to walk. When he rested on the landing of the stairs we could all hear him pant. Then he would lie out on his bed, the sweat drying on his hands and face, and a pretty strong smell emanating from the foot he had in the cast. The dirty toes, with the blackened nails, stuck out at the tip. Lundgren said he showed a fine, promising talent for suffering.

He hobbled out to the tennis courts, on his crutches, every afternoon. If Lawrence wasn't playing he sat in the stands, reading a book. Lawrence had lost his car for the rest of the semester, and when the tennis team had a match somewhere they let Proctor ride along as a sort of manager. He could sit with the sweaters and keep his eye on the extra balls. Nobody seemed to care much about frosh tennis, and it was generally agreed that Lawrence would get what he had coming when he ran into Crewes.

Crewes was a very tall, pimply-faced boy who wore a big white cap, the kind old men wear on winter cruises, and after living for more than ten years in California he was still sallow white. He looked a little underfed

and sickly, even out on the court. But he had a game so
effortless, and his timing was so perfect, that the head
of the racket seemed to contain all the strength he
might need. He stroked the ball with the same power
from both sides. His ground game was so deadly he
seldom had to trouble with his overhead. That looked
a little sloppy, he was so tall, and his long legs looked
awkward, but everything he happened to get his racket
on he put away. Off the court, he hit everything flat, a
sort of slapstroke without any top spin, which would
skid when it hit, and it always hit inside. The talk had
been all Lawrence, in the fall, but in the spring it was
all Crewes. He was thin and weak now because he had
grown too fast. When he stopped growing and gained
a little weight he would be unbeatable. He was that
already. He hadn't lost a set in the last two years.

Early in May, Lundgren vaulted twelve feet in the
frosh meet with Redlands, but the following week, trying twelve in practice, he came down the runway and
stopped the pole with his nose. It was something he
did at least once a year, so he tried to do it early. All
the skin peeled off his nose, and after the bandage had
been applied, which covered most of his face, you could
see that his eyes were turning black. That weekend he
couldn't see well enough to pole-vault, but he thought
he could see well enough to drive, so he borrowed his
uncle's car and we all went to Pasadena to see Crewes
play.

We sat in the bleachers along the service line.
Lawrence had seen the finest players in the world, so
watching young Crewes didn't upset him, but what we
saw worried the rest of us. Lawrence was very fine on
the court, with something that kept you looking at him,

but what you were watching wasn't the tennis so much
as it was Lawrence. But this kid Crewes was just the
other way around. He was nothing at all, but his tennis
was wonderful. He had arms like a girl, but everything
he hit was like a cannonball. He was still so awkward,
and young, that he didn't like to run. Watching him
play, you had the feeling that there must be something
wrong with his competition. This was not what you
felt about Lawrence. His competition often looked
pretty good. But he just went on and beat it anyway.
That afternoon this gawky kid Crewes won two love
sets in about twenty minutes from the fellow who had
taken eight games from Lawrence the week before.
There were no rallies to speak of, no volleys, and when
the kid served his last ball, a nice clean ace, there was
no applause. It looked too easy. We didn't talk about it
on the drive back.

In my own mind Lawrence's goose was cooked. I'm
not sure, either, that knowing that gave me much pain.
I think we all had the feeling that it would do him a
lot of good.

He didn't meet Crewes till the Conference finals, late
in May. They each headed a bracket, and came through
to the finals without much trouble, although Lawrence
was carried to 7-5 in a pair of sets. Proctor told me he
had hoped that three days of tennis would be hard on
Crewes. He was not at all strong, but there was no one
in the league to get him tired. They gave him just
enough exercise to keep him from getting stiff. There
was nothing insolent in his game, he ran around and
picked up all his own balls, and often seemed surprised
that the match had ended so soon. Nobody could wish a
kid like that bad luck. He simply had what it took, and

there was nothing to do but admire it. Lawrence had something too, but I don't think we felt it was going to be tennis. There was a limit to what you could do with that sort of will.

We had the singles finals on Friday, but there were no more than thirty people, including the players, around to see Lawrence brushed off. Four or five months before, half the boys in college would have walked over to Cucamonga, or into Pasadena, and paid money to see Lawrence get what was coming to him. But it had been coming to him too long. Everybody knew he was going to get it, and that was enough. They didn't hate him bad enough to stick around and watch it take place.

I sat with Proctor at the top of the bleachers, where we got the sun. Lundgren came along a little later, wearing his sweat pants and carrying his track shoes, a bright fresh bandage over his healing nose. The bags under his eyes were still curdled blue-black. We were there because we were still solid, and when the slaughter was over we had agreed that we would stand up and yell for Lawrence. It was just about the most we could do, and we were going through with it.

The warm-up before the match was very strange. You can't warm up with a man who never lets a ball bounce. But Crewes didn't seem to know that, and for three or four minutes we had some of the sweetest tennis anybody had ever seen. Lawrence stood at the net, and Crewes stroked those beautiful drives at him. They stopped right when they were sharp, Crewes spun his heavy racket, Lawrence called it and got the serve. He took the down-slope side, since he was not very tall and it helped his slice. But when he walked back to the

base line and bounced one ball, his back turned to the
bleachers, I felt exactly the same as the first morning
I had seen him on the court. He was out there alone.
Just Lawrence, the court, and the ball. For ten or
twelve seconds I thought we had it all wrong and that it
wouldn't really matter who Lawrence was playing or
whether, in the long run, Crewes was the better player
or not. Lawrence was out there alone. He was playing
against himself. The only game he knew was between
him and the ball.

But I didn't feel that way long. In the first game he
served just five times, every one of them sharp, well-
placed, flat serves, and four of them came back just a
little flatter, and right at his feet. He volleyed three of
them out. He hit one into the net. He put away one of
them but it looked like pure luck. Then he took two
points on Crewes' first service, but lost the next four in
a row, two of them aces that his racket didn't touch. He
won only one point in the next game. After just about
twelve minutes of play he was down 4-love. It was really
better tennis than it looked, but it looked bad for Lawrence. The kid just had it. He stroked the ball and it
worked. The worst of it was that Lawrence's serve, a
ball that gave other players so much trouble, seemed
to be made to order for Crewes' flat, slapping drive.
He put it out of play before Lawrence could move into
the court. Crewes won the first set 6-love, and they
changed courts.

Since Crewes was stroking the ball so well, any
player in his right mind would have modified his
serve or tried something else. But not Lawrence. It
was not like him to change. He went right on, robot-
like, hitting the sharp, flat, skidding serve that Crewes

would slap out of play in Lawrence's court. He couldn't seem to learn. It was clear to everybody how stupid he had been. Everything we had admired about Lawrence began to look like something simple-minded, a flaw in him, really, and not something admirable. A granite-like, subhuman pig-headedness. I think we all felt grateful to Crewes for clearing that point up. Lawrence was just plain dumb. Somehow we had all overlooked it. I even began to feel that I owed this kid Crewes a personal debt. He had opened my eyes. He had broken the spell Lawrence had over us. I thought I might even write Crewes some sort of letter, anonymous of course, telling him how much this little lesson had meant to all of us. I asked Proctor what the score was, and he said love-5. I wondered what I'd do when it was over and I had to yell for Lawrence.

Starting the last game, Crewes asked for some new balls. That was perfectly natural. It seemed more than that only in retrospect. It was Crewes' serve and he would naturally like to use some new balls. His first serve was a clean ace—Lawrence didn't even lean his body toward it, he just walked soberly over to the other court. When I studied his face I didn't remark any-thing. He looked just as cool, deadpan, and confident as he had at the start. But about half the crowd in the bleachers got up from their seats after that ace; they didn't want to be around when Crewes finished him off. They hurried off without glancing at the rest of us. Lundgren asked me what time it was, as if he had remembered a date himself, squeezed through the boards at the back of the seats, hung down by his arms, and dropped to the ground. I heard him go off at a trot through the dry brush. Proctor didn't budge, and the two of us watched Lawrence take Crewes' next serve, slap it back at his feet, then come in on the volley and put it away. It didn't seem important to me at the time, but I happened to notice, on that volley, that Crewes' racket turned a little in his hand. The volley wasn't quite clean, and Lawrence slapped it out of play.

As Crewes tossed up the next ball and served it, another five or six people got up and left, leaving about the same number in the stands. They were careful not to look at Lawrence as they walked off. They missed, that is, the turning point of the match. Not that we knew it at the time, but I was watching when Lawrence took the serve and stroked it back just as he had all afternoon. All afternoon that ball had been smashed back at his feet. It was not harder hit or better placed, but it was cleanly hit, very flat, and when the kid reached for it his racket turned in his hand. He took the ball on the wood and watched it float into the net.

There was nothing very unusual about that. It merely made you wonder why it hadn't happened more before. The racket was heavy, and Crewes was not very strong. Everything was the timing, the way he could take the ball just right. I had never seen the kid miss a shot, then stand there like a dubber looking at his racket, but after that miss he stood there a moment, strumming on the gut. Then he came to the net and wiped his sweaty hand on the towel. When he tossed the towel back on the post I saw him glance up, just for a second, at the player in the opposite court. Lawrence was standing at his ease, one hand on his hip. He was glistening with sweat, the band at his forehead had turned a wet, doughish color, but he had the same old look of poise and cool arrogance. No human being could believe he was down 5-love, in the second love set. And Crewes was human. I could see he couldn't believe that himself.

I saw him smile—not at what he saw, but because what he saw forced him to do something—and when that smile just stuck on his face I knew he was beat. He walked back to the line, served the ball well, and even stroked back the one Lawrence hit at him, but that was the limit—he dropped the next one into the net. So the score was 15-40 at that point. Everything he had, and maybe something he didn't, went into the next ball he served Lawrence, and when it came back he didn't bother to run for it. He just stood there, and the referee said, "Game Lawrence, one-five."

I don't know how many of us knew the jig was up. We weren't very many. There were only seven of us in the stands. I think Proctor knew it, and after Lawrence had served his first ball, an ace down the center, I think the referee saw it too. He took a look at his watch as if he thought the sets might run a little long. But they wouldn't. I could have told him that.

Later I heard one of the players say that Lawrence's game kept getting stronger, that he hit the ball sharper, and his flat serve had more pace. I don't think so. It was the same game from the start. It was always a killing game, and he simply never let up. But the man he was playing was a different player—he fell apart. When that racket began to twist in his hand he had a try at lobbing, he went in for slicing, and he mixed chops and pat balls for a spell. He was smart. He did everything Lawrence had failed to do. He did it all pretty well, but it didn't do him any good. When Lawrence put the last point away and the kid turned and threw his racket at it, you would no more applaud than if Lawrence had shot him between the eyes. Which he had. The boy wonder was a dead duck. The jig was up, and we all knew that the man with the finest game in the world was not the same as the world's finest tennis player.

Lawrence walked along between Proctor and me back to the dorms. I carried his rackets, Proctor had the balls he had used in the last set, and Lawrence wore the sweater with the leather on the elbows looped around his neck. The boys who passed us turned for a look at Lawrence's face. He looked about the same, except that he looked very good in a sweat. We sat around in the rooms until he had his shower, then we walked over to the mess hall together, where the news had got around and the shock had had time to wear off. When Lawrence stepped into the hall all the boys that were there stood up. There was no hollering or cheering to speak of; they just stood up. Lawrence put up his right hand, gave them that smile, then Proctor and I took the boy with the clap down the long row of tables to the one near the door, where he liked to sit. Lundgren waited on our table, and I saw him watching Lawrence with his bloodshot eyes.

FOLEY: 7

As he crossed Twenty-third Street a few drops of rain fell on his sleeve. He tipped back his head and a drop splashed on his face. A swirl of wind lifted the curb dust into the air, a cloud shadow darkened the corner, and east from the Hudson, like a jet diving, came the rolling sound of thunder. Big drops, widely spaced, puffed the dust at his feet. Paper boy on the corner slipping tarpaulin over his magazines. Afternoon editions featured tear-stained divorcée moment after her child, kidnaped by husband, reported safe. In pocket of blouse she was wearing Foley could see king-size pack of cigarettes and make out that she was smoking choice of discriminating people, Herbert Tareytons. Proctor gone from the headlines. Flood of news, like river of silt, left deposit over what had been news in the morning.

"Journal?" said the boy.

Foley dropped a coin on the pile, slipped one from beneath the weight, raised it over his head. Wind-whipped sheet of rain, as he walked south, hit him like spray of machine-gun bullets. Or did it? Stopped a moment to consider if that was right. Read it somewhere. Had never been hit by spray of bullets, but as very small boy stray jet from a fire hose had struck him like a wet sandbag in the chest. Rolled back his eyelids. Torn the flesh at the corners of his mouth.

Foley held the paper over his head and cold trickle
of rain ran down sleeve of his trench coat. Felt the cool-
ness where the wet knees of his pants rubbed on his
legs. Rain falling in wind-blown sheets with big hol-
lows, puffed out like a sail. Summer squall. He ran
along the wall of windows to the first open doorway,
ducked inside. Art shop, cards, reproductions along the
walls. Remembered how he used to send Lou Baker
every new Matisse. Did not remember stopping. But
he hadn't sent her anything for five or six years.

He stopped to look at the cards displayed in racks,
one rack labeled MODERN, mostly French, Gau-
guin, Cézanne, Seurat, and Picasso, vest-pocket remind-
ers of reproductions that hung in bus stations, lounge
cars, bedrooms for guests, hallways that were dark and
needed brightening up, dress shops that were chic,
coffee shops that were smart, bathrooms with color
matching shower curtains, and homes where the hair-
oil stains on the paper simply had to be covered with
something. And so they were. The French masters had
anticipated the need.

He found nothing there, but in a box on the counter, as if it had been painted over the weekend, a pair
of haggard lovers floating in a murky, grape-colored
space. The woman bore a certain likeness to Lou
Baker, the woman of sorrows, the Deirdre of Montana,
and the man bore a striking resemblance to Proctor,
the eroded saint. It was called "The Tempest," by
Kokoschka—and was one of those things. A somewhat
unpleasant expressionistic piece—if you thought, as
Foley did, of the pair of them as lovers—with the
flesh daubed on carelessly as if it were peeling off. And
yet lovers they were, very modern lovers, the eroded

salvage expert and his faded blond companion, now sleeping through the tempest that the Senator had brought down upon them. As the current Prince of Darkness, he had power over the elements. He had stirred up a tempest, and this pair of haggard lovers were caught up in it.

Was it uncanny? This painting was dated 1914. Foresight for Kokoschka, hindsight for Foley, but for the lovers, always at the still point, a timeless tempest in an ever-threatening sea.

"We have that particular item mounted and ready for framing," she said. Foley turned, but she kept her eyes off his face. Probably thought he was embarrassed. Odd picture for a man to be looking at.

"I think this little one will do," Foley replied and held on to it while he fumbled for some money, then changed his mind and let her have the card as he paid for it. While she walked toward the front of the shop he turned back to the rack. Photographs. Old and new. Some of them blurred. He peered at an old one—dating back, it was clear, before the fast-lens cameras— sharp contrast of the blurred hand and face but acid etched street detail. Curious feeling, therefore, that these people *existed,* that they were really *there,* but by now, as was clear from their clothes, short of some unusual miracle, some freak of longevity, they would be gone. On the card that he faced Foley could see the Seine, with the towers of Notre Dame. Curious and troubled sensation of the melancholy shortness of human life. River, trees, and towers of Notre Dame still there, but the blurred figures were gone. Who were they? Someone, at the time, had called them by their names. Must have felt as immortal as Foley felt—some-

times. Note on back of card said it was view of the
Seine, with towers of Notre Dame in the distance, but
no mention of the woman with the boa trailing in the
breeze. Just a suggestion of a smile, a living face, under the flowered hat. No mention of the man, several
steps back, who had turned, who had been caught, that
is, in the act of recognizing this woman, or had turned
with the *intent* of recognizing her. Did he know her?
Or did he merely have that in mind? Was this moment
the beginning of life for him—or just another loose
end? Two blurred shadows, caught by the camera,
moving in a scene that was itself immortal, or looked
immortal, like beetles in amber, in that scene so full
of so many timeless objects, the trees and the river,
the history-haunted towers, the bookstalls with their
freight of what was still surviving—a seemingly permanent scene with these impermanent shadows crossing it. That particular river—the one there on the card
—would never dry up or cease to charm this city, and
those trees along the bank would never shed their
leaves. But what about that creature with the Mona Lisa
smile, and the blurred feet? She was not of marble. She
was either going toward or fleeing something. Was this
man her lover or had she still another rendezvous? The
beauty and the mystery of this woman, who had no
name, no face, and no destination, seemed to embody,
for Foley, the mystery, the charm, and the anxiety of
life. All around them was Paris, the immortal city; the
delicate trees cast their permanent shadows, but the
feet of this woman—like the wings of time—were
blurred. Flushed with life, with impermanence, that is,
she moved from one solid curbing to another, troubling the waters on the surface of Foley's mind. Was

that where she now lived? Was this trembling reflection her immortality?

"Fifteen, twenty-five, fifty, one dollar," she said and placed the coins in Foley's palm, pressing down on them, then put into his hand the blue envelope containing the card. "Thank you very much," she said, her eyes on the doorway, where several wet people were gathered, and absently scratched her scalp with the point of the pencil she wore in her hair. "I suppose they need it in the country," she said and turned back to her work.

Not down in Foley's country, Foley was thinking, where the new crop of mold was growing on his books and in the lining of the shoes that he had preserved for twenty years. Glad he hadn't worn that pair, anyhow, as the rain was hard on them. Looked at pair he was wearing, their tops splattered, and through squall of rain blowing up the street saw poster advertising *God's Half Acre,* new nature film. Mrs. Schurz had seen and recommended. Naturally. As good a place as any to sit out the rain. Foley unrolled his paper, raised it over his head, and splashed through the rain into the dark lobby. Elderly woman in ticket booth a little startled, kept her eye on him.

Taking a bill from his pocket, Foley said, "Is the Disney piece now showing?"

"Showing right now," she said, clawed for his bill, pushed out a ticket as if he might be contagious. At the entrance door Foley stopped and took off his wet coat. He opened the door, then stood there as if an invisible hand held him, while stale, sour draft of air blew into his face. Hot, like the wind from a subway grating. He stopped breathing, pressed his lips tight, stepped

forward into the darkness, directly under smell of motor from circulating fan. Inside, the door closed, he
inhaled the same air as if it were clean. Stood in the
dark for a moment, but no usher came forward to
flash a light on him. A bright image flashed on the
screen, reflecting the light back into the room, long
but very narrow, sloping fast, and for a moment Foley
thought it was empty. Then he saw the sailor. Saw the
hat, that is, tipped on his face. Sunk low in first seat
on the aisle, knees up, asleep. At the back, clear at the
back, where the projector was like a bolt hole in a
coal stove, the flickering beam picked up the blond
hair, the wreath of smoke, over a pair of lovers. That
was all. Foley moved down the aisle and dropped into
a seat. With what was left of Schrafft's napkin, folded,
soaked up the rain that had wet his hair, then used
damp sheet to wipe the splatter off his shoes. Hearing
voice from the screen, speaking in farewell tone of
Lowell Thomas on rear-train platform, Foley raised his
eyes just as *God's Half Acre* faded from the screen.
Blurred away, out of his grasp, like that woman on the
French postcard. They were leaving, but over the scene
the narrator's voice hovered for a moment, pressed for
time, reluctant to be torn away. He *knew*. Also knew
that Foley *knew*. God's half acre was not part of *this*
world. Fairy story for adults chased off city streets by
the rain. Grown-up children at the top of the stairs
waiting for bedtime and Winnie the Pooh.

Foley lidded his eyes—the newsreels could give
him a headache in four or five minutes—and wondered if he should wait for *God's Half Acre* to come
around again. Wouldn't have to. Mrs. Schurz had
already described it very well. He was always very

patient with Mrs. Schurz, because Mrs. Schurz was very patient with his cat and on certain rare occasions had taken him in when it stormed. Wiped him off with the towel that hung on the hook with her bag of clothespins. Foley never asked her to feed the cat; the truth was he wouldn't eat a thing but kidney, and Mrs. Schurz believed that all sensible pets should eat table scraps. Not only that, but the cat, Sour Mash, had to have his kidney served au Foley, neatly snipped up, that is, with a pair of green-handled garden shears and dipped—not stirred—into the yolk of a freshly cracked egg. If the egg was not cracked while he stood there waiting he wouldn't touch the stuff.

A cat like that couldn't be left to a woman who had opposing theories on the subject, or, for that matter, to anybody else. He could be left, for brief intervals, to himself. Certain spring and fall nights, with a full moon waxing, Foley had left him to his own devices, but he had stopped when he began to learn what these devices were. But not *that*. No, he really didn't care too much about that. A cat's monsoonlike passion simply came and went. It was one of those things. Over the years Foley had learned to abide with it. But this other passion, as it proved to be, had not been in the Almanac, books on small mammals, or any report that had seen the light of day. For all Foley knew, it had no precedent. It was something new. God's half acre, possibly, had the patent on it. But Foley's own eyes had seen what they had seen, and so had the cat.

One summer morning, as usual, he had got up to salvage a bird. He slipped on his robe, and as he passed the window he reached for his garden gloves, a pair with leather palms that he reserved for this emergency. Through the window he caught a glimpse of the cat. He was coming through the privet with some very strange feathers in his mouth. As Foley stepped into the light he saw that it was not feathers but the tail of a chipmunk, a very small chipmunk; the head was either gone or did not show. Foley stood there waiting for that little point to be cleared up. There was no point rushing out to save what was already lost. The cat crossed the yard to a piece of flagstone, one of the steps leading out to the garden, where he paused and lowered the chipmunk bottom side up. His tiny paws were in the air—a very dead chipmunk in every respect. The cat settled down, in his customary sphinx-style, and, very casually, he reached out with a paw and gave the chipmunk a cuff. Very lightly, tenderly almost, and he did this once, twice more—when the chipmunk sprang up like spring-wind toy and began to dance. He *danced*, his little tail up like a banner, hopping back and forth on the cool flagstone, four, five times—then he suddenly scooted off. The cat, however, had been prepared for that. He was up, pounced on him, and brought him back in his mouth. He lowered him to the flagstone bottom side up, then relaxed once more. After stroking down a spot on his coat he reached out, tenderly, and cuffed the dead-looking chipmunk. Once, twice, and on the next stroke the chipmunk was up. The dance—the same dance precisely—took place again.

That had been more than enough for Foley, and he raced from the house, ran into the yard, and chased cat and chipmunk to the woodpile far at the back. There the cat, as per custom, let himself be trapped. When Foley raised him, by the scruff of the neck, he saw the bright beady eye of the chipmunk peering at him from between the cat's teeth. It was too much: he may have been a little rough, a little overexcited when he put the cat down, opened his jaws, and waited for the chipmunk to scoot away. But he didn't. He took a single hop to the toe of Foley's slipper and just perched there, staring at him, till Foley got the strength to lift his other foot and shoo him away. With the cat he had returned to the house. He had locked the door, put the cat in the kitchen, then walked through the house to his bedroom, where he noticed that his hands and face were covered with sweat. He ran a tub full of cold water and cooled off in it.

Did it really matter that this took place time and time again? All through the summer, with the chipmunk growing fat and having to be carried by the neck, like a kitten, and after putting on her dance lying out on the flagstone with panting sides, like a fat ballerina. Did it matter? Not particularly. It didn't really matter, because to be believed it had to be shared with one of the species—one of Foley's species, that is. One who would believe *that*, in return for some wild yarn of his own. But there was no one in Foley's little world—not even Lou Baker, who believed in vampires—to whom Foley could whisper what he had seen. It finally led Foley to look into Darwin, into a book he had owned but never read, and to spend nights brooding on a creative evolution of his own. Founded on what? Well, founded on audacity. The unpredictable behavior that lit up the darkness with something new. That in some audacious moment of the lunar past, at the mouth of some cave, had resulted in man. A turning on the hinges of his own dark past, toward the light. Through some jeweled chink in Mother Nature's own armor, through some flaw in her own habit of perfection, the glint in some creature's eye shot new rays into the dark. A cat charmer, a lion tamer, a prophet for a new and holy order of chipmunks, who would say to the cat what Joshua had said to the sun. Perhaps, Foley thought, Mother Nature was originating again. Looking over her children to see which one might amount to something. Maybe she had come to feel, quite a bit like Foley, that she had played her cards wrong in the first place and that the time had come to put a few trial irons into the fire. Like that chipmunk. Something really worth while might come out of that. The Origin of a species based on charm, on audacity, on the powers of the dance, and the music that soothed whatever needed soothing in the savage breast. If what Nature had in mind was survival, Man had ceased to be at the heart of Nature and had gone off on a suicidal impulse of his own. And Foley's chipmunk, among others, had got wind of it.

A rumbling sound, so much like thunder that Foley raised his eyes and looked at the ceiling. The blast on the screen, like flash powder, lit up the pattern on the pressed tin ceiling, and the day-old, scattered stubble on the sailor's face. On the screen itself, awesome but familiar, a mushroom cloud bulged from the earth, unfolding slowly, as though the camera had caught some miraculous birth. The flowering of a plant, the petaled opening of some strange, pollen-driven creature of the deep, bursting with the seeds of life, as this one burst with the seeds of death. As if the earth had become a belching cannon's mouth. And then the narrator's voice, the voice of doom speaking out of the smoke rings, out of the thunder, warning Foley, and the sailor, and the pair of lovers, that man now possessed his future in his own hands. He could either save, that is, or destroy himself. On Foley's face, green with the light that seemed to pour from the scene of destruction, there was an expression more troubling than doom itself. Pity for Foley and his kind. Pity for the doom itself. In the voice of the speaker Foley recognized the everlasting disaster-hungry prophet, since men would rather die, in a righteous foxhole, than come and face the battle of daily life. Doom was it? Extinction? Foley could see the saintly, luminous face of Proctor, the quiet smile radiating a power like doom itself. The power to transform, the raw material made immaterial, heavenly. There seemed to be a law that when faced with evil man turned this power upon himself—those who had the power, that is, to turn and face anything. In the light of this blast, in this moment of revelation, they would turn from the cockroach trapped in the tub, Foley trapped in the past, and take refuge in self-slaughter, or the ultimate truth. The agony in the Garden become the agony in the test tube, the sorrows of Werther become the fission of matter, and that last pair of hounded lovers, energy and matter, were now being probed by the finger of Science, bombarded by a hail of questioning protons, to see what light might flash, what thunder crack, when this final pair was torn asunder.

Foley pressed on his eyes, then opened them and gazed on the symbolic zero of Hiroshima, the surrealist's nightmare of man-made dissolution and vacuity.

The camera swept around it, saw that it was bare, that nothing made by man remained in it, then returned to focus on several faint shadows on the asphalt slab. And these? These were the shadows of men—the shadows cast by the blast itself. The shadows of men in the light of their own man-made sun.

Foley pushed up from his seat, groped for his coat, then went up the aisle without looking at the sailor, or the lovers whom the blast left undisturbed. Wrapped up, cocoonlike, in each other's arms. He thrust open the door, stepped into the lobby, and saw on the puddle at the edge of the street the reflection of white clouds coursing across a freshly washed sky. The woman in the ticket booth, her head nodding, appeared to be asleep.

THE CAPTIVITY: VIII

Lawrence and Proctor got away a couple days before the rest of us. Lawrence was going to play clay-court tennis all summer. Proctor was going to work. He had accepted a short-term position with a Manhattan advertising firm.

Lundgren planned to spend the summer in Wyoming, doing a little prospecting around Jackson Hole, and he got a free ride as far as Provo with a Salt Lake frosh. I went back to Chicago on the same mail train that had brought me out.

My mother said she was glad to see me looking so well. Arlene Miller had asked about me when she was home for Easter. She had stopped raising Belgian hares, but her little brother, who was now old enough, had five white rats that he kept in her old rabbit hutch. They were all very friendly, and he walked around with them inside his shirt.

My mother received a letter from the dean, saying that my work was a credit to my father and that I had also given of myself generously. My mother interpreted this to mean that I needed a rest. She thought it better that I not go to summer school or take on outside work. I would do a little reading and help her with a few things around the house.

Arlene Miller did not come home for the summer.

She was waiting on tables at the Dells, in Wisconsin, so the evenings on Byron Street were fairly quiet. There was not much noise after the radios were turned off. One night I went into the Loop to see how Chicago struck me after a year in California, and how the shows stood up after the Colton Visiting Artists course. I found the bands were not quite as smooth as those on the coast. Wayne King was all right, but he struck me as a little monotonous. I didn't care too much for what I heard on the radio. If I heard something pretty good I bought it, like "You're the Cream in My Coffee," and a very smooth version of "You Took Advantage of Me."

In the sports section of the Sunday paper, usually toward the back, with the Want Ads, I might find something about the tennis situation, and Lawrence. One week in July I saw he was playing up at Lake Forest. When his picture turned up in the rotogravure my mother recognized it. She read aloud to me, at Sunday breakfast, that Charles Lawrence, the West Coast sensation, was staying with his uncle, Clayton Gans, while he took part in the Lake Forest tournament. Clayton Gans was president of Gans, Hardwicke & Bollinger. There was no mention of the kidnaping incident. Clayton Gans was big enough, I guess, to put the damper on something like that.

Near the middle of July I had a card from Lundgren, mailed from Jackson Hole, Wyoming, with what I suppose was part of the Hole on the front of it.

This is country, baby.

was all it said on the back. My mother waited for me to bring it up, but when I hadn't brought it up, three days later, she asked me if it was customary for young college men to call each other baby. I said it was not customary, but Lundgren was very tall, sort of shy, and he seemed to be inclined to refer that way to people he liked. As an example of what I meant I referred to *Babe* Ruth. My mother had never thought of it in just that light.

I knew I wouldn't hear from Lawrence, but I was surprised not to hear from Proctor. He liked to correspond. But I didn't get a line from him. I sent off a card or two, one showing the statue of Lincoln by St. Gaudens, with a quote from Rimbaud on the back of it, but he didn't respond. I decided advertising was probably taking all his time.

We had a very bad August, with no breeze at night, and I slept on a sheet in the downstairs hallway, where toward morning it might turn a little cool. Most of the day I spent over in Lincoln Park. I would take along a book or two and sprawl somewhere in the grass. The lunchroom over the boathouse was open, and I would sit there, usually on the balcony, with the sandwich my mother had made and a bottle of Orange-Crush. It was hot on the balcony, but it looked cool out on the pond. On a good afternoon most of the boats were out on it. The water, that late in the summer, was like the duck pond at the Zoo, covered with Cracker Jack, popcorn, crusts of bread, and the boats the kids made out of the Cracker Jack boxes. But it was water and sounded wet when it dripped from the oars. I could hear the creak of the oarlocks even when I sprawled in the grass.

One Saturday in August I sat up to see what the Goodyear blimp was advertising, and watched it go

north along the shore and turn in toward Wrigley
Field. I was still watching it when I heard somebody
on the walk. Hundreds of people went by all the time,
but this walker limped, he took one quick stride, as if
it hurt him, then came down hard on the other foot.
I had to wait till he came from behind the bushes, but
I knew that it was Proctor; he had been walking with
a limp like that for two weeks before he left. I yelled
"Hey!" and put up my hand, but right at that point a
streetcar was passing, and the park was full of kids who
were yelling "Hey" all the time. He didn't hear me,
he went on by, and I didn't yell at him again when I
saw that he was wearing Lawrence's clothes. He had a
pair of Lawrence's dirty buckskin shoes on his feet.
The pants may have been his own—they looked a little
tight in the seat for Lawrence—but he had one of
Lawrence's crew-neck sweaters around his neck. Not
on, just the leather-patched sleeves around his neck.
Under the sweater he had one of Lawrence's T-shirts,
with the short sleeves. The only thing that belonged to
him was the limp.

With that limp he was easy to follow, and we went
around the pond, toured the Zoo, then came back to
the pond, where he bought himself a hotdog and a can-
died apple. He stood there on the pier, watching the
boats mill around on the dirty water, and guzzled down
the core of the apple, pips and all. He kept the stick to
chew on, and headed southeast toward the lake.

I lost him in the crowd around one of the ballgames, then I passed within ten feet of him on one of
the benches along the Michigan bridle path. Hot as it
was, he had put that sweater on. He would have seen
me, but he had his eye on the big apartment house

across the street; on a pair of French doors that stood
open, about nine floors up. There were chairs out on
the balcony, but no one was sitting in them. He kept
his eye up there, as if somebody might, then he crossed
the street and stepped into the lobby—he went around
in the revolving doors, that is, and came right out. He
stood around for a while under the sidewalk awning, as
if that was where he lived, then he walked along the
street where the limousines were parked. He passed
four or five, then he eased over to the curb, like a kid,
and let the fingers of one hand glide along the fender
of that car. It was one of those old Pierce-Arrows, with
the fender lights. He let his fingers just glide along the
fender, and then, with hardly any limp, he went off in
a hurry toward Clark Street, a couple blocks west.

When I went under the sidewalk awning I made
note of the address, painted on the awning, and I had
a good look at the old Pierce-Arrow parked at the
curb. It had Indiana plates, and there were several
racket presses in the back seat. A pair of soiled tennis
sneakers was on the floor up front. I had to run to
keep Proctor in sight, but over on Clark Street he
began to limp, worse than ever, and up near the park
he stopped for a Coke. While he was having a Coke I
sat in the phone booth across the street. It had just occurred to me that the name of Lawrence might be in
the book. There were quite a few Lawrences, as it
turned out, but Mrs. Charles Gans Lawrence was down
in the book at the same address I had seen on the sidewalk awning. Then I looked up Gans, Harwicke &
Bollinger, who had offices in the Palmolive Building,
and since I was sitting there in the phone booth I gave
them a ring. A girl answered the phone, and I asked to

speak to Mr. Jesse Proctor. She was sorry, she said, but the offices were closed on Saturday afternoon. I asked her if she could tell me where he lived, and she said Ludlow Terrace, wherever that was. I thanked her very much, and sat there till Proctor finished his Coke.

Ludlow was a short dead-end street that angled off the park. To get there, Proctor walked through the park, because the grass was easier on his feet, and I sat in the park and watched him walk down to the place where he lived. Ludlow Terrace had once been quite a place. There were concrete flower urns in the yard, a glass-roofed solarium on one side, and out in back, behind the garden, a copper-guttered carriage house. But the solarium was now full of fruit boxes, and a tarpaulin covered the holes in the roof. In the big bay windows on the front there were "Ice" cards and "For Rent" signs.

When I stepped into the hall a woman stood there, talking on the phone. She covered the mouthpiece with her hand and said, "You lookin' for Lois, honey?"

"I'm looking for Mr. Proctor," I replied.

"Second floor, clean to the back," she said and pointed up the stairs with the receiver. When I started up she added, "Clean all the way back, last one on your right." She turned back to the phone and said, "Now wouldn't it be like her to be up there with him! That kid!" she said, then turned to wave me on.

I went up the stairs and down the hall toward the back. All the transoms were open, and someone was playing "Bye Bye Blackbird" on a mouth organ. A woman said, "Will you play somethin' else, for chrissakes?" and for a moment it was quiet. Then "Bye Bye Blackbird" began again.

"You find it okay?" the woman yelled from below.

"Sure," I replied, and on the last door on the right knocked loud enough so she could hear.

"Come in, Sugar," Proctor said, and I opened the door, stepped into the room. Proctor sat at a desk in the back corner, on a piano stool. He had changed to an old pair of moleskins, one of the Colton gym shirts, and wore a towel looped like a scarf around his neck. He sat there gazing at the palm of his left hand. He had the elbow on his desk, the palm facing my direction, and where the fold creased the palm he had drawn a large human eye, using red and green ink. When he half closed the palm of that hand the eye winked. He didn't look at me. He sat there winking the eye for Sugar's benefit.

I didn't speak up because I knew it would give him a start. On the wall above his desk he had pictures of Lawrence, maybe fifteen or twenty of them, cut from all the papers and the college magazines. On the desk he had a loose pile of yellow paper, a jelly glass with a bunch of sharpened pencils, a pint bottle of milk, and a cake of Fleischman's yeast. A box of graham crackers with one end torn open sat in his lap.

"That better, Sugar?" he said, winking the eye again, but when Sugar didn't answer he turned and looked. For just a split second what he saw almost scared him to death. He got up, spilling the graham crackers, and took one step toward me. "Foley!" he yelled. "For chrissakes, Foley!"

"How are you, old man?" I said, and to help calm him down I picked up some of the crackers he'd spilled.

"Old man—" he said, but he couldn't go on, and

wiped the palm of his hand on the leg of his pants. His hand was so sweaty the red and green ink wiped right off. "I'm awfully sorry, old man," he went on. "Thought you were Lois, little chick that lives here." I let that pass, and he said, "Old man, I'm supposed to be in hiding."

"I was going north on Clark," I said, "when I saw you in the park. Saw you cross Clark Street."

"What was it gave me away, old man," he said, "the limp?"

"Well, I did notice the limp," I said.

He shook his head sadly. "Well, I did what I could, mon vieux. Picked a room in the slums, brought in my own food, only took a walk when I needed an airing." He took the towel from around his neck, wiped the sweat from his face. Then he looped it around his neck again and gripped the two ends like a well-trained fighter.

"You didn't want to be seen?" I said.

He took a swig of milk from the bottle on his desk. "Sorry to hurt your feelings, old man, but when you're working on something like a novel—"

"You're writing a novel?"

"When you're engaged in the first draft of a novel, one with the opening scenes in Chicago—" He closed his eyes, spread out his hands, and let me work out the finer details for myself.

"Well, if I'd only known—" I said.

"Old man," he said, "if you knew I was here, you'd naturally wonder what the hell I was doing in *this* place. You'd naturally wonder what old Proctor was doing in the slums. Right? One thing would just lead to another, and when it did I'd probably have to hurt your feelings." He wagged his head, smiling sadly.

"What's your novel about?" I said and glanced at the yellow sheets on the desk. A small pile of typed sheets were in the case for his typewriter. A big photograph of Lawrence, smashing one away, was under the jelly glass full of sharpened pencils. "It wouldn't be about a tennis player?" I said.

He wiped his face with the towel again. "Old man, a book can have Chicago in it, and not be about Chicago. It can have a tennis player in it without being about a tennis player."

I didn't get it. I probably looked it, for he went on, "Take this book here, old man—" and held up one of the books he had swiped from some library. Along with the numbers I could see Hemingway's name on the spine. "There's a prizefighter in it, old man, but it's not about a prizefighter."

"Is it about the sun rising?" I said. I knew that was part of the title.

"Goddam if I know what it's about," he said and opened it up, as if he might have overlooked it.

"Well, it's your headache," I said and turned to see who was rapping on the window. My mother used to make the sound when she tapped with a hairbrush to call me in. The tapping came again, but when I looked at Proctor he had his nose in the book. I figured that must be his Sugar, so I stepped forward, jerked on the cord, and let the blind roll up. Just as I did, Proctor made a lunge for it, but too late. So there we were, facing the window, and about a yard away, across the airwell, was a woman without a stitch of clothes on her,

combing her hair. She was in one of those poses you see
on postcards, and on the postcard it might have been
pretty fetching. Her long blond hair hung to her waist.
The garter rings were bright red on her white legs.

"Keee-rist!" I said, gave a yank on the blind cord,
and brought my hand down on the sill, my knuckles
hitting the edge of a metal ashtray. I didn't feel much,
but when I looked at my knuckles they were covered
with blood.

"Damnation!" Proctor said and passed me his towel.
I wiped the blood off and saw that I'd sliced them
pretty bad. "We better go rinse them off, old man," he
said and led me across the hall to the bathroom, where
I sat on the stool and let my hand hang over the sink.
"Let the chlorine sterilize it," he said and turned on
the cold-water faucet; then he walked back and slipped
the bolt in the door. He still had the Hemingway in
his hand, but there was no place in the bathroom he
could put it, so he just stood there with it, his finger
marking the place.

As he probably felt worse than I did, I said, "I don't
see how you get much work done."

"Opening scenes owe a lot to her, old man."

"There's a poule in it too?"

"Where'd you think he gets the clap, old man—off
the stool seat?"

I hadn't known Proctor knew about the clap at all.
"I understood he got it in Paris," I said.

"Old man," said Proctor, sitting down on the tub,
"we don't have much, but we've got the clap. You don't
have to leave the country to pick up that."

"If I were writing a novel," I said, "I'd have him get
the clap in Paris."

"The Chicago clap is good enough for me," Proctor said.

It was for me too, but sitting there on the stool, after what had happened, I felt the need for conversation. Through the transom we could hear that kid playing "Bye Bye Blackbird" again. The room was nearly dark except for the tub, the rim shiny from people sitting on it, and the white knob on the door, which somebody rattled every now and then.

"Old man," he said, "you think I'm a goddam heel?"

"I don't know what to think," I said.

"Well, I am. I've been a heel for so long, old man, I'm going to make something good out of it. I'm going to write the greatest book a shit-heel ever wrote."

"Baudelaire was no slouch," I said.

"I could make him yell doctor, old man."

I didn't know but what he could. A lot depends on your standards, and he had the highest admiration for Baudelaire.

"I know what Lawrence thinks," I said, but I didn't mean that the way it naturally sounded. I didn't mean to imply that we had talked it over behind his back. "He thinks you've got the gift," I said, and the book Proctor was holding dropped to the floor. He was sitting on the tub, but he didn't stoop over to pick it up. "He didn't mean the gift of gab either," I said. I knew that was what he must be thinking. I had thought so myself, at the time, but it was not what Lawrence meant. I didn't know, as a matter of fact, what the hell he meant.

"This is no bullshit, old man?" Proctor said.

"He said it like he meant it," I said, "whatever the hell he meant by it."

That was all we said about it. Proctor just sat there staring into the tub. I thought he was sitting there mulling it over, but he suddenly got up, came back to my corner, and unrolled about eight or ten feet of toilet paper. Then he went back to the tub and placed it over the slope at the back. He tapped the drain end of the tub with the toe of his shoe, and a big cockroach, trapped in the tub, came up the ramp so fast it nearly spilled over at the top. Then it went around the rim, one game leg dragging, and disappeared through a crack in the wall plaster.

"Proctor Salvage Operations," he said and rolled up the paper he had put down. He came back to the corner for a look at my hand. "How's it feel, old man?"

It didn't feel good at all, but I said, "Fine." I added, "I think I better run along, though, just in case, and get something on it."

"Mind if I put you in the book, old man?" he said and smiled, but when I said, "Me and the cockroach, you mean?" he stopped grinning. I could see that the cockroach was already part of it. I wasn't. The salvage operations hadn't got around to me. "It's all right with me," I said, "but I think you better clear it with the cockroach," then we left the bathroom and walked down the hall to his door.

"It's been a great pleasure, old man," he said, "but I better get on with my packing."

"You leaving?"

"Got to scoot for Brooklyn tomorrow, old man. I'm a heel, you know, but I owe it to my mother."

"In that case," I said, "I'll see you back at school."

"Sure thing," he said, slapped me on the back, then let his door stand open while I walked down the hall.

I passed a tall blond girl who had been eavesdropping on the landing of the stairs. She had a saucer with some pieces of fresh fudge on it, and when I got to the landing she said, "You Lawrence?"

"No, I'm Foley," I said, taken by surprise.

"Just so you're *not* Lawrence," she said, and she stood there on the landing till I reached the door. It made me wonder how much Arlene Miller had grown since I'd seen her last.

The day before I left for school I had a card from Proctor, mailed from Santa Fe. They had stopped at the La Fonda, he said, to pick up some more towels. On the following Thursday I went out on the mail train that got me to Colton by Sunday morning, and I rode up with the baggage man to our new suite of rooms in the dorms. Thanks to Lawrence we now had a tile shower, a fireplace with a gas log, and the *Los Angeles Times* delivered every morning at the door. It was lying there in the hall when I walked up. A big two-column picture of Lawrence was on the front of it. I thought he might have just won another title—they were playing tournament in southern California—but the caption read:

TENNIS STAR SURVIVES

FREAK ACCIDENT

I read that Lawrence, with his college companion, had driven off the road near Williams, Arizona, where the lanterns marking a detour in the road had gone out. His companion, Jesse Proctor, suffered barbed-wire cuts on the arms and face. Lawrence had escaped with a crushed finger on his right hand.

"That you, baby?" Lundgren said, calling to me from the shower; then he said, "I will now sing you a little ditty," and sang, " 'Who's going to bite your neck when my teeth are gone.' "

Then he came to the door of the room, the towel in his hand. The summer at Jackson Hole had been good for him. He was black except for the white saddle at the crotch. He dropped the towel on the floor, stepped on it, ran his hands down his wet body so that the crisp golden hairs all went the same way. Riding on a burro had rubbed some of them off between his legs.

"Pretty swanky little dump, eh, baby?" he said, and we looked at the room together, and the brown imitation gas log in the fireplace. "I miss the smell of the can though," he said and combed his hair. Turning to face the mirror, he said, "What the hell's eating you, baby?"

"Lawrence banged up his right hand a little," I said and held up the morning paper.

Lundgren walked across the rug, leaving his wet tracks on it, and read the article.

FOLEY: 8

A squirrel, like a stone skipping on water, hopped across the asphalt of Washington Square, the surface dark with rain except where the puddles reflected the sky. Foley made his way between them, careful not to shatter what was now at peace. The smell of dogs, wet leaves, and moist earth hovered in the air trapped under the trees. He took a seat on a bench where the leaves dripped rain on the walk. He was reminded—he sat there, that is, in order to be reminded—of Peter Foley, still to be found, unfaded, on the flyleaf of the Latin books on his shelves. There was about *that* Peter Foley something reassuring, and something puzzling. He seemed to be a pleasant sort of character to know; he was fond of his mother, a hard worker, anxious to master the pluperfect subjunctive, and every bit as immortal as Tom Swift or the Rover Boys. He did not change, grow up or grow old, marry the right or wrong girl, come to a good or bad end, or merely peter out, as most men seemed destined to do. No, *that* Peter Foley was out of time, time and the river of silt had passed him by, although a certain erosion was noticeable in the softer parts. The heart, the liver, and the pudding in the hollow round of the skull.

Down the steaming walk, slantwise across the square, Foley could see the mute gallery around the chess players—four men playing, ten, twelve men gathered to watch. Absorbed. Iron filings gathered around the still point. World around them breaking up like an ice pack, but peace on the cake on which they were floating —peace and chivalrous war with the knights and the hazardous life of the pawns. Man nearest to Foley, hat in hand, was avocado-shaped veteran in fireman's braces, fanning himself with the hat, not from the heat but from concern. He could see what was coming. Could hardly bear to wait. Ulcerous price of the terrible gift of prophecy. At his side, clasping rolled newspaper, tall man with wide, forked hips, like a mare, legs of pants spaced out so child could run between them, play London Bridge. Right arm dangling large yellow hand, curiously disembodied in the shadow, palm turned back like fingered flipper hanging at rest. Fingers twitched as if dusting invisible cigarette. Swarthy keeper of vines now an idle white collar, hand reduced to head-scratching, crotch-adjusting, and gestures on the thin air to illustrate a fine point. Five-fingered toy to help idle grownups pass the time. Foley glanced at his own soft house-man's hand, fingers almost hairless, palm almost fleshless, worn down to smooth claw for correcting papers, bizarrely jeweled with old Navajo craftsman's coin silver ring. Also nicotine stains, the egghead's suntan, several pitted scars resembling moon craters, left over from rash of big warts he had chewed on as a boy.

"God bless you!" the voice said, but for a moment Foley missed the man behind it, for no more than his head showed above the signboards and no more than his feet below them. A human sandwich. "God bless you!" he repeated and, seeing something in Foley's face

that disturbed him, he poked an arm from the sandwich and crooked his hand around to point at the sign.
Foley read:

<u>DON'T WORRY!</u>

GOD

HAS

A

LAYAWAY

PLAN

He may have looked relieved as the man turned
away, offered his message to the couple on the bench
across from Foley. "God bless the little one!" he said.
They sat with a baby stroller between them, the little
one pink and sore with a summer rash. The mother
smirked, but the father with an animated face said,
"Kitchy, kitchy, kitchy!" He bent over the child and
made a corkscrew noise, a wide-eyed baby face.

Foley closed his eyes, but on the lids he saw the great
kitchy-kitchy lover, Charlie Chaplin, in his endless
pursuit of the blind flower girl, his face forever pressed
to the window of the florist shop. Another Layaway
Plan. The first. Rapt face of the lover in love with love,
the promises men live by, and the heavenly Bazaar of
America.

"Kitchy-kitchy-kitchy!" the young man said, and the
sour taste of pity coated Foley's tongue. He opened
one eye to watch human sandwich, blessing all as he
passed, cross the square to the men's room, leave his
signboards parked where they would carry on the good
work. Then he glanced at the bride, none could be
fairer, only one of her kind with other lovers unhappy,
thin, sallow-sad girl maybe twenty-six, maybe forty-

one. On her feet a pair of Gimbel's huaraches, plus dirt from cold-water flat.

Foley sounded an Ahhhhh, as if under pressure, and watched father toss his rash-pink child in the air. On his animated face, in his kitchy-kitchy-kitchy, well-advertised concern and security for loved ones, long vacations with pay, carefree old age in ranch-style home, stone's throw from the ocean, cool, tangy breeze stirring flowers along the pickets, flaps on beach umbrella thrown up in the yard shading ever-fair bride from Time's cruel onslaughts, and holding in her lap first bouncing grandchild of the male line. In neat two-car garage, oiling the power mower, friendly head of house smoking his Kaywoodie pipe as up the driveway comes smiling mailman with Rock of Ages monthly insurance check.

Dim and phantom-faint, ghostly as moon shadows, and yet like something tattooed on his eyeballs, over this diorama, hovering, Foley could see familiar shades. The shades of Lawrence and Proctor in this young man, the shade of Lou Baker in this faded bride, and in their dream of happiness, the udder-dripping cow, the oranges that grew to fall in the kitchen window, Foley recognized the bold, faint-hearted shade of himself. Shades of nature, that is, imitating art. The Girl of the Golden West, stars in her eyes, in an up-to-date Gimbel-gunned model, and the man with the golden dreams and the same immortal resolves:

> No wasting time at Shafter's
> No more smoking or chewing
> Read one improving book or magazine per week
> Save $5
> Be better to parents

Shades of shades, but still casting their shadow, the same golden sun lighting up the diorama, where the brooks too broad for leaping were easily leaped in the Elevator shoes. A little rough at the start, even a little sordid, but one fine day—as advertised in *Life*—that brook too broad for leaping would be lapping at the door. A heartbreak dream, with the soundtrack by Chaplin, full of young men still fighting Hemingway's war, still loving and seducing Fitzgerald's women, and believing in perfection—a machine-made perfection—if anything at all. A witness to the power, the glory, and the terrible risks of art.

The sun was still rising, or not rising, but it would not stand still. Coitus interruptus now continuous, the sex life of male, the female, and the gall wasp, given the green light, the VD smear, the analytic and disarming candor that came from a close and detached observation of the erotogenic zones. The *facts,* as anyone would tell you, spoke for themselves. But not for Lawrence, not for Proctor and Lou Baker, not for those shadows on the streets of Hiroshima, and not for those shades sprouting on the graves where the radioactive corpses were buried. They did not speak for these things, nor in this language. They spoke for themselves. The new man, the cybernetic marvel, opened his plastic jaws and said, *I am a fact finder,* then smiled to show his teeth and gums coated with Nature's green. Under a cloud of unknowing, Foley arose, walked south across the square.

Hearing the whinny of Pegasus above him, he tipped his head back, gazed at the sky. The Flying Red Horse? It would not have surprised him. Nor did what he saw.

There on the cooling sky, tossing their manes, were the heads of two big dray horses, protruding from the window on the top floor of a tenement. At the adjoining windows, unperturbed, were human heads. Curious about Foley. Not about horses peering from the windows of tenements. Wisps of straw fell from the blue lips of the white horse as she whinnied, blending with the voices, the traffic noise, and the persistent tang of fermenting manure. Both fine horses, wearing collars, and Foley waited for them to walk out on thin air, flap their wings, and make off for the cumulus peaks. Passing strange, but not at all stranger than Peter Foley, there on the corner, having come from no more than the glint in the eye of a chipmunk with nothing on its mind but a sublime audacity.

Foley walked to Broadway, took a southbound bus for a whiff of sea air or a ride on the ferry, but, passing City Hall square, he saw the gray stone towers of the Brooklyn Bridge. He left the bus and, in the lines of a force like the iron filings around Lundgren's magnet, walked back through the square and out on the overhead bridge promenade.

When he had lived in Brooklyn, in the room beneath the room where Hart Crane had lived and worked on his poem, Foley had walked out on the bridge every day. He was writing no poem, nor anything else, but all that summer he thought he might, and he hoped that living in a house where poems had been written might help. It didn't, but he had a wonderful time.

He had discovered the bridge for himself—that is, Lou Baker had not told him about it—and it was Foley who had told her about Brooklyn Heights. She had taken an apartment across the street, one at the back, with a view of the river and a small balcony where her gentlemen friends liked to sit. The balcony was so small the chairs sat inside, but the feet of the guests could be seen on the railing.

There were plants there now, and television aerials on the roof. Lou Baker no longer had that particular apartment—she had moved farther down the block, beyond the modern cliff dwellings where the roofs were spotted with beach umbrellas. Foley had never been there, nor had he walked across the bridge since the war. A strong wind now blew up the river, flapping the flags on the excursion steamers and whipping up a scud of whitecaps on the slate-blue surface of the bay.

There on the bridge, spooning ice cream from a carton, Lou Baker had turned Crane's phrases on her tongue and let Foley understand that the Brooklyn Bridge was America. A span of art, that is, between the dream and the reality. A bird's wing, no more, across the broken gap of memory. Become a fistful of words, a modern corn-dance ceremony for making rain.

At such moments Lou Baker, a raddled oracle, her Left Bank hairdo like a wig on her gauntness, was nevertheless possessed by the authentic Delphic air. They had not been deceived, she would have him know. They had been possessed by a truth. Perhaps by too many truths, as it happened, every other one a seeming contradiction, but as they eroded, like Proctor, the bedrock truth stuck out. Lou Baker knew it, Foley knew it, and he had watched her yellow fingers fumble at her lips for the tobacco crumbs that were no longer there. Had not been since that Delphic spring in Paris, when she had rolled her own.

As if time had not passed, as if life had not been

lived, as if she were still Montana Lou Baker and that endlessly rising sun had never set.

Gull dung, wind-borne up the river, splashed on the bridge cable vibrating with traffic and left a creamy splatter on the back of Foley's hand. He wiped it on the iron rail along the walk, picking up a smear of rust. As he passed the Squibb tower he inhaled the aroma of the paste.

On Henry Street he paused to consider a row of bottles, packed in straw like eggs, and at the back of the window an advertised special, the square Jack Daniel's bottle with the sober black label. He whistled softly, reading the price. He passed, turned and came back, and with the Jack Daniel's in a tight paper bag he cut through the dim, haunted lobby of the St. George Hotel. Then headed down the street toward the gap over the river, the soft-focus view of Manhattan, seen through the haze of river traffic and tugboat horns. Turning left, on Columbia Heights, heard wind-blown song of street singer, in street shadow himself, but facing windows where the sun was ablaze. From one such window, partly curtained, a coin fell end over end, sparkling, then dropped soundlessly, like lead, in the summer-soft street. Singer did not stoop, but with bird's cocked eye sidled quickly to where he could put a shoe on it, one that was hand-boned, hand-stained, and bench-crafted, but unshined.

THE CAPTIVITY: IX

Lundgren and I were still in bed the morning that Proctor came in and yelled, "Where the hell is everybody?" then went off leaving the door open, as if the rooms needed a change of air.

Later that day, between classes, I saw him waxing the floor in the mess hall, the new barbed-wire scars in a white criss-cross on the top of his head. Another ran along his jaw, like bone showing through his beard. In the evening Lawrence was back, black as an Arab and looking great. There was not a scratch on him that you could see, but he was wearing a pair of chamois gunning gloves. When he came in he gave me that smile and said, "You'll pardon the glove, old man," and put into my palm the good fingers of his right hand. They had saved the thumb. Enough of it, that is, to fill out the glove.

We had our first class rally that night, in the Greek Theater, under the stars. Nobody nominated Lawrence, Proctor, or Lundgren for anything. I was nominated for class treasurer but declined. Sydney Brown, who ran the school Vespers and introduced all the Visiting Artists, won the presidency from Clip Gower, a football man. A resolution was proposed and passed that all members of the class, high and low, should take more active participation in college life. Then the candles were lit, the glee club sang, and the flame of life was passed across the darkness, hand to hand, in the traditional flame-passing ceremony. The Ghosts danced the ghost dance, wearing the white sheets with the skull and crossbones glowing in the dark, and the giant Colton C was lit up on the mountains, blinking like a banner hanging from a blimp, and as we walked back through the wash to the dorms Proctor said, "Christ, what bullshit!"

We came back through Phipps, under the open windows, past the lampshades with the limericks that glowed with the lights off and the beds that were shared by dolls that said "Mummy" and giant teddy bears. We came down through the trees, orange and lemon, across the court where green dinks floated in the fountain, to where the car that had also survived the accident was parked. It was low, with nickel-plated wire wheels, a small visor-type windshield, a cockpit seat, and the word Bugatti under the hood, stamped on the motor. Proctor helped Lawrence cover it with a tarpaulin. The barbed wire had scratched it up but not so you would notice it.

Our swanky suite of rooms had real leather chairs, Van Gogh reproductions on the walls, and a set of Loeb Classics on the built-in bookshelves near the door. They had come out in a crate from Brentano's in New York. Lawrence had told his mother that one of his friends was very scholarly. The north wall of the study was a picture window facing the foothills, the green Phipps campus, and the mountains brown and distant in the summer haze. In December, after the rains, they would move in close. The foothills would turn green, with violet shadows, the gray road up the mountain would turn black, and the rocks in the stream bed would shine in the moonlight as if they were wet. The channel through the wash would would run fire all day, run ice all night.

My room was on the north, facing the mountains, and I could see the rolling dips in the road where the carloads of frosh, coming down from the mountains, dropped so low they were out of sight, the sun bright on the yellow buttons of their dinks. A really good-looking class, better than average; every man in the class would gain weight on the average, neck and lose his first love on the average, smoke and have his first sinful thoughts on the average, but not *above* average. No, just average. A very fine class. No problem like Lawrence, who refused to ground-stroke, no marksman like Proctor, with a hole in his foot, and, needless to say, not a man on the campus with the clap. Just pimples, and the average run of athlete's foot.

Lawrence came back from the hospital with a phonograph that never needed winding and an album of very dirty songs that Dickie had sent him from France. It didn't really matter, however, since they were all in French. In the evening Lawrence would put on the records and let them play till he fell asleep, when Proctor would go in and switch off his light, turn off the machine. Lawrence kept a sponge-rubber grip under his pillow that he would squeeze while listening to the records, the idea being that he would learn to hold a racket again. But that would take time, as the dean said, when he asked me over to talk about Lawrence, and until that happened he had this serious adjustment to make. What to do, that is, with all the free time he now had.

In October we began to see what he had in mind. He would go to bed early, listening to his records, then he would wake up about one or two o'clock, take a shower, and go for what he called a little spin. There was no law against it. It was very safe driving at that time of night. If there was a valley fog he went up the mountains and cruised around in the moonlight, somewhere above it, and if there was no fog he might drive out to Twenty-nine Palms. Or down to Tia Juana, from where he'd bring us back black-paper cigarettes. There was no law against it, if he wanted to do it, but the problem was he didn't like to do it alone. He liked to cruise around with somebody else in the cockpit. Somebody like me.

Proctor couldn't stand the gaff. He had a full schedule and sat up nights working on his novel. Lundgren couldn't make it because his long legs wouldn't fit in the car. When he rode in it at all he had to hang his legs outside. The cockpit was very small, and his knees wouldn't fit under the cowl. So that left me. It turned out that I fit in the seat pretty well. I couldn't spare the time either, not really, but someone had to handle Lawrence's adjustment, and I preferred riding around to taking on his Sophomore English themes. We found a girl at Phipps to do that in exchange for a run of blind dates.

You don't talk much in a cockpit type of car, with your face in the wind. If we started early, a little after midnight, we could drive to Yuma and back before morning, or be in Las Vegas just about the time the winter sun came up. Lawrence didn't drive so fast, on the average, but he just didn't trouble to stop. On the cold, foggy nights we might pull in for hot coffee, but not much else.

As he usually got me up around one o'clock there was not much point in my going to bed, so I would sleep all afternoon, then work right through till I heard him getting up. The day seemed to start for him with that drive rather than to end. He took a shower and brushed his teeth as if he were going out to the tennis courts. It wasn't every night, but I would say we averaged four nights a week. I wore a beret to keep my hair from blowing, and because of the strong draft back through the motor I wore a pair of Proctor's sweat pants, to keep it from blowing up my legs. We could go from sea level to ten thousand feet in less than an hour. Both the fog and the mountains, at that time of the morning, could get pretty cold.

One little problem we had was gas, which we carried in five-gallon oil cans. Lawrence never seemed to know, when he started out, where he might end up. One night we had breakfast in the Harvey House at Needles, another morning we had it in Tia Juana, and we often stopped for chili in a diner outside Bakersfield. One night we drove over and had a moonlit look at Owens Lake. When it was light enough to see we took in Death Valley, then came back across the mountains to the valley and turned up on the campus just in time for my eleven o'clock Chaucer class.

I got in a good nap after lunch, as a rule, but Lawrence got by on the sleep he got in the evening, plus the fairly long naps in his Phipps History of Art seminars. He wore a trench coat in the car, but nothing on his head—his hair was too short to blow around—and for driving he had that pair of finely stitched Swiss gunning gloves. They took on the color and the feel of a good pair of driving hands. He wore them all the time, washed them in the shower, and let them shape-on while they were drying. They gave him the look of a nice welterweight boxer doing a little roadwork.

One night we went to Las Vegas and had coffee in a drugstore with a crowd of Hollywood boys and their women, and one of these babes, after sizing up Lawrence, came over and sat down. She was a fairly smooth blonde of the Marion Davies type. Somebody had told her that letting smoke drift from her nose did something for her.

"You sterilizing something, doll?" Lawrence said, but I could see she didn't mind that. She even liked it, I think. Like Lawrence, it was unusual.

"You boys over here all alone?" she said.

"We drove over here with that in mind, baby," Lawrence said.

"A boy like you think you can get away from women, honey?" she said, gasped in some smoke, held it down, till I thought sure it would come out of her ears.

Lawrence put his gloved hands on the table and said, "A little girl like you ever screw around with a boy wearing gloves?"

It wasn't so much what he said, but how he put it, with the gloves, the palms up, there on the table, and all the smoke the girl had swallowed came out in a rush. She was wearing a short-sleeved sweater, and I could see the gooseflesh rise on her arms. Lawrence didn't make a move, he just sat there, and when this girl thought her legs were steady she got up and joined the crowd standing around one of the pinball machines.

She left her Marlboro cigarette in the saucer of Lawrence's cup.

That happened over the Thanksgiving recess. We didn't have to rush right back to school, so we went up the east side of the Sierra Nevadas to Goldfield and Tonopah. Lawrence seemed to like something about the old mining towns. Under the seat in the car he had the Colt that Proctor had shot himself with. We were never held up or asked any questions, but I think Lawrence wished we would be, and he took shooting lessons on the theory that it was good for his grip.

We came back through Sequoia to Bakersfield, where we stopped at our usual diner, one that featured chili poured over hot tamales and side bowls of chopped onions. When we came in the cook was listening to the scores of the football games. He had a match in his mouth, and when the last score was mentioned he broke off a piece of it, spat it out.

"You hear that?" he said and turned to look at Lawrence.

"Hear what?" Lawrence said.

"USC beat the Bears," he said.

"Ha!" Lawrence said.

The cook nodded his head, then he thought it over, looked at Lawrence, and said, "What do you mean, *Ha?*"

"I mean *Ha*," said Lawrence.

I had no idea what he meant. I had never heard him use it before.

"You didn't expect it?" said the cook.

"What, my friend?" said Lawrence. The cook was an old man, a really old one, so Lawrence had to call him something other than that.

"The Trojans to win," said the cook.

"Nobody ever wins, my friend," replied Lawrence.

The cook looked at me, and I stirred up my chili.

"What the hell you mean, nobody ever wins?" said the cook.

"He means nobody wins them *all*," I said, knowing pretty well he meant more than that. I didn't want him telling the cook just what he did mean.

"That what you mean, kid?" the cook said, but when he said "kid" I said to hell with him. No one who wasn't asking for it would ever refer to Lawrence as "kid."

"I mean nobody wins," Lawrence said calmly. "You can't beat the game."

"What game?" said the cook.

"Any game," replied Lawrence.

"So you're one of those—boys," said the cook. He had it right on his tongue to say "punks," or something like that, but somehow he didn't. He put his hands on the counter and studied Lawrence as if he could see right through him.

"What he means is the game is the *thing*," I said. "If the game is the thing, why, then nobody wins it." That was not too good, but it was a way out, if anybody wanted it. I looked at the cook, and he looked fairly pleased. Then I looked at Lawrence.

"Bullshit, old man," he said.

I think it might have passed over if it hadn't been for the "old man." I was facing the counter, the glassed-in pie case, and the hole where they pushed through the dirty dishes, where a sad-faced woman leaned with her head propped on her hands. When she heard the word pronounced by Lawrence she closed her eyes. The cook took a spoon from the bowl on the counter, rapped it on the counter, then pointed at a sign tacked over the pie case:

PLEASE WATCH YOUR HAT, COAT,
AND YOUR LANGUAGE

"Bullshit," said Lawrence, backed off the stool, took a bill from his pocket, and dropped it on the counter. I followed him down the aisle to the door at the front.

"Give him back his dirty money," the woman said, but the cook just stood there, holding the spoon, and we went down the steps at the side and got into the car. The cook came to the door and watched us drive off.

We did the stretch from Bakersfield to Los Angeles pretty fast. I mean, we did it in about an hour less than usual. But north of Pasadena we ran into smoke; they were smudging in the groves along the foothills, and we could see the pots flaring orange and red like Christmas lights. We stayed up on high ground, out of the valley where the smoke began to gather, cruising along on the narrow blacktop roads between the trees. When the road angled north or opened out into the wash, we could see the fresh snowcap on the peak of old Baldy. Lawrence never said a word, as a rule, but he let the car ease up a bit and remarked that he didn't mind a little snow at Christmas.

I said that I did and I didn't, which was the way I felt. I was thinking of Chicago, where the snow was not white very long. In the abstract I might like snow at Christmas, but in Chicago it was soon dirty slush.

"You say you do and you don't, old man?" Lawrence said and let the car slow up to almost a standstill.

"If you mean the snow," I said, "I do and I don't."

Lawrence brought the car to a stop. "Is there anything you like outright, old man?" I looked at him as if I hadn't caught the gist of what he said. "Anything you really like, old man? Anything you prefer to the usual bullshit?"

We were parked on a sloping piece of blacktop road in a grove of lemon trees. The new crop was nearly ripe, and in the car lights they looked like Christmas tree ornaments. There were quite a few things that I liked, naturally, but I couldn't seem to think of a one of them. Besides, I couldn't take the question seriously. It wasn't like Lawrence. It was completely out of character. He seemed to think this word he'd picked up from Proctor covered everything.

"Don't get me wrong, old man," he said. "I admire it very much."

"You admire what?"

"The way you take the bullshit with the straw, old man," and I could see he meant that as a flattering remark. He didn't have it just right, but I understood what he meant.

"Well, I try to take things as they come," I said.

"I admire it very highly."

"It's not much to admire. I can't honestly say I admire it much myself."

"If I can't do it I admire it."

It must have been at the back of my mind, for I said, "Just what is it you admire in Proctor?"

"What he *admires*, old man. What he admires won't let him down."

"Well," I said, thinking it might cheer him up, "one thing he admires is you."

"You don't say?"

"He admires you very highly."

He shook his head slowly. "Bullshit, old man."

"Just what the hell isn't bullshit?"

I don't think he expected me to put it to him like that. He was sounding like Proctor, and I suppose he thought that nobody ever put that one to Proctor. He thought it over for a while, then without saying a word he got out of the car. He went up front in the lights, then along between the lights to a shallow place in the ditch, where he waded through the weeds to where the pots were lit in a lemon grove. He went along one of the furrows, where the ground was plowed, and as he got close to one of the pots I saw him take his left hand and try to loosen the fingers of his glove. That took time, since he couldn't do much with his right-hand thumb.

"What's up?" I said, but he didn't seem to hear me. I yelled "Hey" at him, but he didn't turn his head. He just stood there, about a yard from the smudgepot, tugging at the fingers of his gunning glove, and without thinking one thing or another I climbed out of the car. He was a good fifty yards away from me. "Oh, Lawrence!" I yelled, playing for time, and as I stumbled through the ditch I tripped over a broken hoe handle. I picked it up without thinking, but I had it in my hand as I ran toward him, and when I got close enough to see what he was doing I hit him on the head. I didn't get him square, because he was stooped over, one shoulder hunched up. He half straightened up, made a quarter turn so I could see his hand blackened by the smudge smoke, then fell on his back.

I think I might have hit him again if he had moved. He was out cold, but he had that goddam smile on his

face. I picked him up, got him back to the car. When
I dumped him into the cockpit some of the black on his
burned hand rubbed off. Not the flesh, just the oily
smudge that had blackened it. The hand was burned
all right, but not so bad as I had thought. Then I wondered if I might have killed him when I hit him with
the hoe handle; the right side of his head was sticky
with blood. But I found that he had a strong pulse. I
propped him up in the cockpit, the visor tipped back so
the cool night wind would blow in his face, then I just
drove around through the smoking groves until he
came to. He had his head on my shoulder, and he left
it there. He didn't say a damn thing. I drove around
another hour, till I felt sure about him, before I took
him back to the dorm, where he climbed out of the car
without any help from me and went up the stairs. I
let him go on ahead while I spread the tarpaulin over
his car. I did that, smoked a cigarette, then I went up
and found him in the shower, with his smudge-
blackened hand sticking out of the curtain, waiting for
me. He stayed in the shower while I covered his hand
with some olive oil from Lundgren's army locker
and wrapped it up in one of Proctor's face towels,
pinned at the wrist.

"Thanks, old man," he said when I'd finished, but I
didn't say a damn thing. All I could think of to say was
that he was a crazy sonuvabitch. I went into my own
room, closed the door, and while I lay wondering if he
wasn't *really* crazy, he played "Sam, the Old Accordion
Man," until Lundgren shut him up. When I knew he
was asleep I got up and turned his goddam light off.
He *looked* asleep, lying on his side so that the bump
on his head was up and the hand with the towel

wrapped around it like a baseball mitt on his chest. It seemed hard to believe that he was actually asleep, but I think he was. He could do just about anything he had a mind to, so he had done that.

They smudged all night up in the foothills, and in the morning when I went to my classes the smoke was over the valley like a dark pool of oil. In the afternoon I got in Lawrence's car and went back to the grove where I had hit him, because when I hit him he had dropped one of his gloves. I didn't want anybody turning up with something like that. They all thought we were crazy, and that would put the cap on it.

In the evening Proctor stepped into my room and closed the door. I thought he was wondering what the hell had happened and wanted me to fill out the story, but I had made up my mind that this was too crazy for *anybody's* book. It would die with me, since I would never write a book myself.

But he helped himself to my cigarettes, sat down on my bed, and said, "I'm not here to question you about the arson, so you can relax."

"I'm relaxed," I said, stiffening. "What's on your mind?"

"How'd you like a little tour of the barbed-wire empire, old man?" He gave me his Lawrence smile and showed me the non-scar side of his face.

"This is conducted?" I said.

"Strictly blue-blood," Proctor said, "personnel all in the family, marriage, fornication, or straightforward blackmail."

"Proceed at less length," I said.

"Exit Guildenstern and Rosencrantz," said Proctor, "enter the noble-browed Horatio." He smirked. He was cool as mint when you swung at him, but when he swung at you he got excited.

"Suppose you step from behind the arras," I said, to cool him off a little, "and give us all the inside dope. The play's the thing, is that it?"

He took a deep drag on the cigarette. He was never so happy as when you were clubbing him with something.

"Harken, Ophelia," he said. "All steam-heated rooms, about thirty of them, all hand-cooked meals, about fifty of them, all hand-picked guests, about sixty of them, all happy and carefree under portrait of the Master, at stud, hanging over fireplace, with seeded non-Jewish girls anxious to meet and correspond with non-Jewish boys."

"So you're not seeded?"

"I'm not seeded, old man," he said. He did not smile. "But in dreams begin responsibilities, and being something of a dreamer, although unseeded—"

"Spit it up in papa's hand," I said.

"You got to take him home for Christmas, old man."

"Look, Proctor—" I stood up. I hadn't expected anything like that.

"I've already put it to him, old man. The coast is clear."

"Why the hell can't he go by himself?"

"You think I'd trust him alone, old man?" he replied, and the way he said it, the tone of his voice, the way he put his head forward as if to thump with it, made clear what I'd sensed all the time. We had all leaned on Lawrence, but now he was leaning on us. And we were all tied to Lawrence, whether we liked it or not.

"Look, Proctor—" I said, but that was all, and later

that evening, his hand still wrapped in the towel, Lawrence stopped by to ask me if I wouldn't like to spend the holidays with him. It would give me a chance to see my mother over New Year's, he said. I said I was sure that would please my mother, especially if Lawrence would stop by with me, and he said he would be glad to, and that was where it was left.

I figured we would drive, but ten days later his grandfather, old Colonel Gans, had a stroke, and Mrs. Lawrence called Charles on the phone and asked us to come by train.

FOLEY: 9

Lou Baker's voice, hoarse and muffled, spoke to him through the tube.

"Who dat?" she said. An old game.

"Us chickens," he said.

"Foley's chick flew the coop," she said, and then the door buzzed before he could answer. He lunged for it, but too late. It buzzed again. Inside, he propped the bottle in the bucket of sand, still there in case of an air raid, paused to take off his trench coat. The hall was hot. Her apartment was five flights up, on the top floor. The buzzer sounded again, and then he heard, clear at the top, the sound of a hall door opened up—and left ajar. Hearing that sound, Foley was glad he had come.

Near the top of the last flight of stairs he could hear the shower drilling on the curtain. Had they just got up? He stood there a moment, cooling off. The draft through the door smelled of roasting meat. Leg of lamb.

He did not knock on the door but said, "Knock-knock-knock," and the drumming of the shower on the curtain stopped.

"That you, old man?" said the voice, and Foley heard the curtain rings slide on the bar. Through the open bathroom door he got a whiff of the steam-laden air. "Come on in," said the voice, although he hadn't answered, for who but Foley, of all the people they knew, would have nothing to say, nothing really memorable, after all these years?

He stepped into a room that was without carpets, almost bare. On the walls were the shadows where pictures had once hung. A set of springs, without the legs or the frame, covered with material that had once been curtains, sat on the floor in the window corner, boxed in with orange crates. A lamp sat on one. In the other was Lou Baker's library. A raddled copy of Petit Larousse Illustré, a Webster's Collegiate with the Greek roots in Greek, a copy of Proctor's novel, in her own translation, and a 1921 Sears, Roebuck catalogue. Years ago, twenty maybe, Foley had browsed in the catalogue. He never seemed to tire of the pictures of watches, and spring-wind trains. There was all the raw material, Lou Baker had said, that was needed to write the great American novel—and twenty years ago they were sure she was writing it herself.

"How are you—mon vieux?" the voice went on, adding that last little touch for Foley, who had not been mon vieux, or very much else, for twenty-five years. Through the bathroom door Foley saw the white foot on the tub, and the grape-colored bruise where a young marksman had shot himself. The foot looked the same, but the leg above it looked thin.

"I'm a little warm," Foley said, and hung his coat in the closet.

"You'll find my wife in the kitchen," the voice continued. "Think she left something burning out there." And Foley was relieved. *That* sounded familiar. Telling you before you thought it what you think.

"I'm glad you found a girl who could cook," Foley

said, slipping the bottle from the paper bag. "Most of
my old friends had to settle for girls with nothing but
jobs."

The feet stepped out of the tub, but they did not
come to the door. They remained on the tile floor, facing the mirror, and Foley said, "If you'll excuse me,
think I'll step back and present a little hair oil to your
wife."

"You'll find her bangs hanging on the towel rack,"
the voice replied. Seemed to be about the same, Foley
thought, and yet— He walked through the door to the
room at the back, where two card tables, covered with
paper napkins, were set up with candles and places
for five. *Five?* "I'll be with you in a moment, old man,"
the voice put in, as Foley had paused there in the doorway.

"Take your time," Foley said. "I understand the importance of that first impression."

"I made that one earlier," the voice said, and Foley
crossed the room toward the kitchenette, a closet-sized
hole clouded with smoke from burning meat. He held
the bottle out before him, stepped to the door, and saw
that she had been waiting there for him, her face carefully smeared with grease and flour for the gravy, her
eyes smarting with smoke tears. A dripping fork in her
right hand, a potholder in her left, she spread her arms
wide, indicating that he should kiss her. He did.
Strands of hair were stuck to her sweating brow. Would
he wipe the falling hair from her eyes? He did. She
turned and poked the meat she had allowed to burn
while waiting for him. He stood there, his face set in
what he hoped was an expression of admiration, while
a very old record dropped on the turntable of his mind.

Love's old sweet song. Same old Baker. Same old refrain.

She felt that, turned him around, ran her flour-coated fingers through her hair, then placed the palms of both hands on her bony hips. A characteristic gesture, the fingers arched and spread, as if covered with something sticky, dating from her Montana childhood—dating from a time when they had been. Foley had seen the photograph. The snapshot of a bony little girl standing in a flower patch. The palms of both hands, as if they were dirty, on her bony little hips. "I'd just done it in my pants," she'd explained. "I guess I do it when I'm embarrassed."

Embarrassed, she raised the floured hand, waved it at the room. "We just decided the hell with it," she said and gestured at the tables set up for five people. She meant the hell with their troubles. That was also Lou Baker, dating from way back. "Oh, the hell with it, Foley," she would say in the flat, cigarette voice that seemed to get the most out of a small range of profanity.

Then she coughed, and he said, "Here's the cherry-flavored phlegm-soother you ordered," and placed the square bottle of Jack Daniel's in her hands. Turning it slowly, she stopped to gaze at the old man himself, a snapshot on the label.

"The old bastard," she said affectionately and wiped a thumb across his face, as if to see him better.

"I suppose you know the rules of the house, old man" —and there he was, in one of Lou Baker's peignoirs, a wet towel looped around his neck. Shaved head bent over, hooked over like a buttonhook at the top. Hunched. From leading, then ducking. Crouch of prize-fighter with a violin player's face.

"Right at this point," said Lou Baker, coughing, "he might be curious to hear that this house *has* rules."

That was Lou Baker. That was what a man who had spent a night with her might expect. But it did not touch Proctor. An almost silly smile made a mask of his face.

"The rules of the house, old man," he continued, "are not to put corn on grape, or grape on corn, or pour corn on the uninvited guest." He smiled at Lou Baker. "Madame Swann's Way is serving Médoc tonight, and our distinguished guest, well known for his palate, would vomit down his corset at the thought of corn on grape."

Foley turned to the tables, the five places, and Lou Baker said, "If I'd known that I'd invited some pickled gentiles to a quiet Jewish wake—"

"If you hadn't known," said Proctor, bowing, "there'd have been damn little pleasure in it."

They'll never make it, Foley thought, they're both too goddam clever and independent. "Who is this pickled gentile?" he said, thinking the *right* gentile might help things.

From the kitchen Lou Baker said, "When you called I thought it must be Friday. You never call on anything but Friday. Then when you said anniversary, I got it—"

"You mean, *I* got it," said Proctor. He had gone back to the bathroom. He began to sing, softly, " 'I got five dollars, got two shirts and collars—' "

"So when we got it," Lou Baker said, "I thought what the hell—let's have a party."

"A great idea," said Foley—and waited.

"So I called up Dickie," Lou Baker said and came toward Foley with two whisky glasses, gave him one,

walked with the other to the bathroom door. Foley
neither sniffed nor studied its color but tossed it off and
felt his eyes water. As the glow spread upward into his
chest he said without turning, "So you called up
Dickie?"

"He's coming," said Lou Baker. "He's bringing Chateau Lafite and someone else's wife."

Had they both been drunk? Kind of reunion you
thought about when drunk. Let bygones be bygones,
etc. Why not? Dickie wouldn't let them.

"A very nice corn, old man," said Proctor. "Calls
for a very nice grape."

"Well, if we must have a gentile," Foley said.

"It was *his* suggestion," Lou Baker replied.

Where was she? Just standing in the other room.
Dialogue between the top and the bottom of the stairs.

"I must say, old man," put in Proctor, "I've been
making suggestions for about thirty years. Some of
them pleasant. First one she ever took."

"Took another one last night," Lou Baker said, and
Foley wondered what man could stand it. Maybe Proctor. Maybe he was *just* the man for that.

"I know we're crazy, old man," Proctor said, "but I
didn't know that *he* was. Think that fooled me. Like
to puzzle it out."

"If you want to know the truth," Lou Baker said,
"I called him just to shame him. Wealthy socialite and
heel seen out whoring with the enemy. Honest to God,
I didn't think he had the guts."

From the bathroom Proctor said, "He's got more
guts than all of us. He's lived for twenty years on absolutely nothing else."

"If you call *that* guts," said Lou Baker.

"I do," said Proctor. "It takes guts to live on nothing. More guts than I've got. I've got to believe in something, hang on *something*—"

"In case you wonder," Lou Baker said, "he's talking about Richard Olney Livingston, heir to the tin-plate fortune and four or five hundred fresh hat-check girls."

"You want to know what I think?" Proctor said.

"No!" cried Lou Baker. "My God, no!"

"I think Dickie *would* have shot him," Proctor said. "I really do."

"Shot who?" said Foley, his mouth a little dry.

"The Senator from Wisconsin," Proctor said softly, and Foley could hear him slipping his belt through the loops in his pants.

"You see, Foley," said Lou Baker. "He's *really* crazy. He used to just sound it, but now he's made it. I might as well tell you that's why I love him. I love crazy men."

As if he hadn't heard a word of that, Proctor said, "If I had his guts I'd have shot him myself."

"Will you shut your big mouth?" Lou Baker said. "Will you ever in God's name learn to shut it? You think I want to go back and go through all that again?" She left the front room and swept past Foley, turned the kitchen faucet on.

"I'm just too goddam dialectic, Foley," Proctor said. He came to the door of the bathroom, stood there buttoning his pants. Foley noted easy way he used the thumb and little finger. Pair of tweezers.

"We've got to think," Foley said. "We've got to try and put two and two together—"

"Do we?" said Proctor.

"You see what I mean?" called Lou Baker. "What the hell can you do with him *but* love him?"

A mocking smile on his face, Proctor said, *"Perche vuol mettere le sue idea in ordine?"*

"That sounds like Mussolini," Foley said.

"A smart man," said Proctor.

"And a dead one," said Lou Baker.

"Well, nobody need worry," Proctor said, "about me." He winked at Foley, but the eye behind the lid did not look at him or recognize him, and Foley turned away, already worrying.

"Anyhow," said Lou Baker, changing the subject, "when he said yes, what the hell could I say? I'd asked him to dinner. I couldn't tell him it was a joke. Then he asked me if he could bring anything, and I said, oh, a bottle or two of Haute-Brion, thinking that might make him see it was a joke. 'Livingston Reserve up country in bomb-cave,' he said. 'How about Chateau Lafite?' "

"Chateau Lafite is all right by me, Lou," Foley said.

"What I mean is—" Lou Baker said, but stopped there. The buzzer was sounding. With the potholder she had picked up Lou Baker walked through the house. While the buzzer sounded she pulled up the front blind, peered down at the street. "Does he think he's going to leave his car parked there?"

"You like to discuss that with him while he's waiting?" Proctor said.

Lou Baker stayed at the window. She tipped her head back for a look at the sky. It crossed Foley's mind, just crossed it, that she might not open the door. She didn't have to. He could still be turned away. What sweeter triumph than to turn him from her door, not answer his bell? But when the buzzer sounded once more she backed from the window, coughed to clear her throat, and faced the speaking tube.

"Dickie?" she said, and they all heard the voice of the man with guts. The playboy who had lived on nothing for twenty years. Then they heard—as through the needle of an old gramophone, the horn missing—the honing voices of a barbershop quartet singing, "The wedding bells are breaking up that old gang of mine."

"Honest to Christ," said Lou Baker, "wouldn't he though!" And they stood there together, facing the door, waiting for him.

What might have happened, Foley wondered, if he had come alone? The woman who stood there, filling the door, a gray-haired, almost massive matron, made it difficult to see the man who stood behind her, her chaperon. He wore a coonskin cap, an eager-beaver expression, carried a sack that rattled with bottles and a tape recorder in an alligator case. A saddle-leather pistol holster slanted across his flat chest. He gazed at them over the woman's shoulder.

"The man who strikes this woman, I'll shoot like a dog," he said.

The woman laughed first, covering her face with her gloved hands, her head wagging, and Lou Baker threw her arms up, crying, "Dickie, my God!"

"I thought I'd take a few precautions," Dickie said, not advancing. "You never know *who* you might run into these days." He rolled his eyes like Groucho, licked his lips, and gave the woman a push.

"You certainly must love him," Lou Baker said, taking the coat and hat the woman was holding, "or maybe you just know him. Maybe you know what to expect."

"I never saw him in my life till one hour ago!" the woman said. It was clear she had been waiting, for that hour, to tell someone. What if the people where they were going were *all* like that? Foley could see that question had been on her mind. "I'm soooo relieved!" she said. "Just coming over here, in that car, I felt so silly—" She looked to see if they understood that. They did. Her tailored suit was gray, and very becoming in spite of the dimensions of her figure. "Wheeeewwww!" she said, not so much from the climb as the close call.

"Where in the world did you find him?" Lou Baker said as Dickie went off with the bottles.

"All I know is, Mrs.—"

"Proctor," said Lou Baker. "This is Mr. Proctor, and this is Peter Foley."

"I'm Mrs. Pierce!" Mrs. Pierce said, blushing. "You wouldn't believe it, but I really am. Married, I mean. And for thirty years!" She threw up her hands.

"Well, you're awfully kind to come to our party, Mrs. Pierce," Lou Baker said.

"*He* said the more the merrier," Mrs. Pierce said, "but I really didn't know—" She questioned their faces.

"We're having a little anniversary," Lou Baker said, but she paused there, wondering what Dickie had told her.

"That's what *he* said, and so far as I can gather"— she smiled at them—"so far as I can gather it's to do with Paris. Is that right?"

"That's right," Lou Baker said, relieved herself. "We were all in Paris just fifty years ago."

"Isn't it the truth?" Mrs. Pierce said. "Just the plain and simple truth?" She looked at Foley as a man who might know.

"It's a long ways back there all right," Foley said.

Dickie came in and said, "Maybe I didn't have one hell of a time!" He turned the coonskin cap so the tail hung in front of his face.

"Oh, I guess we all had a wonderful time, didn't we?" said Mrs. Pierce.

"I mean today," said Dickie.

"Well, I would say that in the past hour—" Mrs. Pierce said and lidded her eyes. That didn't help, so she opened them.

"Now just where *did* you meet?" Lou Baker said.

"I used to be a hostess, honey," Mrs. Pierce said. "I'm still with Air France, and when the news got around about the man who—" She stopped, looked at Dickie, and couldn't go on.

"I'm a boy, but a man at heart," Dickie said and held up his nails, blew on them, then polished them on the tail of the cap.

"I know how you feel, Mrs. Pierce," Lou Baker said.

"About the man who wanted, who said he wanted, a girl who had been in Paris in the twenties. Now if she'd been in Paris in the twenties she was no girl now!" Mrs. Pierce said.

"I didn't say young or old," said Dickie. "Just girl. There's old girls and then there's young girls."

"Well, that was *just* what I got to thinking!" Mrs. Pierce said. "And if that was what he wanted, why, I'd been a girl in Paris myself. I was there chaperoning one of those awful college groups!"

"You'll pardon me," said Dickie, "but Mrs. Proctor is a prominent Delaware Group alumna. Author of that handy pocket guide 'Sex on Shipboard,' including some harbors, each volume with index to—"

"So you answered the call, Mrs. Pierce?" said Lou Baker.

"I must have been simply out of my mind, but I did! I didn't know at *all* what he wanted, but I said I would speak to him and ask him, and he said all he wanted was a girl who had been there in twenty-nine. In May, he said, of twenty-nine. And you know, I was. I really was. So I said if that was *all* he wanted"—she gave him a look, and he leered—"if that was all he wanted, why, I would be free till half-past ten. There's no train or bus out where we live after eleven. Just joking, I said, Mr. Livingston, what in the *world* will I tell my husband, and he said to say that I'd been out drinking with some refugees. Exiles, I think he said, and refugees!"

"Ha!" Proctor said suddenly and startled all of them. They turned from Mrs. Pierce and looked at him. Foley had a feeling that he had heard it—that Proctor, somewhere, had previously said it—but it had not been Proctor. No, it had been Lawrence. Lawrence in the diner just outside Bakersfield. The night he had not watched his language, argued with the cook in the diner, and later that night, in a lemon grove, had tried to burn his hand in a smudgepot. *That* had been like Lawrence, but the "Ha" had been out of character.

"Why, Mr. Proctor," Mrs. Pierce said, edging around so the light was behind her, "don't tell me you're the Mr. Proctor all this talk is all about!"

Proctor said nothing. What she said didn't seem to register.

"Mr. Proctor," Dickie said, "is the current public enemy number one. One of two—or is it three?—one of the three surviving Americans. Visitors will please not taunt the exhibit or throw ground glass into the cages."

"Well, I certainly do like your—pluck," Mrs. Pierce said. She had been about to say nerve, but had remembered, just in time, that Proctor was described as a man who suffered from a failure of it. "Isn't it simply ghastly," Mrs. Pierce said, feeling pluck herself. "I mean, *really?*"

"There's a heartwarming rise in the sale of Mother's Day cards," Dickie said.

Mrs. Pierce gazed at him soberly. "I certainly do admire a man who will stand up to—*it.*"

"You've got the gender right on the head," said Dickie.

"I mean, *really,*" she said, "don't you really think so?"

On her upper lip Foley could see the beads of sweat. Keeping a stiff one. Wondering what the hell she had got herself into. Nest of ex-Commies? Bathroom full of C-day bombs, wireless sets, small, laundromat-size brainwasher, and set of Russian folk songs, sung by Cossacks, for broadcasting over Voice of America.

"In spite of the rules of the house," put in Foley, so casually he noticed his hands were shaking, "I suggest a little corn be laid under the grape."

"Let us now milk the Phoenix, poor bird!" cried Dickie and followed Lou Baker out of the room to where the french windows opened on the river view. "Oh, my America!" he cried. "My Harpies Bazaar! Or is it Three-D movies?"

Lou Baker led him off.

"Hasn't it been just a scorcher?" Mrs. Pierce said; then, catching Foley's eye, "I really thought he must be crazy. I really did. I guess we're all mad these days."

"God help all of those who aren't," said Lou Baker.
She was back with Dickie and the drinks.

" 'This itself was their madness,' " Foley intoned,
" 'that they would not join Dionysus in his madness.' "

Turning, Proctor said, "Who said that?"

"Something Greek," said Foley. "Forget where I
read it."

"It's certainly Greek to me," said Mrs. Pierce and
turned to Dickie, who bowed, kissed her hand, then
sang:

> "Thank ya, fathurrr
> Thank ya, mothurrrr
> Thank ya for meetin' up with one anothurrrr.
> Thank the horse that pulled the buggy that night,
> Thank ya both for bein' just a bit tight—"

He took from his pocket a small atomizer, sprayed
his throat.

"You folks must be in show business," Mrs. Pierce
said and looked at them with admiration.

"You're not far off, lady," said Dickie.

"Do I smell something burning?" Mrs. Pierce wheeled
slowly, sniffed the draft from the kitchen.

"Yes, ma'am," said Dickie. With her drink, Lou
Baker left. "And now, if I may have your attention," he
went on, and screwed his head around, to the left, then
the right, like a man about to pass around some dirty
postcards. "I have here," he continued, slipping his hand
beneath his coat, "a simple cure for the troubles, great
and small, that threaten the lives of us vanishing Americans."

Foley waited for him to take from the holster a toy
gun. One of those jeweled and flashing weapons that

the small fry brandished, then fired, from the rocket ships and bucking broncos in the arcade of every chain store. But Dickie held off a moment, checked the room at his back with a look that was not feigned, then thrust out at them the Colt revolver with which Proctor had shot himself.

"Heavens!" gasped Mrs. Pierce and stepped out of the line of fire.

The gun had been well kept. The barrel and the stock were shiny with oil. Proctor neither stepped forward nor fell back, but his good hand, which held the cigarette, crossed his front and pulled at the lobe of his ear. Foley thought it might be shock. Proctor rocked his head, slowly, as if there might be water in that ear.

From the kitchen Lou Baker called, "We should have gone for a taxi ride. Before we'd eat or drink we'd always ride in a taxi."

Dickie cracked the gun open, blew through the barrel, then snapped it shut. The stunt had not come off. What had he expected? Something positive. Something from Proctor. But Mrs. Pierce said again, "My heavens!" and Foley said nothing. Proctor stood there silently pulling the lobe of his ear.

"It's an awfully quiet party," Lou Baker said and came to the door of the room with her drink. She saw that Dickie's whisky, untouched, still sat on the plywood tray. But she did not see the gun; he stood with his back to the door. "I see that Mr. Livingston is observing the rules of the house," she said. "Upset stomach?" Dickie slipped the gun back into the holster and reached for his drink, but Lou Baker had caught the movement. "I miss something?" she said.

"Just a few dirty imports for us boys," Foley said.

"Mrs. Pierce," Lou Baker said, moving up, "are they showing you those awful wiggly-part postcards?"

"Boys will be boys, honey," Mrs. Pierce said, seeing in Foley's face that this was not funny. "But nothing you didn't enjoy more thirty years ago!" Mrs. Pierce rolled her eyes, sucked air between her teeth, and let her upper half shake as if she had been tickled.

Coming up fast, Lou Baker said, "Is it charades, or just none of my goddam business?"

"Right the second time," Dickie said and buttoned his coat.

She studied his face, the still young-looking face of an aging juvenile delinquent, pimpled along the jaw and boyishly clean-cut. She turned from him and looked at Proctor, who dusted his ashes in his empty glass, sprinkled them on his ice cubes, returned the cigarette to his mouth.

"It's the Colt," he said calmly. "You know, the one I shot myself with."

Foley could see Lou Baker stiffen, like a cat, before she relaxed. She watched Proctor stir the cubes in his glass with his finger, then she said casually, "Well, just so it isn't loaded."

"Mal-hurrrrr-oooozemahn," said Dickie matter-of-factly, "that is the case. They don't sell slugs for the old cannon in the pawnshops no more."

"There's two rules of the house," said Lou Baker, turning to Mrs. Pierce, "no corn on grape is one, and all guns have to be turned in at the door."

"I know just how you feel," Mrs. Pierce said. "It's always the empty gun that kills somebody."

The drink he hadn't touched, Dickie raised to his

lips and finished off. For the length of time it took him to do that, his Adam's apple pumping up and down, Foley was sure that he would put down the glass, then politely leave. With or without Mrs. Pierce, but with the upper hand, and the gun. He had never been a man to take Lou Baker seriously. It brought up the old question of the Livingston prerogative.

Dickie finished off the whisky, stirred the ice cubes, then, in a strangely detached manner, as if answering traffic questions, he said he would observe the rules of the house. Without removing his coat he unstrapped the holster, pulled the belt from his back, and tossed the outfit on the bed.

"Couldn't we all take a ride in a taxi?" Lou Baker said. She looked at Foley, but he had no money; she looked at Proctor, and he said, "In a taxi on the boulevard Raspail, Dr. Hemingstein professed to be bored."

"Do you realize," Lou Baker said, "almost twenty-five years. What *is* twenty-five years?" She turned to Mrs. Pierce.

"It's a long time, honey."

"I mean, what do they call it?" Lou Baker said. "When it's twenty-five, what do you call it?"

Mrs. Pierce looked at them sadly, one at a time, then she slowly smiled. "I suppose you mean silver," she said. "It's silver for twenty-five years."

THE CAPTIVITY: X

When Lawrence and I got back from Indiana we found that Proctor had moved out of the dorm. Lundgren had helped him move over to Hogan's Alley, a collection of shacks where the seniors used to live. Some of the upperclass boys had complained about the noise of his typewriter. Over on Hogan's Alley he could type all night if he wanted to. And he wanted to. He also liked the idea, he said, of being alone.

That left the three of us in the swanky suite of rooms, but we were hardly ever in it together. If we were, Lundgren usually had his door closed. He couldn't stand to hear Lawrence play his phonograph records any more. I didn't mind the records, but I got awfully tired of the showers Lundgren liked to take, sitting on the shower floor and letting the water drum on his back. He took a cold one in the morning and an hourlong hot one every night. Everything in the bathroom was wet with steam and smelled of the olive oil he rubbed down with. After his shower he took about another hour drying off.

As that began to get on my nerves, I did most of my work in the library basement or in the booth behind the radio at the Sugar Bowl. The noise coming out the rear didn't bother me so much.

Both January and February were so foggy that Lawrence and I didn't do much night driving. We would take a little spin in the afternoon, then call it quits. On the weekends we usually drove down to Long Beach, if we were sure Lundgren wouldn't be there, and take in the dance halls along the coast. Neither of us danced, but we liked to sit at the back and watch. The Santa Monica kids had a different style from what you saw at Balboa, or along the strip that Lundgren called the cemetery with lights. That was how Long Beach looked from the foothills, if you felt about it the way he did, and saw the lights through the oilfield derricks like windmills with their heads blown off.

Once a week I'd go by and see how Proctor was making out. A magazine in the East had paid him thirty-five dollars for a story about a pole vaulter, Lindquist by name, who was always running into the pole. But they had cut the story about half, so the reading time was twelve minutes; the magazine featured a twelve-minute story every month. He showed me the check, but he wouldn't let me see what the magazine was.

In February he had a letter from an editor who had read and liked the story and wondered if he might be thinking of something with a little more length. Proctor had about a hundred pages of his novel, but he decided to send the editor just fifty, since he wasn't too sure about the second fifty himself. He thought a great editor might point out something he had overlooked. The editor sent it back with a letter saying that he liked the start of the book very much, especially the fresh quality of the writing, and asked if what Proctor needed was a little ready cash to get on with it. They could let him have a couple hundred dollars if he could indicate, to their satisfaction, just what it was the book was about, and how it would end. But that happened to be what Proctor wanted to know himself. First, just what it was about. Second, just how the hell it should end.

While he was trying to decide we discussed the matter quite a bit. I said I thought he should take the two hundred bucks, naturally. My idea was that he should take the two hundred bucks and go to some place like Santa Fe, or Taos, where he would meet other writers and find a more creative atmosphere. In a place like that he might figure out how to finish the book. But he didn't seem to think so. He seemed to think that Taos was phony as hell.

Every time I saw him we worked over the same old ground. The real trouble was, in his opinion, that two hundred bucks was not a lot of money when you put it up against something like the barbed-wire empire. It just so happened, naturally, that there was a mention of an Indiana family, and certain Indiana families might mistakenly think they were the family he meant. And there was also the mention, at considerable length, of a small, swanky college in southern California, but not in just the terms that might please somebody like the dean of men. The dean was not the type, to put it mildly, to understand the processes of creative fiction, and he might be led to think that he was one of the characters in the book. Put up against the sort of squawk that such people might make, two hundred measly bucks was not much dough. Once he got out in the world, on his own, two hundred bucks would not be so much.

In March I didn't see him for a while, because we had our exams. Then we had a big rain, with a foot or so of very fast water in the gutters, and Hogan's Alley was a solid stream of water about ten yards wide. A stream of it lapped under Proctor's shack all night long. He would come to class barefoot, his pants rolled up, the scar showing blue where he had shot himself, and sit in the back of the class, smelling wet and sucking oranges. It was still raining a little the night he came over to see me. He didn't want Lundgren snooping around, so we walked through the rain to the Sugar Bowl, where he said that they had upped their offer to a clean five hundred bucks. What he wanted to know was, where he ought to go to live on it. Where he could write a book and live the longest, that is, on five hundred bucks.

I hadn't given that particular problem much thought. I gave it some, then said that he might try one of the Great Blasket Islands—if what he wanted to be was alone. If being alone wasn't so important he might try Majorca, or Paris, if what he wanted was a more congenial atmosphere. Some writers did. While living in Paris they had written some pretty good books. Proctor said he was delighted to hear me say so, because in his own mind he had thought of Paris, but *everybody* thought of Paris, and he would hate to end up where everybody was. Then we talked about Capri and Rapallo, where he might run into Ezra Pound, and about St. Cloud, where he just might run into Lawrence. He wasn't sure that he wanted to run into Lawrence, since the book did have a tennis player in it, one from St. Cloud and Indiana, and some people might be led to think it was Lawrence.

We went on in this vein till after midnight, when the Sugar Bowl closed up, then we walked up Hogan's

Alley and listened to the radio in his shack. We went through the Guy Lombardo records that he wanted to save, and asked me to keep for him, and a little after four in the morning I got back to the dorm. I came in through the back, under the lemon trees, where Lawrence liked to keep his Bugatti, but the car was gone, and so was the tarpaulin. He was never off by himself at that time of night. I lay awake for an hour or more, waiting for him, then I slept through till late afternoon, when I heard someone fooling around in his room. I thought it must be Lawrence and called to ask him where the hell he'd been. He didn't answer, so I opened the door and saw a uniformed van man, out from L.A., packing everything in his room into shipping crates. The van man cleaned his room out, roped up the crates, then left them there for further instructions; the shipping labels turned up on my desk.

According to Proctor, the trouble was Lundgren; he knew Lawrence couldn't stand him, the mercurochrome between his toes especially. According to Lundgren, Lawrence had been pretty smart. He had decided to leave before the college threw him out.

There was a little of both, in my opinion. Lawrence had not troubled to take his exams, and nobody else had troubled to turn in a set for him. There was that, there was Lundgren, and there was also the fact that he had gone for a ride, and, being alone, it hadn't been necessary for him to come back. He had probably got over as far as Needles, saw Arizona beckoning across the river, and just kept his eye on the white line, following it east. Over in Flagstaff, having his breakfast, he had probably remembered about his classes, and the Fanny Brice record he had left on his phonograph.

He probably worried about that, knowing Lundgren, and called the van man to come out and pack up.

During spring vacation Proctor got a ride as far as El Paso with a Texas junior, and Lundgren decided to put in the time at Jackson Hole. His uncle from Long Beach, the Army colonel, drove him north to Salt Lake City, from where he sent me a postcard with a little bag of salt.

The first three or four days of vacation I spent in bed. I'd get up in the morning and go for the mail, as if I expected something, then come back to bed and read *The Bridge of San Luis Rey*. One morning I had a card from Proctor, who said he was sailing from New Orleans, and near the end of vacation I had a card from Lawrence. It showed a bullfighter, named Belmonte, down on one knee in the bullring, staring at the bull. It had been mailed from Spain, was signed Lawrence, and on the back it said:

This is no bullshit, old man.

Over the following weekend I packed my books in cartons, which I left in the basement of the dorm, and got off a letter to Mr. Conklin, the Lindbergh man. I said that I was now prepared to take the hop to Paris, or anywhere else. I also wrote a letter to the dean of men, which I planned to mail when I got to Paris, and three days later I heard from Mr. Conklin, Special Delivery. He enclosed a cashier's check for five hundred dollars and said he would like to see me later, if I made it.

I put the five hundred into traveler's checks, applied for a passport, which I arranged to have sent to me in New York, and to put in the time as well as save a little money I bought a bus-trip ticket that would take me through New Orleans on the way.

In New Orleans I wrote a letter to my mother, enclosing a postcard for Arlene Miller, that I mailed in Times Square the night before I sailed. I told them both that I would send them a good assortment of foreign stamps.

FOLEY: 10

"I think it's cooler back here," Lou Baker said, and as they entered the room, dappled with reflected sunlight, it crossed Foley's mind that there had been no mention of Lawrence. Not once. He stopped, raised his empty glass, and intoned, " 'And the sun is unmentioned but his power is amongst us.' "

"Let me give you a refill, old man," said Proctor.

"I like it," said Mrs. Pierce, inhaling the sunset. "Don't you *really* like it?"

"He's like a mole," said Lou Baker. "You wait. The first thing he'll want to do is blow out the candles. Then he'll want to know if the shade on the lamp can't be tipped the other way. Then—"

Peering around quickly, she caught Foley's eye. Nobody listening. Mrs. Pierce had followed the rays of sunset into the bathroom. One thing to say for Baker, Foley thought, without an audience she shut up. Like a clam. Watched her go into the kitchen, poke something.

"Here you are, old man," said Proctor and handed Foley his glass.

Foley placed it on the floor, near the wall, and dropped down on the rumble seat. Seat dated from the summer of '32 when Lou Baker drove Model A coupe to California. Left springs with Foley so she could get into rear of car. Wrecked car near Flagstaff. Dozed off. Blamed it on sudden swirl of dust in the road.

"If anyone had told me," Mrs. Pierce said and stepped out of the bathroom with her jacket off. Moment she set eyes on Foley began to finger the belt line at her waist.

"If anyone had," Dickie said, "you wouldn't have come." He reared back, sucked the air through his nose, and as she stared, fascinated, he flexed the wings of the nostrils.

"Well, now I never—" she began.

"It's nothing," said Dickie, "purely a matter of several thousand years' inbreeding."

Mrs. Pierce made her way around him to the kitchen door. Dickie raised his left arm, balanced the drink on his elbow, then removed a silver case from his pocket, flipped it open, removed a cigarette, lit it with the case lighter, and let the smoke curl from his nose. It rose to cloud the right eye, but he creased his left. *Style,* Foley thought, *Look, Ma, I'm dancin',* Babe Ruth tapping the dirt from his cleats with bat handle, and summer nights full of swing creaks, citronella, and Magnavox horn strains of Paul Whiteman's music, blowing along the North Shore like the flags on the excursion boats. With Richard Livingston the III, hot from the Charleston, cooling off in the breeze that lapped along the pilings, tickling the palm of the girl in the hipless dress whose hand he held. Apple-cheeked, Arrow-collar, jazz-age playboy, knight at arms but not so palely loitering, blasé with life, breeding, and rumble-seat wit— You know the orange juice song? Now *don't* tell me, let me guess. *Orange juice sorry you made me cry!* And she was. Invariably she was.

"Sauce Livingston," Dickie said, peering into the kitchen, "add pinch of barbital, stir, baste lightly under sunlamp."

Foley looked around for Proctor, saw him between french doors on the balcony. Old man's stance, one flippered hand at the rear, stooped so bad he looked a little arthritic, but scar along jowl not so noticeable. Part of the general erosion. Bedrock seam in his face. And still the limp, the gait with the stutter, small chip, fleck in the record dated Xmas, 1927.

"I really think it's *too* small," Mrs. Pierce said in answer to something she had heard in the kitchen. "Don't you think the world has gotten too small, Mr. Proctor?"

Probably thinks he is lonely, Foley thought. Wants to draw him into party, drain off his sorrows.

"I guess it is a small world, Mrs. Pierce," Proctor said, a proper smiling answer for children. Way he was stooped, eyes were naturally always on the floor. Look of animal *almost* human when he glanced up.

"When the world is so small," Mrs. Pierce continued, feeling that her point had been lost on Proctor, "when it's so small there doesn't seem to be room for a simple difference of opinion—"

"Suppose we leave him out of it," Lou Baker said, coming into the room with a bottle and a corkscrew. She looked at Proctor, but he seemed abstracted, so she turned and gave the tool to Foley.

"I don't think I did mention him—did I?" said Mrs. Pierce and looked to Foley for confirmation.

It was Proctor, however, who said, "He who dreams of a woman and does not lay with her shall be charged with a sin."

"Whether we mention *him* or not," Mrs. Pierce said, holding fast to a practical subject, "I just want to say that Mr. Proctor gave as good as he got."

"I would say he gave sterling for plastic," said Dickie and gave the coonskin hat a quarter turn left.

"That's what I really *meant* to say," Mrs. Pierce replied.

"The kid has brains all right," said Dickie, as if Proctor were not present.

"If everybody had brains like that," said Mrs. Pierce, "there would soon be an end to these investigations."

"Have to hold them in Soldier Field," said Dickie soberly. "Nobody but the baby-sitter home to watch 'em."

Mrs. Pierce got that one. "Do you honestly think so, Mr. Livingston?"

"As I understand it," Dickie said, "the accused is charged—"

"He is not *accused* of anything," Lou Baker said and crossed the room to give Foley the bottle. "He was asked to appear—he was not accused."

"As I understand it," Dickie continued, "the charge is that the witness has brains. He has brains. Ergo, he is guilty. Am I not right, Professor Foley?"

"Right," said Foley, put the bottle on the floor, and studied the mechanism of the corkscrew. It resembled, he seemed to remember, something he had once seen for impregnating horses. Mares, that is. " 'Hecho en Méjico,' " he read off the handle, and the sound of the words, the pause they fell into, suddenly made him think of tortillas, frijoles, and the sad nasal voices of the trio at the La Golondrina, on Olvera Street.

"From Taxco," said Lou Baker. "Isn't it marvelous?"

Also from Taxco, Foley remembered, was the crate, a little larger than a doghouse, made of sticks bound together with rawhide thongs, containing eight broken plates and a piece of wood described on the sales sheet as a spoon. This was followed by a letter in which Lou Baker said that she was now taking up residence in Taxco, where Rafael Torres—a Latin lover with obsidian eyes and uncomplicated passions—had opened up for her a vita nova, as she said. *What you won't understand,* she said, *is that it's free of all the goddam complications*—and, she might have added, free of everything else after about six weeks. Her next card— a week before Christmas—re-established her residence in New York.

"Like papa show you how it works?" Dickie said and took the corkscrew out of his hand.

"He's not *hecho* in the right place," said Lou Baker. "Hecho en Chicago. Sounds like a tango."

"You know what Bryan says?" said Mrs. Pierce. "Bryan is my husband, and if I've heard him say it once, I've heard him say it ten thousand times." Mrs. Pierce paused, and just a fleck of saliva showed at the corners of her mouth. "He says the dumb ones shoot you, and the smart ones shoot themselves."

With an effort that brought the sweat to his forehead Foley drew on the cork, heard the pop fill the hollow. "Voilà!" he said and held the cork up in triumph.

"Put it back and do it right," said Lou Baker. "Your face is all red. You didn't follow directions. Directions say pulls any cork without effort."

She stared at Foley, her lips parted, her eyes shouting, *Say something. For Christ's sake, can't you say something!*

"If someone will kindly present me with a decanter," Foley said, "I will decant." He held the bottle to the light, rocked it slightly, then sniffed the cork. "There was a mouse in the cask."

"What you say, madame," said Dickie, turning to Mrs. Pierce, "interests me very much."

"Well, I know it interests Bryan," Mrs. Pierce said. "He says there's hardly a week that somebody doesn't—"

"I'm awfully sorry," Lou Baker said, "to break up this very interesting discussion, but—"

"Seen objectively," Proctor said, very calmly, "I'm afraid your husband is right."

"I *don't* see it objectively," said Lou Baker, "I don't find it interesting, and I don't choose to discuss it. Shall we eat?" She turned to the tables and lit the candles. On Dickie's juvenile face Foley saw the unsettling delinquent smile. Mrs. Pierce wagged her head from side to side, a woman accustomed to the arguments of children.

"Just what do you propose to do about it, Mrs. Schweitzer?" Dickie said.

Foley thought that would do it, that would end it, and he pushed up to do what he could, but Lou Baker was still lighting candles, the flames warm on her face. The hand that held the match seemed steadier than usual.

"Serve the lamb hot, the consommé cold, and the wine at room temperature, dear." Then she turned to them all and said, "Well, let's eat."

"If I may interrupt the panel at this point," said Dickie, sliding the chair under Mrs. Pierce, "to bring you an announcement from Sweet-Bark Dog Food. Mrs. Ida Whiff, of Ridley Park, writes, 'We had a little dog with a very bad breath till we began to cheat him with Smell-Gawn Puppy Pampers.' End quote. Stop evading your dog's friendly lick. He won't tell you, but we will. Pamper your pet with Sweet-Bark's Smell-Gawn—"

"All I wish is that Bryan was here," said Mrs. Pierce.

"Sweet Bark thanks Mrs. Whiff just loads for her letter, and now we return you to our five-star panel featuring Victor, the mutt with all the answers. Now Victor—"

"I see a paw raised," Lou Baker said. "One of the mutts in the audience would like to ask a question."

"Sweet-bark right up," Dickie said.

Proctor moved the candle several inches to the left, so that he could look at Foley, and said, "What would you say it was, old man?"

"What?" asked Foley.

"The good society?" said Proctor.

"If you mean the goods society," said Dickie, "we have it. What'll it be, dry goods or wet goods?"

Lear's fool, Foley thought, a dog must to kennel: whipped out when lady the brach may stand by the fire and stink.

"Sweet as nature's own armpits," Dickie said. "Millions of satisfied foul-mouthed users. Ask for Smell-Gawn, yours for three dated carton tops."

"I could tell you something, but I'm not going to,"

said Mrs. Pierce. They looked at her, and she pressed the paper napkin to her face. It came away wet. "I almost forgot that wine was so warming," she said. "Oh my—"

"We're on the air now, madame," Dickie said, "Sweet-Bark's gold dust is running out of the hour glass—"

"You wouldn't believe it if I told you!" Mrs. Pierce cried, and a series of tremors, in waves, shook her shoulders. She opened the damp paper napkin, pressed it to her face.

"We wouldn't believe what, Mrs. Pierce?" Lou Baker said, and Mrs. Pierce reared back, like a seal out of the water, blurted out, "Tiny—he called me Tiny!" and dropped her head down below the table level, a seal submerged. A bone hairpin fell from her loosening hair to the floor, and they watched the back of her neck discolor.

"He? Who?" Lou Baker asked, as if that might explain it.

"Bryan," muttered Mrs. Pierce through her wadded paper napkin. "Oh dear me, the poor darling!"

"I guess we've all changed, Mrs. Pierce," Lou Baker said and fingered the stem of her wineglass.

"What you wouldn't believe," Mrs. Pierce cried, "is that I've got smaller. Back then I was bigger!" and threw up her arms, rocking back on the folding chair. It gave way without a snap, without a sound, except for the gasp she made in going over, and the rattle of the silver and plates on the table she raised in the air. Foley held the table, Dickie went to the aid of Mrs. Pierce. Thanks to the car seat, on the floor behind her, she was not hurt. She remained there, propped upright in her corset, her head lolling on her shoulders, while Lou Baker wiped the tears of laughter from her face. Weaving like a prizefighter's handler, Dickie fanned the air above her with the small potholder.

"In this corner," he chanted, "Tiny Pierce, tipping the scales at—well, having tipped them—being expertly handled by Montana Lou Baker, ex-paperweight champ, Bryn Mawr twenty-five."

Lou Baker said, "Bryn Mawr twenty-seven."

"Still a master of the little white lie," said Dickie. He looked around sadly, spotted Proctor, and said, "We will now hear a word from one-shot Lasky—"

Foley was sure that they wouldn't, but Proctor began, "I'd say the good society—"

"Oh, my God!" said Lou Baker.

"That's right," said Dickie, "plus all denominations, races, creeds, colors, notions, and Senator McCarthy. Everyman a superman among equally supermen, so there's no hurt feelings."

"Are you a Princeton boy too?" Mrs. Pierce said, peering around Dickie's legs for a look at Proctor.

"No, ma'am," said Proctor soberly, "but I was gored by a Princeton bull. I have a lovely cornada, with Old Nassau license plates."

Lou Baker raised her hand as if to fend off something she saw approaching, then turned the palm inward and drew it slowly down her face. From the pack on the table, not from his case, Dickie took a cigarette, lit it with the candle. When he sucked in the smoke his boyish face had a withered look.

"I have never been so flattered, Mrs. Pierce," he said. "Cornada Livingston. I like the ring of it." He let the smoke hang in a cloud around his head.

"I'm ashamed to bring it up," Tiny Pierce said, "but
I—"

"That's part of the cornada charm," said Lou Baker.
"If you don't know what it is it is very much better.
Professor Foley thought it was an Italian sporting car."

Drawing the fire, Foley said, "I'd heard that Lawrence had hurt himself, so I naturally thought—"

"Lawrence?" said Mrs. Pierce.

"Not *the* Lawrence," said Foley.

"I beg your pardon, old man," said Proctor, *"the*
Lawrence."

"Charles Lawrence," continued Foley, "young tennis
player. If you followed tennis back then you might remember—"

"Didn't he shoot himself—or someone?" said Mrs.
Pierce. She looked around the table at them. "Wasn't
it in the papers?"

"Lawrence had a bad horn wound," Lou Baker said,
speaking slowly, with elaborate care. "He couldn't
stand to be ill. He simply couldn't stand to—"

"This cornada?" said Mrs. Pierce, "you haven't told
me—" She turned to look at Dickie, who said, "Mr.
Proctor, madame, is the world authority on bulls, and
their droppings. He is the author of the widely unread
droppings classic, now out of print."

Mrs. Pierce turned to Proctor, who said, "The cornada, madame, is a blow below the belt. When it is
made by the horn, it is said to be lovely; the man does
not like it, but the bull loves it. When it is made by
college boys—"

"The bull, madame," said Dickie, "evacuates. The
college boy White Wings swoop down to collect it,
analyze it, but come to no conclusions."

Wetting his fingers on his lips, Proctor leaned over and snuffed out one of the candles. "Cornada Livingston's analysis," he said quietly, "is correct. He should have written the book. If he had written the book it would still be in print."

Beyond the candle Foley saw Dickie's sweating face. The coonskin hat made him look like a frontier doll. One that would sweat and make water when the frontier dangers appeared.

"I can't really say," Foley began, "that the spectacle—" He wiped his face with his napkin.

"You mean the poor horses?" said Mrs. Pierce, then added, "Do I smell coffee?"

"I'll get it," said Lou Baker, and Mrs. Pierce went on, "Don't you think it was the age? Weren't we all a bit crazy?"

"A bit," said Proctor, "is not crazy enough."

"When I think," said Mrs. Pierce, thinking, "I think we were all too idealistic."

"Is it idealistic to shoot sitting ducks?" Proctor replied.

"Sitting?" said Mrs. Pierce, getting the picture. "Isn't it idealistic for them to be *sitting?*"

"Madame," said Dickie, leaning forward, "would you please repeat that statement?"

"What did I say?" said Mrs. Pierce. She looked around. "I don't know *when* I've been so warm—"

"Maybe if we left the door open," Proctor put in, got up from the table, and left the room. They heard him open the door, step into the bathroom on his way back.

"What clever thing did I say?" said Dickie. "You think I've given him the last chapter?"

"Once I read a true story," Lou Baker began, "of a man who sent his friends live kittens in shoe boxes. He put fresh lilies in the box with them, and enclosed a card saying, 'Please bury this coffin.'"

"Good heavens!" said Mrs. Pierce, half out of her chair, and dropped down again.

"I thought the story was phony," Lou Baker said. "I didn't believe there were people like that."

"And now you do, dear?" Dickie said.

"I believe in evil," Lou Baker said.

"Of *course* there's evil," Mrs. Pierce said, rising suddenly, for a rebuttal. "Of course there's evil, but there's every bit as much good. If I could just tell you the things people do—unselfish things, just out of pleasure in goodness—"

"I didn't say there were not good people," said Lou Baker. "I just said that I believed in evil. Just like I believe that the sun does not go around the earth. It is a *fact*. It is more of a fact than anything else. I guess I fear it because I *believe* in it."

"Infantile paralysis," said Mrs. Pierce, "is certainly a *fact*. I have a niece in Stamford—but just because it's a fact is no reason to believe *in* it."

"I think I see your point," Foley said, noting the rise and fall of Mrs. Pierce's bosom, the steady, remote serenity of Lou Baker's gaze. "I see your point. I think the modern error has been in the ignoring of the power of evil, treating it as a childish superstition, or worse. Confusing it with sin. On the other hand—" He stopped when he saw Lou Baker's gaunt head wagging slowly back and forth, as if her ears were ringing. Foley agreed. What was he saying? Words, words, words—

"Goodness," Mrs. Pierce said—and for a moment Foley waited for her to say "gracious," but no, she meant *"goodness"*—"is every bit as real."

"It's a very pretty picture," Lou Baker said, "and even cheaper than books on flower arrangement, but it is not something"—she squeezed her small fists together—"in which your guts can believe." Mrs. Pierce stared at her, fascinated. "Why are men of good will," Lou Baker said, "all over the world, good for nothing? Why do men of evil rule the world?"

"I don't for one single moment think they do," said Mrs. Pierce. "I don't for one moment heed the counsel of despair."

"I know," said Lou Baker. "That's what I'm pointing out."

Mrs. Pierce turned to Foley, who said, "People of good will are often blind to the facts. Now take Hitler. In the early thirties—"

"Oh, to hell with Hitler!" Lou Baker cried. "To hell with Mussolini, with Stalin, with Beria! To hell even with McCarthy! Let's take me and you." When Foley leaned back she said, "Let's take me then. Am I a force for good or evil?"

"I'd say we're all a little of both," said Foley.

"You lie!" said Lou Baker. "You know that you lie! And when you lie you are a force for evil!" Her right arm waved in the air, flapping the towel she held like a broken wing.

"Children! Children!" Mrs. Pierce cried, but there she stopped, and Foley thought the roar that filled the room had been too much for her. Her jaw hung slack, the blood drained from her face, and on the no longer panting bosom Foley expected to see the sudden, spurting pump of blood.

"Oh, my God!" Lou Baker said, and on her way out of the room, toward the explosion, she left the towel looped over the arm that Mrs. Pierce, still breathing, had raised to stop her.

THE CAPTIVITY: XI

I spent a week around New York looking for the cattle boats that Richard Halliburton always sailed on, then I booked passage on a Diamond Lines freighter, the *Black Gull*. I had a lower berth, under the portholes and a Swedish artist named Larsen, who sat in his berth strumming a guitar most of the time. We had a Cincinnati janitor, Otto Klug, in the lower berth on the inside, and a Chase Bank clerk named Ruhig in the upper, who was sick all the way.

On the twelfth day out we saw Land's End, then we spent two full days going up the Channel, the smell of the engines in the cabin and the foghorn blowing day and night. We docked in Antwerp the following morning, about three o'clock. The tide was in, and the deck of the boat was high above the street. When the gangplank went down we could hear all the windows facing the dock go up or come down, and then the hooting of the women, but in the fog we couldn't see anything. They emptied their nightpots over the sidewalks as we passed. We sat around in a beer hall until morning, when we could get through the customs, then I went along with Larsen and Otto Klug to the American Express. Larsen bought a third-class ticket to Riga, Klug bought one to Spitz, which was near Vienna, and I bought one on the night train to Paris, to save paying for a room. Then we broke up, as we had seen a lot of one another on the boat.

I mailed a card of the cathedral to Arlene Miller, saying that Antwerp was all that I had expected, and one to my mother saying that I had arrived but the passage had been rough. Then I had a look at the cathedral, the Descent from the Cross as painted by Rubens, and several cafés au lait in an American-style restaurant on the avenue du Commerce.

In the afternoon I went to the Zoo, to keep from running into Otto Klug and Larsen, then I took in a movie until it was time for the Paris train. Emil Ruhig turned up on the train, where he offered me a seat in his compartment, but I said that on European-style trains I liked to stand in the aisle. I stood in the aisle from Antwerp to Paris, and near Paris, early in the morning, I took a live goose through the window and held him till the old woman boarded the train.

We pulled into the Gare St. Lazare about seven o'clock. Coming over on the boat, I'd studied Paris on the maps in my Baedeker, and when I got out of the station I headed down the rue Auber to the American Express.

Three letters and a postcard were waiting for me. One from Troy, Indiana, enclosing an invitation to the wedding of Lawrence and Miss Pamela Crowley, to take place on the 5th of June, in St. Cloud. One from Proctor, forwarded from California, saying that Lawrence had been injured in a novillada, and one from Arlene Miller, giving me a list of the stamps she would like. The postcard was from my mother, who said that she couldn't say she was really surprised.

I couldn't find "novillada" in my pocket Larousse,

so I figured it must be some sort of sportscar, like the
Bugatti, only very likely more powerful. We all took it
for granted he would kill himself in one someday. I
left a note for Proctor at the American Express, saying
that I was on my way to Majorca, but I hoped to find
the time to look him up before I left. Then I had a café
noir at the Café de la Paix, walked down the rue de
la Paix to the Tuileries, sat there for a while, then
crossed the Pont des Arts to the Left Bank. I went along
the quai to the Boul' Mich', where I had a café au lait
and a croissant, then I looked at Notre Dame and
walked up the Boul' Mich' to the Luxembourg. I had
the address of a *pension* on rue Gobineau, but it was
spring, I was in Paris, and when the kids around the
pond yelled "Me voici," I turned and looked. They
pronounced it as Mrs. Josephare had said they would.

In the afternoon I took a room at the *pension*. I had
a shower, then I thought I'd take a nap, since I'd been
on my feet all night, but some American girls were
playing ping-pong down the hall. They didn't play very
well, and the ball would roll down and ping on my
door. The place was full of girls, and one from Welles-
ley had just moved out of the room I was in, leaving
her fingernail polish and four or five bobby pins in the
bed.

I got up around six, walked up Raspail to the American club. Some more American girls were having tea,
playing records on a portable phonograph, and dancing
that open stance way that girls like to dance. A couple
of young men with beards were playing chess and smoking pipes. On some of the stationery the club provided
I got off a short note to Lundgren, telling him that the
Left Bank was lousy with Americans and phony as

hell. Then I walked up to Montparnasse, where I bought a pack of Caporal Jaunes and had a café noir out in front of the Dôme, where the writers hung out. I had a café au lait inside the Coupole, where I read the sports in the Paris *Herald,* then I crossed the street and leaned on the railing at the Métro stop. Three old men were playing sad, whiny music that people seemed to like. I was smoking, listening to the music, when I noticed the English conversation that was going on on the steps of the Métro stop. Both girls were tall, but one had her hair in heavy braids, like the tails of saddle horses, and the other one, a blonde, had it more like Garbo, brushed back. She wore a turtleneck sweater, and it made you think of Garbo right off. They had a man along with them, right between them, and although I couldn't see his face, just the back of his head, I knew that I had seen him somewhere before. I wasn't sure where until he turned, as if he felt me looking at him, and I saw he was the fellow in the leering photograph on Lawrence's desk. He leered at me just the same, as if he still had that French nude in his lap.

He led the girls across the street to a table at the Dôme, clacked a pair of castanets to attract the waiters, and ordered a vermouth cassis for the girls and an amer picon for himself. He called them chicks, and they called him Honey, Bunny, Dickie, and dear. I took a table back under the awning, ordered an amer picon myself, and watched the girl with braids play around with the tips of her gloves. She had a way of showing the tip of her tongue when she talked. I was putting her down as a piece from Goucher, the one who had written some of Lawrence's papers, when she turned to this Dickie and said, "Bunny, you like to take the rap for me?"

"Love it, chick," he said, swapped places with her, then he looked around to see what was the trouble, saw it was me, and came back to my table. He leaned forward on it and said, "Livingston speaking. Would it be Stanley?"

"No, it would be Foley," I said, and let him figure it out.

He did all right, then he said, "I got an extra chick on my hands, old boy. Don't let the slouch fool you. Montana born aus Bryn Mawr chick." That one was Lou Baker, the Garbo type, and the other one was Pamela Crowley. They didn't care for each other particularly. After we were introduced and had a few drinks he asked me to take one of them off his hands.

"I got to feed these chicks, old boy," he said, "but they won't slobber out of the same trough. Montana Lou doesn't seem to like the upperclass type of bitch." I said I wasn't much for that type of bitch myself. "Well, she's all yours," he said, meaning Montana Lou Baker, and slipped me three hundred francs to feed her.

We went over through the Luxembourg to the Café d'Harcourt, on the Boul' Mich'. I spent about a hundred forty on her there, then we had our café noir at the Deux Magots. Just in passing I asked her what she was doing with a Boy Scout like Dickie, and she said he was paying her and a Frenchy to translate a novel. I asked her what novel, and she said the poor boob called it "Querencia," which you couldn't translate, but meant the place in the ring where the bull felt at home. Then

I asked her what the name of this poor boob was, and she said Proctor, Jesse L.

I said I knew certain people who knew him, and she said he was a boob but a talented writer, and it had been something of an education to work on his book. Was it finished? I asked. No, he hadn't finished it. He would never finish it, in her opinion, and she would very likely never finish the translation, since she hadn't seen any of it for several weeks. For all she knew, Dickie might be finishing it himself. I asked her what the trouble seemed to be, and she said Proctor couldn't make up his mind whether to save the hero in the book or kill him off. The book called for killing him off, since the hero had become a bullfighter, but this would leave the author without a querencia himself. He knew that. That was why he couldn't finish it. He was one of these poor boobs who were looking for the great good place, a bullring without bulls, and he would probably end up in the Party or the Church.

"In the Party?" I said—the only Party I knew at the time was the Democratic. But she didn't go on.

"The poor damn boob," she said for no particular reason, then she looked at me and asked, "Am I especially unattractive?"

"You consider Garbo unattractive?" I said.

"You mind answering my question?"

"In my opinion you're a very pretty girl."

"That's my opinion too," she said, "but in more than three weeks he never once kissed me." I looked at her, and she added, "I mean he never even tried to kiss me."

"Who?" I said, thinking she meant Dickie.

"This awful damn Brooklyn boob."

"I thought I knew him," I said, "but I didn't know he was crazy."

"I wouldn't kiss him now if he paid me," she said and put her hand in my raincoat pocket. I don't know whether she knew that mine was there or not. Most of the time we just walked, or stood on the bridges where we could watch the reflections on the water, or sit on the Right Bank and look at the lights over on the Left. Toward morning we walked up the Champs Elysées to a covered bus stop on the avenue Hoche, where she sat in my lap curled up in her camel's-hair coat. I thought she had forgotten all about Proctor, when she brought him up. She began to quote him, and we had something of a little argument. It ended up with my trying to kiss her, and her almost biting the tongue out of my mouth. Then I chased her up the street, and she slammed the door of her *pension.*

I walked back through Paris to the Tuileries. I watched the sun rise on the Eiffel Tower and sat around until the bookstalls opened; then I crossed the river to the Left Bank and had a croissant at the Dôme. I studied one of the maps at the Métro station till I found Proctor's place. He was in a small hotel, Lou Baker had hinted, on rue Duguesclin. It was not much of a street, as it turned out, but some acrobats were showing off on the corner, and most of the people on the street had stuck their heads out the windows to watch. One of them wore a turtleneck sweater, his hair clipped like a monk, and rimless glasses that he had raised to look at the street. He was thinner, and the barbed-wire scar was like a crack in his beard.

"How are you, Proctor?" I said.

"Christ!" he said, as he had in Chicago, put the pipe

he was holding in his mouth, gave a wet suck on it. "Foley, old man, you old bastard, how are you?"

I said I was fine, considering that I'd gone several nights without sleep. I may have looked it, because he didn't question the point. But I had given him such a start I didn't know if he was glad to see me or not; he always needed time to figure out what it was he felt. He figured it out and said, "You like to come up, old man?"

I looked at my watch, as if I might be rushed, but it had stopped at three-fifteen that morning. That was just about the time Lou Baker had clamped down on my tongue.

"I'm here on the landing, old man," he said and pulled his head out of the window to point behind him. Then he left the window, and I heard him open the door on the stairs. The Hotel Duguesclin was five floors high but not much wider than a streetcar. "This is quite a surprise, mon vieux," he said and stepped out of his room so I could step in it. The end of the bed partially blocked the door. Near the window was a table, a chair without a back, one of Lawrence's bags covered with Dollar Line stickers, and a paper bag that had just been crumpled up and thrown aside. On the table was his typewriter, several pipes, a pint-size carton with a wire handle, and a loaf of whole wheat bread with the word HOVIS stamped on it. A Boy Scout knife was sticking up in the bread.

"I was just about to dine, old man," he said, "but I suppose my simple fare—" He waved his hand at the table.

I said thanks very much but I was right now on my way to eat. Some old Chicago friends had asked me to dine at the Deux Magots with them. I could see that he'd taken the bread out of the bag and sunk the knife into it in quite a hurry, for the bag kept crackling as it slowly opened up.

"Don't have the money to waste myself, old man," he said and opened up the flap of the carton, sawed off a slice of bread, and spread a thick layer of sour cream on it. He took a big bite and said, "Never felt better in my life."

"Well, you're looking pretty good," I said, and he was. The beard suited him all right, but he looked more like a rabbi than a writer. It made his jaw seem squarer, and the point of the beard stuck out.

He swallowed down what he had, then said, "What brings you to Elsinore, old man?"

"I guess I felt like a change," I said.

He put the bread down, wiped his mouth, and I thought he was going to ask me about it. But he got control of himself, said, "Christ, what a hole!"

"Colton's not the place it used to be," I said.

"My God, man," he said, "but we were young at the time!" He stopped eating and began to fill his pipe.

"Don't let me keep you from eating," I said.

"I never eat much at one time," he said and tossed me his tobacco pouch. I took out my own pipe, filled it, and he tossed me a box of French matches. Lighting my pipe, I could hear the music across the street.

"You've got a nice place here," I said.

"It grows on you, old man," he said.

We let it grow on us, then he said, "You just get here?"

"I put in some time in Antwerp first," I said.

"Be sure you see the glass at Chartres before you leave, old man."

"I don't have too much time for France," I said. "I want to get into Spain. Brush up on my Spanish." We smoked awhile, then I said, "It's a small world, n'est-ce pas?"

"Too small," he said. To make sure I got that he said, "Fellow from Cornell, a painter, ran into his mother's brother down in Vian's men's room."

"My only uncle is in Melbourne, old man," I said and leaned back so I could get a look at the street. Down on the corner the acrobats were gone. But across the street, on our level, a woman with bright yellow hair stood on the balcony, between two french doors, combing it. The street was so narrow that I could see her hair was dark at the roots. It made me think of Proctor's room in Chicago, but in Paris it would not be necessary to rap a brush on the window or sit in a room with drawn blinds.

"What were you saying, old man?" he said.

"You remember Dickie?" I said. He did. "I had an awful piece of luck," I said. "Ran right into him at the Dôme."

"Well, whatayaknow."

"Recognized him from the photograph," I said. "Same leer on his puss."

"Alone?" said Proctor.

"No," I said, tapping my pipe on the floor. "He was there with two babes."

"Hmmmmm."

"Had this pair of skirts on his hands," I said, "so he passed the Garbo number off on me. Bryn Mawr piece. You know how they are at Bryn Mawr."

"They are persistent," Proctor said.

"Upshot of it was," I said, "he gave me the babe

and key to his apartment. Said he had an extra bed, since Lawrence wasn't in it—"

"Well, wasn't that nice of him," said Proctor and took the knife from the bread, cleaned his pipe bowl with it.

"What's Lawrence up to—now?" I said.

"It is not good," said Proctor.

"He got himself a little gored?"

"A cornada," said Proctor. He placed his hand at his groin, rubbed the spot softly. "Very good for the bull. very bad for Lawrence."

"He must be crazy as hell," I said.

Proctor filled his pipe again. "He is not crazy."

"If he isn't," I said, "you name it."

"I am working on it now, old man."

"He's got everything to live for," I said. "He's got everything anybody could ask for, and what does he do? He runs around trying to get himself killed."

"He was trying to kill the bull, old man," said Proctor.

"It adds up to the same thing," I said. "If what he wants to do is kill the bull, why the hell not get a gun and shoot it? Easier for him, easier on the bull."

"Is it a touchdown, old man," Proctor began, "if you take the football, say, around midnight, and go out on the empty field and put it between the goalposts?" I let it pass. "Is it a touchdown," he went on, "or is it only a touchdown if you follow the rules? There are rules for football, and there are rules for killing the bull. Football is for children, killing the bull is for men."

I could tell the way he said it that he had put it in his book, word for word.

"To quote an old friend of mine," I said, "that's bull-shit."

"Let us talk about something you understand," he said and tossed me his tobacco. He was very calm. I was not calm, so he said, "Did you have a nice passage?"

"How's the bullsh—I mean, book, coming?" I said.

"Pretty good, old man," he said and looked at the sheet of paper in his typewriter. "I got it all but the clincher. I can't kill him off."

"Why don't you let the bull do that?"

Without turning to me he said, "Old man, I guess I'm superstitious."

I didn't kid him. I could see that he was. He looked at the sheet he had in the machine, tore it out with a zip, crumpled it in his hand.

"Okay," I said, "he kills the goddam bull and lives happily ever after."

"There's a bull in this book, old man," he said, "but he's a nice bull. He don't shit in the bullring." I laughed at that, but he didn't. "I can't see him doing it, old man," he said.

"Doing what?"

"Living happily ever after *anything,* old man."

I couldn't either, once I thought about it. To live happily ever after you have to retire. Lawrence couldn't retire.

"Just *who* the hell's book is it?" I said.

"I don't know, by God!" he said. "Maybe it's his." He thought that over, then he said, "If it's his book, and I kill him off in it—"

"I see," I said, although I didn't.

"But my agent thinks that I ought to."

"You've got an agent?"

"Not an agent strictly speaking, old man. But when he saw it, said I ought to have an agent, and when he volunteered his services—"

"Hmmmm," I said.

"Was his idea," Proctor went on, "bring it out in French first. Small, signed edition. Bring it out here first, then when the talk gets around, when the word gets around—"

"Who's doing the translating?"

"Girl with stars in her eyes, old man. Highly admires my stuff."

"She want you to kill him off or save him?"

"You know," Proctor said, "can't get her to say. Think she's probably little squeamish about it." He leaned forward, put his pipe on the table, and took a sheet of yellow paper from the pile on the floor. He rolled it into place and typed a number on the right-hand corner. "Three hundred and twenty-one," he said. "Been there all week."

"I better run along and let you get to work," I said.

"Say *you* were writing the book, old man?" he said.

I thought it over. "How about just goring him so damn bad he can't fight any more, but he can write a book about it?"

He sat there facing the window as if he hadn't heard me. When I turned I saw the woman with the yellow hair pouring wine from the bottle in the wicker wrapping into the glass of a man who sat across from her, a red fez on his head. He was black, not a sooty black, but more like the color of oil smeared on water, or like the blackbirds I had seen under the college sprinklers, worming the grass.

"He'd never try anything so easy," Proctor said, and

for a moment I wondered if he meant the woman. If he meant Lawrence and any woman.

"Is the wedding still on schedule?" I said.

"It's a toss-up, old man, whether I kill him off first or she gets him."

"If she wants him," I said, "I put my money on her." He didn't reply to that, so I got up to leave. "I got a chick from Chicago waiting for me at the Dôme," I said.

"The place is going to hell, old man," he said and stepped out in the hall so I could get out. The window on the stairs looked out on the Cimetière du Montparnasse. Three American girls, one in a dirty slicker, were bent over trying to read what it said on one of the stones.

"I'm thinking strongly of Majorca," I said. "You hear anything from Majorca?"

"They're in Majorca too, old man. They're all over hell. They're even in Russia."

"You hear from Russia?" I said.

"I am in close touch, old man."

When I looked at him he gave me that Lawrence smile.

"Well, vaya con dios," I said and went down the stairs, made the turn at the street, and went off as if I were late for this chick at the Dôme. On the corner where the acrobats had been I stopped to light up a Caporal Jaune.

FOLEY: 11

Proctor stood facing them, the smoking gun in his hand, a look of bemused astonishment on his face, gazing at the finger-size hole in the ceiling of the room. From the hole, as from a cracked hourglass, a powdered dust sifted to the floor.

"Well, I'd say his aim has improved some," Dickie said and made a soft clucking sound, like a chicken.

"You fool!" cried Lou Baker. "You awful fool!" and ran forward and buried her head in his shoulder. He let the Colt hang slack while he absently stroked the back of her neck.

Foley said nothing. His tongue and the roof of his mouth were dry. He gazed, as they all did, at the hole in the ceiling, then he lowered his eyes to a spot on the floor.

Someone below was tapping. Without raising her head, her arms tight around Proctor, Lou Baker rapped a loose mule heel on the floor. The tapping stopped.

"What'll we tell the cops?" Dickie said matter-of-factly. "Cleaning old firearm for homecoming weekend?"

Lou Baker suddenly turned. "You brought it here. Suppose you tell them. You brought it here and you knew it was loaded!"

"I swear to God!" Dickie said, holding up his right hand.

"You swear to *who?*" Lou Baker said. *"Who?"* She looked around at them wildly. "I swear *I'm* going to lose my mind!"

"I swear," said Dickie. "I just swear I didn't know it. The thing looked full of holes." He twirled his fingers to indicate the chamber. "I swear—" he said again, then stopped.

"Go on!" said Lou Baker. "Christ, I'm really curious. I'm just dying to know what the hell it is you'll swear to!"

"Easy, baby," Proctor said, "take it easy now, baby," but when his hand touched her shoulder she spun around and hit him. Not hard, just slapped him with a wild fling of her arm; then, seeing what she had done, she threw her arms around him, sobbing.

"Why don't you and I," Mrs. Pierce said, tapping Foley on the arm, "go and do those dishes?"

Foley turned and followed her into the room at the back. Dickie came along, he tagged along, that is, so close on Foley's heels that he stepped on the right one, said, "Excuse me!"—blurting it out like an overgrown kid. Then he hurried past them both into the kitchen, splashed water on his face. Something about that— nearly everything about it—the sounds he made blowing into the water, made it all seem like the foolish prank of some kid. A big, awkward kid caught fooling with a gun. Foley felt, as he hadn't for years, just the slightest twinge of affection for Dickie, the middle-aged delinquent without a Bible to swear on.

"We can just thank the Lord," Mrs. Pierce said, "that something terrible didn't happen."

"Yes, ma'am," Dickie said. He did not mean to be amusing. It was what he meant. Foley was thinking that the only time Dickie sounded phony was when he was serious, when it was perfectly clear that he was swearing on whatever it was he had.

"You can just give that to *me!*" Lou Baker said, but in the voice of a sensible, exasperated woman, faced, for the last time, by the small fry with the water gun. Then they heard her cross the room to the bathroom, slam the door.

"I'm going to make us all some fresh coffee," said Mrs. Pierce and poured out what was left in the pot, making quite a racket in the sink as she flushed the strainer. Foley and Dickie carried dishes to the sink, folded up the card tables, and leaned them against the wall. Lou Baker's record player, with what was left of the steamer labels and Bryn Mawr stickers, sat in the corner under a pile of old ten-inch disks. The label on the top record had all but worn off. Lou Baker had stuck on a piece of adhesive, a Band-Aid, which read, " 'Wang Wang Blues'—Paul Whiteman."

"I'll be goddamned," Foley said and picked it up, checked to see if it was cracked.

"Don't think I know that one," Dickie said. "How's it go?"

Foley raised the lid of the portable—if Lou Baker owned it, it was portable—and gave the crank four or five turns. Machine about the same vintage as the "Wang Wang Blues." Turntable had a power hum like a deep-freeze. He clawed an old needle out of the cup, screwed it into the head, lowered it to the record.

"Used to hear this—" he began, then had to stop, lift his voice a notch to be heard above the scratching. "Used to hear Whiteman play this when he was out at the Edgewater Beach."

"Sounds like that's where he is now," said Dickie. "That the breakers I hear on the pilings?"

Behind the hiss, the whir, and the rumble was the "Wang Wang Blues." As it should be, Foley thought. Record in about the same condition *they* were, scratched and cracked on the surface, hiss of the "Wang Wang Blues" running underneath.

"Knew the horn in that band," Proctor said, and there he was in the door, smiling at them. A curl of cigarette smoke disappeared up his unbuttoned sleeve.

"Was it Jordan?" said Foley.

"Tommy Gott," replied Proctor.

"He's got what it takes, all right," said Dickie and raised his coonskin hat, arched his back, and high-stepped across the room like Ted Lewis coming on the stage.

"We've certainly improved *some* things," said Mrs. Pierce, stepping into the room with the fresh pot of coffee. "Why, it makes you wonder how anybody ever listened to it."

"See if 'Stars Fell on Alabama' is there," Proctor said.

Foley turned to see, then swung around to face the hall door. Someone knocking. Pounding, that is. They remained there, quiet, and the "Wang Wang Blues" scratched on.

From the bathroom Lou Baker called, "Will someone please see who that is?"

"That's you, son," Dickie said and stepped aside to make way for Foley. Proctor also stepped aside, and Foley crossed the room to the door. The empty holster and belt were thrown out on the bed, and as Foley walked by he flipped the spread over on it. He took a firm grip on the doorknob, opened it. A small, round-shouldered, doll-faced man wiped his face with his hanky, smiled, then said, "You people all right?" On the draft that stirred his hair came the faraway strains of "Wang Wang Blues."

"I'm awfully sorry we disturbed you," said Foley, "but we're giving Miss Baker a sort of little party. Bunch of her old friends. First time we're together in more than twenty years."

"Free to do as you please," he said, wagging his head, "but wife swore what she heard was an explosion. Thought I'd better step up and make sure everybody's all right."

"Well, there was an explosion," Foley said, smiling. "Chateau Lafite, twenty-seven. Great loss to us all."

"Oh, Christ!" he said. "Oh, Jesus! Now ain't that a fright!"

"Forgot and left it on the stove," Foley said. "Guess the heat was just too much for it. Regular damn cannon. Blew the cork right through the wall."

"Well, I'll be goddamned!" he said, and Foley could see that he half believed it. Something to tell his wife, tell the neighbors, tell his friends. Goddam boobs in the apartment upstairs left wine on their stove. "Well, have fun, kiddies!" he said, wiped the hanky around the back of his neck, and Foley watched him pad down to the floor below. In the room at the back "Stars Fell on Alabama," with sharp, rhythmical clicks. Foley closed the front door, locked it, and on his way to the room at the back he saw Lou Baker, at the door to the bathroom, beckoning to him. She opened the door, took him by the sleeve, and drew him inside. She had wrapped a towel around her hair as if she had just washed it, and it gave her gaunt face a curiously medieval air.

"Peter," she said hoarsely, "you've got to."

"What now, Lou?"

"The gun—you've, got to take the gun." She placed her hand on a folded bath towel, and he saw the gun was in it.

"I think that thing's empty now, Lou—" he began.

She cupped both hands to her face, pressing the fingers to her eyeballs, then she parted her hands, the eyes still closed. "I'm asking you to do this for *me*, Peter."

"All right," he said, "all right, Lou—but just what the hell am I going to do with it?" He pointed at the towel. "Slip it into my vest pocket, I suppose?"

"I don't care what you do with it," she said. "Just take it. When you go, take it. Drop it into the river. Into the gutter. I don't care."

"All right," he said, "okay, Lou." He could see the beads of sweat on her forehead, at the pores of her nose, and he wondered if she might be sick. Shock. She was just a little slow coming out of it. Not the same old Baker. Not in that respect.

"I'll see that it's in a bag," she said, and as she had pulled him in, she pushed him out, patting the sleeve of his coat absently. He stood there a moment, listening to a tune he did not know. Le Jazz Hot. Someone strumming a guitar.

"Oh, Foley?" Proctor said.

"Coming," he said, and as he passed the closet slipped out his trench coat, taking it along. "Thought I had some cigars in one of these pockets, but I guess I don't."

But they were not listening. Mrs. Pierce was waiting for the music to begin. Her arms were slightly raised, like the wings of a chicken that was winded and was trying to cool off, but her eyes were lidded and she

swayed back and forth to the clucking of her tongue.
Moving in, but not close, Dickie placed an arm one-
quarter around her, the hand riding on her corset, and
over her shoulder leered at Foley, crying, "Look, pa!
We're dancin'!"

"Foley," said Proctor soberly, "you remember this
one?"

It was not so scratchy. It also had more volume, filling the room. He let it go on cleaning out the groove
till the words began to form, then he said, " 'Baby—
baby, won't you please come home?' Beiderbecke," said
Proctor solemnly.

Foley wagged his head, but he couldn't single the
horn out of the noise. Not often. Just an accent here
and there.

"What's it make you think of, old man?" Proctor
said and raised his hands from his sides, where they
had been hanging, as if the sleeves had suddenly filled
with air. His knees bent slightly, he looked as though he
might just float away. Finlike, and ever so lightly, his
hands paddled the air.

"Good old Chi," Foley said, although that was not
what it made him think of, but he knew that was what
Proctor had in mind. *Good old Chi.* His hot, stinking
room right near the park. The smell of food pouring
out of the transoms, the cockroaches in the bathroom,
and the strip-tease artist hammering her hairbrush on
the glass. *I've been a heel for so long, old man, I'm
going to make something good out of it. I'm going to
write the greatest book a shit-heel ever wrote.*

The music stopped, and Mrs. Pierce said, "But I
can't say I find that so easy to dance to. Not any more!"
she added and fanned her face with a potholder.

"Lady," said Proctor, and when Foley turned he saw the long-suffering mask slantwise on his face, "lady," he continued, recovering his role, "three white leopards, having eaten of my heart, my lungs, and my liver, have now turned to the hollow round of my skull."

"Where do you find the needles for this thing?" Dickie said.

Foley started to answer but saw that Mrs. Pierce was staring at something. Proctor also, at the door at his back, so he turned and saw Lou Baker—Montana Lou Garbo Baker—in her turtleneck sweater and her hair brushed back in a pompadour. Left Bank Baker, her bare feet in huaraches, her long legs in Proctor's pajama bottoms, a cigarette in the holder that collapsed like a drinking cup.

"I thought I'd change," Lou Baker said when the effect had been properly studied, "into something comfy," and slunk into the room.

"I swear," said Dickie, paused. "Well, I swear I made a mistake."

"Didn't we all, dear?" Lou Baker said, bending toward him like a willow for a light, then picked from her lips the tobacco crumbs that were not there. "Isn't somebody going to ask the old bag to dance?"

Foley stepped forward, slipped an arm around her, and felt the heat of the cigarette glowing on his neck.

" 'Body and Soul' okay?" Proctor said, cranking the handle, and they stood waiting till the music started.

"Don't they make a nice couple?" Dickie said. "Chanel Five goes so nicely with Old Spice."

As they shuffled around, Lou Baker said, "Same old elevator dancer, no steps," and he felt the wetness of her hair soak through his shirt. It gave off an odor like a wet suntan. The smell of water when it dried on sun-scorched skin. He said nothing, he avoided the humming that usually indicated how much he liked dancing, because he knew that Lou Baker was in a state of mind. He held her up till the music stopped, and when she put up her face he kissed her.

"Well, who's next?" he said and turned to offer her to Proctor. He was in the corner, bent over the pile of records.

"He'll probably take his records and go home," said Dickie, "if he can't have the last one, the crybaby—"

"Any particular selection?" Proctor said.

" 'Smoke,' " said Lou Baker, " 'Smoke Gets in Your Eyes.' "

Dickie did a tit-tat-toe, then sang,

> " 'Let's begin and make a mess of both
> our bright
> young
> livessssss! ' "

" 'Smoke Gets in Your Eyes' is cracked," said Proctor and held it up. They saw it was cracked.

"They're all cracked," said Lou Baker. Foley glanced to see how she meant that, saw the familiar glazed expression. Her lips were parted. The brightly painted false mouth made her face look green.

"What about 'Stormy Weather'?" Proctor said.

"Cracked!" said Lou Baker and snapped her fingers.

Dickie slipped his arm around her waist. "Music, kid! Let's have it!"

"All cracked," said Lou Baker. "Is no more music."

"Dance without it then," said Dickie, swung her around, and then seemed to lose his balance and almost fell. For a moment Foley thought he was drunk. He was about to say so—kid him a little, that is—when he saw the head of Lou Baker, lying on his shoulder, roll about loosely like that of a doll.

"The lady's passed out on me," Dickie said and held her like a rag doll, her feet just touching the floor, until they pushed up the only stuffed chair in the room and lowered her into it.

Foley sat on a cushion, his back to the doors through which a cool river draft was blowing, fanning the bloodless mask that appeared to be painted on Lou Baker's face. The bright carmine mouth had been wiped from her face by Mrs. Pierce, with a dishtowel. Proctor held the brandy to her lips.

"The excitement," Foley muttered, "along with the wine." He had said that many times, like talk about the weather.

"I can't say I blame her," Mrs. Pierce replied, and she had said that too many times, but now she added, "If I'd been in my *own* place I think I'd have fainted myself." Which was new. It meant the tension was wearing off. Foley was thinking how it seemed to take something—a flood, an earthquake, a dramatic fainting—to pull together what was forever falling apart. Lou Baker sighed, she moaned rather, and as they leaned forward to gaze at her face Foley felt her heel come down hard on his toe. She moaned again, her eyelids fluttered, and Mrs. Pierce said, "Accidents will happen, goodness knows," and daubed at Lou Baker's perspiring forehead.

"Professor Foley," said Proctor soberly, "what is an accident?"

"An accident?" said Foley, then lowered his eyes as Lou Baker brought her heel down, hard, on his instep. His eyes closed, he saw before him the headlines:

TENNIS STAR SURVIVES

FREAK ACCIDENT

"Let me put it this way," Proctor said. "When I shot myself, was it accidental?"

"You mean—" replied Foley, then paused, sucked in his lip, and waited till the heel on his foot stopped rocking. "You mean," he continued, "was it God's will?"

Proctor did not smile. "I mean, was it a crime?"

"How in the world would anybody but God know that?" said Mrs. Pierce.

Proctor kept his gaze on Foley, who said, "I'm not up on just how God would handle it, but I know what Héloïse said to Abélard."

"What did she say?" Proctor said, and Foley noticed that Lou Baker's heel released its pressure. Did she wonder how Héloïse had handled it?

"Héloïse wrote to Abélard," Foley began, thinking how much he was like Proctor, " 'I have brought thee evil, thou knowest how innocently. Not the result of the act but the disposition of the doer makes the crime: justice does not consider what happens, but through what intent it happens. My intent toward thee thou only hast proved and alone can judge.' "

"You believe that?" Proctor said suddenly.

"It is the statement of a woman in love," said Foley.

"But who in the world can judge something like that?" Mrs. Pierce said.

"Your peers," said Dickie, "drawn by lot, providing they don't have a hair appointment."

"If you want to know the truth—" Proctor said, but Foley did not. Not from Proctor. But when he opened his mouth it was merely to cover it with his hand. The pressure on his toe increased, his foot prickled with sleep. "The truth is," Proctor said, since no one had stopped him, "it was no accident. I did it. I shot myself."

Had Foley always known that? Had he been afraid of that truth himself? He kept his eyes off Dickie, wet his lips. "You didn't want to run the quarter?"

"I wanted to run it," Proctor said, his voice rising, "more than I wanted to live. That was why I did it."

"Mr. Proctor," Mrs. Pierce began, "I—"

Proctor smiled. He gazed at them, unseeing, as he had from the front of the morning paper.

"You wanted to show him you could take it?" Foley said, and saw Lawrence, Lawrence in the car lights, walking toward the smudgepot, fumbling at the fingers of one glove. But that was not it.

Still smiling, Proctor shook his head.

"No?" said Dickie.

"No," said Proctor. He looked Foley in the eyes and said, "Any Jew can take it. I wanted to show him a Jew who could give it up."

"*Ohhhh!*" Mrs. Pierce gasped, not at what she heard but at what she saw before her. Lou Baker, as if rising from the dead, slowly drew herself up. The wet towel dropped from her forehead, and she placed her free hand to her face. "You all right, honey?" Mrs. Pierce said and took the hand that Proctor was holding, patted it on the back, then rubbed it briskly between her own. Lou Baker seemed to be all right.

She sat there a moment, her eyes closed. Then she opened her eyes, said, "So the old bag couldn't take it?" She looked around at them sadly.

"You took more than anybody should be asked to," Mrs. Pierce replied.

"How long has it been?" Lou Baker said and turned her gaze on Proctor, who, with the tail of his shirt, was daubing the moisture around her eyes. Foley saw that her face went forward to meet him, and held the pressure of his hand, like a stroked cat. "Was it long?" she asked him.

"It was long for me, baby," he said. That was why she had asked him, she saw it was true, and in her bloodless face there were patches of color. Leaning back, she took his hand to steady herself, held on to it.

"What in the world time is it getting to be?" Mrs. Pierce said.

Foley glanced at his watch, but it was Dickie who said, "Twenty past ten."

"I've just got to run then," Mrs. Pierce said, and Dickie replied, "I'll run you over to the station, Livingston-Fargo Ulcer Transit." He saluted, clicking his heels, but only Foley had his eyes on him. "Think Gallagher and Shean less popular today," Dickie said and buffed his nails on his sleeve.

"Think I'll ride along with you if you don't mind," Foley said. "Last train my way is about eleven too."

"I happen to know that it isn't," Lou Baker said.

"Later trains to Philly," Foley said, "but last local out of Philly is about twelve-forty. I'm not cruising in the suburbs on my salary."

"You could perfectly well put up here," said Lou Baker. "We've plenty of room, haven't we, honey?"

"What's that, baby?" said Proctor. He hadn't been listening.

"I've got to get back and feed the cat," said Foley.

"That damn cat," said Lou Baker, who only liked kittens. "Is it the same damn cat as last time?"

"He'll be ten the sixth of next month," Foley said.

"Everybody else's cats die young," said Lou Baker, "the gods love them. But Foley's cats love Foley."

"They like regular habits," Foley said, getting up. "They're like me." He walked into the front room, where he found his coat lying out on the bed, a paper carton beside it. The carton was tied with a cord, and he could see that the gun lay in it crosswise. As he picked up his coat, the pair of haggard lovers—Kokoschka's storm-tossed lovers, floating in their tempest—slipped from the inside pocket of the coat and dropped on the bed. Foley stooped for the postcard, then leaned forward and slipped it beneath one of the pillows. As he stood up, he heard Dickie say, "Want a hand with that coat?"

"Think I'll just carry it," Foley said and placed the carton inside the coat, folded over the tails. "Warm night," he added, "little warm myself."

"Let me perk up just a bit," Mrs. Pierce said and stepped into the bathroom, stood facing the mirror. She ran a comb through her hair, said, "In spite of *every-thing*, it's been the grandest party. Honey"—turning to Lou Baker— "I forgot my glasses." She rolled her lips back from her teeth. "Did I get any on them?"

"What lovely pearly teeth you have, grandmother," said Dickie.

"Isn't he a character?" Mrs. Pierce said, picked up her handbag, looked in it for something. She found a packet of mints, chlorophyll. "Anybody else like one?"

"Thank you," said Lou Baker.

"Don't thank her, thank Nature," said Dickie.

"I hear they make you glow like a watch," said Mrs. Pierce, "but I can't say that I believe it."

"Mesdames et Messieurs!" Dickie said, raising his hand for attention. He stepped forward and bowed to Lou Baker, took her hand in his own, kissed it. "Doll, it's been *real*."

"Oh, Christ!" said Lou Baker.

"That's the way they're doing it now," said Dickie.

"I can't believe it," said Lou Baker. "I *won't* believe it."

"You think we're different, eh?" Dickie said.

"I think we *were* different," Lou Baker replied. Under her gaze Dickie lowered his eyes, flicked the levers on his watch. "They *say* it's been real, but we *were* real," Lou Baker said.

Dickie whistled softly, paused, then sang, "Oh, he could dish it out, and she could take it—"

"They could *both* dish it out," Lou Baker said and turned and threw her arms around Proctor. Over her shoulder Proctor gazed into the hall without smiling. His hand stroked her head.

"We'll be in touch," Dickie said, backed from the doorway, herded Mrs. Pierce down the hall to the landing.

"If Bryan had the faintest notion—" Mrs. Pierce began, and as they went down the stairs Foley saw the lovers, he saw their legs, that is, right where he had left them in the door. One of Lou Baker's mules dropped off the foot that rose from the floor.

"They make a nice pair of kids, don't they?" said Dickie and pushed out the glass side-wings of the windshield, so the draft down the river would not blow away their talk. There were yellow pier lights shining on the water, but the river looked cold.

"Is it *their* anniversary?" Mrs. Pierce asked and turned from Foley to Dickie.

"Their twenty-fifth," said Dickie, playing with the throttle.

"It's been hard on both of them," she said, "hasn't it?" Foley agreed, his head wagging, and she said, "You're married yourself, Mr. Foley?"

"No, I'm the withered appleseed," said Foley.

"You're so quiet," she said as if she hadn't heard that, "I would have sworn you were married."

"He's a very nice item," Dickie said, "if you're looking for something in drop-seat flannel."

They came off the bridge into City Hall square, swung around it to the right, then headed north on Broadway. Almost empty. A vacant Broadway bus coasted by. The wind in his face, the open car, made Foley think of the long night rides with Lawrence. They had been real, but it seemed a little crazy to think of it now. Time and the river, man's hunger in his youth, and the shadow of the ghost, the middle-aging voyager, cruising down a street where the fires of the city were banked for the night.

"Is this the same street?" Mrs. Pierce said. "It wasn't like *this* when we drove over."

They crossed Eighth Street, curved past Wanamaker's, crossed Fourteenth with the changing lights, and Foley said, "You can let me off around Thirty-second, little walk do me good."

Did Dickie hear that? He did not reply. In the windshield Foley saw that his eyes reflected the lights. As they shifted from red to green, running up the dark street like a phosphorescent zipper, a perceptible change appeared in his face. He leaned forward on the wheel. The tires increased their whine on the cobbles. Foley watched the floating needle drift up to fifty, hover there, drift past, as the row of green lights went up to where the night seemed to end. The smoking neon glow over Times Square and Forty-second Street.

"If you'll drop me off here," Foley said again, pulling in his head so Dickie would hear him, just as they flashed into the open on Thirty-fourth, then tunneled again. The coonskin hat squashed low on his head, the tail flying out behind him, Dickie was not in the car, not in New York, but in the current that passed from signal to signal, in the green lights that exploded, like a rocket, far up ahead.

Leaning toward him, Mrs. Pierce said, "I think Mr. Foley wants off," and she nudged him, but another light passed before he was able to bring the car to a stop.

"You say you want out, old man?" he said and let one tire screech along the curbing. Foley groped for the handle of the door, let himself out. Mrs. Pierce gave him her hand, and he smiled at her friendly, motherly face.

"It's been a great pleasure, Mrs. Pierce," he said. "You were very kind to come to our crazy party."

"I don't really know when I've had so much fun,"

Mrs. Pierce said. Did she wink at him? Or was it merely a tic in that eye? Tired. Sort of thing a little too much high-life brought on.

Dickie reached Foley a hand, said, "It's been simply realer than life, old boy," and the eyes under the coonskin cap were those of a Space Cadet.

"We'll keep in touch," Foley said, who had flunked a student for talking such gibberish.

"Next time you come up," Dickie said, giving an urgent flick to the throttle, "you give me a blast, old man, and we'll have lunch."

Foley nodded, stood there with his right hand raised in the air. The car went off, leaped off, actually, leaving a dark film of rubber on the asphalt, and the arm that Mrs. Pierce had raised to wave clamped down on her hat. Up ahead, toward the captive future, the lights changed from red to green.

THE CAPTIVITY: XII

After I left Proctor I walked back to the *pension* and went to bed. I didn't sleep, but I lay there till four, when the girls began to fool around with ping-pong, then I got up, shaved, and walked up Raspail to the American club. They were serving tea again, and the girls were dancing to American jazz. A few English boys were also dancing, if that was what you could call it, and the American boys were playing chess or reading Balzac. I walked up to Montparnasse, used the men's room in the Dôme, then took a table near the walk at the Coupole. I hadn't been there ten minutes when Montana Lou Baker strolled by. I let her go up one side, down the other, then I moved to a table where she couldn't help see me. She saw me and said, "Boy, is this seat taken?" and sat down on it. She had on the same dirty camel's-hair coat, but underneath she wore a cashmere sweater.

"Where are your chums?" I said, though it came out more like "thums," because my tongue was still sore.

"You have a very nice cedilla," she said. "You should go to Spain."

"I am thinking of Majorca," I said, "to get away from the States."

"They've gone to Laperouse," she said, indicating that sort of thing was beneath her. "She simply *adores* riz de veau Melba, and he said you should take me to Fouquet's."

"What do they serve at Fouquet's?" I said.

"Nothing you should eat before breakfast," she said and turned away from my café noir. I tried to think of something cutting, but her standards were too high. "We'll sit here for a while," she said, "then we'll take a walk till you feel better." She patted my hand, turned down her coat collar, and as she ran a comb through her hair I caught a whiff of a scent she hadn't been wearing the night before.

We didn't go to Fouquet's, as it turned out, or anywhere else. When we took the walk that would make me feel better we went past Foyot's, near the Luxembourg, but it was full of famous people of the type she didn't like. We walked from there down to St. Germain, where we stopped to eat at the Deux Magots, and the garçon she liked complimented her again on being with me. They discussed me as if I weren't there. He stood by our table, his tray under his arm, and after they had finished discussing me they discussed anything that popped into his mind. Lou Baker had a nice nasal Delaware Group type of French. After the café noir we had brandy, which set her up but made me sleepy, and to wake me up we went for another walk. We went down the Boul' Mich' to the bridge, sat for a while on the Ile de la Cité, then went along the quai on the Right Bank, under the trees. When we stopped to rest she would lean her weight on me. There were people on the walk behind us, cars going back and forth over the bridges, but the thing about Paris was that we seemed to be alone.

After a while I said, "What did you do with your-self all day?"

"We went out to see Lawrence," she said.

"How is he?" I said.

"The cornada is very good," she said, "with a white rag, like a wick, in it, and he is very brown, like a Spaniard, and smoking Spanish cigars."

"The smoking is new," I said.

"He has a different model now," she said.

I didn't want to talk about that, so I said, "What did you do next?"

"Proctor kissed him, Pamela kissed him, then Dickie and Mrs. Crowley Senior kissed him, but I did not kiss him because I could not get near the bed." She paused. "You get the picture?"

"Very well."

"It will be even better," she said, "when you read the book."

"He puts everything in it?"

"He puts in everything that happens." She waited, then said, "Now he's waiting for something to happen."

"Maybe he needs a new chapter?" I said.

"They both need a new chapter."

"Don't you worry about Lawrence," I said, "he'll turn something up."

"Lawrence watches Proctor, Proctor watches Lawrence, Lou Baker watches both Proctor and Lawrence, but nobody watches poor Dickie but Pamela." We sat there, and she said, "Everybody copies somebody—why the hell is that?"

I didn't know. I wondered who I was copying.

"I used to copy my older sister," she said, "my older sister copied Aunt Martha, who the hell Aunt Martha copied I just don't know." I didn't probe her, so she said, "We're all just a bunch of carbon copies."

"Not Lawrence," I said. "Lawrence is an original."

"Lawrence is worse than anybody," she said. "He's never been Charles Lawrence a minute of his life. He's always copied something, and right now he's copying Lawrence. He's waiting for Proctor to give him tips. He's so goddam good there isn't anybody left but Lawrence and God."

"Why do you hate him so much?" I said.

"Why does he make it so goddam hard? He isn't human. How can you copy something like that?" She leaned back to look at my face, then she took hold of my coat and tried to shake me.

To calm her down I said, "I'm not sure I agree with you, Lou."

She stopped trying to shake me and laughed. It was a very phony laugh. She stopped and said, "Well, now isn't that darling. Well, now isn't that the greatest piece of goddam comfort. So he doesn't agree. Well, now isn't that just too sweet." I tried to get up, but she stood up and pushed me down. "You're so goddam calm," she said, "I could kill you!"

I don't know how I looked, but I wasn't calm.

She laughed her phony laugh again. "But if I'm going to kill you I should do it here, and not back in the States. You know why? Say why."

"Why?"

"Because back in the States it would be crime, unless I was with child and you were his naughty dada, but over here, even without a child, it is a Moment of Truth!"

"Look, Lou—"

"In Spain there are bulls, in Paris there are girls, so you have your choice of a lovely cornada, which runs into money, or a nice touch of clap, which comes fairly cheap. In either case you have had your Moment of Truth. You can go back home, and if you are lucky you can have it again in a taxi, preferably horse-drawn, driving slowly through Central Park. That shows you have lived, and if you have lived you can write a book. 'Querencia' is taken, so you'll have to call yours 'The Moment of Truth.' "

"Look—" I said.

"Do you hate me?"

"Why should I hate you, Lou?"

"Oh, my God!" She stood up, and when I reached for her ran off. I let her go, because her pumps were still in my lap. She got a pretty good start before she knew that, not being so calm and collected herself, then she just kept going since she was the kind of girl she was. I let her paddle along, her coat almost dragging now that she had no shoes, then I walked to the opposite corner and picked up a cab. I showed the cabby the shoes and said I thought I knew the little girl who had dropped them, and what I wanted to do was just follow her along. He seemed to find that understandable. A girl who dropped her shoes along the quai was not something strange to him. So I got in the back, where I found a few hairpins, just as Lou Baker had predicted, and we went along the quai to the Pont des Arts, where we picked her up. I mean, where we drew up on a level with her. In her finest nasal Delaware Group French, she told the cabby she was out for an airing, which was something she was accustomed to taking in her bare feet. If the gentleman tourist

wanted her shoes he was welcome to them. She would
toss in her panties if he would go away and leave her
alone.

That was how it was at the Pont des Arts, but passing the Tuileries she rested for a moment—we all
did, that is—then we headed up the Champs Elysées.
A tall girl, she had the usual flat pair of feet. When
it was perfectly clear she wouldn't make it she tried to
flag a cab herself, but there weren't many running at
that time of night. If they were, they seemed to understand that sort of thing. Near the Rond Point she tried
to duck into the woods behind the Palais de Glace, but
in that coat I soon headed her off. She pulled my hair
and pounded on my chest, knowing that I was calm and
collected, then she let me carry her back to the cab,
where she sat in my lap. The cabby drove around for
another hour or more. Then he drove out to the
avenue Hoche, where he let us sit, charging me nothing, under the trees across the street from her *pension*.
Later he brought me back through the Trocadéro,
looking very fine at that time in the morning, and
across the river between the spread legs of the Eiffel
Tower. A mist hung over the trees but the morning sky
was clear. As it was getting on toward four in the morning, and since I still had the key to Dickie's apartment,
I let him drive me down to Lawrence's place on the
rue Bonaparte. He charged me only twenty francs
coming back, and when I tipped him another ten he
said after such a fine night I should have a good sleep.

I didn't, however. I don't think I slept at all. The
scent she had been wearing was in my hair, when I
rolled over it was on the pillow, and I lay wondering if
I had the nerve to fight bulls or not. To be gored, to

have a lovely cornada with a white rag in it, like a wick, and then to go back and get myself gored again. It didn't seem likely. The bull would know this right off the bat. If I was the rubber stamp of some Viking, one who was extremely calm and collected, not even love would make a good bullfighter out of me. I would have to be admired for being a different rubber stamp.

Dickie didn't show up at all, and in the morning, when the phone rang, I let it ring for a while, before I got up to answer it. I thought it might be Lou Baker, and it was.

"Lou?" I said, recognizing her voice, but she didn't seem to recognize mine.

"You're awfully goddam clever," she said, "you must feel awfully proud."

"This is Foley, Lou," I said.

"Oh, my God! Where's Dickie?"

"He isn't here right now."

"Oh, God! He's probably out passing them around."

"Passing what around, Lou?"

"The book. The poor boob's book."

"You mean *his* book is out?" I said.

"It's out," she said, "but he'll never know it. Dickie brought it out without his name."

"You mean—?" I said.

"There's nothing on it but *Querencia*," she said.

"His name isn't on it *anywhere?*" I said, but she had hung up, or was cut off, and I put the receiver back on the phone.

The blinds were drawn at the windows, but the morning light filtered into the room. Around the walls were the swords used by bullfighters, a cape spread wide to show the bright red lining, and several shafts, like short javelins, framing a blown-up photograph of a bullfight. The bullfighter was standing with his back to the camera, stiffly erect, his feet close together, while the blurred hulk of the bull, the curved horn tip showing, charged up through the cape. The man held the cape as if the bull were going by on tracks, like a train. The cape was like a mail sack made to catch the hooks as the train went past. I could see the pigtail down the bullfighter's back, and in the charge of the bull the cape billowed out like a flag attached to a post.

I had never seen a bullfight, but I had seen Lawrence, as blurred in action as this charging bull, go up toward the ball the way the curving horn went up through the cape. The game was not so different—the way Lawrence played it—as one might have thought. The cornada was the bull's ace, the stroke that had no comeback. But if he charged and missed, he had no comeback himself. A serious game. The sort of game Lawrence liked to play.

I may have stood there five or ten minutes—anyhow, I was still there, right beside the phone, when it rang again. For what seemed a long time I let it ring. I wasn't playing the game, any game, and I didn't have to answer the phone. But it seemed as if that bull would hang in the air and the red-lined cape billow out forever, so I picked up the receiver, said, "Hello?"

For five or ten seconds I thought nobody was there. Then I heard her inhale, gasp nearly, as if she had been holding her breath, and she said, "He's dead. He's dead, Peter." Then she hung up.

FOLEY: 12

In the men's room at Penn Station, Foley took the pistol from the Gimbel's carton, found a piece of paper clipped to the barrel with a rubber band. On it Lou Baker had scrawled:

See you at the next hearing.
Foley's Chick

He slipped the gun into the sleeve of his trench coat, rolled it up carefully. The coat under his arm, he boarded the train, walked through the crowded coaches to the smoker, found a seat on the aisle opposite the water cooler. The GI near the window had a bump on his forehead, a freshly bandaged eye.

"This seat taken?" Foley said and, getting no answer, turned to the sailor behind him.

"He's back in the bar," the sailor replied, "but he's tight as a mule's ass. You might as well take it."

"Think I'll step back for a drink myself," Foley said. He hesitated with the folded coat in his hands, then placed it on the seat to hold it. "Mind keeping an eye on the coat?" he added.

"For a small commiseration," the boy replied, but without removing the gob's hat from his eyes. The coach was full of sailors, soldiers, and a cloud of eye-smarting cigarette smoke. As the train began to move Foley walked down the aisle, feeling the tunnel pressure build up in his ears, and in the third coach back he stepped from the aisle to let a soldier pass. He came weaving down the aisle with his GI cap full of ice cubes.

" 'Scoose me," he said as he passed Foley and smiled to show the boy behind the cloud of gin. He was dark, a blue beard along his jaw, but the coach lights gave him an ashen pallor, as if a barber had freshly tal-cumed his face. From a candy-striped cord, tied in a bow behind his neck, dangled a little boy's toy bugle. In the clip for the music, a horizontal Petty girl. " 'Scoose me," he repeated, rocking with the train, and Foley placed a hand on his shoulder to support him. The curve held them together, and the reflection Foley saw in the streaked coach window was that of a father, an affectionate hand on the shoulder of his son. "Thanks, pop," the boy said, and as the train left the tunnel he lurched away.

Foley kept going, through one coach, then another, till he reached the bar. He found it nearly empty. A woman reading *Life*. Two sailors asleep. He ordered bourbon, leaning from his chair to point behind the bar at a particular bottle, one of the miniature whisky bottles that he didn't have. He tried a new one every trip. He kept them on the bookshelf 'with his Loeb Classics. They indicated that Foley took his culture, like his Greek, straight and on the rocks.

His head in the car door the conductor called, New-ark, Newark, next stop North Philadelphia, reminding Foley of a clever passage from his own works. *Junction City, Kansas City, New York City, Sui City*—Foley muttered, but not smiling, not so pleased with himself as he had once been. Who would be next? The steady

erosion of the liberal mind. Winant, Matthiessen, For-
restal, and—Foley paused, swallowed the name that
next rose to his lips. But not Foley. Lou Baker would
say he lacked the guts. Foley would reply no, he had
the guts but he lacked the conviction, the habit of perfection, that would lead him to believe that even *that*
settled anything. For one thing, he didn't want to leave
something someone else would have to clean up. Except the general mess. Except the world in a hell of a
mess.

He also lacked the temperament for despair—or the
passion, as Lou Baker would describe it, who liked to
say that no man had ever killed himself with thought.
Foley had replied no, that Lawrence had done precisely that, being as good as dead once he had made the
decision. The actual shooting little more than an after-
thought. A testament to the effect that the decision
had taken place. Pity had led Proctor, pity and im-
perfection, to put an end to the great quarter-miler,
but it was perfection, the terror of it, that had killed
Lawrence. The knowledge that he might be caught
with perfection on his hands and still be discontent.

Foley thought too much, as Lou Baker had pointed
out, ever to get around to anything like action, but
there had been a night—two or three nights after the
bombing of Cassino—when the complex problems of
his own inaction were simplified. Was it worth going on, was it worth the suffering—or was it not? Was
it true that life, as he liked to put it, *ne vaut pas la
peine d'être vécû?* He always put it in French. It made
it seem more impersonal. It was hardly his *own* life
that he meant, when he phrased it like that. Like Hans
Castorp, that shy lover who made his true love in a

foreign language, Foley found it easier, in that language, to make his peace. To face his Maker in a more musical, impersonal tongue.

Juger que la vie vaut ou ne vaut pas la peine d'être vécu.

There had been the night when he had come to the decision that life was not worth the pain of being lived. If he had been a man of the caliber of Lawrence he would have died on the spot. But he was merely Peter Foley, and he did not die of thought.

He had gone to bed early—an old and cagey maneuver to escape from the world and Peter Foley—but he had not slept, and lay there trapped with this Foley in the dark. They had made this little dialogue of Good and Evil—Diogenes Foley with his magic lantern— and he had proved to himself that Evil was a sad miscarriage of the Good. No more. That it lacked a soul it could call its own. It rooted in the ground where the Good lay bleeding, brought low by environment or some political cunning, but the Good would not die because only the Good could not be explained. It came without motives, like sunlight, and suffered or did not suffer evil, but Evil was simply inconceivable without Good. Evil marked the spot where some good had fallen, like the X in the photographs in newspapers, and it owed what life it had to this tragic circumstance. That was how he argued. Insofar as he believed, that was what he believed. It seemed to make sense, it had about it what a Greek might have respected, but it did not have, as Proctor once said, what it takes. What did it take? It took something that would explain what had happened to Peter Nielson Foley the day he had spent in the induction center and come out 4 F.

It seemed a small thing, in the abstract, to make him so upset. He had walked into the induction center with a typewritten statement of seven pages, which they would read, stand amazed, and then lead him off to wherever they tortured pacifists. Mimeographed sheets of this statement had been sent to friends, submitted to and read by the college authorities, and it was well known that Professor Peter Foley stood where he stood. Where that was the statement pointed out. It had taken him several months to write, leaned somewhat heavily on Thoreau and Tolstoi, and appeared to represent the philosophical turn of Foley's life. A stand. He had stepped forward and taken it. He had packed up his books, found a home for the cat, bought the plain workman's clothes he would wear in prison, and in a suit of this type he had made his appearance at the induction center.

It might have been different if he had found the man in charge. He did not. Nobody seemed to know who he was. In the meantime he was asked to strip, and with the statement in one hand, his clothes in the other, he joined the line of nude, summer-hot, and smelling men. In the next ten hours nobody asked him about the papers he was holding, and he returned them, unread, to the pocket of his new coat. Into those seven pages he had put his *coeur mis à nu*. It had seemed a fine thing, in his study, it had been warmly applauded by his friends, but in an empty loft with several hundred nude men it was not the same. Le corps mis à nu was something else again.

The experience found Foley unprepared. He had

lived in the world, he thought, for a good many years.
He had seen hundreds of assorted males in the nude.
But he had not seen several hundred piled together,
their pitiful drapery over one arm, herded like whores
from one checkup to another one. He found it hard to
conceive, when he thought of it at all, that the campus
he had left really existed, or that a man named Foley
had typed out a statement he took seriously. There was
no connection, none at all, between the seven typewritten pages in his hand and the nightmare world in
which he passed the day. He had failed the army, but
he had passed, with flying colors, through the gates
of hell.

Through the windows that opened over the street,
and through which they were observed until the nov-
elty passed, the commonplace noises of the everyday
world blew in and out. The state of the world, the ballgame at Shibe Park, organ music for eating, band music for dancing, string music for relaxing, soft music for
listening, with the background music of the pianola
in the penny arcade. Life went on. Nothing seemed to
have stopped. Wolf calls, police calls, fire calls, com-
mercials, the crack of the rifles in the shooting gallery,
the click of the balls, the ringing of the bells in the pinball machines. Trains came up from Washington, down
from New York, the legs and hips were added to a girl
on a signboard, and a giant in red pants, advertising
bone meal, tossed packages of flower seed through the
windows. A helicopter made a landing on the station
roof to speed the mail. A peddler sold rubber monkeys, copulating, but hearing-speaking-seeing no Evil,
and plastic walnuts for the shell game to swarthy sailors
from the Argentine. Business as usual, as aimless and

as pointed, and what had seemed so depressing to Foley in the morning, the shapeless, extravagant waste of living, looked almost beautiful to him in the afternoon. Were they free, these people, to do as they liked? To eat foot-length hotdogs, hoot at the girls, crank the handles of machines with caged fan dancers, or make love in the seats of cars at the back of parking lots? Unaware, or if aware not caring, that men like themselves, brothers and keepers, were parading like molting storks in the loft of a building where the signs fined you for *Spitting* and men stood in line holding pint milk bottles of warm, cloudy piss.

A commonplace day, like all others, the sun rose and set, like the others, but not on the one in the limbo of Foley's mind. That day had the durable, changeless pattern of Dante's hell. The same faces appeared, the same scabrous bodies, and the same hoarse croaking of voices. All there but the Leader. In place of the Leader was the line. It went out through the door ahead, came in through the one behind.

At Foley's rear was a Mr. Folger, Andrew Folger, a farmer, who had got up at dawn and driven in with baskets of sweet corn. The corn could be seen on the truck in the parking lot. One of the tires was low, and Mr. Folger often referred to it. A middle-aged man. His hands and face, including the dark patch at his throat, seemed to have come along with his body through some mistake. They were brown and weathered, while his body was pink and white. A nest of auburn hair lay on his chest, dangled a vinelike streamer on the curve of his belly, then ended abruptly where the friction of his belt had worn it off. He stood with his arms folded on his chest. This concealed the brown hands in his armpits, but there was no place to hide his head, or his face, clapped on the white shoulders like a carnival mask. Spots were found in one lung, sugar in his urine, and cavities in his teeth. On the parking lot his tire went down and the sweet corn dried in the sun.

At Foley's front was Mr. Fogarsi, or Fugarcy, or Focharsi, since it was spelled two ways on his papers and he wasn't quite sure himself. A Latin lover, with blue-black hair and a fawn-colored sport coat with built-in shoulders, Mr. Focharsi wore charms on his ankle, at his wrist, and around his throat. A woman's hair was braided through them all, and they would not slip off. Mr. Focharsi had teeth like ivory but was not able to remove his socks. They had become, over the months and years, part of his feet. Athlete's foot had made them a living part of himself. When this was clear, and when his feet had been dipped in a solution to reduce the odor, he was permitted to put on his patent leather shoes and wear them around. They had loose cleats, for tap dancing, at the heel and toe. Mr. Focharsi could dance, which he did for a living, putting down "dance man" as his vocation, but in the setting-up exercises it was found he could not bend at the knee. When the intern cried "Down," and they all went down, Mr. Focharsi stayed up. On his face was the expression of a man whose heart had stopped. It was thought that the meaning of the word was not clear to him. Other words were tried, several of them suggested by Peter Foley, the learned professor, but Mr. Focharsi's knees did not understand one of them. When the call came his head went down but his knees stayed up. He was taken from the line for further experiments.

Foley could bend at the knee, his lungs showed no spots, he read the lines off the cards and heard the ticking watch, but his pump, as the intern described it, was not so good. It clopped. When he did the bends it clopped and leaked. It was not a piece of plumbing the army wanted on its hands.

Foley received this news around eight o'clock, a little more than ten hours after he had entered, statement in hand, the door he was now free to go out. He felt nothing. Nothing that he thought he should feel. The shock had worn off, but he did not even feel relief. *Nothing.* So he had come to know, in spite of himself, what hell was really like.

He put back on the clothes he had carried all day, pulled the clean socks over his dirty feet, waved to Mr. Focharsi, and went down the stairs to the street. The everyday street, full of the commonplace, everyday scene. The neon signs flickered, the traffic was noisy, the sailors in the penny arcade gulped hotdogs with the gaze of men one hour from the battlefield. A commonplace scene, as American—as the book jackets said— as a filling station, but Foley found it stranger than the nightmare he had left at the top of the stairs. More unreal. Harder to account for, that is. Given man for what he was, his corps mis à nu, how had he ever put together anything that worked, or woven socks that would slip on and off a man's feet? Where did he get the lips that would smile, and the legs that would bend at the knee? Mr. Focharsi put the question. His knees put it, that is. Faced with the baffling commands of life, they refused to bend. They held fast. Mr. Focharsi seemed to be willing, but his limbs were not. Froglike, he was caught midway between a hopper and a man.

Foley had walked the eight or ten miles back to his room: he had taken the long way, following the river, crossing and recrossing all the bridges, as if a leap into the river was what he had in mind. He did. He thought about it. But the thought passed. It seemed to be as pointless as the other thoughts he had.

Long after dark, after midnight, he had reached the sleeping college campus, where he sat on the wall along the pike and took off his socks and shoes. The socks in his pocket, carrying his shoes, he had wandered barefoot around the moonlit campus, sitting for a while in the empty bleachers of the football field. Along toward morning he had gone to his room, but not to sleep. He lay out on the bed listening to the clopping hammer of his leaky pump. He had often suspected the worst, and now he knew. One day, like Mr. Focharsi's knees, he would bend no more.

In this state of mind, or absence of mind, he turned to a thick book he had been reading—had bought, in fact, to read at his leisure while in jail. He opened the book—toward the end, for he thought he might not live long enough to read it—and found himself scanning, with professional detachment, several lines of verse.

> There flies a gray bird, a falcon
> From Jerusalem the Holy
> And in his beak he bears a swallow . . .

Something about these lines, the gray bird, the falcon, and the day he had just passed at the induction center, gave him the feeling he had stumbled on some strange revelation, some gift of prophecy. So he had read on, some thirty lines of it, which turned out to be a poem, a Serbian poem, dealing with the Tsar Lazar and his defeat at Kossovo by the Turks. Of this Tsar Lazar, Foley had known nothing, nothing at all until that moment, but this gray bird, this falcon, seemed to fly like a portent through his own life. This Tsar Lazar, whose destination was heaven, was asked to choose between the heavenly or the earthly kingdom, and of course he had chosen the heavenly. The price of this kingdom, this eternal victory, was that he and his army of seventy thousand men would be slaughtered by the Turks on the field of Kossovo. This had occurred, and the poem closed:

> All was Holy, all was Honorable,
> And the Goodness of God was fulfilled.

These words should have quieted Foley's troubled heart, but the clopping increased. He gulped for air: despair seemed to smother him like a hood. What did he feel? When he was able to feel, he felt sold out. Sold down the river with the Tsar Lazar and his army of seventy thousand. Down the river with Saint Lawrence, the self-slaughtered matador, down the river with Brother Proctor, the self-styled martyr, and down the river with Sister Baker, who kept the chronicle straight, like the Venerable Bede. Last but not least to be sold down the river was Foley himself. Crouched on the battlefield, as if in hiding, or about to leap into the arms of God, but, like Mr. Focharsi, unable to bend or flex his knees. A true symbol of the froglike passage he had made through the earthly life.

Did they lack conviction? No, they had conviction. What they lacked was intention. They could shoot off guns, at themselves, leap from upper-floor windows, by themselves, or take sleeping pills to quiet the bloody cries of the interior. But they would not carry this war to the enemy. That led to action, action to evil, blood on the escutcheon of lily-white Goodness, and to the temporal kingdom rather than the eternal heavenly one. That led, in short, where they had no intention of ending up. The world of men here below. The god-awful mess men had made of it.

In this peaceful manner the Prince of Darkness ruled everywhere. The bloody plain of Kossovo was as wide as the world. Everywhere that men of good will could be found they stood in queues of happy victims, waiting to spill their pure blood on the field of Kossovo. Black lamb and gray falcon, a gut-deep urge that in surrender was the moral victory, in death and defeat the lasting possession of the lasting world. But this one, this bloody cockpit, this temporal kingdom and battle-ground, could be left, *must* be left, that is, to shift for itself. The Proctor-Foley salvage operations applied to vermin, not to men.

Foley suddenly remembered, with shame, the pious meetings of the pacifists he had attended, where it was known that the doing of good, or of evil, was a devil's snare. The doing of anything led to action, all action was blended with evil, but one could *be* good, one could only be good, by sitting on one's hands. Otherwise they would get bloodied in an earthly, temporal fight of some sort. Settling nothing. For what was ever settled here on earth?

A cold draft blew on his neck, and Foley turned to see a young GI, carrying a trench coat, push through the door and weave down the aisle to where he sat.

His uniform was soiled, where he had just been sick, and there were drops of water on the tin horn of his bugle. One side of his face was still colorless and bruised with sleep.

"This yourn?" he said to Foley and held the trench coat out over the aisle.

"Why, yes," Foley replied, "thank you very much," and the young man tossed the coat over the back of a chair. A fold in the skin cut across the bruised side of his face like a scar.

"Like a drink?" Foley said to be friendly, and the young man closed his eyes as if to think.

He thought, then said, "I'm gettin' off here," but he did not leave. "I'm gettin' off here," he repeated, then furtively, as if his fly were open, he spread wide the flaps of his topcoat and groped for the handle of the pistol he had thrust, like a pirate, between his pants and his belt. Before handing the gun to Foley he sniffed the barrel.

"Ahhhhhh," he said, as if it gave off an incense, then placed it carefully on the table.

"An heirloom," Foley said casually. "In the family for years. I'm very much obliged."

The young man belched, bowed with a sober, military air, and started away before what Foley had said penetrated his mind. He stopped, centered in the aisle, and began to smile. A secret smile, from the way he blushed, but one that Foley knew very well. An old smile, the shameless smile of Proctor smelling bullshit. The young man did not speak; he stood remote and erect, as if digesting the smile with pleasure, then he lurched off as if hidden gears had suddenly meshed. It was clear that he hoped to reach the door before he laughed. He managed, thanks to the conductor who had propped the door open, then it slammed behind them as the train braked to a stop.

A moment later Foley saw him on the train platform, seated on his duffle bag. He held the bugle clasped in his hand, and as the train began to move he spotted Foley at the window, wildly waved the bugle, then held it to his lips. There was no sound, but a flaming paper streamer with wagging fingers at the end leaped toward Foley, struck the glass, and thumbed a red-paper nose. Then it returned, with a snap, into the mouth of the horn. The young man threw up his arms, rocked over backward, as if the recoil had been too much for him, and as the train pulled out Foley saw his polished boots waving in the air.

That was all, but at the back of Foley's mind, glowing like a lantern slide, he saw another bugler. One that wore, in the fog-strewn evening, a canary-yellow slicker, a nautical hat, and the air of a man riding to the hounds, while he solemnly chanted:

> "Strawberry shortcake
> Huckleberry pie
> Girls go to Oxy
> I wonder why."

At the moment of crisis, as the signals floated up from the huddle at the goal line, the young man took the horn from his slicker, stood up, and sounded a blast. No bugler, the sound that he made was not of this world. More like a shriek, a loon's cry in the darkness, so that players, umpires, and spectators wheeled to see what comet, unknown and unpredicted, crossed the night sky. As one had. Perhaps, as one always would. Cruising around in the dark, in the void, just for the hell of it.

Foley slipped on his coat and walked through the car to the rear platform. They were crossing the Schuyl-kill. On the water he could see the band of coach lights. Down the river the flicker of car lights on the bridges, the neon glow over the city and the moon, lit up from below, as if part of it. A signboard that had been turned off for the night. No longer a goddess, not much of a wonder, more of a tide-making mechanical marvel—and yet it was still, like Foley himself, part of the night. Destination unknown, resolution uncertain, purpose unclear, source undetermined, but a slit in the darkness where the eye of the chipmunk might peer out. A crack in the armor where the bugler sounded a wild, carefree note. An island in space where young men were still careless with themselves. Casually, as if flipping a coin, Foley tossed the heirloom over the railing, but he did not hear it splash or see white water where it fell. The rails clicked, the train left the trestle, and as they pulled into the Philadelphia station the conductor stepped out and reminded him that this was his stop.

He went along with the ten or twelve people who got off. He used the escalator, followed them up the ramp, and found the last train waiting on the local platform. In the smoker he took out and lit up an unfinished cigar.

At his station—within the station (the insects were getting to be a nuisance)—he saw the tramp he had passed in the morning stretched out on a bench. He lay facing the wall, his head resting on the bundle tied up with the rope.

Lights burned in the dorms, and as he circled the pond he heard birds stir on the water, rise flapping, and drip water on his face as they passed overhead. In the window where, early that morning, he had seen Mrs. Schurz in a cloud of gray flannel, a lamp now burned, lighting up the tiles on the porch roof. That would be, he knew from experience, something about the cat. Mrs. Schurz did not wait up unless there had been trouble in Paradise. Unless God's half acre, by cat or man, had been disturbed. He went around to the back, hoping to miss her, but as he turned the key in the lock the window directly over his head went up.

"Oh, Mr. Foley?"

"It's me, Mrs. Schurz," he replied.

"A man was here to see you," she said. That was all.

"A man?" he asked.

"He wouldn't tell me his name or a thing, Mr. Foley. He just said he had to see you personally."

"I see," he replied, opened the door, stepped out again as Mrs. Schurz called, "Mr. Foley, I want you to know that I don't give snoopers any satisfaction. If he got any, I want you to know it wasn't from me."

"I appreciate that," he said. "Thank you very much."

"It was none of my business, and I told him I didn't think it was his."

"Thank you kindly," Foley replied, closed the door, set the lock, paused in the dark hallway leading back to his room. Mrs. Schurz lowered her window, water dripped on a saucer left in the sink. Drop, drop, drop.

I am eroding, the witness had said. Leaving bedrock. A white scar across the mind indicating where the anchor might have dragged. A broken link in the chain where a man had been torn from his captive past.

He heard Mrs. Schurz sag into her bed, then he walked down the hallway to his study. The smell of the orange he had peeled in bed was strong in the room. A sprinkling of moonlight and soot lay on the yellow pages in the fireplace. He struck a match on the hearth, took from the pile of yellow pages the sheet lying on top, the last page of the book, and saw that the morning splatter of bird dung had dried. He left it. Proof positive that there, at that point, the book had stopped.

The match that he held burned down to his fingers, blackening the nail. He cupped the flame to his face, as if he might see, within it, a moment of truth. A draft down the chimney brightened the flame, sprinkled more soot on the yellow pages, and the reflection that he saw in the study window smoked like a flare. Cupped in his hands was not the dying match but a smoking smudgepot. Into the flame Lawrence dipped his hand, and with the sightless smile of an antique statue he turned and gazed into Foley's face. The lips silent, the gaze already remote, he peered toward Foley from a sacred wood that slowly receded into the changeless past. A blurred, shadowy figure, caught by the camera, nameless in a scene that seemed immortal, like that woman of mystery in the postcard view of the Seine. Suspended in time, like the ball that forever awaited the blow from the racket, or the upraised foot that would never reach the curb. A permanent scene, made up of frail impermanent things. A lover like Lou Baker,

a saint like Lawrence, a martyr like Proctor, and a witness like Foley. So much fire and water, so much fear and
wonder, so much smoke and sprinkling of soot. But in the
burning they gave off something less perishable. How
explain that Lawrence, in whom the sun rose, and
Proctor, in whom it set, were now alive in Foley, a
man scarcely alive himself. Peter Foley, with no powers
to speak of, had picked up the charge that such powers
gave off—living in the field of the magnet, he had
been magnetized. Impermanent himself, he had picked
up this permanent thing. He was hot, he was radioactive,
and the bones of Peter Foley would go on chirping
in a time that had stopped. No man had given a name
to this magnet, nor explained these imperishable lines
of force, but they were there, captive in Peter Foley—
once a captive himself.

With his blackened fingers he struck another match
on the bricks. He read again the last scene, the death
of Lawrence, the hollow voice of Lou Baker over the
phone; then he sat in the dark until her voice seemed
to blend with the stirring birds. The cat clawed at the
screen, and he walked through the house to the kitchen
door. A new day was breaking, the dawn like a sheet
of clear ice on the pond. He took out his watch, started
to wind it, and saw that the time—the captive time—
had stopped. At two o'clock in the morning, the first
day of his escape from captivity.

Printed December 1995 in Santa Barbara
& Ann Arbor for the Black Sparrow Press by
Mackintosh Typography & Edwards Brothers Inc.
Design by Barbara Martin.
This edition is published in paper wrappers;
there are 200 hardcover trade copies;
100 hardcover copies have been numbered & signed
by the author; & 26 copies handbound in boards
by Earle Gray are lettered & signed by the author.

Photo: Barbara Hall

Long regarded as one of the most gifted American writers, WRIGHT MORRIS received the National Book Award in 1956 for his novel *The Field of Vision.* His most recent novel, *Plains Song,* won the 1981 American Book Award for Fiction. He is the author of seventeen other novels, several collections of short stories, books of criticism and a number of photo-text volumes. In recent years Black Sparrow has published *Writing My Life* (1993), *Three Easy Pieces* (1993), *Two For the Road* (1994), and *The Loneliness of the Long Distance Writer* (1995). He and his wife make their home in Mill Valley, California.